5/9/

To Heidi

With best wishes

Thanks for your support...

Warm regards

Duke Southard

MW01248905

A Favor Returned

by Duke Southard

Duke Southard

Peter E. Randall Publisher
Portsmouth, New Hampshire
2000

ACKNOWLEDGMENTS

To the McCarthys, Nobles, Tepes, Gares,
Mendenhalls, Jeri, Pam, Kim, and Alex:
Thanks for your encouragement and insights . . .

To Robert Newton Peck:
Thanks for your candid and helpful commentary . . .

To Peter Randall, Publisher, and Doris Troy, Editor:
Thanks for your patience . . .

Printed in the United States of America

Peter E. Randall Publisher
Box 4726, Portsmouth, NH 03802-4726

Distributed by University Press of New England
Hanover and London

To Barbara, for her infinite patience,
especially during this project,
and for her unrelenting support
for whatever I've tried to do . . .

To my father, who was not Ethan Becker
and who I hope would have been proud . . .

JENNIE'S SYLLOGISM

There is a just, merciful, and LOVING God;
Earth is a planet filled with unhappy people;
THEREFORE, there must be an afterlife, a better place.

JENNIE'S COROLLARY

The LOVING God places some people on Earth
to help others be happier; unfortunately,
He doesn't explain the process to anyone!

—Jennifer Proctor Becker

Memorial Day 1950

PROLOGUE

I knew that my father had to be dead. I jumped from my prime viewing spot atop the old pickup truck, my legs already churning through the air so that I was running before I even hit the ground. By the time I got even close to the scene of the spectacular but terrifying crash, hundreds of spectators had already sprinted to the scene, eager to be able to say that they saw what was left of the driver when the story appeared in the morning paper. After the first surge of panic and sickening fear drained away, I continued hopelessly to battle my way through the crowd. As a ten-year-old boy, I had already learned only too well the manly lesson that grown-up boys do not cry, and I fought the tears as long as I could. Finally, there was no holding back. Sobbing uncontrollably, I stopped fighting and just stood there. What had just happened did not even seem real anymore, but I knew it was.

When I felt the light touch on my arm, I whirled around, expecting that somehow my mother had found me in the pushing and shoving crowd. Instead, I saw a girl about my age staring into my eyes with a look that frightened me yet in some strange way made me feel better.

"Would you like your father to be all right?" she asked quietly.

For the minute, it seemed as if we were the only people in the whole world. To a ten-year-old boy who worshiped his dad, it was a pretty stupid question with only one possible answer. Looking into her eyes, my stomach fluttered like it does every time I stepped up to bat in Little League. She was very pretty, her short blond hair forming a glowing halo around her face in the afternoon sunlight. I had the odd sensation that I could answer her one-sided question with a yes or no. All I could manage to mumble was a shaky, "We need him." My eyes seemed locked onto hers. Their calm deep green hue comforted me, and everything seemed all right again.

"Then you shall have him," the almost ghostlike girl said in a calm, matter-of-fact way.

The cheers of the crowd should have easily drowned out the girl's reply. I knew that the noise could only mean that my father had survived the crash. I had seen enough race-car accidents to know that hundreds of people can be awfully quiet when they think someone is dead. Instead, the shouts and applause faded into a fuzzy background as I continued to stare at the girl, the softly whispered words coming through to me loud and clear.

"You understand, of course, that this favor will need to be returned sometime later," she had whispered as she vanished into the gathering crowd.

I wondered if I would ever see her again.

Memorial Day 1950

A DAY AT THE RACES

This day began as the adventure of his life for Ross Becker. Since he started coming to the races with his father several years before, he had been relegated to the wooden grandstand of the half-mile dirt track to sit with his mother. He had watched longingly across the way at the chaotic but yet somehow organized order of the race cars and crews scattered helter-skelter around the infield. Finally, today he would be allowed into the pit area.

Ethan Becker had decided that this Memorial Day holiday should be one that his son would remember. By necessity, Ethan was a part-time dabbler in weekend racing. The reality of the budget prevented the hobby from becoming an obsession that would rattle even further the already shaky family financial structure. The small-time racing circuit was enough to feed his passion for speed but the only rewards were the occasional one-hundred-dollar purse and the weekly thrill of risking his life with other drivers, all of whom most people thought either reckless or crazy. Perhaps today would be the day when Ross would be completely won over to the hobby that filled so much of Ethan's time and so often decimated the Beckers' weekly finances.

The moment Ethan's truck and trailer rolled to a stop, Ross jumped out and began to walk toward the pits, sensing the exhilarating tension of the drivers and crews as they set about preparing their cars. The throbbing roar of the engines as they warmed up seemed to create a collective adrenaline rush for all who were close by. The boy ran from one car to the next, inhaling the atmosphere, a strange combination of anxiety and fear mixing with gaiety and camaraderie, a sense of tempting fate but being confident that it was on your side.

The half-mile oval at Laurelwood was carved from a deep pine woods. The owners of the track had visualized a miniature version of the brickyard at Indianapolis, with grandstands located on both straightaways and open spaces around the perimeter for family picnics. Their magnificent dreams, as so often happens, clashed with the reality of financing the venture. The project needed to be scaled down considerably and the track had now all the amenities it was likely ever to have. Only one grandstand had been built, facing the infield and lining most of the first straightaway. From this vantage point, the fans could observe the start and finish of the race, and from the third row up had a solid view of the far side of the track. Beginning at the first turn, a white, wooden fence was constructed around the entire outer edge of the track, more as a marker for the drivers than a safety net to keep the cars from soaring into the tall pines surrounding the oval. Each turn had been banked sharply, allowing the drivers to maintain speed through the corners without flying off over the embankments at each end of the track. Only a very few of the drivers who came to Laurelwood expected to rise to professional levels in the racing world and the track suited most of the hobbyists just fine.

Ross tuned into his imagination, and he visualized not the small dirt track in Laurelwood, New Jersey, but instead the pit area of the Indianapolis Speedway. The crews huddled around their open cockpit sprint cars could just as easily been hovering over a sleek, low-slung Indy car in Ross's mind. He was absorbing the atmosphere through every pore, his excitement building by the second. He found himself slowing when he walked by a particularly attractive car, eavesdropping but not understanding much of the technical engine jargon surrounding it. He knew that if his mother ever heard any of these discussions, she would never allow him back in the pits again. The very descriptive language the men used would have had his mouth washed out with a bar of Ivory soap.
He carefully noted the superstitions that Ethan had explained were part of every race driver's ritual. There could be no green cars, no number 13, no women in the pits, no pictures before the race; the list was endless and it varied with each driver but Ross was sure that his fourth-grade teacher at St. Luke's would be certain to call it all devil's worship. As this thought of his favorite nun at school flashed through his mind, an indefinable but clearly

physical feeling of dread spread through him, a foreboding so strong that it almost made him nauseous. It passed as quickly as it came, however, and he was off to his father's car to watch the final preparation for Heat Two, a race that Ethan Becker had promised to win for his son.

Ethan's pit crew, actually two friends and an acquaintance, rolled the car to the starting line for its push start. Ethan, hunched in the cockpit, thought about the odd feeling that had seemed to filter through his entire being as he finally relented after several days of discussion and decided to permit Ross to stay with him in the pits. Before every race day, Ethan was convinced that he had experienced a premonition of death. It was the sort of feeling that could not be shared easily with anyone else, especially for men like Ethan Becker. Even after discovering that this sense of doom happened to be quite common, Ethan refused to allow his domineering male ego to be compromised by admitting to any kind of fear.

To all who knew him, Ethan Becker was simply the man in charge. Despite a slim, too thin build for his height, he had a wiry and sturdy physical presence. Most of his acquaintances and even his closest friends had at one time or another felt the fury of his ferocious temper, and everyone knew to avoid doing anything to make him angry. His angular face, its most prevalent feature a sharp, jutting chin, had an appealing ruggedness, with deep-set dark blue eyes that could unnerve any woman with their penetrating gaze. A thick shock of curly light brown hair effectively hid his slowly receding hairline. He carried himself with a rare kind of authority that, in spite of his slight frame, inspired a sense of respect bordering on awe or fear, depending on how well one knew him. Although not handsome in the movie-star sense, he had a certain physical appeal and easy but enigmatic charm that most women found irresistible. He reserved his toothy grin for the ladies and kept everyone else guessing about his mood with a half smile, half smirk that was impossible to interpret. Ethan Becker could only be described as a paradoxical and dominating force in the lives of those who knew him.

One night, at a gathering of his buddies, a few too many beers loosened inhibitions and some of the drivers began talking about the intense, almost sexual feeling of power a driver experienced when in the cockpit of a race car. The discussion quickly ran the gamut from the exhilarating excitement of approaching the green starter's flag to the more profound subjects of fear and even the death wishes that some of the drivers joked about being an integral part of their psyche. Ethan had just listened, never indicating that he could identify with much of what they were saying. As the starter truck bumped the steel cage protecting the rear of his car and began to push, he realized that the feeling of this morning was quite the opposite of his usual foreboding death prophecy. Instead, an extremely comforting knowledge that he would live to go to work the next morning had settled over him. Then, the luxury of being able to think was gone as he was forced to concentrate on the mechanics of getting his car jump-started. Instinctively, Ethan began to follow his strategy for this heat, which, with any luck, would qualify him for the feature event and its one-hundred-dollar payoff later that afternoon.

Ross watched intently as his father's car was pushed from the line. He tried to imagine the tension that Ethan had often attempted to describe. The roar of the sixteen sprint cars now circling the track was increasing by gradual but constant steps. Starting positions had been arranged by the time trials earlier in the day and the drivers now jockeyed to arrange their cars, the two-by-two rows undulating and snaking their way around the oval. Ross had scrambled onto the roof of the faded pickup.

"Good thing Dad is out on the track," he thought, having experienced a solid tanning on two occasions when caught sitting on the family car. He knew that it would not have mattered to Ethan that he was on the truck; another good tanning would have followed. Ross glanced across the track at the grandstands, only a few open seats showing. He knew that by now his mother, for reasons he could never fathom, would have left the stands and would be in the rear seat of a friend's car, her rosary beads clenched in her hand.

Fay Becker often acted as foil for good-natured joking from her brothers, but never more than when they teased her about her rosary ritual on Ethan's race days. When they taunted her about doing more laps around the beads than her husband did around the track, she responded with the unshakable conviction that her ritualistic prayers were what kept Ethan safe.

It took two laps around the oval for the cars finally to be in their proper position for the start. With the crowd seeming to be drawn out of their seats by the approach of the now perfectly aligned, wheel-to-wheel rows of thundering cars, the starter raised the green flag over his head. He paused, checked one final time that everyone would get a fair start, and dropped his flag with a dramatic flourish as the first row of two reached the starting line. To Ross, now standing practically on tiptoe on the roof of his truck, the deafening roar of the engines was enough of a stimulus to allow his imagination to spirit him into the cockpit of his father's car. He became the driver as the cars, with throttles wide open, careened into the first turn.

Much of the excitement for the occasional racing fan comes from the pure danger of speed, coupled with the fact that drivers are human and make errors in judgment. A very large segment of those in attendance on this Memorial Day would have fit into this category. Although none would ever admit it, the possibility of seeing a spectacular crash did influence their decision to attend the holiday races. Not that anyone really wanted to see someone hurt, but, after all, it was the drivers' choice to provide this sort of entertainment and everyone knew that they were well aware of the risks.

By the third lap of the eight-lap race, the field had been cut in half. Much to the subtly hidden but still obvious dismay of the occasionals, the reduction had not come about because of accidents. Homegrown race cars often had the disconcerting habit of being unable to hold together for an entire race, even one of short duration.

With the various mechanical problems causing the cars to drift into the pits on a regular basis, Ethan Becker worked his way from his fifth row start to now challenge for the lead. Al Stuart, a good friend of Ethan's and another of Ross's heroes, was pushing his powerful Offenhauser to its limit. He held the inside, confident that his car could match the challenge as Ethan moved out to his right and placed his left wheel within inches of Al's right rear tire.

As they passed the grandstand, the crowd roared approval of this close and dangerous race. Ross, beside himself with the awe of a ten-year-old in any new and exciting experience, strained to see his father's number 21 pass Al's car before they entered the first turn for lap four. Instead, what he saw in an instant was that something had gone terribly wrong, and he knew that his father was now in mortal danger. On so many back-road tests, Ethan always would tell Ross that a good race-car driver can overcome almost any situation on a racetrack. The one exception, mentioned as though the machine made the conscious decision, was a car that was not handling properly. Ross always just agreed, even though he had no idea what exactly "not handling properly" meant. In this devastating instant, he knew. Ethan was struggling with the wheel and the car was not responding. Ross had absorbed hours and hours of driver conversation over the last several years, truly understanding very little of it. Now, in what was a bare few seconds of time, meaningful pieces came back to him.

"Never brake or even slow down in a staightaway, son," they would say. "You'll get run over!"

"Get the car under control, Dad!" became a virtual shout from his subconscious. As Ross watched helplessly, it was horribly apparent that there was no way out for Ethan as the car hurtled toward the first turn with its thirty-five-foot embankment just beyond the fence. Later, when Ross replayed the scene over and over in his mind, vividly reconstructing every single image, he would remember seeing Al Stuart's shoulders sag as he glanced over to his right to watch the struggle between man and machine just as the car exploded through the fence.

Memorial Day 1940

When Jeanne and Robert Proctor married, the stock market crash of 1929 existed only in the minds of the most pessimistic of the gloom-and-doom prophets. They and the rest of the country remained in a state of mind that would not allow them to consider the obvious. The beautiful future for all Americans was in serious jeopardy and attention needed to be paid to what was happening. The Proctors fell into the category of the deliberately blissful ignorant. The optimism of the roaring twenties stayed with them and they could not wait to bring a child into this bright and cheery world. They were young and healthy; there was no reason not to expect that a successful pregnancy would follow the wedding ceremony in a quick and orderly fashion. The adorable cottage with the white picket fence and the swing in the yard was ready and it was just a matter of time before the baby's nursery on the second floor was filled. Unfortunately, reality often seems to seek out the most romantic, stepping in to crush dreams and turn optimists into cynics.

The twelve years following the Proctors' wedding were increasingly difficult, as nothing seemed to be going according to plan. The childless marriage was especially trying for Jeanne. Like so many women in similar circumstances, she was convinced that something must be wrong with her. The fact that the doctors could not determine the cause of her inability to conceive caused a deep frustration, a pebble-in-the-shoe irritation that neither of them could readily identify. What had been a very happy marriage began to suffer.

Jeanne waited for three months of missed periods before she dared to tell Bob that she was indeed pregnant and that their nearly twelve years of waiting were over. He could barely contain his happiness and felt that finally his dream might be coming true, although many years late. He was sure that a man of his age would not be called into the service, even if the United States entered the war in Europe. His expanding textile business, which had seen the hard times of the Depression, would be likely to flourish further in a war environment. While he preferred not to think about war, he knew that there would be money to be made if the country had to gear up to fight.

While age was working to Robert's advantage, the doctor expressed considerable concern about the effect of a pregnancy on a woman of Jeanne's age. For her part, Jeanne felt more like a woman of twenty-five than of thirty-eight and did not give her doctor's warning any attention. After all, wasn't this the same doctor who had finally told her it was highly unlikely that she would ever get pregnant?

When Jeanne started labor on the night before the holiday, the usually well-organized Bob Proctor became the typical father-to-be, even though he had sworn he would remain calm. By the time they arrived at the hospital, Jeanne's labor was well under way and the doctor felt it was sure to be a holiday baby. Bob's only regret, of little consequence to him, was that his favorite spectator event of the Decoration Day holiday was a trip to the local dirt track to watch those open-cockpit sprint cars race. He always thought about how exciting it must be to drive one of them but was far too practical to consider getting involved in such a hobby. Instead, he would be satisfied simply to watch those crazy drivers risk their lives to entertain a small group in the grandstand for a paltry purse at the end of the day. He would gladly set aside his traditional trip this Memorial Day in order to be sitting in the waiting room with the other expectant fathers. He already was imagining the scene when the doctor opens the door, announces that Robert Proctor is the proud father of a baby boy and the passing of cigars begins. He even was enjoying the fantasy of bringing his little boy to ball games, circuses, and perhaps the holiday races he himself enjoyed so much.

When the door to the waiting room swung open, all four of the fathers-to-be practically jumped from their chairs. Bob instantly recognized Dr. Judson and immediately on the heels of that recognition came another. Something was wrong. For whatever reason, Bob simply walked through the door into the hallway and waited for the doctor to follow and give him whatever bad news had to be delivered. In his usual monotone, Dr. Judson began to spout medical terminology until Robert screamed, "What in God's name is happening?" The doctor took a step back at the aggressiveness of Robert's approach but now knew that the news was best delivered quickly and with no time to soften the blow.

He breathed deeply and announced, "Your wife died during the birth. I'm terribly sorry but there was nothing that could be done." Bob Proctor's reaction was not the ordinary response that the doctor had seen before. He did not ask about the child at all. Only after a minute or two of absolute silence did Dr. Judson begin to give some details of what happened.

"Had Jeanne been younger," he said, "I believe she might have survived the birth. It was a very difficult delivery and we just were unable to stem the hemorrhage."

The doctor had to put his hands on Robert's shoulder to make sure that he had his attention.

"Mr. Proctor! The baby survived. She's doing very well and..." Judson's voice faltered as he gathered enough air to blurt out the rest of his announcement in a single breath.

"There's one more thing. Before Mrs. Proctor lost consciousness, she said to be sure to tell you that she loves you. And, Mr. Proctor, something else, something that did not make much sense to any of us. She wanted to tell you that she knows your daughter will be worth the sacrifice."

When a shaken and ashen-faced Robert Proctor was taken in to see his wife, he looked down at her, struck by an obvious aura of peace surrounding her. He reached for her right hand, raising it toward him as he bent over her. He held it to his cheek, looked down at her, and said simply, "Thank you." Then, he knelt by the bed, put down his head and sobbed until the nurse came to take him to see his daughter.

Memorial Day 1942

The Johnsons, a large family even for the heavily Catholic neighborhood they called home, were about to endure what was becoming a much too common event as the war spread its cloud of gloom over the world. The visit from the captain, accompanied by the priest, had confirmed exactly what they expected when Ross, barely two, saw the two uniformed men approach the large but deteriorating farmhouse. The youngster, impressed by the shining medals adorning the chest of the military man, was well aware of the importance in the faith of the uniform of the priest. His exclamations had bought the family running but in seconds he saw the usual happy-go-lucky nature of the brood drain from them like water from the bathtub. Whatever it was that replaced the cozy, safe feeling that always surrounded his grandmother, he knew that he did not want it to happen.

By the time Father Gallagher raised his hand to knock on the door, Susan Johnson's cascade of tears told Ross that something utterly terrible had happened. Knowing that her life and that of her eight children was about to be changed forever, she could only whisper, "But we need him." She gathered her courage and opened the door. The expression of sheer panic on her face told Father Gallagher and the captain that they need not say anything except "I'm sorry." The two men dutifully mumbled the words, virtually in unison. The explanations, the clichés, the romanticized version of their father's death were all for the benefit of the children. To Susan, none of it really mattered. All she was feeling was the blurred realization that her sweat-drenched nightmares had come true. Her husband of nineteen years, the robust and always smiling Irishman with the bright red curly hair was gone. She recognized in that microcosmic instant that she had referred to her Sandy as gone hundreds of times. That is what professional sailors are most of the time. His long stints in the Merchant Marine and now the US Navy had brought Susan much sympathy from the other women in the neighborhood. The frequent joke among her friends was that Sandy had the instincts of her other pets, never being "gone" when she was at her most fertile.

The captain, his many war medals reflecting the crumbling faces of the family around him, assumed his best professional demeanor. He straightened into the classic military posture and began the routine of explaining options for the rituals of the next week or two. Susan felt overwhelming sadness for the eight children, now arranged behind her by size, as though about to march through a physical education class. "The children always feel this sort of thing the deepest," she thought. They idolized their father, no surprise since he perpetually arrived home from his exotic trips with the expected, even required souvenirs. Then he would spend his leave enthralling them with suspense-filled stories before sailing off to yet another adventure. They, of course, had no idea that an integral part of most of his adventures involved virtually any female companionship he could find. Susan, however, was painfully aware of this penchant her handsome husband possessed but had long ago made the conscious choice to accept it with her usual stoicism.

Fay, the eldest, now held Ross tightly, feeling much more like a young child than an eighteen-year-old mother. What she had thought was to be her release from the second mother, chief babysitter role of the oldest daughter of the family had not worked as she had planned. At fifteen, quickly maturing into womanhood, she became an easy target for the older, sophisticated Ethan Becker, locally famous as an expert automobile mechanic, despite being only eighteen. As Susan was forced to supplement the family income with a position in the cafeteria of the nearby high school, Fay saw the inequities of her homemaker responsibilities increase to what she thought were unbearable. Her hasty marriage to Ethan created a small but tasty bit of gossip for the neighborhood but, unfortunately for Fay, only resulted in a larger trap instead of an escape. Ethan could not land the well-paying automotive job he expected and they were forced to move into the already-crowded Johnson household. The neighborhood gossips were delighted when their suspicions were confirmed and Fay and Ethan's infant son was added to the family. Fay grew more and more discouraged as the duties of motherhood were not of the romanticized, live-happily-ever-after type but rapidly became pure drudgery. She watched enviously as her brothers and sisters left for the carefree life of school. There were many days when, after her mother and husband had driven off for work, she would look around at the housework to be done, sit down and simply stare out the window, angry tears of frustration filling her eyes.

The inevitable tension in a young teenage marriage was compounded by the close quarters of eleven people living in the small farmhouse. In her worst moments, Fay would secretly wish that Ethan had not become part of the closely knit family. Her siblings welcomed Ross as just another brother and she thought they probably would all be happier without the temperamental Ethan acting like the obnoxious older brother of all of them. Now her father, who she had been sure would one day come back and save the family from the silent, stoic desperation of the lower middle class, was never coming home again.

Fay had continued to mature into a quietly attractive young woman, her light brown hair with a reddish tint falling softly below her shoulders in a natural pageboy cut that would have made some film stars envious. In the three years since her marriage to Ethan, her dark brown eyes had lost much of their sparkle but none of their natural beauty. A lovely, smooth complexion enhanced the effect of her high cheekbones and gave her a Lauren Bacall look. A perfect row of slightly protruding teeth pushed against her upper lip, seeming to force her mouth to smile to be comfortable. Her mother's hand-me-down cotton dresses, fitting loosely, could not cover the voluptuousness of her figure, yet she had such little self-confidence that her entire demeanor assumed the qualities of a woman twice her age, a slight sag in her shoulders already apparent.

Fay's dazed, light-headed state was interrupted by the sound of a car on the gravel driveway. "Ethan!" she thought. "Why didn't his errand keep him just a little longer?" She was not in the mood to give him the attention he always demanded. She knew that even in this situation, he would not be happy sharing her with both Ross and now her deceased father whom he barely knew. Once again, she felt the ever-present knot of resentment and bitterness expand ever so slightly in her stomach.

As Ethan turned into the driveway, guiding the old rumble-seated Ford coupe through the break in the tall hedge, he noticed the official US Navy sedan parked near the front porch. Immediately, he felt the sick, sinking feeling in his belly, knowing that something was not right but afraid to let his mind speculate about what that might be. He quickly parked the car under the huge walnut tree in the backyard of the farmhouse, feeling the same dreaded anticipation anyone experiences at the beginning of a "I've some bad news" phone call. He felt that this excitement would not be all that bad. He knew only one person in the U.S. Navy and that was Fay's father. His relationship with Mr. Johnson could only be termed strained at best but since the father of the house was home so rarely, it barely affected him at all. He pulled on the car door handle, only to have it come off in his hand once again. With more frustration than anger, he reached through the open window and released the door from the outside. As he made his way toward the porch, the whimpering sounds of women crying drifted through the somewhat dilapidated screen door. The harsh squeal from the rusty spring caused everyone in the parlor to turn toward him, looking at him as if he were an intruder at a family party. Ethan saw the gathering through the long hallway leading from the kitchen to the small living room, or parlor, as they liked to refer to it. Even at that distance, their emotional state was obvious. The now common but troublesome thought again came to him: "How could I have let myself get into this situation?" What had seemed like an interesting seduction of fifteen-year-old Fay had left him with a two-year-old son and her large family which seemed constantly to be involved in a conspiracy against him. As he approached the group, he knew that once again a family crisis was on the horizon.

Memorial Day 1950

As Ethan came off the last turn, he knew the car was not handling the way it should. It seemed to be fighting him all the time. He felt fairly confident that he would be able to finish the race but that was all.

"God dammit! I hate going into the pits halfway through a race," he shouted out loud but to himself, as there was no one else to hear. He quickly made the decision not only to finish the race but also to fight this machine until it gave him a chance to win. He knew that Al Stuart would not make it easy for him even though they were the best of friends. He thought he could pass on the straightaway. "The grandstanders will love this," he thought. As he pushed the pedal to the floor, he felt something snap in the steering mechanism. At over ninety miles an hour, they had passed the grandstand and were heading into the first turn. He had put his left front wheel right on top on Al's right rear but realized that the machine was not responding to his coaxing. In what was just an instant in time, he knew he was going to crash. He could not make the car turn at all. It seemed to have a mind of its own and was heading straight for the wooden fence marking the edge of the track, the embankment looming beyond the first turn. His last thought as the car sent the fence boards flying in every direction was of his son who was seeing all of this. "Probably sitting on top of the goddam truck," he thought as his hands flew to his face for protection.

The sprint car became airborne as it sailed into the forest that surrounded the first turn. Cutting treetops as effectively as a lumber mill power saw, the car then tumbled to the ground, coming to rest upside down in a small clearing. Ethan dangled by his seat belt, marveling that somehow he was still alive. When the adrenaline careening through his veins had slowed enough to allow him to begin to assess his situation, he understood that he remained in extreme danger. He was still trapped by the exhaust header that ran down the side of the car and knew that the white-hot pipe would cause third-degree burns if it were touched. His mind was in turmoil. Miraculously, he had survived the crash. He had to get out before the inevitable fire started. Twice, he had witnessed racing buddies being fried after surviving the initial accident, and the fear of being burned to death was about the only one he would admit to anyone who would listen.

As he hung there, upside down, thinking about his best course of action, he heard the shouts of the crowd coming from up on the track. Just as he tried to maneuver to see if any of the spectators had made their way down the embankment, he saw two hands come from nowhere to grasp the steaming-hot exhaust pipe. The hands were connected to a burly man about fifty whom Ethan thought he recognized as part of Al Stuart's pit crew. Standing directly behind the man, Ethan noticed a girl of about ten. Even from the dazed, upside-down perspective in which Ethan found himself, he was keenly aware of the presence of this child. He saw the huge, muscular man glance back at the girl. After she simply nodded, the man, using his bare hands, lifted the exhaust pipe away from the car. Ethan unsnapped his seat belt and dropped to the ground. In the time it took him to get to his feet and begin to think clearly again, both the man and the girl had vanished. Ethan, in an instinctive response mode, ran to the bottom of the embankment and scrambled partway up the soft sandy incline, slipping back every few feet. He knew that he had to warn any would-be rescuers, now assembling at the top of the hill, to clear the area. He looked up and gave the traditional "I'm all right!" wave and acknowledged the cheers of the crowd, knowing that he had likely disappointed some of them by not being ripped to pieces. When he made the top of the hill, he ran across the track and pushed through the crowd to find his son sitting on the ground and shaking.

"I'm ok, Ross, boy!"

Ross answered calmly, "I know." And then the ground shook as number 21 exploded and burst into flames, sending a fireball of aviation fuel into the air above the tall pines.

After finding Ross, Ethan checked to see that Fay had come through the ordeal with her faculties intact. He found Fay's mental state just as he expected it would be, bordering on a controlled hysteria. She seemed almost surprised to see him but recovered quickly. It was apparent that once again she had convinced herself that her rosary beads saved the day. Ethan just shrugged and returned to the pits, circulating among the other drivers and crews. Almost to a man, they congratulated him with more enthusiasm than if he had won the race, well aware that Ethan's survival could only be described as a miracle.

Ethan found his way to Al Stuart's pit area to thank the burly Charlie Beckholdt for saving his life by moving the exhaust pipe. He found only one of Al's crew working on getting the car ready for the trailer transport home.

"Hey, Billie, where's Charlie?" Ethan called, fully expecting that the answer would be "at the local hospital tending to the severe burns" he must have received when he touched the exhaust pipe.

Billie acted rather surprised at the question and responded with a shrug of the shoulders. "I thought Al would've told you, Ethan. Charlie took sick in the middle of the week and far 's I know, he's still home in bed." Now it was Ethan's turn to be surprised.

"I'm sure that he helped me out of the wreck today, Billie." Charlie Beckholdt was not someone likely to be mistaken for someone else, even by a man hanging upside down by a safety belt in a race car about to explode.

"Well, Ethan, I know you don't make many mistakes but you've got this one wrong, for sure," Billie said, now convinced that Ethan better have his head checked at the hospital after all.

While Ethan was on his search, Ross also was wandering through the entire area. He was wearing his father's helmet as a badge of honor, with numerous deep gashes where it had been struck with tree limbs slicing through the number 21 on the side. His wanderings had a different purpose. He also had someone to thank, but she was nowhere to be found. He wound his way through the maze of cars and crews in the pits asking all of the regulars about the beautiful young girl. No one was of any help in locating her, which completely frustrated Ross, who had convinced himself that she was the sole reason his father came through the accident virtually unscathed. From a distance, he saw his father standing by the burned-out skeleton that was his car and the lilting voice of the girl came drifting up from his subconscious.

"You understand, of course, that this favor will have to be returned later" she had said.

The most startling event of the incredible day occurred minutes later, after Ethan saw his son come running over to the old number 21, the helmet bouncing crazily over the too-small head of the boy.

Al Stuart had not only won the race after the accident delay but also went on to win the feature race and take home one of the largest purses in the history of the small track, a handsome $235. Ethan saw him striding across the infield as though he had a mission. He went directly to Billie and the rest of the crew, who were just completing the loading of the car on the trailer. Even from the three or four hundred yards away, it was plain that Al was carrying more of a burden than that $235. When all of them finally got together, Al looked around, made eye contact with each of them and tried desperately to control himself.

In a carefully restrained but shaking voice, Al struggled to force out the words that seemed to be choking him.

"Charlie's dead," he said. "When I got to the purser's office, there was a message to call Mary. She said his heart just gave out. I don't really know anything else right now."

Ethan, now visibly affected, protested. "It can't be," he said. "He helped me get out of the wreck. I know he did!"

The other men, now in shock at the horrible news about their lovable friend, Charlie, just turned and stared at Ethan.

"Hey, Ethan, it's been a long and bad day all around," Al said, in as kind and gentle a tone as he could muster from his quivering, emotional voice. "Why don't we just get out of here?" In a somber, sad silence, the men proceeded through the final preparations to make the trip home.

Charlie Beckholdt's Funeral

At Charlie's funeral later that week, Ethan knew he was simply being patronized when he attempted to explain to anyone about the somewhat miraculous appearance of Charlie to help him get out of the car. Even his closest friends would just nod and agree amicably when he knew they were thinking his explanation was the result of the shock and trauma of the accident. Much like the old proverb about a lie told often eventually becomes the truth, Ethan began to doubt his version of Charlie's intervention after hearing so many of his racing comrades dispute it. Most of the people he told would more likely have believed Fay's account of his survival in such a catastrophic crash. The mechanical repetition of her story at poor old Charlie's funeral to anyone who would listen became more than slightly obnoxious, as though she were trying to impress everyone with the profound depth of concern she felt for Ethan. In a matter-of-fact way, she would describe hearing the collective groan of the crowd as the car disappeared through the fence. Then she would say almost by rote, "I squeezed the rosary in my hand, kissed the cross, and knew he would be all right." Ross first heard this line as they were driving home from the track late that afternoon. At the time, he wondered what his parents would say about the young girl and the promise he had made. He had decided that for now it was best not to anger his mother with such a fantastic story. He also was busily trying to sort out in his mind how the Catholic Church could tell the difference between the superstitions of the race drivers and the belief that clutching a rosary could save a life.

A major topic of conversation at Charlie Beckholdt's funeral was the story of the accident in the local paper the day after the holiday. The small track usually was barely mentioned in the *Courier Gazette*. The coverage never amounted to more than a paragraph hidden away on the sports page. On this particular Memorial Day, an apprentice reporter had decided to take his new camera with manual shutter speeds on a test run at the races, an obvious choice to see if indeed it could stop action as effectively as its maker proclaimed. He had stationed himself at the first turn of the track, just outside the fence. This position gave him a head-on view of the cars as they came down the straightaway and roared into the turn. He had decided that the second race would be the last he would try to photograph until the final feature event. As he watched Al and Ethan careening toward the turn in a very close race, he began taking pictures. The three that appeared on the front of the *Gazette* were the object of much discussion, especially among the drivers at the charming Charlie's final party. Ross, the proud son, carried the front page with him to school every day and eventually was told by his favorite nun that he was not to look at that newspaper in class again. The first picture was taken just as Ethan realized the hopelessness of his situation and made the futile gesture of putting his hands over his face. The young reporter used his speed shutter to excellent advantage and captured the speeding car's initial impact with the wooden fence. The side-view shot of the car with one wooden slat flying through the air seemed to show a driver on his way to certain death, huge trees and a thirty-foot drop in front of him. The paper, naturally enough, carried a disclaimer that had the driver died, they would not have run the picture.

The second and third photographs were apparently taken within seconds of each other as the reporter made his way down the embankment toward the accident scene. Both were of the car as it rested in the small clearing, upside down and leaning over to expose the cockpit. The center frame clearly showed the driver hanging upside down, held in by only his safety belt. His arms were in a raised position as though trying to unsnap his belt. The exhaust pipe was diagonally across the only escape route out of the cockpit. The third and final published picture was quite obviously snapped by the photographer as he tried to keep his balance coming down the hill toward the car. This was the photo that caused the most discussion: it showed Ethan crawling through the very spot that seconds before had been blocked by the hot exhaust system.

When Ethan extracted the paper from the bushes where the inaccurate news carrier usually threw it, he didn't look at it until he sank down on the bottom front step of the porch. In a corner of the crooked porch, Ross sat brushing their large and, by most criteria, vicious German shepherd, Mikie, when he saw his father unfold the paper, open it, and stare at the front page. After a full minute, Ethan said, softly but loud enough for Ross to hear, "He must have seen that little girl and Charlie or whoever the hell it was!"

"Dad, what little girl?" Ross left Mikie unattended and tiptoed over to see what his father was seeing. He couldn't resist asking the question. He had thought of nothing but the girl since the accident.

"There was a little girl there with the guy, Charlie or whoever, Ross." Ethan spoke the words with such an unusual combination of agitation, conviction, and reverence that Ross decided in an instant that this was the time to tell his father about his little girl.

"Dad?" The father-son relationship had plenty of room for admiration, respect and for hero worship. It was not a relationship that allowed Ross to open himself to possible ridicule by talking about problems that he was convinced his father could never have had. The thought of telling Ethan about the girl at the track was never even a consideration until Ross heard his father mention a girl. While his mother would have punished him for lying, his father would have simply laughed at him in that way of his that always made him cry, but, of course, never in public. Ethan had gained his son's admiration and respect but it was certainly not rooted in his compassion and understanding. Rather, it came from an awesome fear far beyond what most young boys felt toward their fathers. To tell his father about this girl would take as much courage as Ross could extract from his somewhat uncertain self-esteem.

"Dad, I know who that girl was; or, at least, I saw her right after the accident." Ross made this statement in almost cowering fashion. He was never sure how his father would react to anything. Ross had learned a lesson early and often: Children were seen and not heard, especially in the Becker household. The truth was that Ross was terrified of his father and regretted instantly his announcement, as his father spun to face him on the porch.

Already Ross was beginning to plan his defense, both physical and emotional. When Ethan demanded loudly, "Come here, boy!" the familiar churning in his stomach let Ross know that he could be in for a whole lot of trouble. He slowly approached his father, who seemed to be in quite an emotional state himself, a state that Ross rarely witnessed.

"What in hell are you talking about? If this is another one of the stupid stories you're always making up, you'll have more trouble than you can handle!"

Ross now felt that he had a made a serious mistake and decided to retreat out of physical range. The accusatory tone was common, one that Ross and his mother heard often enough. It frequently followed the desperate attempts of both son and wife to please Ethan in some way. They were both realizing without ever talking about it that these attempts were becoming more and more futile. Neither one had the slightest idea why but each kept trying just the same.

If there is such a thing as negative encouragement, Ross felt it as his father pressed him about this girl. He was surprised when Ethan actually appeared to listen to him with some degree of interest, and he wondered why his father seemed to have a reason for believing him this time.

Memorial Day 1950

THE PROCTORS

Bob Proctor had spent his usual two hours at his wife's gravesite, alternately weeping and cursing, just as he done for each anniversary of her death for the last ten years. His life had evolved into what some thought was an unhealthy relationship with their daughter.

At the beginning, no one blamed him. Jennie was all he had and the fact that he became a loving and doting father was initially seen by his friends as positive. After all, hadn't everyone known a husband who harbored a well-hidden but abiding resentment toward the child who was the cause of a beloved wife's death? In the case of the Proctors, those who gloried in gossip would not hesitate to point out the almost obsessive devotion that Bob exhibited in every area of Jennie's life. All of this speculation was lost on Robert Proctor. If someone were to point out that getting on with his own life was long overdue, he would have dismissed the idea immediately. The final words of his dear Jeanne, as delivered by the now disgraced Dr. Judson, had become a virtual creed to live by. "Your daughter will be worth the sacrifice," the doctor had repeated. It only made sense to Bob that his wife had made a deathbed request, one that required him to be sure that Jennie was protected from what he saw as an increasingly dangerous world. If that request meant spending an inordinate amount of time with her, then so be it.

Since Jeanne's death, Bob attempted to date on just two occasions, both of them utterly disastrous. An engaging and successful businessman, Bob Proctor certainly was an infinitely eligible single man who had the attention of most of the unattached females in town. Not particularly handsome but more than adequate by most standards, he could easily pick and choose those women who might interest him. In spite of the abortive attempts of his friends and neighbors to play matchmaker, he plainly and simply was not interested in another relationship. His devotion to Jeanne was now transferred to Jennie; from his perspective, there was nothing wrong with that. From an outsider's view, Jennie had some need of protection. She was not a physically strong young girl; most who knew her would describe her as wispy, even frail, a child who needed to be watched especially carefully for the many dreaded childhood diseases. Emotionally, she seemed much the same. Her thin but beautiful face always carried an expression of concern, about what was anyone's guess. She was widely regarded by her teachers as the most sensitive student in her school, a trait that should have made her an easy mark for the incessant teasing of elementary-age schoolboys.

On one occasion in second grade, her teacher found her clutching the chain-link fence around the schoolyard, her body shaking with the force of her sobs. After hurriedly removing her from the gathering crowd of classmates and calming her enough so that she could talk, Miss Charles had tried to find out exactly what caused this emotional trauma. Jennie, when she could finally explain, described in a halting voice how she had seen a small squirrel struck by a car as it tried to cross the street.

"I did my best but I couldn't help it," she managed to say before once again the uncontrolled tears were flowing. Miss Charles, who was well aware of the other twenty children on their way into her class, concerned herself with calming Jennie once again. She never did frame the question that had quickly come and just as quickly gone in the activity of the moment. The question was rather obvious but Miss Charles surely had no way of knowing that Jennie herself couldn't have answered it at that time.

"What exactly might you have been doing to help the squirrel, Jennie, especially through the tall chain fence?"

Now in fifth grade, Jennie had been through almost six years in the same school. Her teachers in the close environment of the small elementary school came to expect what would have been some bizarre behaviors in other children as just the norm in Jennie. The most remarkable observation, one that they made over and over again in private but never in the insecurity of group faculty meetings, was that all teasing of Jennie had gradually stopped. Even some of the most vicious of the developing class bullies would have no part of using Jennie for a target of their cruel jokes. Some of the staff felt that Mr. Proctor's close involvement with all that happened in her life had a dampening effect on the other children. Others thought that it seemed as if the children held Jennie in awe, but none could determine any possible reason for this feeling; however, it was a sense shared by more than just a few.

Bob Proctor, now in an almost ritualistic mode after his visit to Jeanne's grave, raced through a shower, glanced at the clock, and saw that he needed to prod Jennie to get ready for the annual trip to the races. The relationship between father and daughter was so loving that Jennie never questioned the annual Memorial Day outing. Even though she was not very fond of the noise and the fumes, sitting with her father in the grandstand had its moments. She knew that Bob was not often happy. In spite of her repeated attempts to make him smile, the turned-down corners of his mouth seemed locked into position, preventing any effort on his part even to appear happy. Jennie never balked at going to the races thinking the outings would put a slight enthusiasm into his demeanor. For one afternoon at least, her father seemed interested in something beside her.

"We're leaving in fifteen minutes," Bob hollered up the stairs to Jennie. He knew that she was never late. He could not recall ever needing to discipline her at all. He really did look forward to the picnics, the trips to the amusement parks, the races, the Jersey shore, anything that kept Jennie within easy reach. At least when they were together, he didn't have to worry about the threats of the world around them. On very rare occasions, usually at night when the nagging, creeping depression kept him awake, he worried that he was not being fair to Jennie. Always, he would turn his thoughts to how much she liked spending time with him, then he could shunt aside the disquieting thoughts. She never mentioned having friends over or wanting to go to any school activities, so his desire to keep her insulated was validated in his mind. Today, the vicarious excitement he drew from watching the sprint car drivers stupidly endanger their lives would, as always, be enhanced by having his daughter right there next to him.

The second race of the day featured one of the top drivers on the small racing circuit. Al Stuart had always been one of Bob Proctor's favorites because of his utter recklessness, although race fans were fairly evenly divided in referring to this trait as fearlessness or stupidity. As Bob and Jennie watched from the fourth row of the grandstand, the race turned into what the true fan really wanted-a close two-car race between Al Stuart and Ethan Becker. Bob watched intently as the cars came past the grandstand, separated just by inches. He stood with the crowd and shouted encouragement to his favorite but in an instant realized that the second car, the car driven by Ethan Becker, was headed directly at the fence on the outside of the first turn. The exciting dread of seeing this spectacular crash about to happen was tempered by a sudden awareness that he did not want Jennie to see it. He quickly turned to his left to shield her eyes. At the same time that he heard the impact of the car striking the fence, he saw that Jennie was gone. His fascination with the crash was replaced by the utter terror of a parent who has lost his child. Stepping on the feet of the other spectators in his row, he pushed his way to the aisle and frantically looked around. The "occasionals" were straining to see what they were sure was a fatal accident. Bob had no patience with their lack of compassion nor with their pushing and shoving. An urge to begin screaming for Jennie rose in his throat. He fought the desperate panic of a man sinking beneath the surface for the last time before drowning.

Jennifer Proctor

Robert Proctor was well aware of the only reason he had not slipped into an abyss of despairing grief in the first few months after Jeanne died. His baby, his beautiful daughter, became the center of his life. The last words that Jeanne spoke assumed a life of their own. Bob missed his wife terribly. Although he would never admit it, he felt mired in the angry stage of grief that questioned God, the doctors, the hospital, even Jeanne herself. Before he realized that Jennie was recognizing him, he found himself behaving in completely irrational ways, cursing pictures of Jeanne.

"How could she have been so stupid? I didn't want her to get into a dangerous pregnancy." "The doctors warned her that she was too old!" The cataloging of his assigning blame would continue until he could feel himself falling over some sort of edge, a frightening cliff that he lacked the courage to peer over. His tirades usually ended with him doing something completely stupid, like throwing a picture across the room, always followed by a loss of all emotional control and the inevitable onset of almost hysterical sobbing. In this state of mind, he did not seem to be aware of his child, even though he was adamant that when he arrived home from work, the daytime baby-sitter was to leave immediately so he could take over. Jennie, in infancy, just appeared to wait for him to work through his nightly ritual. Only when he finished would she indicate that she needed some attention. Bob's unusual, but in his view normal behavior in his situation, ended abruptly on a ghastly hot summer evening in the middle of June when Jennie was just short of two weeks old.

As he always did, he instructed the sitter to leave even before he had come into the living room. He generally felt a bit of guilt in being abrupt with a fifty-year-old widow who was so conscientious, but his guilt disappeared as soon as he entered the house.

What he did not need were stories of possible instability floating around the neighborhood; he was more than capable of handling his parental responsibilities, despite the concerns of his friends and neighbors. It was best not to let anyone become aware of his occasional lapses into irrationality.

As the screen door slammed behind Mrs. Thompson, Bob suddenly was aware of a soft gurgling sound emanating from the baby's bassinet in the nursery. Slowly, he made his way through the house and up the stairs to the special room he had prepared with Jeanne more than twelve years before. As he entered the room, the usual deep sadness settled over him and he began to prepare himself for yet another bout with misery. Soundlessly, he approached the bassinet from the direction that he knew would be above the baby's head. Carefully remaining just out of Jennie's sight, he peeked over the side. He was startled to see her lying on her back with her eyes following very closely the colorful fish mobile suspended above the crib. Up to this time, she had seemed unaware of the world around her. To Bob Proctor, Jennie represented all that he had lost and nothing of what he had gained. Now, as he looked down on her and saw how her eyes reacted to the mobile, he felt his throat tighten and tears once again form in his eyes.

In desperation, he said aloud, "God, Jeanne, I want you here for this! You deserve to see her growing!" In a moment, his imagination flitted across the years, through a first communion, through a first date, through a prom, and dozens of other events that parents of two-week-old infants usually haven't begun to think about.

"You'll miss it all, Jeanne. I don't know how I can do it without you!" He became aware that the soft sounds coming from the bassinet had stopped. He slowly dropped his right hand from his eyes, the attempt to stem the tears futile as usual. It was just a meager few seconds before his eyes could focus once again. When they cleared, he found himself feeling somewhat self-conscious. Jennie, his beautiful daughter, was staring at him. All of her typically quick infant arm and kicking motions had stopped and she was simply centered directly on him. As he returned her gaze and she continued to stare back at him, he wondered how it was possible that an infant's eyes could be so penetrating. In that instant, he knew that the old maxim about the eye being the window of the soul was true. He had the unshakable feeling that Jennie, his tiny daughter, ever so helpless, was looking directly into the depths of his soul. In that watershed moment, he knew he would be having no more irrational tirades. Suddenly, the overpowering effect of the child in the small crib swept through him and he knew what Jeanne had meant. In later years, when it seemed the entire neighborhood was discussing Mr. Proctor's unusual, some said obsessive, level of interest in Jennie, Bob knew that it really was not important. Jennie had let him know that when she was two weeks old.

As the weeks turned into months and Jennie grew more beautiful by the day, Bob often returned to that blistering summer evening in his mind. That moment he had felt his very soul touched by a two-week-old infant. It had been the most unnerving and unsettling experience of his life yet, in a way he could never have understood, extremely pleasant and even uplifting.

The proverbial war clouds were clearly gathering in America and it was simply a matter of time before the country was drawn into the conflict. Bob Proctor's precious daughter created a deep ambivalence toward the prospect of war. His factory would be a hearty beneficiary from an extended armed conflict, yet he was deeply concerned about the effect an all-out world war would have on the future, especially on Jennie's. He agreed with the unspoken assessment of many government leaders that there is nothing like a good, old-fashioned war to expand the economy and put some momentum into the business growth of the country. As he sat with his beloved Jennie, barely eighteen months old, cradled in his arms and listened to President Roosevelt speak of the day that would live in infamy, he wondered what the future would bring, and held onto her just a little tighter.

Jennie could only be described as precocious. Her father never liked the term because he felt it had a negative connotation, and there was nothing about Jennie that was negative. People marveled at how such a young girl could be so poised and self-assured. She seemed to have a special sense that helped her know exactly what to do or say in every situation. Bob attributed her expansive vocabulary to his nightly bedtime reading, even though there were occasions when she used phrases that he simply could not explain. Her eyes, which he knew had once penetrated the depths of his very being, became a darker green and yet contained the lively sparkle so typical of intelligent and enthusiastic youngsters. Bob came to expect that Jennie would be at the center of events that could not be naturally explained. Now, when something unusual happened, he just shrugged it off, knowing with an innate certainty that she truly had a unique power, a gift that he dare not question.

When Jennie turned three years old, she awakened Bob at three in the morning and told him he had to go to the Baranellos' farmhouse across the road.

"Something is wrong with their toaster," she announced in a matter-of-fact tone. In a typically fatherly fashion, Bob tried to persuade Jennie to return to bed, but she was not to be dissuaded. Bob reached over and turned on the light, thinking how wonderful it was to have finally gotten electricity. He turned to face his daughter, ready to draw on his most persuasive parental psychology, but when he looked into her eyes, he knew he had to walk across to the Baranellos' farm.

Slowly and deliberately, Bob found his way through the darkness, wishing the streetlight project had not stopped a half-mile up the road. How could he tell his neighbors across the street that Jennie, at age three, wanted him to check their toaster? In the time it took for him to reach their door, he was still struggling with what he thought might be a plausible reason for a middle-of-the-night visit. He rapped loudly on the door, secretly hoping that he would fail to rouse anyone. Finally, he could hear movement on the second floor. He was sure that he also heard the muttering and swearing of the old Italian farmer. Then, the clumping down the stairs was followed by a short exclamation of frightened surprise, the kind that creates an instant stomach churning in anyone hearing it.

"Something is very wrong," Bob thought as he tried without success to peer through the thin layer of dust covering the window. He could hear the commotion inside, and, putting aside neighborly politeness, rushed through the unlocked door. He went right down the hallway to the dimly lit kitchen. In a single glance, he was able to take in the entire scene. Frank Baranello was frantically pumping the hand water pump in the sink, filling the bucket he had under the faucet. In the far corner of the typically large farmhouse kitchen, several old appliances were plugged into the single electrical outlet through a cheap adapter. In the seconds Bob required for the entire scene to sink in, Frank had finished filling the bucket. He motioned to Bob to watch out and headed toward the corner with the appliances, a corner that was rapidly filling with smoke from the smoldering but obviously live fire created by the frayed, shorted-out wiring in the old toaster. The single bucket of water was sufficient and extinguished the blaze.

In the same seconds, Bob Proctor became keenly aware that he had left his three-year-old daughter alone in the house, something he never did. It did not take very long for him to realize that had he not done as Jennie wanted, the old wood-frame farmhouse and its occupants would have been a tragic front-page story in the weekly newspaper. In the excitement of the moment, Frank Baranello did not ask Bob why he was there, a fact for which Bob was thankful. By the next morning, he hoped he might have a logical story to explain his knocking on the Baranellos' door at three A.M. He surely did not want to try to explain Jennie's behavior, especially to devoutly Catholic neighbors who believed that the power of Satan was much more likely to intervene in earthly affairs than would the power of saints.

This incident and others like it, although perhaps not always so dramatic, made Jennie's request of April 12, 1945, seem normal.

"Daddy, please turn on the radio. Something has happened," Jennie said.

Bob, having learned the difference between Jennie's flighty appeal for something like an ice cream and a seemingly urgent request like this, walked over to the huge RCA console radio that acted as the centerpiece of their living room. He flipped the on switch and the radio came slowly to life as the tubes warmed up. His favorite station, WCAU, was always on the dial. Instantly, he recognized the announcer's voice as the newscaster instead of the usual entertainers or soap operas. Bob and Jennie sat on the large, green overstuffed sofa. They stared at the two cloth-covered speakers on either side of the mahogany console, as though a face might appear, attached to the voice now drifting across the room. The deep, resonant voice was somber and Bob and Jennie listened to a repeat of the bulletin issued just moments before.

"President Roosevelt died at 3:35 P.M. this afternoon at his home in Warm Springs, Georgia. Harry Truman has been sworn in as President of the United States and will assume his duties later today in Washington."

Summer 1944

THE DROWNED KITTEN

Ross Becker, at four years old, provided the Johnson children a ready mark for the typically good-natured teasing that large, poor families often depend on for entertainment. Fay (the oldest and Ross's mother) had just turned nineteen, so the family consisted of nine children between the ages of four and nineteen. The fact that Fay had married Ethan Becker carried no influence with her brothers and sisters. To them, she was not an older married woman but just their older sister, subject to the same household rules and family traditions as the rest of them. Her husband, Ethan, was simply there, getting in the way on occasion but mostly referred to as the Phantom, a character from a popular movie serial currently in the theaters. Much like the celluloid Phantom, Ethan could disappear at a moment's notice, primarily to his workshop that he had declared absolutely off limits to the rest of the clan. Everyone shared the old farmhouse that the family rented, but the shaky garage, as Ethan called his construction, was available by Ethan's invitation only.

The Faxons had kept the house itself for income after they built a magnificent new home with the substantial revenue from their dairy farm. Surrounded by corn and potato fields, the house served as a residential haven for the large mice population found in the fields of any farm. The obvious solution to the "rascally rodent" problem, as Susan Johnson referred to it, was to develop a population of barn cats equal in number to the mice, or least so it seemed. Over the course of several years, the cats fell victim to constant inbreeding, a situation resulting in more than the usual amount of deformed kittens.

One warm Saturday morning in July, Toby Johnson, the oldest of the four boys, found a litter of newly born kittens under one corner of the porch. He quickly discovered why the mother cat had apparently abandoned them. All six animals were severely deformed. This was not the first time that this situation had arisen and an unintentional tradition, a rite of passage, had been established for the children in the family. On a rotating schedule and in a humane fashion, each of the children was required to dispose of any deformed kittens. The local veterinarian could have been contacted but even his nominal fee put this option out of reach for the Johnsons. Sandy decided that this would be a wonderful lesson for the children in the ways and realities of life and death, and Susan, gentle soul that she was, agreed with him in this instance. Even with Sandy gone, the tradition continued, and the sisters and brothers looked at their schedule to determine whose turn it was to mature a little this time, taking care of the six kittens Toby had found. Harold, now nine years old but the youngest and by far the most mischievous of the Johnsons, was next in line for the task. As the older brother, Toby usually acted as a protector for his brothers but this task became more unpleasant the older he got and he was more than delighted to let it fall to the happy-go-lucky Harold.

The favorite and surely the quickest and most humane method for the execution was to draw a large pail of water and submerge each kitten for just a fraction of a second and the deed would be finished. A second part of the tradition was the necessity that all of the children would observe the process, also as a growth experience. Toby, accommodating as ever, had already drawn the bucket of water for Harold to use and the family now gathered in the open backyard to observe the ritual. After Harold took two of the kittens from the box and, from the human perspective, put them out of their misery, it became quite clear that he was not enjoying this experience. He searched the faces around him, looking desperately for a way to shift the responsibility. His sad eyes struck upon Ross, standing behind the inner ring of Johnsons. As though the thought spontaneously and simultaneously appeared in every sibling's mind, all turned to look at Ross, now in his defensive, back-tracking mode. Ross actually turned to run but Ethan wrapped an arm around his waist and lifted him off the ground, feet still in full flight.

"He's too young, Ethan; PLEASE DON'T!" Fay was pleading but all of them knew what needed to happen.

Any other day, Ethan would have been at work but this Saturday was one of his few days off. Fay knew that without Ethan there to force the issue, she could have handled the rest of the family. Ross was, after all, only four years old, but instead she just gave up without a even a whimper.

Ethan carried Ross into the middle of the family circle and set him down by the bucket and the box with the remaining kittens in it. He reached into the box and handed Ross one of the worst of the pathetic animals, a shiny black kitten with a single patch of white on its chest accentuating the grotesque stubs that would have served as front paws.

"Here, Ross. You need to do this."

Ross wrapped his small hand around the stomach of the tiny creature and held it over the bucket.

"Do it quickly so it doesn't suffer, Ross", Toby hollered from the circle. With one motion, Ross pushed his arm into the bucket, so far that the tattered sleeve of his T-shirt touched the top of the water. When he pulled his arm out, the dripping-wet kitten looked as if it had been frightened to death, eyes bulging and body rigid in the small boy's hand. Ross turned his hand slightly to look at the animal, glanced at his family around him, dropped the dead cat, and ran crying into the house. He practically fell up the stairs and then flopped onto his bed, stuffed his head into his pillow, and continued to weep.

Back in the yard, his father, with no show of emotion, announced to the gathering, "The first time is always the hardest; he'll be fine." He then turned and walked toward his car, parked near the homemade garage.

Barely a week had passed from the time Ross had his coming of age with the drowning of the kitten. Even sleeping in the row of beds with the four Johnson boys all in the same room did not stop his recurring, fleeting nightmare, a nightmare from which he always quickly awoke and then quietly went downstairs to his grandmother's room. No one else in the house would be awake but somehow, as he pushed open her bedroom door, Susan Johnson would know he was there and invite him in for comfort. A few soothing words from her and Ross would be ready to return to his bed and could then sleep the rest of the night. This night, the sixth since his kitten experience, he awakened right on schedule with the short nightmare, a vision of the kitten he had killed stiffening in his hand and screeching in silence.

As he slowly climbed from the bed and prepared to venture down the stairs to be comforted by Susan, he heard muffled voices coming from his parents' bedroom down the long corridor of the second floor. By now Ross was quite good at not being heard as he found his way around the house in the dark. He tiptoed down the hallway. The door to the bedroom was ajar and Ross could see into the dimly lit room. The sparse furnishings took shape as his eyes grew accustomed to the poor light. Ross could see the old wooden double bureau across the room, the small lamp providing just enough light to reflect its stained top, with its chipped brown paint, in the hazy mirror. His eyes traced the cracks in the plaster of the bare wall toward the four-poster double bed, yet another piece of old furniture handed down through at least two generations.

Fay was in the bed and the covers were all askew. His youthful eyes had by now completely overcome the murky half light and he realized that his mother was holding a pillow over her face, muffling the sounds she was making. One thing he knew for certain; she was in pain. At the foot of the bed, a man in dark clothing was bending over and seemed to be examining his mother, much as he remembered the doctor examining him for appendicitis. Next to the bed, standing but slouching slightly, Ross saw the unmistakable silhouette of his father. For more than five minutes, he watched in fascination and complete silence, straining to see details. Finally, the man who was bending straightened up and turned to his father, holding something in his hand. The muffled sounds came louder from beneath his mother's pillow. He wondered how everyone in the whole house could still be asleep. Then, the man holding the object turned toward the shaded light from the bureau lamp, trying to allow Ethan a better look at whatever it was. As he turned, a streak of the light reflected off the man's hand and, in that instant, Ross almost screamed. His nightmare of minutes before became real as he saw that what the man was holding had eyes and could easily have been the dead kitten. It was about the same size and seemed deformed but looked much more like one of the rag dolls that his aunts constantly had draped over their beds. Whatever was taking place in that room, Ross was sure that he was not supposed to be watching. In his now practiced quiet pace, he slowly eased his way back down the hall and inched his way into bed. Over an hour later, he finally fell into a somewhat fitful sleep and did not hear the quiet footfalls of his father and the doctor as they went down the stairs.

Ethan Becker

At any time of the day or night, if he wasn't working, Ethan could most likely be found in the makeshift garage he had slapped together in the backyard of the Johnsons' house. Only under extreme duress would he choose to come into the house, a house where he increasingly felt like an intruder. His feelings that a family conspiracy against him was always in progress were enhanced any time he was in a gathering of Fay's brothers and sisters. Susan, the matriarch, tolerated him, especially after he landed the job at the local Ford agency and was able to contribute to the weekly income. The other siblings were barely civil. Ethan was definitely not one to express himself in any way that might show vulnerability, so he chose to ignore them as much as possible, feeling that the problem rested with them, not him.

This especially beautiful spring afternoon, he pulled his old '36 Ford coupe out of the garage and was going through his usual routine of taking things apart and putting them back together again. Gas rationing prevented any but the most critical driving but he was determined that his car would be ready when this seemingly endless war was over. He smiled to himself as he thought about the providential attack of appendicitis that had sent him to the naval hospital in Bainbridge. But for that, he might have suffered the same fate as poor old Sandy Johnson. He was quite satisfied not being a war hero, especially a dead one. His honorable medical discharge provided him with a solid head start on the men his age who would be returning from overseas with all sorts of medical and psychological problems.

As he leaned across the fender, peering into the wonderfully grease-ladened six-cylinder engine, he heard the old screen door slam and Fay's voice echo across the yard.

"Ethan, come quick. Hurry!" she screamed.

Ethan knew from her trembling voice that something was wrong.

"She's always overreacting," he thought. "Solve your God damn problems yourself for a change," he whispered viciously under his breath.

He grudgingly pulled himself out from under the hood and began to walk slowly toward the house.

"The President's dead, he's dead!" Fay was now sobbing loudly.

By the time Ethan reached the porch, he realized how reminiscent the whole scene was. The family were reacting just as they did about three years before when the news of Sandy Johnson's death reached them. Although not usually a political person, Ethan had no time for Roosevelt. He believed what the conservatives were saying: Roosevelt had manipulated everything in order to have the general population see him as the country's savior. Ethan was convinced that the attack on Pearl Harbor could have been stopped but that it was to Roosevelt's advantage to be sure that the United States entered the war with popular opinion behind him. Although he would not say what he was thinking to Fay at this moment, he was not that sorry to see the President being replaced by the incompetent Harry Truman.

"Damn, Fay. That's awful!" Ethan said, squeezing as much sincerity into his voice as he could without appearing artificial. He could hear the crying and sobbing coming from the house and really wanted no part of it.

"I've got a lot of work to do on the car, Fay. Why don't you go in and try to comfort your family? Send Ross out to me if you want." He gave her his usual perfunctory and meaningless hug, turned, and started back across the yard to his car.

The bright April day was in contradiction to the mood of the household. Ethan again wondered how he had gotten himself into this box. He increasingly felt that he had been trapped and the avenues for escape were becoming more limited. Fay was beginning to act as if she owned him and the responsibilities of fatherhood were infringing on his valuable time with his car.

"I couldn't care less about that communist Roosevelt," he thought. "People don't know the harm he was doing to us. Maybe the next guy will be better but for sure we'll get a Republican elected next time." His thoughts tumbled together as he arrived at his precious car.

"This is what makes me happy, right here. The family and Roosevelt can go to hell for all I care!" Once again, he thanked whatever eternal master plan there was for the fortuitous burst appendix at Bainbridge Naval Station several years before.

As Ethan once again leaned into the engine compartment, he heard the unmistakable roar of Al Stuart's car as it rumbled into the driveway. He had met Al two years before at a small auto repair shop and they struck up a solid friendship right from the start. Both were interested in racing and often spoke of building race cars together as a business instead of a hobby. The shared interests and the fact that Ross idolized Al strengthened the friendship to the point that much of their time was spent together. Ross loved to see Al coming. He always had a ball, bat, and glove with him and would spend hours on a Sunday afternoon playing catch with Ross. His unending supply of patience and good natured humor was welcome around the Johnsons' and Ethan was happy to have someone relieve him of many of his fatherly responsibilities. Fay did not seem to mind either, actually enjoying Al's company also. To Ethan, the situation looked positive for all concerned.

"Wonder if Al heard about the President?" he mused.

Al's car had stopped halfway down the driveway. Ethan lifted his head out from under the hood and looked back up to the house. Fay had gone back in and brought Ross out onto the porch. Al jumped from his car and signaled the usual exuberant greeting to Ross. Ross jumped into Al's arms from the top of the porch steps and Fay managed a smile through her tear-stained face. Al put Ross down gently and went up the steps to Fay.

"I heard the news, Fay. It's really a tragedy. He's done so much for the country!" Al said, surprised to feel his eyes fill with tears. A tall man with a stocky build, Al could have been taken for a rugged western movie star, one whose looks are overshadowed by their on-screen heroics. He could not be called handsome but his face always had a soft, kind expression, an empathetic look that everyone found appealing. He just seemed to care. His tousled brown hair gave him a slightly unkempt but not at all sloppy appearance. A gentle and sincere aura coupled with his warm hazel eyes radiated a subtle seductiveness.

Fay, who had just managed to get her emotions under control, now lost them again. She was genuinely touched by Al's reaction and mildly surprised, although she knew Al to be considerably more sensitive than Ethan. In a spontaneous reaction, she moved toward Al and reached out with both arms. Ross moved between them, and all three shared a warm and comforting hug. Fay found herself thinking how lucky she was that the two men in her life, her husband and his best friend, both managed to escape the horrors of serving in war. Al, like Ethan, had the good fortune to be released from duty after enlisting when he suffered a debilitating long-term injury in basic training. The two friends often joked about the circumstances of their discharges, Ethan claiming that his appendicitis was much more painful than Al's broken leg. Al's unique modesty prevented him from reminding Ethan that his injury came about as he tried frantically to save a comrade from certain death under the wheels of a troop transport vehicle.

"So, where's that husband of yours, as if I needed to ask? Come on, Ross. Let's go find your dad."

Al realized that he and Fay were still holding each other's hands after the hug and he gently squeezed hers in a friendly, things will be OK kind of way. Then he was off to the backyard with Ross in lockstep behind. Fay watched them go, smiled through her tears and turned to face once more the corporate mourning going on inside the house.

As Al and Ross approached the dilapidated garage, they could see only Ethan's bottom half sticking out from under the hood of his car. Ross, in the typically playful way of a five-year-old, ran slightly ahead of Al and when he was just a few feet from Ethan hollered "BOO!" The exclamation caused Ethan to jump and loudly bump his head on the sharp edge of the hood. Ross recoiled, knowing that when his father turned, his temper would have gotten the better of him and it was best for the cause of that flaring temper to be well out of physical range.

"God dammit, boy!" Ethan's voice practically blistered the air. "Don't be such a clown!" His rage softened a bit as he realized that

Al was directly behind Ross and was observing the rather unpleasant reaction to a small child's innocent prank.

"Come on, Ethan, it didn't kill you, for God's sake. He didn't mean anything by it."

It was becoming more and more impossible to ignore his friend's almost irrational outbursts, as they were exhibited with a disconcerting frequency.

"What in the hell's bothering you these days, Ethan?" Al asked the question in his usual good-natured way, knowing that Ethan would not take offense as long as he was the one asking.

"There is really nothing bothering me. I'm probably on edge with all that crying in the house over a guy who has practically ruined our country." Ethan was now rubbing the small bump on his head and looking fiercely at Ross as though his small son had meant to hurt him. The boy's slight and subtle backward body motion was not lost on Al and he sensed that Ross spent much of his time in a defensive posture when he was around his father. Al wondered how anyone could not enjoy being in the company of such a fun-loving young boy and felt a strong pang of jealousy that Ethan had this wonderful wife and son, yet didn't seem to want to spend any time with them. He knew he would treat them differently if they were his family.

In a very short time, the tension of the head-banging incident was gone and the car became the focus of attention for the two men. Ross continued to hover just out of reach until he was sure that his father had returned to an absorption in his car and his best friend. When he dared, Ross moved closer and just stood between the two men, now busily engaged under the hood. He could see nothing but the fender in front of him, but that was enough as he listened to the conversation about the engine, none of which he understood. That was not important to him; he was standing between the two men who were virtually his entire male adult world. He could not have been happier as he looked up, from one to the other. As he glanced at his father's profile, Ethan's face grimacing in deep concentration, Ross thought of the day when his father came home with the news about his new job. It was one of those rare occasions that Ross could remember Ethan actually seeming to be happy.

The local Ford agency had been looking for a knowledgeable mechanic to work in the parts department and Ethan's reputation led the general manager to contact him. They wanted someone with a sound mechanical background so that when customers came in looking for parts that they couldn't even name, the counter man could lead them to the right place. Ethan certainly filled the requirements and, in the short time he worked there, quickly earned the respect of customer and boss alike. He was in his element; everything surrounding him had to do with cars. Already he was known as a company man, finding ways to save the agency money and to manage the department more efficiently. Most of his suggestions were put into practice, and he realized that he had a natural aptitude for business as well as for automobiles. This combination was readily marketable, as the industry was poised for phenomenal growth whenever the war ended.

As Ethan and Al stood hunched over the Ford coupe, their conversation took a turn from the mechanical side of the automobile under them to a wider, more philosophical discussion of the automobile business in general. Al noticed that since Ethan had taken the job at the Ford garage, his conversation increasingly became directed at what he could see was the potential for his future. Al also became very aware that Ethan seemed to be feeling Fay's connection with her large brood of brothers and sisters were somehow standing in his way.

"I know that Mr. Manley has his eye on me," Ethan was saying as Al wiped the silver carburetor for what seemed the tenth time. "He really seems to like my suggestions and the way I handle even the hardest-to-please customers."

Anything that Al had heard of John Manley had not been positive. He knew the owner of the agency was not a favorite among the small farmers in the area. The generally accepted story was that he had little compassion for those who were struggling against the continuing intrusion and competition of the large corporate farms. Financing of farm equipment was a relatively new concept but one that John Manley had quickly grasped. It was quite a lucrative endeavor to sell high-priced equipment to the local dairy and vegetable farmers who could manage a fair down payment but often could not keep up the monthly payments through the off season.

Mr. Manley, behind closed doors with Ethan one day, laughed as he described one of Ethan's neighbors trying to explain why he couldn't make a payment.

"It's not the downs, it's the monthlies that get me," the farmer had said. Ethan knew the farmer well and was uncertain as to how to react. After some hesitation, he decided that the discreet thing to do was to simply join in the laughter.

John Manley, a perceptive business man, quickly saw that the larger corporations would gladly buy the slightly used power equipment that he repossessed after the three-month grace period for missed payments. The price would be reduced, making the impersonal corporate world happy but still supplying a substantial profit for the agency.

"Be careful whose respect you try to earn, Ethan," Al answered in his usual no-nonsense tone of voice. "You're still living in this town and not everyone thinks you're working for a guy with much common decency."

Even young Ross, from his vantage point below the two men, could sense the edge in Ethan's response.

"That's the trouble with people around here, Al. They can't stand to see someone get ahead. Nothing that Mr. Manley does is illegal. People got to pay their bills. If they can't manage themselves, then they face the consequences."

"Come on Ethan!" Al put down the wiping rag and straightened up from under the hood. "You know he's taking advantage of the situation. We're in a war, for God's sake. Lots of these people are caught in a bind and can't get out. They get desperate, think better equipment will help, and put themselves over the edge. Manley saw that cars were not the answer now; not with gas rationing, and butter and sugar stamps and all. That's why he went heavy into the farm equipment."

Ethan now came out from under the hood and stood facing Al. Ross did not have to see either of them to feel enough tension to take a few steps back.

"Can't blame him for that, Al. He's smart and he's the kind of guy we all should be admiring, not criticizing. This country's all about free enterprise, not a social state like Roosevelt wanted!"

It was clear to Al that his friend was becoming agitated, and from past experience, he knew that this was neither the time nor the place to try to win the argument. The best way to diffuse the situation would be to switch the attention to Ross. The young boy had gradually inched his way backward and now stood almost ten feet away, his face carrying the worried look of a five-year-old well acquainted with arguments between adults.

"Hey, Ethan, do you think it might be good for all of us to take a nice long walk down through the park? We'll get Ross and Fay away from here for a while. I think it might help everyone to get a little exercise."

Thinking quickly, Ethan sidestepped the invitation. Walking in the park was not exactly his idea of a good time.

"Actually, I'd love to do that but I've got some things here I want to finish up. Why don't you all start out and I'll catch up with you if I can?"

Al just shrugged and called over to Ross. "Go fetch your mom, Ross; we'll take a walk and stop by the playground for a while on the way home."

As the boy sprinted toward the house, Al glanced back over his shoulder at Ethan for some small indication that he would be catching up, but he had already disappeared into the so-called garage.

Glad not to have to hide his relief, Ethan took quick refuge in the small shed that served as both his tool storage and, sometimes, his personal hiding place. His car could be squeezed into the space between toolboxes and parts of every size and description but he usually reserved that ordeal for winter when he couldn't work outside. He had readily agreed to Al's plan for Fay and Ross. "Let them take a walk, the longer the better," he thought. He could direct his attention to his car and not have to deal with the turmoil of the family. In the distance, he could still hear the wailing of the women, and if Al could get Fay and Ross away, he would have no reason to go into the house at all.

Ethan was sure that his friend was well aware that he would not really be interested in catching up with them. Despite their political and sometimes deep philosophical differences, Ethan knew that they understood each other and that Al didn't mind being the surrogate father for Ross at times. At least he and Al could communicate, an aspect of his relationship with Fay that was becoming nothing but a memory.

Memorial Day 1950

Bob Proctor practically pushed at least ten people down the concrete stairs as he fought the parental panic that had him running in circles. How could he have been so stupid? With his mind and his heart racing at nearly equal speed, he arrived at the railing of the grandstand and searched frenetically in both directions. The grandstand crowd had moved almost as one body to get as close as they could to the scene of the crash that had occurred just moments before. Bob felt himself falling into despair. He had the sensation of each thought playing itself out in triple time on a movie screen in his head. The race was stopped and an eerie hush settled over the track, almost duplicating the dust settling as all the sprint cars gradually came to a halt in the pit area. Bob frantically tried to hold onto any positive thoughts as they came up on his personal mindscreen. From deep in his subconscious, Jeanne's voice whispered what was quickly becoming his personal cliché: "She be worth the sacrifice."

In that instant and having no concept of why, he stopped worrying and instead calmly began to find his way through the crowd, knowing that his Jennie would be all right. He found himself at the section of the grandstand where most of the people had gathered to watch the ambulance make its way to the first turn of the track. The hush was now a deafening silence. The occasionals, not truly race fans, fought back a collective feeling of guilt, knowing that the potential for this kind of accident had brought them to the track in the first place. Now that the crowd was convinced the driver had no chance of survival, a gloomy cloud of reality hovered over them.

Bob became much more aware of his surroundings and of the unbearable corporate tension in the spectators. Wherever the knowledge came from, he knew that it was not going to be *if* he found Jennie but *when*. He relaxed enough to be drawn into the group empathy for the driver lying at the bottom of the embankment.

Just as he heard the low hum of the crowd, he felt a slight tug on the back of his shirt. Simultaneous with his quick turn around to see who was trying to get his attention, the hum became a full-fledged roar. Jennie, in her usual simple, heartfelt way, put her arms around her father and hugged him. The increasing volume of the spectators' cheers was drowning out her words. Bob could make out just bits and pieces of her soft explanation, but that was not important at the moment. Here was Jennie, unharmed, and he could not avoid the joyful tears that came to his eyes. He would get the whole story later, he thought. Now, he could not help but be drawn to the reason for the incredible din of the racetrack crowd. He turned from Jennie, although firmly holding her hand, and looked at the broken fence where the race-car had left the track just moments before. The driver had made his way up the embankment and, through whatever miracle, seemed to be all right. He was waving vigorously and appeared to be trying to move back the crowd. The throng of spectators responded to his waves with muted enthusiasm, aware that they had witnessed a most unlikely event. Bob, in his highly charged emotional state, absorbed the scene and thought to himself that the race fans were reacting as if they had seen Jesus resurrected from the tomb. The excitement generated by the entire incident had a heartfelt but subdued quality. Then the crowd involuntarily and collectively retreated a step or two as the exploding fuel tank sent a plume of black, greasy smoke high into the air behind the raised right hand of the driver. The atmosphere over the track assumed a surreal quality, as if the huge gathering had just had a mass illusion, an event they found somewhat frightening, and they could not quite believe what they had witnessed.

Much of what Jennie said when she first made her presence known to her father was lost in the confusion and noise of the moment. What Bob did hear did not make much sense, but he was so relieved that it did not matter.

Her beatific smile matched the sparkle in her eyes as she said, "I sure helped the squirrel that time, Daddy! Now, someone owes me a favor."

Fay Becker

THE ROOSEVELT WALK

When Ross bounded through the screen door with the energy and enthusiasm five-year-olds are constantly able to generate, the solemn sense of grieving for their beloved president was momentarily lifted. His excited calls to his mother brought Fay hurrying out of the huge farmhouse kitchen onto the porch. She arrived just as Al Stuart came up the steps and stood looking through a gaping hole in the screen door.

"Come on, Fay!" Al exclaimed. "We're all going for a good walk down to the park and get out into this beautiful sunshine. It's way too nice a day to keep cooped up in the house."

Fay thoroughly enjoyed Al's occasional boyish enthusiasm and her lighthearted amusement showed through her pleasant smile. Al stood there, his energy matching Ross's as they waited for her response.

"I think I'd really better stay here with everyone, considering everything." The look of disappointment that washed over Ross's face made Fay regret the quickness of her answer. She could see that he really wanted to do this and realized also what a terrible environment the Johnson household was at the moment for anyone, let alone an exuberant young boy. While Ross used just his facial expressions to convince Fay to come for the walk, Al decided to use his good humor to persuade her that it would a good thing for her to do.

"If you don't go, Fay, we'll have no one to fetch the ball when Ross hits it. We need you along as a shagger!"

"Oh, that's just great, Al! No one wants me for me for my company, only as a slave. I get enough of that here!" Even in her attempt to stay within the lighthearted and good-natured kidding of the moment Al knew that there was more truth in that than he cared to think about. The edge of bitterness in her voice was impossible to ignore.

"OK, I'll go, but let's not make it too long a trek and I'll only agree to chase a limited number of balls!"

"Truth be told, Fay, I love to take Ross on these outings but I was hoping you'd go along, for your company, not as a ball chaser. Thanks."

Fay turned to go back into the house but glanced over her shoulder at her son. He had moved closer to Al and she thought the two of them seemed to be a perfect match. As her eyes moved from Ross to Al, a subtle and disturbing nervousness flitted through her stomach. Al indeed was a good man and very attractive. His mouth always appeared poised to break into his wide, disarming smile and his dark brown eyes radiated a rare and deep sincerity. Fay hoped, with a twinge of guilt, that Ethan would not catch up with them on this particular walk in the park.

Fay quickly went into the house and let everyone know where she was going. Then, the three of them set off down the road for the three-quarter-of-a-mile walk to the park, which the town was trying desperately to maintain within its limited budget.

Ross loved the recreational area. The grounds were situated on a donated piece of land between two of the larger vegetable farms. One of the few streams that ran all year meandered through the center of the fifty-six-acre parcel. Two huge cannons, placed there shortly after World War I, guarded the entrance. The New Jersey coast lay over fifty miles to the east but the entire eastern seaboard lived in a paranoiac and irrational state of fear that somehow the inept German Air Force might mount a Pearl Harbor-like attack. Civil Defense authorities tried mightily to allay the fears without success and felt compelled to schedule regular blackout drills as far west as Philadelphia. Whenever the air raid sirens went off, usually in the middle of the night, Susan Johnson was the first to the boys' dormitory-style bedroom to roust them out of bed. As she made Ross lie flat in the bathtub, his active imagination would always take him to these two cannons. He just knew that these guns were all the protection they needed from whatever was causing the terrifying sirens to be blasting out such a warning. The cannons faced northeast and provided a bookend kind of backdrop for the plaque containing the names of the local servicemen and women who had perished in the line of duty. There had been substantial discussion among the town fathers regarding the best way to handle the expansion of the plaque as the list continued to grow at a frightening pace.

As Ross clambered onto the base of one of the cannons and slowly shinnied his way out to the end of the seven-foot-long barrel, Fay and Al walked over to the two marble benches in front of the large memorial. The stone wall with the brass engraved plaques was taller than either one of them and actually made a rather dramatic impression, with its long rows of names, forty-five in each of the eight columns. The last two columns had been added recently by the town to ensure that the maimed and injured veterans returning from overseas and the current war would be able to find some evidence that their comrades ever existed.

Fay and Al watched Ross climb all over the steel gray cannon, all of its moving parts long since sealed with the innumerable coats of paints that kept it from rusting into nothingness. Then, in silence, they turned around and found a seat on one of the benches facing the memorial. It had been a quiet walk from the Johnson house to the monument and Al had the strong sense that Fay did not feel much like trying to make conversation. Up to this point, there had been only the usual perfunctory comments about innocuous topics like the weather. Now, sitting within inches of each other, they felt almost mesmerized by the sheer numbers of names staring out at them from the cold stone.

Roosevelt's death somehow made the names a little more real. Yesterday, these long lists would have been just and only that—long lists of faceless and meaningless names engraved in brass and encased in stone. In the somber silence, as they sat on the marble, cool despite the spring warmth, both thought about the memorial. They knew that every once in a while, a long-lost relative or friend would come by to see if there might be any tangible reminders that someone they loved had indeed been on the planet.

With Ross continuing to scramble up and down the cannons just behind them, Al sent a sidelong glance from the now blurring list to Fay, whose attention was riveted on the monument. She slowly stood up from the cool marble seat and approached the beckoning memorial. Al looked on as she approached the huge brass lists and reached out her hand. Although he couldn't read the name that her fingertips were slowly tracing, he knew that it had to be that of her father.

Al knew very little of Sandy Johnson, and most of the information he did have had come from Ethan. Sitting behind Fay as she ran her fingers over this very special name, Al began to think that it was a big mistake to have brought her and Ross to this particular place at this particular time. He could see her progress from introspective reminiscence to outright grieving in a matter of seconds. Even from his vantage point behind her, he knew that she was crying. Fortunately, Ross continued to be occupied by the World War I relics and was oblivious to his mother's increasing distress.

Al, now in the awkward position of one who knows he should do something but has no idea what, stood and tentatively approached Fay, still with her fingers touching the name on the wall. He gently placed his hand on her shoulder, a gesture meant to provide comfort. He was shocked to see that it apparently had the opposite effect. Without even acknowledging his presence, Fay spent the next two minutes sobbing, her head just dropped on her chest. Al quickly removed his not-so-comforting hand and tried to decide what to do next. Feeling somewhat self-conscious and not at all sure what his role was, he gradually concluded that he needed to calm Fay down before Ross caught on to the mini-drama occurring at the wall.

Al reached out, this time with both hands, put one on each shoulder, and softly turned her around. He was truly startled by her appearance as she lifted her head to look at him. The depth of emotion evident in her eyes would have been obvious even to a complete stranger. The sobbing subsided and was replaced by quiet but full-flowing tears. Al knew that the proper thing to do was to wrap his arms around Fay and give her the sort of hug that good friends reserve for times like these. Something vague and undefined held him back. All he could do was keep his hands on her shoulders, feeling useless, and wait for her to gather herself together. When finally she was able to speak once again, she looked up at him and in a carefully controlled voice said, "Nothing is working out, Al." With that, she removed his hands from her shoulders, where they had lain somewhat lamely for what seemed forever, and brushed by him on her way to find Ross. Al, left standing there staring at the wall of names, focused only on one of them—Earl "Sandy" Johnson, 5/29/42.

The long walk, which Al had envisioned as a release for Fay, instead served as a catalyst for something perhaps more important. After the emotion-filled moments at the monument, most of the rest of the walk through the park and back to the Johnson household was relaxed. Ross always ran ahead, darting down to the small stream and back to them, much like a puppy constantly checking to make sure they were easily available. Fay calmed considerably and seemed intent on explaining to Al why "nothing is working out." Speaking in a wistful tone, never making eye contact with him, she shared details of her life that he could not have guessed. At times it appeared that Fay was speaking to some unseen companion, Al's physical presence seeming to envelop them, providing a safe haven. To Fay, the protection she felt was like being in the confessional at St. Luke's.

During the next month, Fay wondered on a daily basis how the emotional breakdown she had suffered on what her mind now called the "Roosevelt Walk" was affecting Al Stuart. She relived practically every word on her conversation with him, realizing that he probably thought she was exaggerating the desperate nature of her situation. Perhaps she was, slightly, but she hoped the exaggeration for effect would accomplish at least part of her purpose. She knew that it could never hurt having a man of Al's caliber sympathetic to her cause.

Circumstances did not allow them to be together for even a minute since then, and she still wondered what Al's reaction had been to some of the revelations she shared that day. She had deliberately made herself vulnerable without any fear, feeling a deep trust in Al and sensing that he was as honorable a man as she had known in her young life. She was now more than grateful that he had dropped into her life.

One hazy, hot summer afternoon in late June, as she sat in the old rocker on the porch shucking fresh corn for dinner, she heard the familiar sound of Ethan's Ford coupe winding down through the gears as he approached the driveway breaks in the tall hedge. It was early for him to be home from work but her initial concern disappeared as he drove past her toward the backyard. Uncharacteristically, he was smiling and waving as he went by, so she knew that nothing had gone wrong at work. She heard the engine shut down and the immediate opening and closing of the creaky driver's-side door. Ethan came around the corner of the house in record time and Fay frantically tried to anticipate what in the world was happening here. He took the three steps to the porch in one leap and went directly to Fay, pulled her out of the rocker, and hugged her. Still holding an ear of half-shucked corn, she responded as well as she could with a one-armed hug back. Ethan moved her away from him, removed the ear of corn from her hand, and put it on the rocker. He gently took both of her hands in his and made the announcement that explained his unusual, if not bizarre, behavior of the last few minutes.

"Fay," he said, an excitement in his voice that she had not heard in a long time, "We're moving; we're getting our own place!"

Fay knew how desperate Ethan had been to, as he termed it, escape from the Johnson asylum. She had not been aware of any plans for such an immediate and quick change, but for at least an instant his genuine enthusiasm made her put aside her normal resentment for his unilateral decision-making process. Her own growing excitement was tempered only slightly by a vague uneasiness about the suddenness of whatever this all meant to her and to Ross and to her family. For the first time in recent memory, Ethan had actually given her a greeting that seemed to indicate that she still was part of his lifetime plan, a realization that actually surprised her. The initial giddiness quickly wore off and now she decided to embark on the possibly dangerous mission of asking Ethan some of the many questions busily arranging themselves in her mind.

Al Stuart

THE ROOSEVELT WALK

As Al Stuart lay in his bed the night of the President's death, he tried unsuccessfully to extract his mind from the turmoil of the events of the day. Not only did Roosevelt's death affect him; that was not entirely unexpected. Everyone knew the condition of the President's health and the poor man had been through a prolonged period of stress unlike any president before him. Al experienced the profound sadness that so many were feeling but he also could not let go of parts of the conversation with Fay on the return trip from the park. Al knew he had been included in a side of Fay that he found fascinating at the same time as it was somewhat frightening. He had no idea what made Fay suddenly so comfortable using him as a confidant but he admitted silently that he did not mind at all.

As much as he considered Ethan and Fay his best friends, he often worried about their relationship and the effect it had on Ross. After the conversation, or rather Fay's monologue, since he had cast himself in his usual role of good listener he was even more concerned. He lay awake, listening to the early spring peepers outside his window. He reconstructed every word of the lengthy conversation.

Fay had a way of speaking that never took a direct route, and at times Al thought she deliberately and vaguely was leading him somewhere but he had no idea where. Some of her "things aren't working out" speech he already knew. The death of her father, the crowded living quarters in the Johnson house, and the continual financial pressures of the young marriage were all rather obvious. What kept Al awake for a substantial part of the night was her answer to a question he asked just to try to lighten the tone of what was becoming for him a somewhat depressing walk.

The question came just as Ross completed one of his reconnoitering forays to the stream. When Ross was close enough to hear, Al innocently and light-heartedly called him and asked when was he going to have a little brother or sister to chase around. Fay's reaction had Al searching for some explanation. All she said before the tears came once again was, "That's something else that's not going right, Al." For the second time on this walk, Al felt completely useless but did not know what to say. After composing herself yet again, she said simply that Ethan had taken care of that possibility a year or so ago. The subject was dropped and Al was left to wonder what it was that she meant.

Although he didn't even come close to realizing it at the time, the long walk on the day of President Roosevelt's death had far-reaching ramifications for Al that he couldn't have imagined.

Memorial Day 1950

FAY'S ROSARY

I knew that my rosary on this day, all those Hail Marys and Our Fathers, could only be interpreted as blasphemous and probably no one but God Himself would have dared to imagine why this particular race day was far different from any other for me. I took great care to behave exactly the same as I always did, seeming to cower in a friend's car as Ethan's race car roared around the track. I grasped the ever-present rosary beads tightly in my hand just as I always had; I repeated the ritualistic prayers over and over again just as I always had. My praying rite on this day had its usual purpose, some sort of divine intervention for my own good. The startling difference in the sincerity of the Holy Rosary today was that I was pleading not for Ethan's protection but for forgiveness should Al's nebulous and secretive plan succeed. Just two nights before, he had been adamant. "Things will work out now, Fay. You deserve better!" Al had been so vague but I sensed that he had made an irrevocable decision, a choice that made me shiver whenever I thought about it. My only viable option at the moment was to continue to pray.

Al's original suggestion that I simply ask Ethan for a divorce was dismissed out of hand. I knew that Ethan would likely kill us both. On any number of occasions, his malevolent and scornful eyes told me he could be capable of that level of violence. Whatever the details of this choice, I was sure that his admonition to not worry, that he would work things out, necessitated a lot of praying. The single part of my supplication that was not truly hypocritical involved Ross. I prayed for him with more conviction than I could pray for myself. Ethan's decision to allow him into the pits for the first time on this day of all days had been a complete surprise and I could only hope that whatever was to happen would not be too painful. I wished that he was with me but all of this was, after all, Ethan's fault, all blame resting clearly and completely on him.

Anyone passing by the car would have thought that I was deep in fervent prayer, never realizing that my prayers contained much more desperation than devotion, a frenzied call to an outside force to bring some meaning to my confused life.

Collins Heights

THE MOVE—SUMMER 1945

The Beckers' move from the crowded farmhouse became an occasion of mixed emotions. Ethan was running from house to car with the few belongings that he and Fay had managed to collect for their own over the last several years. Fay realized quite clearly that this family home, as uncomfortable as it had been, was still a haven for her. Her siblings, her mother, and even the house itself surrounded and protected her so many times when it seemed her world was crumbling. Now she was leaving it for what Ethan kept telling her was their fresh new start, a chance to be on their own without the Johnson family interfering in their lives.

She and certainly Ross saw things differently. The house was always full of activity and fun. Neither of them could imagine what it would be like living in a five-room apartment, just the three of them, without the tempering influence of Fay's large family to keep Ethan under control. Ross sat on the steps of the back porch and watched as Ethan's car filled with the sparse belongings of the Becker family. Looking in the window of the Ford coupe, he thought the piles of clothes on top of lamps, an old toaster, and a broken caned chair reminded him of the annual rummage sale they always attended in the basement of St. Lawrence Catholic Church.

The move was not going to be that dramatic but it was so different from anything the family had experienced that it was causing an intense excitement for everyone. Fay's brothers and sisters, happy that Ethan would no longer be around to harass them, worried about who would now watch out for Ross. Susan Johnson had the usual maternal concern for her eldest daughter, a concern that had blossomed even more a year or so before with the strange appearance of Dr. Judson at the door late one night. Ethan had passed off the doctor's visit with what to Susan was a completely unsatisfactory explanation that Fay had stomach cramps and wanted Dr. Judson to check them out. Since that night, what had been a cool relationship between her and her son-in-law turned to one of bare toleration. Now, she had to face her very real fear that Fay would be out of her protective reach.

Each member of the family watched as Ethan completed the last loading of clothes into the car and walked back to the house. The Johnsons were never at a loss for emotional displays and this event was made for emotion. Although the Beckers were moving less than ten miles away to a large, older home that had been converted to four apartments, one would have thought the move was to a different country from the reaction of Fay's brothers and sisters. When Ethan finally slid into the driver's seat, turned the car around, brought it to the side of the porch, and leaned on the horn to get Fay to come, the entire family gathered on the porch to wave goodbye. The sisters were openly crying while the boys formed a protective circle around their mother and stood in silence. Fay came through the tattered screen door and gently took Ross's hand. Almost in a daze, Fay guided Ross first to his grandmother for the obligatory goodbye kiss. Susan's eyes instantly filled with tears but she did not make a sound. Ross hugged her tightly and, in the way that children have, practically broke her heart with the simple words, "I'll miss you, Grandmom." Susan could not respond but instead answered by enfolding the boy in her arms and squeezing him. Ross inhaled the unique grandmotherly essence, a wonderful combination of baked bread, starch, and warmth. Finally he squirmed, and she knew it was time to let go. In the car, Ethan became increasingly impatient with the whole scene and hollered to those on the porch to get it over with.

"We're only going ten miles, for God's sake!"

Sensing his agitation, Fay made the rounds and said goodbye to the rest of her brothers and sisters in quick successive order. She again took Ross's hand and they slowly walked down the steps and across the yard to where Ethan had stopped in the driveway. Ross clambered into the tiny back seat of the coupe and perched atop the piles of clothes. Fay had barely closed the passenger-side door closed when Ethan started down the driveway. He glanced at the Johnsons, standing on the porch, looking as if they were watching a loved one's funeral. His single thought was "Thank God I'm getting away from this!" The perfunctory wave he tossed out of the window in their direction made Susan Johnson wonder how often she would be seeing her eldest daughter from now on.

Ross watched through the rear window until the car went through the opening in the tall hedge and pulled onto the highway. His hesitant, almost plaintive wave the family observed as the car disappeared around the hedge made the Johnson clan unconsciously draw closer together until they looked like a football huddle.

His attention now turned to the road ahead and the natural exuberance and enthusiasm of a five-year-old on a new adventure took command. Ross had traveled this road before but now everything assumed more importance, especially as they approached their new hometown.

Although this part of southern New Jersey was geologically like a tabletop, somehow the developing small town of Collins Heights became known simply as the Heights to the citizens of the area. Ethan made the left-hand turn from the highway and drove slowly through the business section. Ross, even at the tender age of five, observed how the main street, with its many different types of shops, fairly sparkled with the pride of ownership and community collegiality. Every sign and every storefront appeared freshly painted and there was not a single scrap of trash along the curb or on the sidewalks. Ross couldn't wait to be walking around this town between his mother and father. The memories of the emotional goodbyes of less than half an hour past were already beginning to fade.

The warning lights at the railroad crossing signaled all cars to stop but Ethan squeezed by the short line of waiting vehicles and made a right turn onto Virginia Avenue. The street ran parallel to the railroad and in less than a block they arrived at their new house. A long freight train with multicolored boxcars and open coal cars spewing black dust began passing in the opposite direction. Ross was enthralled and could not believe his good luck to be living where from his own front porch he could watch trains go by.

In contrast to Ross's increasing excitement, Fay maintained the silence that characterized the ride after leaving her family behind. Ethan had tried a whole range of subjects but had been unsuccessful in getting her to talk about anything, giving up in disgust.

"Finally we're getting somewhere and she doesn't seem to care," he thought with frustration.

The large white house was built around the turn of the century and had certainly been one of the showplaces of the burgeoning community, just seven miles from Philadelphia. Ethan guided the car into the black-cinder driveway and under the sheltering carport type of roof that came off the wide veranda surrounding the first floor. Like Ross, he also was excited and was out of the car practically before it stopped. The last cars of the freight rumbled into the distance, a red lantern swinging from the back of the caboose.

The Beckers climbed up the steps and walked across the veranda to the side door leading to their second-floor apartment. Ethan and Ross clambered up the stairs, pausing briefly at the landing where the steps turned at a strange forty-five-degree angle, rising five more treads before the dark brown mahogany door with a large silver 2 blocked their way. Ethan nervously fumbled for the key, then opened the door.

Ethan thought about how much needed to be done to turn this house into the profit maker John Manley promised it would be, but Ross could barely contain his youthful enthusiasm and ran from one room to another, everything a new discovery. Fay began to catch some of the excitement but found it somewhat smothered by a recurring but disturbing thought, one that just reinforced the feelings of guilt of the past year.

"I wonder if Al will come to visit us as often now that we live farther away." She pushed the final part of that thought out of her head whenever it intruded. On those rare occasions when she did let it linger a bit, she realized that she was thinking, "I hope so."

Ethan had taken the idea to buy the apartment house to John Manley and further ingratiated himself with his boss by his ambition and vision. The detailed plan, well thought out and described to Mr. Manley but, of course, not to Fay, was to renovate the four apartments and live in the largest one. The others would generate sufficient income for the Beckers to live virtually rent-free. Manley saw the potential and readily invested the five hundred dollars to get Ethan started.

By the time of the big move, it was clear to all who worked at the Ford agency that Manley was grooming Ethan for some management role. A new position of assistant service manager had been created for him and everyone knew that Ethan was the person their boss would ask to carry out the repossessions of equipment and vehicles from the financially strapped small farmers in the area. Although this would have been an unpleasant job for most, Ethan seemed to relish it. John Manley became Ethan's mentor and felt he had found a philosophical compatriot. Not only was Ethan a competent and loyal employee but he learned quickly as well, and like Manley himself, put aside all compassion when it came to business. Ethan's dedication to work meant long hours at the agency and little time for hobbies or home. Any spare time was taken up with either working on the apartment house or his race cars. Many nights, on coming home from work at seven or eight o'clock, he would take a sandwich Fay had made and immediately go out to the garage just to sit and look at the cars while he ate.

For Ethan, one of the most attractive aspects of buying the apartment house was the large garage that sat at the end of the long cinder driveway. Ethan quickly adapted one of the three bays to house his sprint car and a second one became home for his coupe or for Al's race car. The third turned into a extensive tool storage area which Ethan organized with his usual fanaticism for details. The driveway was more than one hundred yards long and the sprint car made regular slow test runs back and forth.

Within a few weeks of the move to the Heights, the Beckers' garage became a magnet for several of Ethan's friends who shared his interest in building race cars. Sunday mornings, even before Fay and Ross left for eight o'clock mass, Ethan made his exit to the garage, usually not to be seen again until dinner. By the time the Mass ended and Ross and Fay walked the half-mile home, the usual group would have gathered. Fay always was amazed that this Sunday-morning event became a ritual in the space of just a few weeks. Ross would see the cars back by the garage and bound up the steps to get changed into old clothes so he could be around the men and absorb some of the car and race talk. Fay would prepare enough coffee for all and send Ross to tell them it was ready. Each of the group would make his way up the wooden fire escape at the back of the house to the second floor, Fay passing the steaming coffee cups out the back door of the kitchen so that the grease-encrusted shoes would remain outside.

Al Stuart was the only one who would remove his shoes and stop in for a brief visit with Fay when he came to get his coffee. With each passing Sunday, she found herself looking forward to Al's visit with more enthusiasm. She was a bit unnerved when she realized that she was thinking about it even during the church service. Al was painfully quiet but easy to talk to, and the visits went by all too quickly. She had the feeling that Al enjoyed her company in a friendly sort of way and any regrets she had about the "Roosevelt walk" had long since disappeared. At first she was afraid that she had let her guard down and shared probably too much, but that worry was replaced by the awareness that Al had taken her father's place as her shining hope for escape.

Al, for his part, began to look forward to the visits to Ethan's new garage and the spacious, well-organized work area. In a short time, he had expanded the twelve-mile trip from his home to a twice-a-week basis as he and Ethan became more involved in building the cars. Saturday and Sunday mornings were now etched into a sort of permanent calendar and he rarely varied from the routine. Had he been punching a time clock, it would have shown his arrival was always within a minute or two of seven-thirty both mornings and he usually was busily engaged by the time the rest of the group filtered in.

As excited as he was about the work they were doing on the cars, he often found himself watching the clock for the time when Fay had the coffee ready. Quite deliberately, he would be the last to climb the rickety fire escape so that he could catch up with her news as they stood in the kitchen sipping their coffee. When he allowed himself to think about it, he realized that the attraction of the cars and Ethan's garage was not the only reason he never missed a Saturday or Sunday. Even for just the few minutes they had, he thoroughly enjoyed Fay's company. During the week Al, in his sincere and honest fashion, forced any thoughts of Fay to remain within what society would call the bounds of propriety. After all, wasn't she his best friend's wife? The Catholic Church had carefully constructed the so-called occasions of sin with the intention to dampen the inevitable temptations when any male and female spend any time alone. Al and Fay, admitting nothing and by unspoken agreement, fell into a pattern of avoiding those occasions. They both knew that the Catholic religion seemed blissfully unaware of how powerful the "occasions" were and how difficult it might be to subjugate the sexual chemistry that the Church barely admitted existed. The only safe avenue for them to remain close friends meant keeping their relationship pure and chaste, words the nuns constantly echoed in the classrooms, no matter what subject they were teaching at the time. As a simple precaution, Al rarely even mentioned Fay during the many hours he spent working on the cars with Ethan Becker. His connection to Fay, innocent in word and deed, was not so innocent in thought and he remained concerned with the decorum of the situation. He often thought how proud the old nuns from his grammar school would have been had they witnessed the few hugs that he and Fay shared, the hugs being affectionate but stiff, and certainly pure and chaste.

Fay took up the challenge to use the move to the new house as a catalyst to reverse her deteriorating relationship with Ethan. She couldn't seem to please him no matter what she did and her frustration with his apathy toward her was overpowering.

With Ross going off to school, she spent most of her time alone in the apartment. The homemaking necessary in the small living quarters was minimal. The largest room of the four faced Virginia Avenue, a triple bay window looking over the tarred roof of the veranda toward the front of the house and the railroad. Sparsely furnished, the room was dominated by an overstuffed sofa with a green satin slipcover effectively hiding the soft cotton stuffing leaking from innumerable holes in the under fabric. Two mismatched parlor chairs, one a favorite of Fay's, framed the bay window, separated by a rickety old light pine table that wobbled under the weight of the bulbous painted pottery lamp atop it. A walnut end table held the telephone and a small RCA radio. Ethan's imitation leather recliner, the newest piece in the room, held down one edge of the frayed area rug, the heavy sofa keeping the other side firmly in place. The walls had no decoration other than the large, garish, purple flowers on the dark blue background of the wallpaper. Fay always turned her favorite chair toward the window whenever she sat down, a deliberate avoidance of the depressing, claustrophobic atmosphere of the room.

The two bedrooms and kitchen were equally plain and simple and Fay could accomplish a thorough cleaning in just an hour or two a day, leaving her with long blocks of time to fill. When she broached the subject of taking a part-time job at the local A & P, Ethan would have no part of it. The discussion, more of a pronouncement of Ethan's philosophy, was brief and, as usual, unsatisfactory to Fay.

"Wives keep the home fires burning," he had said. End of discussion.

When she finished what she referred to as her morning chores, as if she still lived with the Johnsons, she often took long walks around the small town. Her contacts with other women were somewhat restricted to those she met at PTA meetings at St. Francis Grammar School. One beautiful October morning, her walk took her past the home of Rose McGowen, a young mother with a son in Ross's class. Rose was sitting on the front steps of her large Victorian home and waved to Fay as she walked by. Fay hesitated at the gate and Rose stood and motioned for her to come in. It was the beginning of a daily coffee klatch and a close friendship that Fay would treasure for the next three years, after which she would wish she had never met Rose McGowen.

The public transportation system in Collins Heights consisted of a bus line running the length of Tilton Pike, ending in Center City Philadelphia after crossing the bridge over the Delaware River. The bus was far more convenient than the commuter train to the city, having many more local stops within each of the small towns on the route. The Tilton Pike was just a block over from Virginia Avenue, making the bus trip to the city an attractive option for Fay, even if all she could do was window-shop in the huge department stores like Gimbel's and Strawbridge's. About once every two or three weeks, Fay would be able to hold out the twenty-cent carfare from her food budget and made the exciting trip into the city. Walking up and down the streets, she absorbed the apparent purposeful direction of the bustling crowds. She secretly wished that some of that purpose could somehow rub off on her as the throngs brushed against her, on their way to who knew where. With the war over for just a year, the country seemed to be looking forward to an unprecedented future, one filled with optimism and enthusiasm. At home, Fay had trouble catching any of the fervor but here, in the city, it was palpable. A person could feel alive here, excited, and the bus trip home invariably became a depressing letdown, but never depressing enough to discourage her from making the trip again as soon as she could.

When Fay planned an excursion to the city, she packed Ross a lunch instead of having him walk home from school during his lunch hour. She could time the beginning of her trip to coincide with his departure for school, allowing almost six hours before she had to be home to greet him. Fay never told Ethan about these trips, of course. She knew he would not understand and, worse yet, would not take the time to listen to her explain why she liked to do it. But she happily anticipated sharing anything new she saw or felt on the excursions with Al during one of their five-minute conversations in the kitchen. She knew she could count on his dazzling grin and his usual exclamation-"That's really neat, Fay!" And she always knew that he meant it.

On a cold morning in late November, Rose McGowen called and specifically asked Fay over for coffee. It was a day that Fay had especially prepared for. She had actually saved enough money not only to trek into Center City but also to go to the Horn and Hardart Automat for lunch. To the city's businessmen and secretaries, lunch at the automat was not exactly a treat but it was quick and the food was passable and reasonably priced. To the occasional small-town visitor, the automat represented an adventure and Fay did not feel silly in the least looking forward to her escapade into the land of automated food dispensers. With her departure time delayed an hour or so by her visit with Rose, Fay thought of postponing her city trip for that particular day but her childlike excitement led her directly to the bus stop on the corner of Green Street and Tilton Pike. Immediately on finding her seat in the usual spot in the middle of the bus, she started to regret her decision. She hated to feel rushed when she visited the city and this day especially she had wanted to inhale the full effect of the environment, including serving herself lunch in the busy automated restaurant.

After a fifteen-minute ride through the series of villages, the bus made its way around the circle and headed for Spaulding Boulevard, leading to the Benjamin Franklin Bridge. A large billboard, one of the first of its size erected along the side of the boulevard, blazoned the name of Manley Motors in black-shadowed letters four feet high. It was impossible to miss from the bus and Fay made a spontaneous decision. She would get off at the new Manley Motors building and surprise Ethan at work. The timing would be just right for them to have lunch together. She actually found herself getting excited at this prospect but wondered vaguely how Ethan would react. Dismissing any uneasiness, she decided that he would be glad to see her. Perhaps he would even introduce her to some of his coworkers. The unsettling thought that she might seem slightly desperate in grasping at this connection with her husband forced its way to the forefront of her mind. On a rational level, she confronted the issue by telling herself that he should be happy to see her. On a deeper, perhaps even subconscious level, she was not sure at all why she was about to do it, not willing to admit that she really wanted to keep all of her possible future opportunities open and available.

"After all, we are married!" she thought, realizing that she had almost spoken the words aloud. At the same time, she became determined to allow the spontaneity to bloom and see what might happen. Emotionally, she easily convinced herself that Ethan would let her into his world at the Ford agency. The pit of her stomach let her know without a doubt that she was about to take a big chance.

The last stop before the bridge came on them quickly and Fay pulled the cord, ringing the buzzer to let the driver know she wanted to get off. As she came up the aisle, she could see the driver's questioning glance in his rear-view mirror. He had seen Fay any number of times before and she always got off at the same stop in the city. The bus came to a hissing halt just as she reached the bar separating the passengers from the driver. He opened the gate and took her ticket, asking as she went down the two steps to the door if she was all right. Fay just smiled back at him and managed a nonchalant wave. The door opened and she quickly stepped from the bus, heading back toward Manley Ford, two blocks down the boulevard.

At ten minutes of twelve, Ethan Becker stood at the second service desk, intent on the paperwork in front of him. Bill Perry, the service manager whose job Ethan had been eyeing since he came to work for Mr. Manley, was speaking with a regular customer at his post just in front of Ethan.

"Hey, Ethan. Take a look!" Bill and his customer were staring through the glass door leading into the showroom and Ethan knew instantly why they were staring just by Bill's tone of voice. There was an unwritten but firm understanding among the men working at the dealership. The agreement, which any male would deny if questioned, went into effect when any reasonably attractive woman entered the building. The lines of subtle communication among the male workforce immediately connected. Depending on the proximity of the female in question, the signals took the form of an exaggerated cough, a low, barely audible whistle, a hand or arm gesture, or, if the subject was sufficiently distant, the not-so-subtle exclamation, "Take a look at that, will you!"

Ethan, the most enthusiastic supporter of this system, dropped everything and moved to Bill's desk for a better view. He stared, unbelieving, as Fay crossed the showroom floor toward the door to the service area. In a moment of wildly confused feelings, he thought in turn about how beautiful she looked, dressed in the only suit she owned, a pale green, figure-hugging wool two-piece. Quickly following this, a powerful jealousy took over as he saw behind Fay a trail of salesmen watching her swaying movements through the showroom, their salacious eyes focused from her cinch belt downward. By the time Fay finally passed through the foyer into the garage section and approached Ethan, it seemed as if every power tool in the shop had stopped. Ethan knew without looking behind him that the mechanics had begun to salivate along with the salesmen. Fay would be the topic of discussion at lunch, he was sure. He quickly converted his next thought into words.

"What in the hell are you doing here, Fay?" The question came out so harshly and angrily that it practically made her knees buckle. He saw the fear flash across her eyes but it was instantly replaced by a defiance he found disconcerting. He glared at her and forced the defiant look from her face. By now, the ogling men realized that Ethan had some connection with this woman and they tried to make it seem as though they hadn't noticed her, returning busily to what they had been doing. Ethan had assessed the situation correctly. Fay would be the reigning topic of gossip at the lunch tables on this day. What he had not assessed correctly was the direction the discussion would take. Instead of the usual crude remarks about the physical attributes of the woman and how each of them would like to handle those attributes, most of the talk would center on two questions, neither of which anyone would have the nerve to ask Ethan himself.

"Why in the world does Ethan keep this woman hidden from the world?" None of his colleagues had met Fay before.

"Why in the world is Ethan always sniffing around other women when he's got that at home?" To most of them, Ethan seemed to have an insatiable appetite for seducing women. No one could remember a new female employee whom Ethan did not try to seduce or, in his crude vernacular, plunk. Most of the men were sure that his success rate was high; he was disarmingly enchanting and unabashedly forward when around women.

When Ethan had recovered sufficiently from the shock of seeing Fay, he knew he did not want any kind of scene here at the workplace. His initial outburst forced Fay through a gamut of emotions, from fear to defiance back to a sad sort of fear that ended with tears welling up. He moved closer to her, took her arm and ushered her back into the showroom as coworkers fought to show a lack of interest in whatever was going on, an effort most of them found impossible. Ethan asked one of the salesmen for permission to use his closing office for a minute, and soon Fay sat looking up at a pacing Ethan, obviously struggling to regain control of the situation, whatever that might be.

"So, why did you come, Fay?" Ethan asked the question with obvious sincerity, as though it was beyond him to believe that she would actually just want to see him.

"Just a surprise, Ethan. I thought we could maybe eat lunch, you could show me where you work, meet some people. I thought you'd like it, Ethan; otherwise I wouldn't have come." Fay felt that she was, as usual, on the defensive, trying to explain everything she did. Ethan clearly did not appreciate her surprise. The sales closing office had dividers, only about five feet tall, so the sales manager could hear everything that a salesman told the customer and make his counter plan accordingly if the customer should begin to walk out the door. Ethan, aware that these walls did have the proverbial ears, decided it was in his best interest by far to diffuse this situation and turn it to an advantage.

"You just caught me off guard, Fay. I'd love to have lunch with you and show you around." Ethan announced this in a calm tone of voice, easily but not obviously heard by the salesmen out on the floor. He knew they would spread the word around the dealership that Ethan and Fay would be out and about. He also knew that they would all observe another unwritten law-what happens here stays here. There is home and there is work and the salesmen especially would not be interested in having their wives know what they did in their off-the-sales-floor time.

"I did have an appointment for lunch but it's not until one o'clock. Just give me a minute and I'll rearrange it." With that, Ethan returned to his desk to make the call. Fay entertained herself looking at the cars spread around the showroom floor, sliding in and out of the driver's seat of several of the vehicles as the entire sales force circled around, always in good position to observe Fay as she exited, her skirt sliding up to her thighs. Not quite twenty-two years old and extremely naïve, she had not had the experience of being the center of attention and really had never thought of herself as very attractive at all. As she looked through the glass at Ethan making his phone call, she felt a slight heat in her cheeks and realized she was blushing.

"So far," she thought, "this is better than I ever expected."

Bill Perry, several feet from Ethan's desk, once again thought how fearless Ethan was. Here he was surprised by his wife's visit and still has the nerve to flirt with the operator. All he could ever get the Bell Telephone operator to say was "Number please" and here was Ethan carrying on a conversation. By the time Bill decided to try to hear the smooth line that Ethan apparently had perfected, he only heard Ethan whisper "Goodbye, Rose" into the receiver and then set it into the cradle.

As Ethan squired Fay around the dealership that afternoon, she thought her decision to visit him had been a brilliant one. All she wanted to accomplish seemed to have worked. She had even gotten to meet the famous Mr. Manley, along with many of the other key people in the dealership. Everyone treated her with respect with the minor exception of John Manley, whom she thought to be patronizing, if not condescending. Fay had heard so much about Manley, little of it from Ethan, and expected a more imposing personality. She was flattered by the attention she received, her naivete still refusing to allow her to accept the effect she could have on men.

Fay hoped Ethan would offer to drive her home after their lunch but he didn't. His reason was quite believable; she knew he must have work to do, so she checked the schedule and crossed the boulevard to catch the bus back to the Heights. She would be home in adequate time for Ross and she actually enjoyed the bus ride. For the first time in a long time, her thoughts were not only of sharing experiences with Al Stuart on the weekend but also that perhaps Ethan might come home earlier than usual. The afternoon had gone so well after his initial shock at seeing her. Once again, she optimistically looked forward to some improvement in her future, whatever direction it might take. When the bus reached her stop, she cheerfully said goodbye to the driver and walked briskly toward St. Luke's Grammar School to meet Ross. She wanted to share a little of the afternoon with him on the way home.

At exactly five-thirty that evening, Ross and Fay were sharing what in 1946 would have been considered a wartime dinner. Fay had boiled a few potatoes, opened a can of DelMonte sweet peas, and heated them along with a can of Spam, one of Ross's favorites. Young boys found a certain fascination with inserting the metal key attached to the top of the can into the metal strip and opening the lid like a can of dog food, exposing the marbleized and compressed product of some sort of meat and filler.

The sound of a car on the gravel driveway sent Ross running to the rear bedroom window, where he could see whose car it was. Loudly and with considerable surprise in his voice, he called out to his mother.

"It's Daddy, Mommie; he came home early just like you hoped."

Fay, excited that maybe all she had thought this afternoon might be coming true, slid out of her chair and peered out of a kitchen window. She saw Ethan close the garage door across behind his car. He came up the fire escape steps the boys always climbed for their coffee and Fay had the door open to meet him, anticipating a positive kind of evening, maybe even one with Ross going to bed a little sooner than usual.

She could admit to herself that since the afternoon attention of the men at the agency, she had been feeling somewhat lusty and hoped Ethan might be in the same mood. As she lay soaking in the bath after getting home, she resisted the urge use her usual method of relief from pent-up sexual energy, a method the Catholic Church would call a venial sin, but a serious one. Over the last few years, Ethan's increasing lack of interest in her had continued to degrade her self-esteem but she had discovered that a long, languorous afternoon bath had a rejuvenating effect. She could never bring herself to admit to the priest in the confessional what she did during these baths to feel a little more like an adult sexual being. Sometimes, after one of these sessions, she would smile as she tried to imagine the scene in the confessional, wondering how many rosaries she would have to say for penance to have this sin cleansed.

"Father, forgive me for I have sinned. It has been one week since my last confession. Three times I have lain back in the tub during a bath and caressed myself to a shattering orgasm while daydreaming about a man other than my husband."

Ethan reached the top of the stairs and was framed in the rear door of the kitchen. Fay's stomach did a flip-flop when she saw his face. All thoughts of a pleasant evening with husband disappeared. Ethan's face was an angry red with a dark and ominous tinge. She quickly recognize the fury in his eyes from past experience but there was much more in his expression today. Irrationally, she began to fear for her life. Ethan had never threatened her physically, although she had no doubt he was capable of that level of uncontrolled rage.

Ross had just come around the corner to greet his father but stopped short in the doorway. He also recognized the look on his father's face, the kind of look from which he had backpedaled many times in his short life. There was trouble here; Ross had no doubt of it, and he took one step back into the hall to wait it out.

"What's wrong, Ethan?" was all Fay could muster in the time it took Ethan to cover the five feet separating them.

"Don't ever pull a stunt like that again!" coincided with a stunning backhanded blow across Fay's right cheek, sending her splaying across the floor. Ethan spun on his heels and left the same way he had come, leaving both Fay and Ross in tears, trying to pick up the pieces of the crushed emotions that seemed to be strewn around Fay as she sat cross-legged on the floor.

On Saturday of the week of Fay's wonderful-turned horrible-visit to Manley Motors, Al Stuart arrived, punctual as usual, to work on the cars with Ethan. As studiously as he avoided talking about Fay with Ethan, he indirectly involved her in his inane and harmless question, "So, how's the family, Ethan?"

"You would not believe what that bitch did on Wednesday, Al." Al cringed as he always did in the face of Ethan's crude references to women, his cringing tempered by a rising anger because this reference was not about just any woman. Ethan summarized his version of the events of that day, ending with the vague but not veiled threat that she would think twice before surprising him again. Al found something discomfiting in the tone of voice and the attitude with which Ethan related the incident. He wanted to go get his coffee immediately and check on Fay's well-being but couldn't come up with a viable reason to go to the house. Instead, he just turned to the work at hand and tried to forget the ugly image of what Ethan might have done to make sure that Fay did not surprise him again. After what seemed like days, Ross finally came into the garage and announced that coffee was ready.

As had become the ritual, Ross took the short walk down to Pop's Confectionery earlier that day and picked up the usual Saturday morning order. He now would fetch his father's coffee and one of the delicious homemade blueberry muffins, plump and still faintly warm. Dutifully he would deliver them to Ethan, who had the remarkable ability to continue to work on the greasy engines while balancing his morning snack at the same time.

Al waited until he heard the door slam on Ross's return trip before he started up the creaky old fire escape steps to the rear door of the kitchen, thinking about how often he had made the trip. Desperately wanting to have a minute or two alone with Fay before Ross returned, he was grateful that this particular Saturday, the rest of the usual crew had not arrived, so he would not have to contend with them. He felt a need to be sure that Fay was all right, a feeling heightened by Ethan's harsh description of the events of several days ago.

He knocked lightly on the door at the same time as he looked back over his shoulder and saw Ross enter the garage. From experience, he knew that Ross would not return for at least ten minutes. He could picture the shy, young boy, standing by his father, shuffling his feet and waiting to be told exactly what to do, living in fear that he might do the wrong thing. Ethan would take a small sip of coffee, hand the cup back to Ross, expecting him to be close enough for the second sip and a bite of muffin whenever he decided he wanted it. Al had seen the routine so many times that he could count on it. On this day, for some ill-defined reason, Al's usual depth of empathy for Ross was diminished somewhat and he realized that his anxiety to see Fay probably was the cause. He knocked again, this time a little harder.

When she called out, "Who is it?" Al began to experience the reaction he had every time he saw her lately. The sound of her voice and the knowledge that she was physically close made him feel like a teenager, the nervousness in his stomach quickly translating into a quiver in his voice and a wobble in his knees. He had to take several deep breaths to gather himself together before answering simply, "It's Al." It occurred to him that she never asked that question before, automatically sending back a friendly "Come in" to any of the Saturday-morning boys.

When Fay heard Al respond, she came out of her bedroom and stood in the hallway just outside the kitchen. She softly invited him in, carefully staying in the slightly darkened hall.

"The coffee is in the pot on the stove and the muffins are on the counter, Al." Fay said this in a clipped, mechanical way, a tone of voice that Al found very unnerving.

He thoroughly wiped his feet on the thick mat by the door and walked straight to the white porcelain cabinet that housed the cups. His nervousness was replaced by the undeniable realization that Fay had seen some trouble that week, probably more than he had guessed from the sketchy information supplied by Ethan.. As he reached for one of the heavy mugs, he heard Fay shuffle into the kitchen. When he felt her presence close behind him, he turned, ready to give his normal restrained but good-natured greeting. He had always resisted the urge to hug her, even in a nonthreatening, friendly way. Al did not know where even a friendly, non-pelvic hug could lead and was not willing to take any chances. As he completed his turn and faced her, she moved directly toward him. She pulled the tie around her waist and allowed her bathrobe to fall open. The glimpse of her nakedness forced Al's eyes to the floor. His physical reaction to Fay's presence embarrassed him, the intensity of it causing his face to turn bright crimson. She moved into his arms before he could react, but just as suddenly recoiled and backed up two steps, pulling her robe closed. She reached awkwardly for the sash with both hands and quickly tied the white terry-cloth robe shut.

"I'm so sorry, Al" was all she managed to mumble before the words became muffled sobs and she fled back down the hall to her room. The door closed firmly behind her and Al was left standing in silence in the kitchen. The entire incident could not have taken more than two minutes and already in Al's mind it took on surrealistic qualities. Stunned, he turned back to the stove and filled his cup from the bubbling coffeepot. Once again, Fay had left him feeling useless, unable to help with whatever her problem was. His enervated mind flashed back to the Roosevelt walk and Fay's desolation at the war memorial. Irrationally, he thought of going to her in the bedroom but reason and cowardice prevented that. He reached into the icebox, took a fresh quart of milk, pulled off the cardboard lid and poured just a touch of cream from the top into his coffee.

"What in the hell happened here?" Al thought. Whatever it was, any doubt about the potential for damaging the status quo with Fay and Ethan just became limitless. Al used his return trip to the garage to visualize the incident with Fay once again. He walked through it from beginning to end, dwelling on the momentary view of Fay's naked body a bit more than he thought he should. His arrival at the bottom of the steps coincided with the image of Fay's face as he raised his eyes from her breasts to look into her eyes. The image contained a troublesome recollection. In a flash of insight, he knew that what he had hoped to be an inaccurate memory in fact was correct. Her right cheek, covered with rouge, was swollen and bruised.

"That bastard!" Al would not have dreamed that four years would pass before he would have the chance to make Ethan Becker pay for what he had done.

Manley Motors

THE STRIKE

Manley Motors flourished more than ever in the two years since the war ended. The entire country, acting with unprecedented enthusiasm and optimism, drove the economy until it equaled the war-driven prosperity of the early forties. The booming industries of steel and rubber could now concentrate on the production of peacetime products instead of the war effort. America became hungry for the freedom offered by the automobile, and dealerships around the country prospered as never before. The average worker, eager to please and to share in the wealth generated by all aspects of the automobile industry, happily worked long hours under intense pressure to increase productivity. With a certain degree of naivete, they believed that the system would reward them. Only after watching their employers reap huge financial dividends for several years without equitable compensation for their efforts did unionism begin to have an appeal.

John Manley and his managers met for one hour every day immediately after lunch. Mr. Manley treated them with respect, almost as his equal, provided that they agreed with his business philosophies. He was well aware that people like Ethan Becker possessed matchless expertise in areas crucial to his business. He also knew that he must keep those people satisfied or they would easily take their experience and competence elsewhere. The profits of Manley Motors rose at an incredible pace and John Manley expressed gratitude to his managers (whom he called his lieutenants) through generous weekly bonuses and incentives. Universally, the managers of the three major departments (parts, service and sales) remained content and willing to agree with their boss on all counts. The pool of workers available to fill the positions in the increasingly large Ford agency proved to be more that adequate. The managers of the various departments knew that a direct correlation existed between the payroll of their department and the size of the weekly bonus and the monthly or yearly incentives. As Manley pointed out on a tiresomely regular basis, the largest expense in any department is always payroll.

"Keep your expenses to a minimum but get the job done." At the close of one of the daily meetings, John Manley issued small, framed versions of this quotation, which happened to be his own. After the ceremonial distribution, he added, with a smile, that this would always result in more money for those in charge. This very philosophy, adopted as gospel by his "lieutenants," wreaked havoc on the dealership for several months in the spring of 1948 and almost put his future general manager in prison.

The workforce at Manley Motors consisted of seventy-six employees, having grown from forty-seven at the close of the war. The enthusiasm and loyalty most of them carried into their work was exemplary. The general work ethic of the employees could have been credited with success of the business, as it was with similar companies in the South Jersey area. Manley Motors differed in its belief. John Manley believed that his company's success was the result of his leadership skills and business acumen, abilities he managed to share with his handpicked leadership team. Among these elite few, Ethan Becker was chosen for grooming as his future general manager, the business rapidly becoming too large and complex for Manley to oversee.

During the whole of 1947, the energetic employees of this burgeoning company patiently waited for a "sharing of the wealth" through raises or bonuses, but none was forthcoming. The grumbling had started late in the year and when the Christmas bonuses turned out to be as paltry as the previous two years, the grumbling grew louder and more obvious.

Jed Carver, one of the dealership's best mechanics, dared to threaten Bill Perry, the service manager, with quitting if he did not receive an adequate raise, and was summarily informed that his services were no longer needed. John Manley gave Ethan Becker the pleasure of ushering Jed into the mechanics' locker room and informing him of the decision. Jed could pick up his one-week's severance pay from the comptroller as soon as he gathered his personal things and turned in his keys. Ethan watched for Jed to come to the main office suite, and it was obvious to all that he seemed to take great delight in ushering him to the door after Jed had his check in hand. Ethan did extend his hand and wished Jed an insincere "Good luck." Jed ignored the hand, instead just staring at Ethan, simmering hatred rising in his eyes. Ethan shrugged, turned, and walked back through the showroom.

After Jed's departure, several of the mechanics contacted the local chapter of the AFL and invited a representative to come to the dealership to speak with the entire group. Bill Perry easily discovered the names of those responsible for the invitation and passed them along to John Manley. Manley said nothing to them, quietly hiring replacements first. Then, in rapid succession, he called each into his office. Without a hint of compassion or sympathy, he told them to clean out their lockers. They no longer worked there. He could not by law interfere with his employees investigating a union affiliation but, by God, he could send a strong message about how he felt about it.

After that, the meeting with the union representative took on a whole different dimension of importance. The meeting had to be held at a time and place when all employees could come and resulted in almost one hundred percent attendance, other than a few who were ill. Of those attending, seventy-one employees voted to set up a local chapter of the American Federation of Labor. A second vote sanctioned an election and further authorized those elected to pursue a collective-bargaining agreement.

The outcome of the union meeting infuriated John Manley and his managers. Three weeks later, they were enraged even further by the newly elected president of the union's request in writing to start contract negotiations. By the end of February, all hopes of any negotiations had disintegrated and the local union, with unanimous membership, voted to strike against Manley Motors on the first day of spring, March 21, 1948. The membership remained solidly convinced that they were in the right and believed that within the three-week period, management would certainly understand the value of being reasonable. The union members did not know that John Manley had decided that he would not, under any circumstances, be bullied into a corner by people he perceived to be unappreciative and selfish. He and his leadership team, led by Ethan Becker, decided to let the strike take place, feeling that the determination of the employees would fade rather quickly in the face of a few weeks without pay. With each side waiting for the other to give up, the issue seemed to be ignored as though nothing was happening.

When March 20 arrived, there was only hushed conversation around the agency. At the daily managers' meeting, John Manley simply told his team to be sure to come to work tomorrow and that he had notified the police of the strike threat. They would be on hand to see that the picket lines were orderly, and he expected the daily meeting to take place as usual the next day.

For their part, the employees had their plan under way, with signs all painted and various time slots assigned to the shifts of pickets. Each shift knew exactly where they were to station themselves around the building. The whole scene the day before the job action took on an unreal quality; no one truly believed that it actually would happen.

March 21, 1948

Ethan Becker did not do anything unusual on what turned out to be a glorious first day of spring. The temperature warmed quickly into the fifties before he left for work at 7:30. He could easily have forgotten all about the ridiculous strike threat, knowing that he had at least an hour to spend with Rose before he was scheduled to arrive at the agency. He loved the situation that took Jack McGowen away on sales trips on a regular basis. At least one morning every week, he had the luxury of drawing his inspiration for the day from Rose. He never had to worry about Fay dropping by to see her best friend that early in the morning, as getting Ross off to school was her first priority. And Rose truly was inspiring. The time they spent engaged in the various sexual sports provided Ethan with daydreams enough to last for days and, and best of all, she required no commitment. She just enjoyed the uninhibited adventures and seemed as interested in them as any woman he had ever known. As he showered and prepared for the day, the strike, should it be happening, stayed in second place, far behind his anticipation of frolicking with Rose for a while. After a quick breakfast of toast and coffee, he grabbed his light sports jacket and headed for the door. Ross and Fay were each in their rooms and Ethan just shouted his usual apathetic goodbye as he closed the door behind him. Neither Ross nor Fay knew he left until the car roared in reverse out of the gravel driveway.

Ethan drove immediately to his rendezvous with Rose, following the plan they had put into practice during the last few sessions. The small diner where Rose picked him up had a parking lot in the rear, making his car invisible from the road. He jumped in the back seat of Rose's old Hudson for the two-minute ride to her house. Before he scrunched down out of sight for any nosy neighbor's benefit, he reached from behind and slid his hands onto

Rose's breasts, kissing her neck and lightly chewing on her right ear. Rose just chuckled.

"Can't you wait even two minutes?" she asked, knowing that she could hardly wait either. After spending a superbly inspirational hour with Rose McGowen, Ethan bade his goodbye to her, but first checked calendar dates for the next morning that Jack would be away. He left, looking up and down the street to see that no one happened to be walking by, and slid into the back seat once again. Rose joined him a minute later and the two of them spoke not a word on the way to the diner.

"Thanks for the ride, Rose," Ethan said, a verbal leer in his voice as he left the car. By the time Rose left the driveway, Ethan had his '39 coupe revved up and heading for what he thought might be a very interesting day. He did not notice Jed Carver, the former Manley Motors mechanic, watching intently from the corner window seat of the diner.

The scene at Manley Motors succeeded in surprising even the usually unflappable Ethan Becker. He could see the trademark black-and-white police cars with the single red lights atop them from at least a half-mile away. His attention on the trip from the diner to the agency had flip-flopped between thinking about the marvelous sexuality of Rose McGowen and the excitement of facing down the ungrateful workers-turned-strikers at Manley's.

He let his mind linger just a bit on Rose. He loved her lack of commitment to her husband, to Ethan, to almost anything but her own pleasure. Not especially attractive, she was probably fifteen or twenty pounds overweight. Naked, she had the look of a wood nymph painted by an old Dutch master, exaggerated curves in all the right places. Her most attractive facial feature was a sensuous wide mouth. She had a nose like the Wicked Witch of the North, a severe crook just above the bridge. Her eyes were a dull brown until they became involved in some sexual sport, when they would turn smoky and sultry. A lusty electricity emanated from her when in the presence of men, but he had noticed that she was an entirely different person around her women friends. He was certain that Fay would never suspect anything. The thought of the hour with Rose faded as he focused his mind on the strikers.

He pictured arriving at the dealership and finding them all at work as usual, ready to apologize to Mr. Manley for any worry they might have caused. What he never expected to see was a very large group of people, numbering more than the seventy-five employees, milling about and blocking the two employee driveway entrances to the business. The three police cars, not so fondly referred to as black-and-whites, were arranged to allow traffic to enter through the two driveways, with one on each side and one in the middle of the two openings. Ethan had little time to react to the scene before habit turned the wheel into the first entrance. The picketers walking back and forth had the entrance blocked and he had to brake quickly to avoid running through the crowd. His car turning off the street had attracted everyone's attention, including that of the three policemen, now out of their cars and watching with a surprising degree of disinterest.

Ethan brought his car to the sudden stop and considered his options. He took in some of the signs passing in front of him. Each one he saw increased his anger and in direct proportion decreased his patience.

"Where in the hell do these people think they get their food money," he thought. "We should fire the whole bunch of the ungrateful bastards."

MANLEY UNFAIR! proclaimed one sign.

SHARE YOUR WEALTH! another announced.

Ethan felt the color rising in his face. "This is America, Godammit. It's a free country. Fucking communists better get out of my way." This last thought synchronized perfectly with his foot depressing the accelerator and clutch, making his hopped-up car engine roar at over four thousand RPMs. The picketers, including some spouses and even a few small children, stopped their movement through the driveway and stared at the car. In an unspoken but unanimous decision, the group in front of Ethan's vibrating and rattling car stood their ground, staring hard back at him. To Ethan, with his adrenaline pumping at full bore, everything seemed to be happening in slow motion. The closest policeman started to move toward the crowd, appearing to be ready to make them separate and let Ethan through. His diminishing patience now approached a zero tolerance and he had no intention of waiting for the inevitable discussion that would delay his entrance even more.

"These people have no right to keep me from going to work and by God, I am going in."

The final thought gave life to Ethan's left foot, which began to slowly release the clutch, the engine still at full throttle. As the car inched forward, several of the strikers realized what was about to happen and approached Ethan's car as it crept toward the gate. Ethan recognized Frank Cresti immediately, one of the leaders of the union movement at Manley's. Frank assumed a position directly in front of the silver bulls-eye hood ornament and waited until the bumper touched his legs. Ethan slammed the clutch pedal to the floor and the coupe stopped, the engine still racing. He rolled down the driver's window and screamed out at the gathering crowd around the car.

"Get out of my way or someone's going to get hurt."

Although his attention remained centered on Frank at the front of the car, his peripheral vision told him that the automobile was surrounded. He glanced to his left and noticed the policeman leaning on the entrance gate, observing but showing no signs of becoming involved. In that brief instant, Ethan knew he wouldn't be getting any assistance from that direction, not that he wanted any. At this point, he was beyond his initial irritation into the much more dangerous realm of controlled anger, a realm that could quickly turn into rage. A blinding fury, the kind that juries use as reason to acquit jealous spouses who murder their partners after finding them in bed with someone else, overwhelmed Ethan. The escalating anger seemed to spread to the workers surrounding his car. As he released the clutch, they began to rock the car. Frank leapt from the front of the vehicle and now positioned himself on the driver's side, his hands pushing on the roof directly above Ethan's head. The rocking of the car became more violent. The wheels came off the ground, first on the right, then on the left. Ethan slammed the floor shift into reverse as the wheels spun in the air each time the car came off the ground. Finally, when it appeared that the vehicle teetered on flipping onto its side, the strikers backed off. As the car righted itself, the tires screeched into action. The coupe lurched backward and Ethan brought it to a stop about fifty feet from the attacking picketers. There was no logic to what was happening. As he surveyed the scene, Ethan did not see a line of human beings. What he saw represented a threat to his very way of life, a system where there were superiors and inferiors. While he believed in the philosophy that every human being needs someone to feel superior to, he left it up to his workers to find someone they could control. That did not happen to be his problem. He made managerial decisions and his workers implemented them. Everything needed to be kept that simple. If these people strung out before him thought they deserved more of the pie, they had to work harder at doing what they were told.

"They're ruining everything and I'm not going to let that happen" was his last thought before he noticed Frank Cresti looking at him from the middle of the driveway. Frank, drawing on the strength of the crowd around him, slowly raised his right arm and sent the universal obscene gesture of derision in Ethan's direction. Some say that seeing red is a figure of speech, but Ethan, after blanching and rubbing his eyes to make sure he did not mistake what he saw, pulled the stick shift down hard enough to force it against the seat into first gear. The engine had never retreated from its fully revved state and the tires squealed and sent the black coupe hurtling toward the gate, the bulls-eye pointed directly at Frank Cresti. The dramatic turn of events finally forced the policeman to make a halfhearted move toward the crowd, now running in two directions, leaving Frank momentarily alone in the middle of the driveway. Inexplicably, Frank did not run to either side of the gate but turned and sprinted toward the employee parking lot, Ethan's car gaining on him at every step.

"My God, he's trying to kill me!" The comprehension seared Frank's mind, but at the same time prompted a more logical response. He spun on his right foot and angled back in the direction of Ethan's careening car but on a line toward one of the police cruisers parked by the farther gate. Ethan could not make the adjustment quickly enough and threw his car into a spin trying to reverse directions. The car came to a stop, and the incident ended as quickly as it had begun. The police, well aware now that they had not exactly responded with dispatch, recovered from their apathy and rushed to Ethan's car. As he exited, they escorted him to one of the cruisers with a great deal of pomp and ceremony, as if they had prevented what might have been an unspeakable tragedy. John Manley could hear the jeers and shouting from the strikers, even in his well-insulated office, as the police car drove off through the crowd.

John Manley commanded as much influence in the local police forces and courts as any powerful politician could hope for. His wealth drew into him the social circles containing the lawyers, judges, and politicians who were forging the futures for the entire southern section of the state. In just a matter of two telephone calls, his soon-to-be general manager was released from the holding cell at the local jail and the charges, originally attempted murder, were reduced to minor assault. Manley believed in taking care of his own and he had great plans for Ethan Becker. If he was the least bit upset over Ethan's irrational behavior, the anger never surfaced. The next day, when the police patrolled the gates in a more active fashion and the pickets were instructed to allow in anyone without harassment, Ethan drove through the glares of the workers to his meeting with Manley, not sure what to expect. The *Courier Gazette* had carried a front-page photo of the strikers rocking Ethan's car, the picture taken from an angle that made the incident appear uglier than it actually was. The reporter had an entire roll of film from the day's activities but one additional phone call to the newspaper's owner from John Manley ensured that any pictures of Ethan chasing down a picket with his car would not be used. The article about the strike contained no mention of the confrontation between Ethan and Frank Cresti, placing most of the blame on the union for its recalcitrance in refusing a generous last-minute management offer. The increased police presence at the picket lines and the negative publicity the union received from every media outlet forced the employees to accept a minimal settlement, the details of which were not released.

In the short space of two weeks, the abortive attempt by the striking workers at Manley's to improve their working conditions had come to an end. Fully half of the workforce at the dealership turned over during that time. Newly hired employees were informed that union activity could not be tolerated. All employees were not required but were strongly encouraged to sign an agreement in principle supporting this view. Those who rebelled found themselves under such subtle but impossible pressures that they either conformed or left for other work. The one big happy family portrayed to the outside world through advertising by the management of Manley's was now a reality, achieved by crushing the spirit of the workers and molding them into the docile mentality of a flock of sheep. Some of those affected by the transformation, particularly Jed Carver and Frank Cresti, did not appreciate being relegated to the barnyard.

The morning after the strike at Manley's began, Fay fetched the *Courier Gazette* from its usual perch top on of the huge rhododendron bushes surrounding the veranda. She already knew the story of Ethan's excursion into the world of union busting, or at least as much as he chose to tell her. She crossed the porch toward the entrance to the apartment, unlocking the paper from its neatly packaged newsboy fold as she walked.

"How can they train these boys to fold the papers so well I can hardly get them apart, yet can't train them to throw them onto the porch instead of all over the yard?" she wondered, half out loud but with a faint smile. She'd be sure to make Ross hit the porches during his newspaper carrier career.

As she opened the paper, the picture on the front page made her stop walking. There was Ethan's car, being tipped over by the hooligan unionists, as he called them. She quickly scanned the article for any reference to her husband but found none. The photo rather dramatically showed Ethan in physical danger from what seemed a violent mob. Her family's life had become more comfortable with Ethan's improving job situation at Manley's and they, as Ethan constantly reminded her, owed an allegiance to his employer.

In her limited and protected view, the union truly did seem a threat to the continued success of Manley Motors. Observing her husband under attack by the uncontrolled rabble of the unionists served to reinforce her strong feelings that the movement toward aggressive union rights could victimize Mr. Manley, the benevolent owner. Often, Ethan was somewhat less than compassionate when he spoke of the employees at Manley's but he repeated his opinion so frequently that Fay innocently adopted it as her own. She looked closely at the photograph again, surprised that Ethan had downplayed the apparent danger he faced. She thought she would try to squeeze more information out of him when he came home that night, especially with the paper as a reminder.

The paperboy usually arrived at about the same time every day and she looked forward to reading the paper, from front to back and word for word, while Ross did his homework in his room. She loved to see the warmer weather coming, as winter made finding things to do with Ross difficult after the paper was read and his schoolwork finished. He loved to listen to the radio, lying on the floor next to their new RCA console, a huge piece of furniture that relegated the small table model to Ross's bedroom. His creative mental pictures of Jack Armstrong, the Shadow, and the Phantom played across the single cloth-covered speaker. Fay preferred a walk to the park and sitting on a swing while he ran from sliding boards to seesaws and whirligigs.

She made her way up the steps, calling to her son as she entered the apartment.

"How's the homework coming, Ross?" The usual answer came drifting back from his room. "OK, Mom." It was her signal to hunker down in her favorite overstuffed living room chair and begin her trip through the news of yesterday. On a normal day, the newspaper ritual would consume about a half hour, a worthwhile escape from the boredom of keeping house. The *Gazette* was thinner on this day and she marched through it quickly, noting that not much of interest happened the day before other than the beginnings of the strike at Manley's and the attack on Ethan's car.

"Probably enough excitement for one day," she thought, still angry with the lowlifes who would stop a man from coming to work. She skimmed through the article again, without much concentration, vaguely registering the usual news story staples of who, what, when, where, and how. She already knew most of the details, Ethan having been more forthcoming than usual about that particular day at work. Fay reached the back page of the paper, reserved for the most part for human-interest stories. These she enjoyed especially, her sentimentality rising to the surface as she read about rescued pets, a reunion of long-lost relatives, highway good Samaritans and generous philanthropists. Only on a rare occasion could get through the entire section without tears. She never regretted immersing herself in one or two of the stories, vicariously reliving a good time in someone's life. When she performed an honest self-analysis, she felt that she deserved a good time or two in her life as well.

As her eyes scanned this favorite section of the paper, a disquieting question worked its way to the surface of her mind. The question had to do with the "when" part of the lengthy front-page piece about the strike. She reached down to the floor and retrieved the first section, quickly finding her answer in the second paragraph.

"Strike leaders had assembled the pickets and observers at exactly 8:15 A.M., timing the beginning of the picketing with the official start of the work day at 8:30." Fay put down the paper and resumed her scan of the back page, wondering why Ethan had not already been in the dealership before the picketing began. He had left the house that morning with a solid hour of lead time. She decided to ask him about it, if the right moment presented itself. With a slight, unhappy smile, she admitted silently that "right moments" in her relationship with Ethan were rare occasions indeed.

A headline over a small piece in the bottom left corner of her favorite page caught her attention.

"Boy Caught on Train Track Saved" led into a brief description of the incident, another potentially tragic accident with a happy, heartwarming conclusion.

The Boy, the Train, and Jennie

Almost every afternoon, nine-year-old Danny Charboneau walked home from school with several of his friends, quickly changed into old clothes, picked up a cigar box full of steel toy soldiers, and headed for his favorite battlefield, a steep embankment leading down to a double railroad track. The commuter trains coming out of Philadelphia always slowed as they passed under the trestle separating the Heights from Lyndeboro, its neighbor to the south. Danny and his friends constructed the mock battlefield for their soldiers just over the town line in Lyndeboro, in the shadow of the trestle. The young boys regularly attended the local movie house, always placing themselves directly under the huge and gaudy chandelier in the center of the ornate old theater. The films ran continuously and they could sit through at least two shows before the manager caught on and arrived with his flashlight to escort them kindly to the door.

Before their unceremonious exit, they were enthralled by the romanticism of war as portrayed by John Wayne and Robert Ryan. The leap from the movie screen to their tiny soldiers presented no problem to the active imagination of nine-year-olds. Some Saturdays they would spend the entire day on the field of battle, the conflict ebbing and flowing up the hill and down again, interrupted every two hours by the rumble of the freight trains heading for the Berlin Sand and Gravel pits. The distant rumblings of the trains as they approached created an exciting distraction from the raging war on the hillside. The boys would call a truce to watch as the steam-spewing locomotives chugged past, the acrid coal pungency hanging in the air and mingling with the wave of the engineer from the cab. Small side bets on the number of cars in the train kept their attention as they counted, the clackety-clack of the wheels providing a hypnotizing pattern of sound. The friendly wave of the conductor from the caboose signaled that it was time to resume the war on the hillside. The boys often added another element to the passing of the trains: When they heard the whistle blow as the train approached the Collins Heights station, they knew they had about six minutes to spread a few pennies on the track. After the long freight finally passed by, they usually could retrieve the pennies and entertained themselves arguing over which was flatter or more elongated, laughing at what the train had done to Lincoln's face. Some of their classmates believed in the old wives' tale that a penny on the track could derail a train, but this claim they summarily dismissed as ridiculous.

On the twentieth of March 1948, Danny could not convince any of his friends to come to the trestle to play and decided to go by himself, as he had done on any number of occasions. His tin soldiers provided more than enough company and he could dig a few hidden foxholes to surprise his friends on the weekend. He also loved to be at the trestle during the late afternoon on weekdays to watch the trains switch tracks, the slower freights switching to a side track while the passenger commuters roared by.

The switches were fascinating to all of the boys but Danny, an exceptionally inquisitive young man, developed a keen interest in the timing required to keep the trains running smoothly. His natural curiosity coupled with the normal adventuresome spirit of nine-year-olds almost cost him his life.

Bob Proctor arranged his work schedule so that he always arrived home before Jennie. He had no worry whatsoever about her dependability and knew that she would do exactly as she was told. That confidence in her still would not allow him to have his eight-year-old go home to an empty house after a full day at Lyndeboro Elementary School. The early spring sun developed a warmth for which he was grateful as he rocked gently back and forth on the green metal glider on his porch. He watched as Jennie alighted from the school bus at the corner, waving goodbye to her schoolmates as they scattered throughout the quiet neighborhood. He smiled as she skipped down the street, stopping now and then to admire the first blooms of the daffodils bordering the neighbors' walk. At times like this, as the world came alive again after the desolate winter, he often thought of Jeanne. In that part of his life, the world never came alive; the desolation continued. He had never been able to accept Jeanne's final goodbye on her terms. He could not imagine his life without Jennie. The precious little girl hopscotching down the sidewalk toward him had become his anchor to the real world but he still waited for the proof that Jeanne's sacrifice, which he still viewed with a degree of anger, would be worth it.

"Jeanne should be here," he told himself adamantly as Jennie jumped up the steps and ran into his arms. They had developed a ritual over the last two years and perfected it now. Rituals often have a way of becoming meaningless after so many repetitions but this one remained deeply sincere.

"I missed you today, Daddy," Jennie would say.

"I missed you, too," Bob would answer. "And were you a good girl in school today?"

"Of course not," was Jennie's required response. Then they would share a firm hug and Jennie would vanish to her room to change into play clothes and do her homework.

Jennie's unusual talent, as her teachers referred to it, remained in evidence but her father decided that it would be best for all concerned, especially Jennie, if her abilities were downplayed a bit. It had nothing to do with the other children. They seemed to be in awe of her and yet loved her just the same. The same qualities that bring out fear and suspicion in adults usually draw admiration from the hearts of children. The youngsters at Jennie's school were well aware that she could do some extraordinary things, but that simply did not bother them any more. If Jennie said that something might be going to happen, it would be well to listen. They accepted her talent in much the same way that they knew that Bobby Lucas could do every math problem with little or no effort. He could do math; Jennie could see things happening before they happened. To the children, that was all right. To the adults, it was somewhat more troublesome, but Jennie was such an adorable and lovable child that the occasionally jarring incidents were overlooked. With the warm sun on his face, Bob Proctor had drifted into a late-afternoon nap in the glider. Jennie startled him when she let the screen door slam behind her as she ran across the porch.

"Daddy", she announced, "We've got to go to the trestle."

Bob had long since learned that when Jennie approached him with that tone and attitude, he could not refuse. He was thankful that it did not occur on a regular basis but knew that when it did, he needed to respond.

The Proctors lived two blocks east of the railroad connecting Philadelphia with the southern sections of New Jersey. The railroad noises bothered them considerably for the first few months after they had moved to Lyndeboro, especially at night. Eventually the clacking wheels and the whistles blended in with all the other sounds of the neighborhood and they were no more noticeable than a blue jay squawking at some poor little sparrow.

As Bob and Jennie left the porch, they heard the whistle from the four o'clock commuter as it entered the Heights station to the north.

"We'd better hurry, Daddy," Jennie said, her soft voice indicating a degree of concern that made them pick up the pace. They arrived at the trestle in minutes. The ground under their feet rumbled slightly with approach of the train, still two miles away. They crossed Virginia Avenue and stepped over the curb, looking down the embankment that was Danny Charboneau's battlefield.

"Oh my God!" Jennie and Bob saw Danny simultaneously. He had his back toward the Heights and the approaching train and was pulling violently at his right leg. Instructing Jennie to stay exactly in that spot, Bob alternately ran, tripped, and stumbled down the hill, stepping in Danny's newly dug foxholes, one after the other. The ground shook more definitively as the locomotive approached. Bob stepped up onto the railroad bed and jumped across the northbound tracks to Danny, whose foot was wedged between the track and one of the powerful switches, which had snapped back into place after redirecting the 3:30, freight onto the side tracks.

Bob figured that he had about one minute to free Danny's foot. Frantically searching for any sort of tool, he noticed that the manual switch lever, used when the new automatic switches fail, had a removable bar for releasing it. In two long steps he was at the manual switch, pulling the bar loose. The engineer of the train, characteristically piloting his locomotive with his head hanging out of the window, began blowing the whistle in panic as he saw the two figures on the track, now just a half-mile away. He knew from their actions that they were not there by choice and he leaned on the emergency brake cord. The giant wheels of the locomotive stopped quickly but the engine, with its ten passenger cars behind, continued to be pushed along, the steel wheels screeching as they slid down the track.

Bob pushed the bar as far as he could into the small opening between the main track and the switch and pulled with every ounce of strength he could muster. Danny, his face tear-stained and black and his pants dripping wet, used the extra inch that Bob had given him to pull free. Bob pushed him violently down off the bed and jumped himself. The two of them became a tangle of arms and legs in the small valley between the railroad bed and the hill rising up the west side of the track.

Seconds later, the huge engine, its wheels still locked, came skidding by, the noise of metal on metal deafening as it passed. In the pure terror of the moment and in his position lying on his back, Danny could see the faces of the frightened commuters pressed against the windows as the passenger cars ground to a slow, inexorable halt. The train came to a complete stop with the caboose aligned with Bob and Danny, who were struggling to get to their feet. One of the conductors, slightly overweight and still holding his signal lantern, jumped from the rear of the caboose and stumbled over the rock bed as he tried to run toward the two people who caused the incident. His face bright red from both the exertion and his burgeoning anger, the conductor set down his lantern and reached out one arm to each of the fortunate survivors. Within seconds, the engineer and several other conductors were huddled around Bob and Danny, an emotional mixture of concern, anxiety, relief, and fury swirling in the air.

With his usual calm demeanor, Bob quickly explained what had happened, diffusing some of the hostility aimed in his direction. The attention and concern of the railroad employees turned rapidly to the passengers on the train and, in just another few seconds, Bob and Danny found themselves standing alone. They could see the conductors running up and down the aisles of the last few railroad cars, checking on the welfare of the passengers.

The two clambered up the hill a few steps, startled by the loud whistle of the locomotive. The caboose conductor, now calmed considerably and with a more natural coloring to his face, leaned out of the caboose door and waved his lantern to signal a clear track. The slow response of the huge commuter train to an emergency stop actually prevented injuries within the train itself. The gradual slowing of the train had kept the passengers from being thrown around, and apparently the engineer felt it was safe to continue the trip, a memorable one for the commuters.

As the caboose pulled away, the pudgy conductor, who minutes before seemed to be having an apoplectic attack, waved a friendly salute to Bob. Danny lifted his blackened and tear-streaked face to his life-saving benefactor, really seeing him for the first time.

"Thanks, Mister!" was all Danny could manage as together he and Bob started across the tracks to Jennie, who stood at the top of the hill, a broad, knowing smile on her face.

"How'd ya happen to be here?" Danny asked after they had negotiated the embankment, avoiding the minefields and foxholes of the mock battlefield.

Bob cast a quick glance at Jennie, deciding again that it would be best not to add to her reputation.

"You're quite a lucky young man. We were just out for a little walk and happened to see what was going on. It could've easily gone the other way, you know."

Bob correctly sensed that this was not a good time to deliver a lecture on the danger of playing on railroad tracks. The boy's knees still shook slightly and he needed to get home to a safe haven as quickly as possible. Danny refused Jennie's offer of having her father get the car and drive him home, mulling over already what he would tell his parents, if anything. With luck, no one would have to know about the incident. Danny pictured a vivid scene in his mind, a realistic portrayal in which his parents forbade him to play in his private war zone by the railroad tracks again. It would be the kind of punishment to make a nine-year-old boy create a delicious series of lies to avoid.

Danny assured Bob Proctor and Jennie that he was all right, in convincing enough fashion that Bob believed him. People are never prepared to thank someone for saving their lives and young boys are less prepared than most. With a self-conscious "Thanks again," Danny left the Proctors as he half sprinted, half skipped down the street toward home.

When the story appeared in the *Courier Gazette*, Danny and Bob Proctor were both relieved to see that the reporter allowed the "who" in her story to remain anonymous. She had experienced the train ride personally but had been seated on the opposite side of the car from Danny and Bob. She wrote her brief article based purely on the facts as given to her by the conductor and the engineer, feeling that good Samaritan stories often are more effective if the identities of those involved are not revealed. Somehow, universality is attained if everyone can imagine that he or she could have been the hero or heroine, a possibility enhanced by anonymity. Danny and his friends continued to wage their battles in the shadow of the trestle, but Danny's fascination with the switches on the tracks had been thoroughly satisfied.

Bob Proctor filed away the experience in the compartment of his brain reserved for what he called "Jennie's Miracles." He thought he would save them all for when he saw Jeanne again. As the years disappeared rapidly into the past, his belief that he would see Jeanne again became firmer and more unshakable. For Bob, the belief probably did not exist in a religious realm, for he was not that religious. More likely, it existed only in the human desperation that keeps most people sane, the belief that there must be something more than this. Bob often thought of the Thorton Wilder play *Our Town*. "Something is eternal," he had reasoned. "It just HAS TO BE!" He truly believed that Jennie's miracles would eventually prove Jeanne's strange prophecy for Jennie, but still had no idea how. The dramatic scenario of his first meeting with Jeanne in the ethereal eternity took many forms, but each version contained a wonderful episode in which he regaled his beloved wife with all of Jennie's marvels, her almost divine interventions. He imagined that the story of the boy and the train would surely be one of her favorites.

Fay put down the paper, wondering about the man who appeared at just the right time to save the boy from certain death. She loved happy endings and optimistically clung to the slim hope that her life would continue in the positive direction of the last year. Her marriage to Ethan obviously had its rocky moments but the success he was having at Manley's seemed to have a mellowing affect on his home life as well. At least once during the week, he actually would eat dinner at home, sitting with Ross and her for the entire meal before going to the garage to work on the race car. She had learned the lesson of separating Ethan's work and home life well and waited for special invitations from Ethan before visiting him at work. Since her abortive visit to Manley Motors more than two years before, she was extremely careful not to anger Ethan. She made a concerted effort to avoid occasions that would send him into an abusive rage. Her efforts did not always meet with perfect success, as there were times when Ethan's irrational and unreasonable behavioral quirks took control.

As she reread the article about the strike and tried to combine the newspaper account and the photograph with what Ethan described, she experienced the unsettling feeling in the pit of her stomach that Ethan had probably lost control during the incident. She knew that it would be best for all if she did not pursue the truth of whatever happened that day. In a rage, whether rational or not, Ethan could be a frightening person. The section of the newspaper piece that kept demanding her attention was the "when." The timing did not add up; there was no question in her mind that Ethan should have already been in his office when the strikers were assembling for the picket lines. She would continue to wonder where Ethan was in that hour before he arrived at work, but her instincts were not too subtle as they virtually screamed at her not to question Ethan. As she once again set the paper aside, calling to Ross about his homework progress, she could never have predicted how she would discover the answer to her bewilderment about Ethan's missing hour the morning of the strike.

Jed's Revenge

Jed Carver followed with more than casual interest the story about the Manley strike. He picked up the paper at the local delicatessen he had adopted as his lunch supplier since going to work for the small Ford agency just south of Lyndeboro. He ordered the special, a double cheese steak sandwich smothered with fried onions, the roll absorbing the delicious grease from the cooking process. As he waited for his meal, he picked up the *Gazette*, absently perusing it.

In spite of his undeserved reputation as a union troublemaker, Jed had no difficulty whatsoever in landing a job. Good mechanics were scarce; outstanding craftsman like Jed were almost impossible to find. He was without a job for exactly one day after his embarrassing dumping, a scene that made his stomach churn whenever he thought about it. His deepening resentment over how he was treated at Manley's, especially the humiliating exit forced on him by Ethan Becker, rose to the surface once again as he looked at the front-page picture of Ethan's car being rocked by the pickets.

"Should've turned the damn thing over with him in it," he thought to himself.

He knew that sometime, somehow, he would get even with Ethan Becker. What he had seen through the window in the diner the previous morning might provide him with what he needed to extract a small amount of vengeance from Ethan's hide.

Among the traits that made Jed an excellent mechanic was a photographic memory. Whether it was a page from a documentation manual for a new engine or transmission or observing a man he had come to hate climbing out a woman's car behind his favorite diner, Jed could remember every detail. As he read the article with a voracious interest, Jed knew with certainty why

Ethan had not been in his office before the strikers gathered at Manley's. He would have a little fun thinking about how to use that information for the most effect. As he thought about Ethan Becker, he remembered with his usual clarity the appearance of Ethan's wife at the agency a couple of years before. He decided that the beautiful young woman would be interested in knowing how her husband came to be involved in the picket line. Perhaps Frank Cresti, whom he recognized in the photograph as the man directly in front of Ethan's car, had some ideas when they met for lunch on Saturday. He began to contemplate some of the many and varied scenarios for getting even with Ethan Becker.

Frank Cresti and Jed Carver met on a regular basis at the Empire Diner for lunch on Saturdays ever since Jed had been shown the door at Manley Motors. In the time they worked together, the two had formed a close friendship and determined not to let the separation on the job break up the friendship as well. Jed looked forward to this particular Saturday luncheon with more than the usual anticipation. He knew that Frank would be very interested in what he saw on the morning of the strike. He also had a rather strong feeling that Frank might be searching for a way to extract a bit of retribution for being chased around the Manley lot by a maniacal Ethan Becker.

The two men shared the usual friendly handshakes, augmented by firmly placing each other's left hand over the right and squeezing, a gesture indicating the depth of their friendship. After Jed mentioned in a good-humored fashion the drastic measures Frank would take to get on the front page of a newspaper, their bantering settled into a more serious vein.

"The bastard almost killed me, I really believe he would've, Jed. If you'd seen the look in his eyes..." Frank's voice trailed off, as though he was transported back to the Manley parking lot.

"What happens now, Frank? He's got to be prosecuted, for Chrissakes. Something's got to happen to him." Jed's anger began to show as his voice developed a slight quaver.

"Nothing, Jed. Well, something ...he got a fifty-dollar fine for attempted assault and all the other charges were dropped. Must have something to do with Manley's connections, that's all I can see. It's just a bitch, that's all." Now it was Frank's voice that took on the slight trembling, a shaking coming not from nervousness but from a gut-wrenching resentment.

"Well, Frank, maybe we can do something to make good old Ethan Becker's life a bit more interesting. Nothing like he's done to us but just a little something to kind of get his attention." By the time he finished, Jed's voice had become a conspiratorial whisper.

For the next hour, as they shared all the good that comes from close friendship, most of the conversation focused on the best way to expose Ethan's relationship with the woman they could identify for now only as the "Hudson" woman. Frank volunteered to try to identify the woman, using whatever secretive methods he found necessary. They agreed it would be a shame to involve Ethan's good-looking wife in the process but, in the end, their plan had to include her as well.

Another Move

The largest apartment in the Beckers' house spread out over the entire first floor. In a town with limited apartments, it was among the largest and most desirable, once the tenants became accustomed to the various noises emanating from the railroad track just across Virginia Avenue. The location, within easy walking distance of the downtown area, added to its attractiveness. Ethan was glad when the tenants who had moved in shortly after Ethan and Fay bought the house informed them that they would be moving into their own home and would need to break their lease by three months. On the surface, Ethan gave a stern, Dutch-uncle type of speech to them about the importance of keeping a lease agreement, but it was a halfhearted attempt. He knew that he could rent the apartment for considerably more than he was getting from them.

The Crowleys apologized profusely, afraid that Ethan would not allow them to break the lease without a stiff financial penalty. They had counted on using at least two months of the rent for new furniture and Ethan, uncharacteristically generous, surprised the Crowleys by agreeing and charged only one month's penalty. He was already counting on the increase in rent to put more money into good old number 21, his favorite sprint car.

In some ways, he hated to lose the Crowleys. They were good tenants, causing no problems and being very understanding of the need to test the race cars in the driveway that ran directly under their bedroom window. He certainly would miss Amy Crowley, an extremely attractive woman, even though he never found the courage to approach her to be more than just a downstairs neighbor. Rose McGowen was as close to Fay as he dared venture for satisfying his appetite for women. Even that had often proved to be dangerous, but it was always well worth the risk. He had decided early in the Crowleys' tenure at the apartment to pass up any opportunities that Amy might present.

Ethan planned on being quite selective when it came to choosing the next occupants of what was sure to be one of the most sought-after apartments in Collins Heights. Fay was excited when she discovered that the Crowleys might move away. She had already begun planning the move downstairs when Ethan put a crushing stop to her idea. The spacious full-floor apartment would be superfluous for their small family and he knew the second floor could never bring anywhere near the income. This happened to be one of those disagreements that Fay knew would be a lost battle, and she had learned that she needed to pick her battles carefully.

Just short of two weeks after the Crowleys announced their intentions, the Faxons announced theirs. The old farmhouse where the Johnsons had lived since 1940 was not generating enough income to make keeping the house a viable prospect. The Faxons' dairy and vegetable farm, while substantial by local standards, could not compete with the expansive southern New Jersey farms being bought by companies like Birdseye and DelMonte. The Faxons made the difficult but financially brilliant decision to subdivide their acreage into two parcels, keeping a ten-acre tract surrounding their house and selling the other two hundred with the Pike frontage to a commercial developer. There was no question as to what would happen to the rental property of the Johnsons. The romantic old house had fallen into such disrepair that fixing all of its problems would be a financial nightmare. The building had absolutely no commercial value and would most likely be a victim of the bulldozer within a day of the final settlement on the property.

When the phone rang and Ethan heard Susan Johnson's voice on the other end of the line, his heart skipped a beat. Everything had been going too well and something in Susan's voice told him that this was not going to be good news. His mother-in-law obviously did not want to speak with him, and he quickly called Fay to the phone.

"It's your mother," he shouted, a sharp edge in his voice.

"Grandmom!" Ross heard the call in his bedroom and raced out, grabbing the brand-new dial phone he had learned all about in school two days before. He barely had time to say hello when Fay took the receiver from him and immediately wanted to know what was wrong.

Ethan watched Fay's expression pass quickly through the stages of concern to relief. Her mother did not like to talk on the phone and usually reserved her calls for an announcement of death or some equally despairing news. It seemed to Ethan that Fay's mind had shifted into high gear and his normal lack of curiosity disappeared quickly when he heard her say, "I've got a great idea. Let me speak with Ethan and I'll call you right back."

"What's going on?" Ethan asked, something telling him that he did not want to know.

"Faxons have sold their property. Mom and the kids have to leave the house."

Fay's announcement did nothing but add to Ethan's rapidly increasing anxiety.

"And...?" Fay could sense the agitation in Ethan's demeanor and she struggled to find the right words to describe her great idea. What plainly was a fine idea a moment before now paled before Ethan's silent but frightening demand to know.

Fay thought for just an instant before realizing that this battle, if it was to be one, had to be fought.

"Why don't we offer to let them live in the apartment downstairs, Ethan?"

"They can't afford it, Fay. You know that. We can charge a substantial amount for that place and your mother can't afford it. That's the end of that. Period."

Her husband's voice began the sentence softly but by the punctuation mark he was shouting. Ethan's mind whirled. For almost four years he had been out from under the Johnson family roof, a roof that to him seemed always to be ready to collapse under its own weight. He had felt forever trapped, outnumbered by the brood. Even though the group had lost some of its numbers through marriage and simple adulthood, he knew there were still enough of them to throw the noose of dependence back around his neck. After four years of freedom, how could he stand to have them in the same house again?

Fay took her normal two steps backward, a technique she had

learned from their son, both of them perfecting it and using it to advantage in any confrontational situation with Ethan. They used the backpedal method, not as a sign of weakness but rather of practicality. If the situation happened to be one that would bring Ethan to a boil, it always was better to be beyond arm's length. Fay didn't know what would come of the present standoff, but just wanted to be sure that she stood clear of immediate physical danger. Ross retreated into the hall, standing at his bedroom door ready to bolt to his bed. On several occasions, he witnessed violence in his house, and his best defense, physically and emotionally, was to hide in his room until the storm subsided. He usually was ignorant of the cause of his parents' arguments, coming on them quite by accident. He generally would make one feeble but futile attempt at asking them to stop, but this time he could predict the outcome. He knew what this fight would be about and he wanted no part of it. The excitement of hearing his grandmother's voice on the phone disappeared, replaced by the dread that once again his parents were about to argue. Decided not to wait for the inevitable, he slipped into his room. For just a fleeting moment, he remembered the night years before when he stood silently outside his parents' bedroom in the dark, knowing something bad was happening. The physical escalation of the battle in the living room left him feeling equally helpless now. He leaned against the inside door jamb, listening intently.

Fay held her ground, having determined that this battle had to be fought, even if not won.

"Ethan, they've no place to go now and it just makes sense to rent them the downstairs place. If we charge just the same rent as the Crowleys were paying, my mom and the other kids could swing it. It would be great having them so close."

Ethan began to feel as if he was being pushed into a final corner, surrounded on three sides by Fay and her family. He knew he had no acceptable reason to refuse the Johnsons to take the apartment for the same rent as the Crowleys. He searched his now wildly active mind for a way out but, for once, knew he had to give on this one. How could he explain to anyone that he refused to let his in-laws move into such a perfect situation? He weighed the pros and cons, putting everything into mental columns. The only con that he could say aloud was the loss of increased rental income. The other negative in his mind he would be unable to explain to anyone, even his best friend, Al Stuart. With his in-laws in the same building, he knew his life style would have to change. With them in the same town, he would need to be much more careful in his "activities outside the home," as he referred to them. Basing his argument on the rental issue alone, he gave the appearance of thinking only of the welfare of Fay and Ross.

"Wouldn't the extra money come in handy?" he asked Fay. He watched her face for any change in determination but it was not forthcoming. Either she saw through his argument, knowing that he wanted the extra income to spend on his cars, or she was sincerely caught up in the excitement of having her family close by once again.

"OK, Fay. But to be fair, they will have to be treated like the other tenants-no special privileges," Ethan said in his firmest voice, trying to salvage some small degree of satisfaction from the predicament.

Ross, hardly able to believe what he heard, inched his way into the hall so he could see his parents face to face in the living room.

"I'm going to want a lease and an insurance contract agreement, even if it is your mother," Ethan was saying, still desperately trying to make it appear that he remained in charge, even as he waved the white flag.

When Ross reached the archway into the living room, his heart stood still as Fay threw her arms around Ethan and kissed him. She felt Ross's presence in the room and turned to him, looking absolutely radiant.

"Grandmom's coming to live here, Ross! Won't that be fun?" The look on his father's face left no doubt that he did not share Fay's unbridled enthusiasm. In a dichotomy of feelings that he did not really understand, Ross's urge to squeal with youthful excitement was suppressed, tempered by the knowledge that this skirmish had resolved itself much too quickly. The defeated but still menacing glare in Ethan's eyes clearly meant to Ross that the move to bring his grandmother closer might not be that great an idea after all.

Manley's Practice Oval

Laurelwood Raceway opened for the season in late spring. Al Stuart and Ethan Becker couldn't wait. All winter long they spent uncountable hours working on perfecting their cars in the garage behind Ethan's house. As the season approached, they went on jaunts all over southern New Jersey in search of open areas where they might test the cars with wide-open throttles. The driveway by the house lost much of its appeal after several hundred short trials up and down its full length of three hundred feet. Much like the preparation for any sport, the early-season practices for auto racing finally become a bit humdrum. Any driver who has experienced the thrill of operating a sprint car under full throttle, throwing it into the characteristic sideways slide coming out of the first turn, tires very quickly of driving the car back and forth in a short driveway.

About six miles from the house in Collins Heights, John Manley had held an option on a three-hundred-acre parcel of land for several years. With his usual far-sighted thinking, he anticipated the outward expansion of the New Jersey side of the Philadelphia suburbs and had leased the huge tract with an agreement to buy. He envisioned expansion of his own business and was well aware that this prime piece of land would be the envy of developers within a few years. When Ethan approached Manley with the request to use some of the parcel as a practice ground for his cars, his boss readily agreed. Manley's only contingency was that his prize pupil take care of himself.

The business value of Ethan's involvement in racing was not lost on John Manley. The automotive parts industry held out the promise of huge profits and Ethan's contact with so many of the mechanics in the area through racing provided a substantial boost to the parts department sales at Manley Motors. Ethan assured

John Manley that he would be very careful and called Al immediately after the conversation to pass along the news that they had a proving ground for their winter work.

The first Sunday after the approval to carve out their own racing oval, Ethan and Al invited everyone who had been one of the garage boys during the long winter to come over and help load the two sprint cars onto the trailers. The men arrived early and had the cars prepared and loaded before Ross and Fay even returned from Sunday Mass. From more than a block away, Ross could hear the thunderous roar of number 21 as Ethan inched his way up the ramp onto the trailer, the powerful engine racing but Ethan controlling the forward progress with the clutch and gear box. By the time Fay and Ross had walked the last block home, a three-car entourage had formed behind the trucks with the trailers and race cars. Last-minute checks of the trailer connections, tools and supplies took about ten minutes, enough for Fay to protest that the men had not yet had their coffee. Even as she mentioned it to Ethan, she sensed the palpable excitement among the men and knew that her coffee and doughnuts were not about to slow the progress toward the practice area.

After Fay went back inside, only Al Stuart opted for one of the doughnuts and bounded up the rear stairs as the others waited, shaking their heads impatiently.

Al had time to come to the rear door, grab one of the jelly-filled pastries Fay offered and say, "I'll talk to you later." She knew very well that his craving for a jelly doughnut had much more to do with her than with his breakfast. She just smiled, reached out, and squeezed his hand.

"Ok, see you later," she said as he backed out of the door. Since her embarrassing scene with him over two years ago, the friendship between them had deepened. There was much more going on in her head than she could admit. She was not nearly so vulnerable now as she was when she failed miserably in her effort to show him how she felt. For whatever reason, Fay relived the infamous bathrobe scene again in her head now as he stumbled down the stairs, reacting to the shouts of his friends below to hurry.

"What a stupid thing to do," she thought. No matter how often she remembered opening her robe while trying to hide her swollen cheek, she always came to the same two conclusions. First, she did not know what she expected to accomplish, and second, she must have looked so foolish. The fact that neither of them ever mentioned the incident only served to convince her that it was a pointless thing to do. Now, two years later, she could face the fact that she had feelings for Al far beyond their friendship. The sexual tension electrified the space between them whenever they were in the same room, but, other than her bathrobe scene, neither of them would allow themselves to acknowledge it. Fay easily convinced herself to reject the feelings based on her supposedly deep religious beliefs and decided for the time being to continue to keep that side of the relationship alive only in her fantasy world. Al would be the first to admit in his own mind how much space Fay occupied in his daily thoughts. He would have had to be completely numb not to sense the magnetism between them but lived in fear that if he acknowledged it, brought it out into the open, he would lose her all together, an outcome he rejected out of hand.

Fay went to the front bay window and watched as the two trucks with their precious cargo on the trailers behind pulled out of the driveway. Ethan, in the front of the caravan, was engrossed in the scene and never looked back. In the second truck, Al had glanced up at the second-story bay window, but she decided that perhaps she only imagined his slight wave. She stayed at the window until the last car disappeared down Virginia Avenue. Ross had come through the rear kitchen door and gone directly into his room, not wanting his mother to see the tears of yet another bitter disappointment. He had been sure that he would be asked to come along to watch as the cars were being truly tested for the first time this spring.

Jed and Frank

In less than a week, Frank Cresti discovered the owner of the Hudson. It was a surprisingly simple process. Casual inquiries as the shop mechanics were at lunch led to a discussion about why someone would bring a Hudson into a Ford agency for service. During the conversation, Mark Soroka mentioned that Bill Perry always assigned him to work on the dark green, late-model Hudson. He had no reason for it except that he did have slightly more experience with cars other than Fords. Frank, trying not to act too interested, inquired about the owner of the car.

"Only saw her once but what a sexy lady, a little hefty but all the more to squeeze," Mark said, throwing a meaningful leer in Frank's direction.

That afternoon, after Frank had cleaned up, using a little more Boraxo than usual on his grease-smeared hands and arms, he stopped by for his regular flirting time with Annie, the part-time evening cashier. Annie started work at five o'clock and her booth by the showroom floor was a popular place for the male employees as they left work. She could be counted on to be wearing a tight Betty Grable-style sweater and the men enjoyed the momentary inspiration she provided for the long ride home. Frank occupied a special place in Annie's routine because he actually talked to her and seemed to be interested in how she was doing. When she saw Frank coming, she flipped her long brown hair to be sure that it flowed over her shoulders and greeted him with her pert, saucy smile. Frank quickly ran through the formalities of inquiring about her life in general, ending always with a rhetorical and harmless question about her love life. He closed the conversation with the usual "See ya tomorrow, Annie." In what to Annie seemed an afterthought, Frank turned back to her and asked for a favor, "just for curiosity," he said.

"Is there any way of knowing how many Hudsons we service here, Annie—just curious, you know?"

"What a silly question, Frank. This is a Ford agency, you know," Annie replied in a condescending but joking way.

"Sorry, Annie—pretty stupid of me..."

"The only one I know of for sure is the one that Ethan Becker brings in once in a while. I remember because I'm always on duty when he pays the bill after everyone has left." Annie had no reason to be suspicious of Frank's motives and continued to expand her story as her memory allowed.

"He said the car belonged to a close family friend and to keep all the records in his file so that she would get his discount."

Frank, on the verge of getting all of the information he wanted, struggled to remain casual, almost uninterested.

"The thing I was most curious about is the years, Annie, you know, how old the cars are."

A service customer came up behind Frank, ready to pay his bill. Annie, efficiently pushed her rolling stool over to the file cabinet, pulled open one of the drawers, and grabbed a file. She rolled back and handed it to Frank through the slot in the bars.

"Look for yourself while I help this gentleman, OK?"

Frank stepped aside to let the customer up to the window. The file tab at the top of the folder had a green background, indicating an employee designation. BECKER, ETHAN (HUDSON) was typed neatly on the flap. His body shielded the folder as he turned away from the showroom. When he opened it, his service-trained eyes knew exactly where to look on a work order for the customer's name. Quickly scanning the first page he found exactly what he wanted printed under Ethan Becker's name. The car, the famous Hudson Jed had seen behind the diner, belonged to Rose McGowen of Collins Heights. The plan that he and Jed had devised could now be implemented.

Frank Cresti was so anxious to share his information that he drove by Jed Carver's house on his way home from work that very day. He found Jed pushing his lawn mower through the thick growth of spring grass in his back yard. When Jed saw Frank turn the corner, he gladly stopped his mowing, thankful for the excuse to rest. They walked over to the large weeping willow, brushed aside the low-hanging branches, and sat down on the two rusting metal lawn chairs Jed had just brought out of the cellar.

Jed remembered Annie well from his days at Manley's, having done more than his share of harmless flirting with her. Frank related the whole story of his extracting the information on the "Hudson woman," ending with a simple question.

"So, when are we going to drop this little bomb on our friend?"

Jed thought for a moment and concluded that Sunday might be good. They knew that Ethan had this racing car hobby that kept him busy whenever he was not working at Manley's, so probably Sunday would work well.

"Who's going to make the call?" Jed asked, knowing that all the details had already been worked out.

Frank just laughed. "She won't ever remember your voice, you know. I think about ten-thirty would be a good time, soon after nine o'clock Mass is finished. Do you want me to come over and sit with you to hold your hand?"

"Get the hell out of here, I can handle it. Actually, I want to handle it. I just feel bad for Fay Becker, but she'll be better off knowing anyway." Jed said this in such a way that it was obvious to Frank that he was trying to convince himself that it was the truth. They both thought, almost in unison, that no one is better off knowing this type of truth.

Frank reached into his pocket and pulled out the piece of paper with Rose McGowen's name on it. "Collins Heights" scribbled under Rose's name was the only other writing on the paper. Jed would have to call the information operator for the number, but neither man saw that as a problem.

Frank stood up, handed the paper to Jed, and shook his hand.

"Good luck, Jed, and have fun!" As he started across the lawn, the thick damp grass clippings sticking to his shoes, Jed called to him.

"You really think this is a good thing to do, Frank?" The question hung in the air, suspended there from a cloud of doubt overhead.

"No question about it, Jed, no question at all", Frank called back, not really believing his own answer. His next thought he kept to himself:

"I only hope to God that Ethan Becker never finds out who did it."

The First Test

The first day of testing their race cars had gone better than Ethan or Al even dreamed. A large area of John Manley's land was used for a gravel pit, Manley allowing a few contractors take out fill dirt for various projects around the area. His fee for the privilege had been quite reasonable but he made the conditions very clear. With his eye toward the future of the land, he stipulated to anyone who extracted gravel or fill dirt that the pit was always to be leveled. He did not want the expense of additional construction work when it came time to develop the land and the terms for use of the pit were unequivocal.

The enormous amount of excavated gravel had left a level hollow almost a half mile in every direction. Because of their agreement with John Manley and the value of the gravel, the visiting contractors took great care to smooth the surface as they moved outward from the center of the pit. To a driver passing by on Route 70, the hollow wasn't visible at all. Ethan and Al had spent several evenings planning how they could best use the hollow for testing their cars but never thought that they would be able to design their own race track. Being invisible from the road made the area perfect for keeping away the curious, who otherwise might be attracted to the roar of the cars. The contractors' heavy loading machinery and mammoth dump trucks had packed the surface to a perfect racing consistency.

Much of their first Sunday at "the pit," their unoriginal nickname, was spent carefully measuring and laying out a half-mile oval. All of the tracks they raced during the season were half-mile dirt ovals, a perfect distance and surface for the "big cars," a pet name for their sprint cars that separated them from the "midgets," which used quarter-mile asphalt tracks. Setting up the track was a supreme test of the patience of the two anxious drivers and their companions. Finally, at two o'clock, after several hours of making certain that everything was accurate, they readied their cars for the first trials. Having taken the trucks and other cars around the oval dozens of times, the drivers could no longer contain themselves.

Together, Ethan and Al climbed into their cars, parked side by side, only ten feet separating them. The trucks, driven by their equally excited friends, moved up slowly behind each car, setting the bumper against the steel grid protecting the rear of the cars. Ethan and Al agreed that the first trials should be conducted at least a quarter of a mile apart. Ethan signaled for the truck to begin the push start and within just a short distance the engine thundered into life. Al watched as the dust kicked up and Ethan's car screamed into the first turn of their homemade oval. He waited until Ethan brought his car out of the broadslide coming off the second turn and then gave the signal to his crew to begin his push start. Within seconds, he too was roaring into the first turn, his first stint of the season behind the wheel under way.

The rest of the afternoon passed quickly as the two drivers forced themselves to be conservative, treating the cars with the same degree of gentle care that one would treat a home-built sailing vessel on its maiden voyage. By the time the crew loaded the cars back onto the trailers for the trip home, they could not stop smiling through their emotional and physical exhaustion. Already, they hoped for good weather for the next weekend, anticipating another day of pure enjoyment, the characteristic bellowing of the Offenhausers echoing through their memories.

The unmistakable throbbing whine of the race car engine awakened Fay out of a sound sleep.

"What in the world?" she thought, as she clambered out of bed and went to the window. Ethan had told her everyone would be very eager to get started after the success of the previous Sunday, but she had not anticipated that they would be this anxious. She had set the old Westclox Big Ben alarm for the usual Sunday-morning wake-up call at 7 A.M. and knew that it had not yet gone off. The early-morning sun angled into the window, its warmth already established. She could not believe that the boys had the cars out of the garage at 6:45 on a Sunday morning and had managed to get one of them running already. "That'll make us popular with the neighbors," she thought, covering her personal agitation with the concern for the surrounding neighborhood. Seeing Al's car parked under the basketball hoop at the end of the driveway extension presented her with the only positive aspect of the scene. She hoped that perhaps today they might get a chance for a little longer visit before they all retreated to the haven of the homemade racetrack at Manley's pit.

Ross came wandering out of his room, and rubbed his eyes. "Why are they here so early, Mom?" he asked.

"I'm not sure, dear, but your father didn't tell me they would be here this soon. Would you please put on your old clothes and go tell them that I'll have the coffee ready as soon as I can?"

Ross raced into his room, threw on a pair of old dungarees and a T-shirt, shoved his feet into sneakers without even putting on socks, and was out the rear door in less that two minutes. He loved being around the cars and listening to the men talk. Just being in the environment made him feel grownup and Ethan's friends always made him feel welcome. He bounded down the wooden steps two at a time and ran across the backyard to where Ethan and Al huddled over the front of Ethan's car, the engine idling noisily. Al turned first and greeted him warmly.

"Hey, Ross, what are you doing up this early?" he shouted, his wide grin making Ross feel like one of the boys.

Al's greeting made Ethan also turn from the car. When he saw Ross, he gave a small, lukewarm wave and asked him why he was there. Al once again couldn't help but notice the reaction of the young boy, who now seemed flustered, as if searching for some validity to his very existence.

"Mom said to tell you she'd have coffee ready soon," Ross managed to stammer.

"Tell her not to bother; we're going to stop at the diner for breakfast this morning on our way to the pit. We're real anxious to get going." Ethan turned back to the car as he spoke. Ross responded with a flat, sad "OK, Dad," realizing that he wouldn't be going with the crew this Sunday. In contrast to his approach to the garage minutes before, Ross started across the yard with sagging, disappointed shoulders, walking at an old man's pace back to the house.

By the time Ross reached the top of the fire escape, glancing back disconsolately over his shoulder, the driveway and garage were alive with activity. The trailers for the race cars were lined up with several of the men pushing the cars into position for loading. As Ross reached for the screen door, he turned back with one last youthful hope that perhaps his father might call to him to come with them. He stood there, his hand cupped over the doorknob but not wanting to turn it and go in. With the ever-present hope of a young boy, he continued to watch the caravan forming, the vehicles being aligned for the trip to the pit. Al Stuart, pushing his car from the rear, looked up and made eye contact with Ross across the distance. He removed one hand from the car and waved, his natural smile giving Ross a minor boost but also ruining the optimism of moments before. He reluctantly opened the door and went in to tell his mother that her coffee effort was wasted.

The loud, insistent buzzing of the Sunday morning alarm clock could barely be heard over the sounds of the vehicular procession crunching over the gravel driveway as it passed under the partially open windows on the second floor. Ross ran to the front bay window and watched the trailing cars disappear down the street. Fay overcame her own disappointment at not being able to communicate with Al and walked over to Ross, hugging him from behind.

"Your dad will take you soon, Ross, I'm sure. He probably just wants to make sure it would be safe for you, that's all." She said this with as much conviction as she could muster, trying hard to convince herself as well as young son. If Al had anything to say about it, Ross would be with them right now. Fay had no concern about the dilemma of Ross missing Sunday Mass to be with his father as she thought they would be going after the nine o'clock Mass ended. She knew if the issue came up, there could be no equivocating on her part-a mortal sin is a mortal sin and she would not put Ross in that kind of eternal jeopardy. Ethan would poke his usual fun at her religious superstitions, as he called them, but she would not cave in. Missing Sunday Mass was not an option for either Ross or her. She decided to worry about that possibility when it occurred.

"Well. Let's eat breakfast and get ready for church. It's going to be a beautiful day; maybe we'll walk down to the park this afternoon." To Ross, a walk to the park came in a distant second to being where the race cars were but it represented a positive Sunday afternoon activity and some of his spirit returned. By the time they walked out of the door headed for the St. Luke's, his disappointment with the morning's events had been replaced by the eternal optimism of an eight-year-old boy.

Vengeance Is Mine

As Ross and Fay began their walk toward St. Luke's, Jed Carver's wife, Loretta, was taking their large Doberman for his daily stint of terrorizing the neighborhood. Ike, muzzled by the Carvers only because the gentle dog had such a ferocious appearance, loved to go for extensive walks and practicality made Sunday mornings a convenient time. No sooner had Loretta left the house than Jed picked up the phone. He thought he recognized the operator's voice, having heard the familiar "Number please" spoken in so many different ways. Of course, he had no idea who she was or what she looked like, but after hundreds of "Number pleases," he had fun imagining the owner of the phantom voice at the switchboard on the other end of the line. He knew he would miss the personal contact with a real operator when the spread of the new dial phones covered his town. For now, all he wanted was to speak with the information operator and find out Rose McGowen's phone number.

"Information please," Jed said. After a brief wait, Jed heard another of those personal but somehow impersonal, disconnected voices. "Information-how may I help you?" Even this voice sounded familiar to him.

"The number for McGowen in Collins Heights. Sorry, I don't have a street address."

"There is only one that I have, sir. A John McGowen on Garden Avenue."

"That must be it, Thanks!"

"The number is Lincoln 7-4546." The line went dead.

Jed pushed the disconnect button on the cradle of the phone and lifted it again. Amazingly, the same operator's voice came on the line. "Number please?"

Jed recited the number and listened to the two short rings. He prayed that Rose herself would answer although he was prepared for any eventuality.

"McGowen residence, this is Rose speaking." Jed loved the way some people forced a formality, even in the way they answered the telephone. Why not just a simple "Hello," he wondered.

In a low monotone, Jed recited what he had practiced over and over again.

"I understand you are very, very good friends with Ethan Becker. I'm sure that his wife and your husband will enjoy finding out just what good friends you are. Hope you've enjoyed your time together. I think it might be coming to an end."

Jed set down the receiver gently and smiled. He tried to visualize that poor woman's mental state right at that moment but gave up. He picked up the receiver again. "Number please?" It was definitely a different voice. He knew Frank's number by heart. "Fairfield 3-8643."

"Part one is completed," he said quietly when he heard Frank's voice. Both men felt as if they were playing an adolescent telephone prank on a local merchant. They chatted briefly, wondering aloud what, if anything, Rose McGowen was doing now. Frank wished Jed good luck with phase two, knowing that this went far beyond the old "Do you have Prince Albert in a can" trick, a prank pulled so many times by children home alone with the telephone as their only recreation. All a drugstore proprietor could do was sputter when told, "You better let him out. He's suffocating," knowing he had become a victim when he heard the giggling on the other end of the line. If this telephone prank played out the way they intended, Frank and Jed knew that much more than sputtering and giggling would be the result.

The nine o'clock Mass ended sooner than usual and Fay and Ross arrived home a little after ten. They had decided that the day should not be wasted. The ground had lost all signs of frost and today began for the first time this season to give back some warmth of its own. Ross begged his mother for permission to ride his bike south along Virginia Avenue, maybe even as far as the trestle separating Collins Heights from Lyndeboro. The thought of the recent newspaper article about the dramatic rescue on the railroad track by the trestle made her hesitate and almost automatically say no. She relented only after extracting his solemn promise that he would not go near the railroad and would be home by twelve so they could eat lunch and then go to the park. Ross rushed ahead of her, changed into his play clothes, and was out the door in record time. Fay marveled at the resiliency of young children, remembering how distraught at being left behind he had been just a few hours before. She felt somewhat resilient herself, the warm spring day offering her some of the same sense of renewal it was providing to the flowers and lawns.

Once inside the apartment, Fay whisked from one room to the next, opening the windows wide, enjoying the warm cross breeze blowing through the house. She went into the bedroom and rather languidly took off the layers of church clothing, standing close enough to a window to allow the soft, warm wind to touch the increasingly exposed areas of her skin. She found her thoughts drifting to the occasions of sin, the thoughts she could never bring herself to confess. During times such as these, Al Stuart's face became an intrusive presence. She forced herself to stop thinking and turned to her closet. She hung up her dress and folded her silk slip, replacing it in the top drawer of her bureau. As she stood by the bed, the breeze blowing the curtains away from the windows, she needed all of her self-discipline to keep from lying down and letting her fantasies carry her away. Instead, she again went to the closet and this time snatched a pair of old slacks and a print blouse from the hook on the inside of the door. As she pulled on her slacks, the telephone rang in the living room. She started toward it slowly, making sure that it was their ring, and arrived at the telephone table just as the second pair of long rings finished. She picked up the receiver and gave a cheerful hello. Twenty seconds later, her world fell apart.

Jed Carver slowly set the telephone receiver back into place. He tried to imagine how he would react to a phone call like the one he had just made:

"Hello, Mr. Carver. Are you aware that your wife spends at least one hour a week in bed with a man named...?" The name wouldn't matter. He would be devastated. The one factor he and Frank had not considered was that this Rose McGowen was Fay Becker's good friend. It was just as well. Jed knew that in the short space of twenty seconds, he had thrown a big rock into the pond and the ripples would be spreading out for a long time, probably a lifetime.

As much as he hated Ethan Becker, a sense of guilt and sadness swept over him. Feeling like a modern-day Macbeth, he picked up the phone once more to report to Frank that the deed was done.

Ross enjoyed riding his bike. Before he left for his ride down Virginia Avenue, he went to his cache of balloons in the basement and removed just one from the package. Since it was Sunday, he didn't want to make too much noise but he loved imitating the blatting muffler sounds of the race cars. Partially filling the elongated balloon with air, Ross was careful to leave enough of both ends hanging loose so he could tie them around the front sprocket of his Schwinn. He had learned through harsh experience that if the balloon was too hard, it would break soon after the ride began. A soft balloon had a much longer life span once it was tied and flipped over into the spokes of the front wheel. There were four places on his bike available to accommodate the balloon mufflers, two in the front and two on the back. He knew that on a Sunday-morning ride, a single noisemaker would have to do. Satisfied that his muffler would last at least much of this trip, he set off down the street.

Immediately, his vivid imagination kicked in and he was no longer on his Schwinn but behind the wheel of a powerful race car, roaring down Virginia Avenue with the sound of his blatting balloon muffler streaming out behind him.

South of the business district of Collins Heights, Virginia Avenue became a strollers' delight on the warm, sunny spring Sunday. Vehicular traffic was minimal. Anyone with someplace to go would use the Pike running parallel to the railroad and the avenue, just three blocks over. Ross cruised through the many families taking advantage of the beautiful weather, taking what President Truman had popularized as their "morning constitutional." A lively, good-natured spirit energized the spring fever running rampant up and down the avenue.

Just ten minutes into his ride, the trestle crossing the tracks and separating the Heights from Lyndeboro came into Ross's view. His mother's warnings surfaced immediately. He had no interest in going onto the railroad tracks but his natural curiosity caused him to bring his bike to a stop at top of the hillside where he could look down on the series of switches where the young boy came close to losing his life. Several boys about his age, perhaps slightly older, played in the dirt along the hill, making the sounds of a fierce military confrontation taking place among their toy soldiers. The pitched battle demanded all of their attention and none of them even noticed Ross up on the street. After observing for a few minutes, he turned his bike to head back toward the Heights. The blat from his balloon as he gained speed caused the boys to glance up briefly but he had already disappeared from view.

Less than a block from the battlefield by the tracks, Ross noticed a father and a young girl, hand in hand, coming toward him. They appeared to be fully engaged with each other, their attention riveted on their little world, not the surrounding environment. As Ross blatted past, the girl glanced sideways and waved. He had already passed when he realized that she had actually waved to him. He looked back over his shoulder but there was no sign that they had even seen him. He decided the wave was an illusion, but the image of their obvious closeness stayed with him for the rest of the ride home. He thought of his brief and only contact with his father that morning and felt just a twinge of jealousy as he sped his bicycle toward home and his mother.

Ross turned his bike into the driveway, skidding on the gravel but managing to stay upright. His muffler, having lasted for four miles, gave one last blat and popped just as he came to a stop. Leaning the bike against the side of the house, he ran up the stairs onto the front porch. He thought fleetingly of how great it would be when the Johnsons moved in downstairs as he passed the door to the lower-floor apartment. Taking the stairs two at a time as he always did, he was at the first landing in four bounds, turned on the landing, and jumped up the last four steps, opening the door and landing on the top stair all in one motion.

"Mom, I'm home!" No immediate answer came and Ross turned toward the kitchen. He could see his mother facing the gas stove, her back to him. "Hey, Mom!", he hollered, and repeated the superfluous "I'm home!"

"After you eat this sandwich, we'll go to the park, ok?" She said this without turning around and Ross crossed over to her, the image of the father and daughter still crowding his mind. He came up behind Fay and wrapped his arms around her waist and squeezed. A stifled sob escaped but Ross didn't recognize it. He quickly apologized for squeezing too hard and let go. Fay brushed by, mumbling something he did not understand. When she got to the hall, she turned back and said simply, "Just eat your lunch and we'll go."

Not until he sat down at his place, his jelly sandwich placed neatly in the middle of a napkin, flanked by a huge glass of milk, did Ross realize that his mother was crying in her bedroom. He slid off his chair, picked up half of his sandwich and tentatively tiptoed down the hall.

"Mom, are you all right?" Ross had seen his mother cry before but he generally knew the cause. This time, he worried that he should not have taken his bike trip, but he couldn't imagine what might have happened.

"Why are you so sad, Mom?" he asked in a plaintive eight-year-old way.

"I'm fine, dear. Just let me get myself together and we'll go." Ross could tell, even through the closed door, that her voice was shaking. Few things in a child's life are more traumatic than seeing his mother cry, but one of those things is seeing a mother cry and not know why. Eight-year-olds finding themselves in that situation tend to think immediately that it must be something very serious and, worse yet, that they may somehow be the cause. Ross began to get very nervous and then he thought of his father testing the race cars. A cold fear shivered through him.

"Mom?" Ross felt tears beginning to come. "MOM!"

Fay opened the door, saw her son, and reached out for him. "Everything is all right, really, Ross. You don't need to worry or be upset. Everything is fine." As she pulled him to her, she could feel the reassuring hug drain Ross's worries as only a mother's hug could.

"Why don't you bring your sandwich along and we'll walk the long way to the park. We'll stop by Pop's and get an ice-cream soda on the way." A mother's hug and the promise of one of Pop's ice cream sodas had the power to remove all kinds of fear and trepidation from any eight-year-old. Within minutes, Fay and Ross were on their way to the park the long way, a route that would take them directly past the home of the McGowens, one of the Beckers' closest friends. Fay thought of Al and Ethan and wondered what the rest of this day would bring.

The trials and testing at what was now a swirling dust bowl were going well. Al Stuart opened the throttle of his powerful machine as he thundered down the straightaway of the roughly measured racing oval. Close behind but at a safe distance, Ethan guided his car through the dust trail raised by Al's car. The exhaust fumes from both cars formed a cloud over the oval, blending with the thick, choking dust. An outsider would surely wonder what the attraction of breathing such a mixture could possibly be. The two men in the cars careening around the track barely noticed as the excitement of the speed became all encompassing, their concentration focused on a blending of their own, the relationship between man and his machine.

Although the oval they had constructed was well away from the road and hidden by trees, the noise raised by the two cars did attract the attention of a few curious passersby. The buffer zone created by the huge tract of land owned by John Manley provided ample protection from police interference for disturbing the peace of a quiet Sunday morning. The beckoning call of the warm, early-spring morning had brought out more than the usual number of spectators, all of them standing in a group, at least one hundred feet removed from the cars and trailers of the crew and another hundred feet or so from the track itself.

Al and Ethan had an implicit trust in each other and gradually developed a habit that now was a ritual. After several laps around the half-mile oval, they would guide their cars to a stop, set the hand brake, and, leaving them running, would quickly switch from one to the other. The familiarity a driver developed with his machine often would lead to overlooking a small quirk in the handling of the car or the sound of the engine and the two friends knew how helpful a second opinion could be. This Sunday was no different, even though both drivers were convinced that the cars could not be performing any better. A ritual in racing easily falls into the category of superstition and the testing of each other's cars before a race quickly ran the gamut from habit to ritual to superstition, a superstition that neither one would dare to ignore. As the cars rolled into the pits of their homemade racetrack, the two men, in almost simultaneous motions, reached their right hands out to the hand brake lever just outside the cockpit and pulled them back. The cars idled roughly as Ethan and Al jumped out and traded places, glancing at each other and smiling. The shared experience of driving one of these cars made any words unnecessary. The looks exchanged from behind the dust-caked goggles indicated a satisfaction with their own cars and almost shouted silently, "Isn't this the greatest?" Within a few seconds, both men had slid down into the cockpits, released the brakes, and began to move back onto the track. Trading places and testing each other's cars became an obligatory ritual. Racing superstitions had a way of being elevated to religious rite, rites much like Sunday Mass attendance, and equally dangerous to ignore. Missing Mass placed that mortal sin blemish on your soul, dooming you to the everlasting fires of hell. For most race drivers, ignoring a racing superstition put your physical body in the same danger.

The rest of the day passed quickly, too quickly for the racers and their friends. The cars had been thoroughly tested and had proved to be ready for the season. The irony was that Al and Ethan would return them to their bays in the garage and tinker some more during the coming week, necessitating yet more testing the following weekend. As the cars were loaded on the trailers and the caravan departed for home, Ethan felt content and gave Fay and Ross little thought, blissfully unaware of the turmoil he would face when he arrived home.

Fay, desperately trying to keep herself under control, reached out for Ross's hand as they walked down Virginia Avenue toward Main Street. She had not held his hand as they walked for at least a year and Ross cast a quizzical glance in her direction but gently took it anyway. He knew that something had upset her before they left and he decided to go along with whatever she wanted.

"Are you sure you're all right, Mom?" he asked once again. Even to her young son, the barely perceptible sag in her shoulders was impossible not to notice. She just nodded and they proceeded to make the left turn onto Main Street. The brightly colored sign for Pop's Confectioneries stood out from the neat row of signs for the other shops along Main Street. Ross wondered briefly why she chose to take the long way to the park but the promise of a Pop's ice-cream soda overshadowed everything. He loved going to Pop's.

Nelson Hiller, whom everyone called Pop, had been the proprietor of the confectionery for so long that he was now an institution in town. The unique aspect of Pop's personality was his obvious love for people. He never seemed to care if his customers bought anything; he just enjoyed talking with them. His homemade candy and bakery business had boomed and he had expanded it into a soda shop, complete with four booths along the wall and a counter with eight stools. Children would beg their parents to let them turn in the empty soda bottles from home for the one-cent refund, hoping to save the ten pennies needed to buy one of Pop's innovations, a beat-up-a cross between an ice-cream soda and a milk shake. In the two years that Ross had lived in Collins Heights, he had become one of Pop's favorites. More often than not, he would take the Main Street route home from school just so he could wave to Pop, who was always in full sight as the children return from classes.

As they entered his shop, Pop called his usual cheery greeting.

"Hey, Ross, good to see you. Even brought your mom along. Are you treating her?"

Pop's banter could go on forever, stopping only when another customer came into the shop.

Fay paused, waiting to see where Ross wanted to sit. As he scrambled onto one of the stools at the counter, Fay quite accidentally made eye contact with Pop. There probably was no finer observer of human nature in the whole town of Collins Heights. His six feet four frame, topped by tousled white hair framing a lean, happy face etched with character lines, towered over Fay. He peered at her over the gold-framed glasses perched on the end of his nose and started to inquire about her health but his instincts made him look away. He knew that something was very wrong but it was the kind of wrong that even a best friend would hesitate to ask about. His attention quickly turned to Ross, loving the fact that children usually left their sadness at his door as they entered.

"What'll it be, boy, as if I have to ask?" Pop asked jovially.

"A chocolate beat-up, of course," Ross answered, smiling.

The counter was arranged so that Pop could reach practically every ingredient without losing touch with his customers. No matter the age of the patrons sitting at his counter, he could keep them mesmerized with his constant chatter and eye contact as he reached to his right and his left and mixed whatever they requested. With the only other group in the shop sitting in the far booth, sipping on a variety of shakes and sharing one of Pop's huge banana splits, he could devote his attention to Ross and Fay.

Ross, who always seemed to blossom in Pop's presence, lost his innate shyness and became rather talkative. He informed Pop about his father being away for the day, testing his race car, and rambled on about walking to the park. Fay sat in silence, barely reacting with a nod if the occasion called for it. Pop, with his homespun wisdom and perception, knew that she was physically here sitting on the stool but she certainly was somewhere else in that pretty little head of hers. He poured Ross's beat-up out of the mixer into a tall green glass and set it down in front of him. Beads of moisture had already formed on the outside of the glass and ran in fits and starts toward the counter. Pop reached into the five-gallon container of vanilla ice cream and scooped out a small portion, placed it carefully in a small bowl and slid it across the counter toward Fay. She smiled and said thanks, but Pop marveled that someone could smile with her mouth but frown with the rest of her face. He again made eye contact. At that moment, he thought she had the saddest eyes he had ever seen. They both looked away. The heavy wooden door opened, the chimes just above it ringing loudly, and Pop, relieved to have an excuse to move away, welcomed another group of youngsters, who headed for one of the booths.

After just five minutes, Ross sent loud slurping noises throughout the shop as he came to the bottom of his beat-up. Fay hushed him, placed fifty cents on the counter, and got up from the stool. Pop returned from taking the dishes from the back booth into the kitchen in time to call after Fay's back as she exited the shop.

"Thanks for coming, you two. Hope all gets better for you, Mrs. Becker." The door had just about closed when Fay caught it. She felt a need to respond but had no idea what to say.

"Could it be that obvious?" she wondered.

"Thanks, Pop. I'll be fine" was all she could manage before the door closed and left her standing outside.

In the brief time they spent in Pop's, Fay had lost her nerve. With no explanation to Ross, she once again took his hand, grabbed it actually, and pulled him back the way they had come.

"I've decided that we'll just go the short way to the park, Ross." She didn't know for certain what it was that sent her almost scurrying in the opposite direction of Rose McGowen's house. As they walked briskly down Main Street toward the intersection with Eighth Avenue, she realized that the "it," whatever the "it" happened to be, indeed must be obvious. Pop had known that something was wrong and he hardly knew her. What if by some chance Rose coincidentally was outside, working in her yard or her spectacular flower garden? Fay had no idea how she would react when she saw Rose. If a near stranger like Pop Hiller could see through the cool veneer to the controlled fury raging inside, surely Rose would see something as well. She could never be comfortable confronting Rose based on the information she had received in that perplexing twenty-second phone call. Probably spending the rest of the day sorting out the best course of action was a smart thing to do. Ethan would not be home until late in the afternoon, perhaps not even then if the boys decided to stop by the tavern for a few beers. The park would be a good place to think, and from previous experience she knew Ross would be content to spend the whole day there if she let him.

When they arrived at Hatcher Memorial Park, a recent name change from the simple Collins Heights Park, Fay went directly to the large swing set in the northeast corner of the grounds. Sitting on one of the swings, she could watch Ross as he sampled every piece of playground equipment throughout the five-acre park. It would also provide a small sense of isolation, as it was set off from the main routes around the park. She selected the last swing closest to the chain-link fence and sat down on the splintered wooden seat. The swing swayed ever so softly as she looked out over the early buds about to explode on the trees. In a week or so, the leaves would have burst forth, one day buds and the next full-blown leaves. She loved spring, with its positive energy, its promise of renewal, and its beauty. This, she decided, would be a good place to think clearly about the devastating news brought by the morning phone call.

She thought of Ethan's mother, who, in her strange, often weird way, usually made so much sense. Alma Becker had always refused to have a telephone in her house: They brought bad news more often than good, and she believed, she wanted her bad news delivered to her in person, or not at all. She equated the "disembodied voices," as she called them, with the voices she claimed she heard sometimes at night, passed-on loved ones speaking from beyond the grave. As hard as Ethan tried, he could not convince his mother that a phone was nothing more than a modern convenience.

"Old Alma never would know that her husband was being unfaithful if it meant getting the news by phone," Fay thought dejectedly.

Fay moved from her perch on the swing only occasionally to walk around a bit, then returned to let her mind go once again. She spent about three hours of reflection, bordering at times on spiritual meditation. The most troubling aspect of the whole process was the regular intrusion of thoughts of Al Stuart. In a series of complicated, mind-bending twists, she found herself feeling guilty about what, up to this time, was a platonic relationship with Al. She had a great deal more trouble convincing herself that it was entirely innocent. The intimacy of the episode in her kitchen two years earlier easily could be rationalized; she had been vulnerable at the time and her behavior was simply an anomaly. However, there was no denying that she planned it and lost her nerve only at the last minute. If indeed Ethan and Rose McGowen were involved in an affair, they had taken that one giant step beyond the bounds that Fay had established as acceptable limits for her relationship with Al. Her fantasy world continued to be centered on Al but that was where her involvement remained-in a fantasy. She always had difficulty with the concept of sinning through thought, word, or deed. The theology that stated that a sin in deed is the same as dwelling on a sinful thought did not make much sense to her. She could not fathom placing a physical act on the same plane as a thought that might have slipped through the subconscious barriers of the mind. On any number of occasions, she let herself drift into a reverie around her languorous, even erotic afternoon baths, her conscience convinced that she did nothing wrong.

By three o'clock, Ross began to tire of the swinging and sliding and spinning and climbing. At about the same time, Fay reached some firm conclusions about how she would handle this potentially explosive situation. When her young son came running over, she was ready to take the walk home, far more confident and at ease than she felt just a scant few hours before.

An unquenchable thirst held the boys at its mercy. The full day of racing, coupled with the work involved in keeping everything running, and the dust and heat of the powerful engines were enough to produce dreams of the ice cold beer awaiting them in Mel's Tavern, just minutes from the pit. Without saying a word to each other, a knowing glance followed by even more knowing smiles traveled around the group after the cars were loaded onto the trailers. The men quickly piled into their vehicles, and the caravan, trailed by dust and exhaust fumes, left the pit for the renaissance of the tavern. After the few short blocks, they trooped into the tavern in single file, Al Stuart bringing up the rear.

Inside, Mel's atmosphere consisted mostly of poorly lit booths and a long bar with a unique kind of barstool, one with a tall back wrapping around into arms. The traditional joke among the regulars was that Mel had to buy this type of stool because he never refused anyone a drink, no matter what state of inebriation the customer had managed to attain. The high backs and the arms were a necessity to keep the patrons from falling off the stools and getting hurt. Mel's had other strengths in its favor, though. No women except for the well-worn waitresses dared enter, so the language never needed to be toned down. Many of the men considered it a haven from their wives. Mel and his well-trained bartenders were masters of the art of mental reservation, never quite lying to the inquiring wives' phone calls but not being entirely forthcoming either.

"No ma'am, I don't see 'im" constituted the most common answer, always uttered as the bartender faced the blank wall behind the ornately carved bar.

Ethan, Al, and their cohorts found an empty booth toward the back of the tavern. Eve, one of the waitstaff, came over and solicited the drink order. Ethan ordered draft beer for everyone, on him, in celebration of the performance of the cars that day. Using much the same technique as a western movie hero would down a shot of whiskey, each of the group chugged the first draft in seconds. Eve, watching from behind the bar and knowing that the size of her tip depended on her overly attentive service as well as the depth of cut in the front of her dress, hustled over with another round, ready to serve it as the men set down their first glasses. The unquenchable thirst was brought under control with the first draft and the second could be savored a bit more. Al Stuart was the only one who once again guzzled the beer without taking a breath. When his beer disappeared, he stood, obviously preparing to leave.

"What the hell are you doing, Al," Ethan barked. These sessions generally went on for several hours and Al had never bailed out before. "We've got some more drinking to do!"

"Not for me today, fellas. I'm going to head home. Tough day tomorrow, you know?"

The positive strength of the relationship among the men led to a gentle chiding from his friends but they all knew that Al must have a good reason for leaving after just two beers.

"Hey, Al, tell Fay I'll be along as soon as I can. Give her one of your patented excuses for me, will ya?" Ethan bellowed, knowing unequivocally that Al would not lie for him but not really caring what he told Fay.

"Yeah, sure, Ethan. See you some night this week, OK?" Al threw a dollar bill on the table for his second beer and his part of a generous tip for Eve's low-cut dress. He turned and left quickly, the bright sun still high enough in the sky to hurt his eyes as he opened the solid mahogany door and left the dark tavern.

* * *

When Fay heard the truck slowing out front, her heart flipped in her chest. Ross, lying on the floor listening to the radio, jumped up and ran to the bay window. Having made the decision to take a direct approach with Ethan, she could not wait to get it over with. The day had been so warm that she would have been surprised had they not stopped at Mel's and she didn't expect them back for hours. Caught off guard, she frantically searched her mind for the perfectly worded opening she had prepared for Ethan when he came through the door. She had rehearsed her little speech over and over and now, with just a little effort, it was scrolling past her eyes.

"It's Al, Mommie," she heard Ross say. Her heart flipped once more, this time with relief. "There's nobody else here." Ross left the front window and ran through the house to the back kitchen door.

"I'm going down, OK?" He opened the door and stood on the landing just outside.

"Of course, dear. Ask Al to come up for minute after he gets his car unloaded."

Ross negotiated the fire escape down the rear of the house and stood waiting as Al guided the trailer smoothly back the driveway toward the garage. He stopped, leaving enough room to back the car off the trailer and maneuver it into the bay to the far left of the garage. Ross watched, fascinated as always, as Al went from one wheel of the car to the next, disconnecting the chains holding the car on the trailer. A noisy and grimy process, Al did not count it among his favorite parts of racing. After the connections were released, he slid the ramps from their holders on the trailer and locked one end on the trailer and let the other end come to the ground. He pulled the external battery to the back of the truck and connected the cables to its terminals, then to the temporary battery in the race car. He looked over at Ross and motioned to him to climb onto the trailer. With youthful exuberance, Ross scrambled onto the trailer. Al reached across and swung him up into the cockpit of the car. He reached inside the cockpit and pushed the small starter button. The engine sputtered to life and Al hollered for Ross to give it a little gas. Al disconnected the battery cables from the car as Ross pushed tentatively on the gas pedal. The engine revved slightly and Ross smiled broadly at Al's thumbs-up sign. Al stepped across the trailer and climbed into the cockpit with Ross. He depressed the clutch pedal, pulling the gear shift lever toward him and down into first gear. He slowly increased the RPMs and let out the clutch slowly. The car crept forward until it reached the ramps, then Al let it go, purely for Ross's sake. The dirt-encased car rolled down the ramps and came to a bumpy stop a few feet from the end of the ramps.

"WOW!" was all Ross could say. Al had no idea how special an event this was. Ross's memory of his first time in a moving race car would be forever linked to Al Stuart.

"Mom wants to see you when you get finished, Al. Thanks a lot!" Ross clambered out of the cockpit and stood close to the car, just listening to the throb of the engine as it gradually lost its intensity. Al throttled down and guided the powerful car into its bay. The usual explosive backfire was the exclamation point as the engine shut down.

Fay watched the entire scene from the kitchen window, smiling at Al's patience with her son. Even from the considerable distance, she sensed the unmistakable admiration that Ross had for Al Stuart and regretted being unable to put her own gratitude for his friendship into words. She wondered how she would react when Al stopped by after "tucking his car in for the night," as he so often put it. Her palpable vulnerability had to be showing as clearly as it had on their fabled Roosevelt walk.

"And I thought things weren't working out then!" The irony made her chortle pathetically. Already she regretted having Ross ask Al to stop by. As she watched her son and his hero each grasp a garage door handle to close the two heavy, barnlike doors, the sensation of an impending daytime nightmare enveloped her. More convinced than ever that her desperate emotional state would pull her under if she talked with Al about anything but the weather, Fay drew back from the window just as Ross and Al came out of the side door of the garage and started toward the house. She felt an indefinable dread settling over her as the thumping footsteps on the wobbly fire escape moved closer, shaking the small, gilt-framed Johnson family photograph hanging in the hall. She successfully willed herself into what she unquestionably knew had to be a strong and positive temperament as she visualized again the upcoming scene with Ethan. She had not prepared herself for managing the always difficult level of feeling that boiled to the surface whenever she found herself in Al Stuart's presence.

Fay heard her son laugh as Al reminded him about his mother's absolute "wipe-your-feet" rule and she knew they were at the rear door of the kitchen. As they simultaneously knocked their feet against the door jamb, then followed quickly with the obligatory rubbing the shoes across the bristles of the welcome mat, Fay silently edged down the hallway, becoming almost one with the wall, and slipped into her bedroom, gently closing the door behind her. She just needed a few more seconds to think, to gather herself, to put on the old happy but phony face she had mastered.

"Hey, Mom!" Ross called out. "Al's here and guess what! He let me ride in the cockpit of his car!"

Even with a closed door between them, Ross's excitement penetrated into her room. Reaching for the tarnished brass door knob, Fay knew that her deep brown eyes had their most radiant sparkle, a genuine glow that always appeared when she saw Al. As she tried to force a smile to match her eyes, a sense of hopelessness and despair washed over her and she knew it would never work. The naturally happy gleam in the eyes when greeting a person deeply cared for cannot be hidden, any more than a faked smile, no matter how wide, can force the lines of sadness from a face. Finally, with a resoluteness that took her by surprise, she turned the knob and opened the door.

Ross opened the icebox and stood there, peering into the lower compartment, rummaging for the unopened quart of milk with the cream still on the top. Al, standing behind him, assumed the slightly awkward posture he generally seemed to have in Fay's presence, his shyness showing clearly but in a way that Fay found especially endearing.

"So, how'd the practice go, Al?" Fay asked the question more as a courtesy than to gather any information. In the more secret parts of her mind, she could freely admit that racing held little interest or excitement for her. In the truly secret niche, the part of her mind reserved for her and her alone, she could admit to one good thing about Ethan's obsessive hobby. It did keep him fully occupied, therefore keeping him out of the house and away from her for frequent, extended blocks of time, time that she guiltily treasured for its peacefulness.

"Oh, everything went well, Fay; thanks for asking. Ethan said he'd be along soon. The boys just needed to wash down some of that dust, you know?" Even when engaged in the simplest of conversations with Fay, Al appeared to be on the verge of blushing. He consciously made sure that he stayed out of what he referred to in his man-to-man talks with himself as the three-foot circle, the space he needed to have between Fay and himself.

As a youngster, Al had been given two small horseshoe magnets for Christmas. The polarity of the magnets fascinated him and he would spend hours pushing them toward one another until the attraction began and they would clamp themselves together. He then would reverse them and watch the repellent action. Whenever he thought of Fay, especially after the "robe incident" of two years before, he developed an analogy between his three-foot circle and the magnets. The blinding attraction he felt if he drifted into the three-foot circle could easily be referred to as magnetic. "Must be my magnetic personality," he would say to himself, knowing that, from his perspective, that certainly could not be true. There was no doubt that by whatever name-electricity, chemistry, magnetism-something drew him to Fay. As clearly as he knew that, he knew just as clearly that nothing could or should be done about it. How much easier if the repellent force of magnetism would operate in the three-foot circle.

Ross found the bottle he was searching for and poured a tall glass of milk, never shaking the cream from the top. The milk took on the color and thickness of a vanilla milkshake from Pop's and Al and Fay just smiled at each other. Ross made his way down the hallway to the living room, balancing the full glass as carefully as any eight-year-old could. The late-afternoon sun pushed its way through the heavy gold burlap curtains on the front bay window and Ross settled in by the RCA console radio to listen to the Sunday-afternoon episode of the "Lone Ranger." As the Ranger and his faithful companion Tonto began their adventure, Fay sat down at the kitchen table, inviting Al to do the same. Al slid one of the metal frame chairs out from under the table and sat at the far end.

For reasons she could not begin to understand, and despite the sturdy promises made to herself in the bedroom, Fay looked across at Al and felt her eyes fill. Not a word was spoken, but Al knew something serious had happened while they were at the test track. He knew also, whatever the consequences, that he was going to hear all about whatever was causing Fay to crumble before his eyes.

"Oh, Al." The simple phrase caught in her throat. A visible depression settled over Fay as her words assumed a life of their own. In just a matter of minutes, the events of this beautiful Sunday morning were retold, Fay managing to hold her rampaging emotions in check during the whole story. Al sat at the far end of the table, spellbound but rapidly being drawn into the whirlpool of sympathy the story deserved. By the end, Fay's strong voice finally developed a quiver and dropped to a whisper.

"It was Rose, Al. How could she do it to me?" She reached into the pocket of her blouse, drew out a lacy white handkerchief, and began to cry very softly.

Al once again found himself in the position of knowing that he should do something to comfort his friend across the table but somehow he felt a stronger fear of infiltrating that three-foot circle. He glanced down the hallway toward the living room, hoping that Ross had not heard any of the conversation. The only evidence that Ross was anywhere in the house was the deep voice of the masked man filling the room, and, no doubt, Ross's imagination as well. As he looked over at Fay, an inevitability of the circumstances came over him. The feelings rising in him from the pit of his stomach were powerful enough to make him shake. The circle could have been as wide as the room and it would not have mattered. When Fay lifted her reddened eyes from the handkerchief and they locked onto his, he slowly pushed back his chair, never looking away from her. In two steps he stood next to her. He reached down and took her hand. The "William Tell Overture" wafted in from the living room, and in an ironic bit of timing, signaled some crucial moment in the life of the Lone Ranger. Fay remained rooted in her chair as Al squeezed her hand with his and gently lay his other hand on her shoulder. He felt her shudder but knew that it was not meant for him to move away. His left hand lay locked on her shoulder, two fingers resting on the bare skin exposed by her sleeveless blouse. The overture from the next room was winding down, leading into an advertisement for the Breakfast of Champions and Al knew that Ross would probably be up and running to the kitchen at any second. He removed his hand from Fay's shoulder, but continued to gaze into her upturned eyes. He squeezed her hand rather forcefully and, realizing that he had not uttered a single word, said, "It'll be all right, Fay, I promise." He thought once again of the magnets, hopelessly and irreversibly tumbling toward each other, finally clamping together in a death grip.

In the years since Al realized that Ethan sometimes physically and verbally abused Fay, he had been extremely careful about becoming involved in what he knew should not be his business. He had every reason to believe that Ethan and Fay argued on a frightfully regular basis but his self-made promise to help Fay if he ever had the chance had never come to fruition. On those occasions when he faced the truth, he readily admitted that he could fall in love with Fay.

Since he had known her, he had no real interest in any other women. As a reasonably attractive young man, he certainly had his share of brief romances, most of them transitioning rapidly from acquaintance to physical intimacy to dissolution. He had even double-dated with Fay and Ethan on occasion, but found it difficult to direct his attention to his date when in Fay's presence. His friends, including Ethan, or especially Ethan, kidded him about his lack of girlfriends. The good-natured mocking always assumed that Al's "girl problem" was the result of his relentless, overriding shyness. None of them would have imagined his private adulation of Fay Becker. And Al would have been mortified if the depth of his feelings for Fay became general knowledge. Until this Sunday afternoon in April, he kept himself content by being a solid, good friend, always staying clear of those troublesome Catholic occasions of sin. Fay's strange behavior the day of what Al had cataloged in his mind as the "robe incident" made him realize that perhaps there were some feelings on Fay's side as well but, through a concerted effort on both their parts, though they never spoke about it. The question now became quite a bit more complicated.

Al was not the least bit surprised by what Fay had told him about his best friend. His curiosity led him to wonder why Fay seemed more upset with Rose than with her own husband. It was as if she might have expected Ethan to be involved and would have been prepared to accept that. The betrayal by a good friend was another matter entirely. As expected, Ross came bounding down the hall and into the kitchen. In the background, the radio blared the virtues of Wheaties, leading into an announcement that all those Lone Ranger fans out there should watch for the special package of their favorite cereal for the Ranger ring with its secret decoder inside. Al and Fay, although physically in close proximity to each other, gave no indication that anything at all had happened. With Al Stuart in the room, Fay kept from making eye contact with Ross, as his eyes, slightly above his hero's belt-buckle level, were always looking up. She stuffed the dampened handkerchief into the pocket of her slacks and Ross could have no idea of the content of the conversation between Al and his mother.

"Thanks for the visit, Fay, and you too, Ross. I think I'd better get along and see what I can accomplish at home." Al looked down at the young boy and promised that the next time, he would give him a longer ride in the car. From the other room, Tonto and Kemo Sabe came riding back in time with the "William Tell Overture" and Ross once again left the two, now very good friends, alone in the kitchen as he galloped back to the radio.

"Somehow, I don't want to be here when Ethan gets home, Fay. Just remember what I said. It's going to be all right. I'll see to it." Al started for the door and Fay followed him. When he stopped and turned to say goodbye, she nearly bumped into him. As they stood just inches apart, the tension became unbearable. Fay defused the heady, exciting, but frightening moment by putting a hand on each of Al's shoulders, leaning forward on tiptoe and giving him a light, chaste kiss on the lips. She took great care that the only part of her body contact his was her lips.

"Thanks, Al. I know you'll help all you can. I really do appreciate you. You're a special person." Even as Fay finished the sentence, Al had his hand on the screen door, pushing it open. He took one more step to the landing and let the door close behind him. Fay's eyes had their usual, moving sparkle that even the screen between them couldn't hide. It became the type of wordless goodbye that in truth accomplishes more than any long speech ever could. Al quickly descended the shaky steps, and began seriously to consider what he could possibly do to help Fay and her young son.

After Al Stuart left the apartment, Fay immediately went into her bedroom and checked herself in the mirror. She did not want Ross to grasp the gravity of the day by seeing the bleakness of her eyes. He appeared to be perfectly content to continue lying on the floor by the radio, listening to his programs. Even the nuns and her parish priests agreed that listening to radio programs provided an imagination stimulus for young children. She recalled a few weeks before when she asked Ross what the Lone Ranger looked like and he came up with an incredibly vivid picture from his mind. It was not at all what she had pictured, but, of course, that didn't matter.

Her plan for the meeting with Ethan began with asking Ross to walk down to the local A & P, less than a block away, for a tin of coffee. The Eight O'Clock coffee would have to be ground and the whole errand would probably take at least thirty minutes, especially if she added a side trip to Pop's for some penny candy as a reward. Ross would not believe his good fortune, visiting with Pop twice in the same day. Fay felt fairly certain that Pop would strike up a conversation with Ross, taking a few more minutes at least. Even the most volatile of their married arguments lasted a minimal amount of time and she had the uneasy feeling that this one would be very brief. By the time Ross returned home, the house would be quiet once more.

Fay hated the arguments, for no other reason than they were so upsetting to Ross. Over the years, she had become more and more stubborn, refusing to be bullied and silenced by Ethan's bellowing. Her scornful taunting, which she had in fact perfected, had in their recent bouts brought on the frightening physical threats.

Most of the time, Ethan would control himself and the threats remained just that. She actually took some delight in managing to push him to the violent stage. To Fay, having him apologize the day after he blackened an eye or bruised a cheek allowed her to chalk up a win in the argument column, regardless of the sincerity of the apology. Most of the disagreements centered on some inconsequential detail, forgotten practically as soon as the shouting started. This one, at least, would have some validity to it. An unfaithful husband and a conniving best friend. "I guess it doesn't get much more valid that that," she had thought as she laid out her plan.

Finally, as Fay sat in the overstuffed chair by the bay window, a gorgeous spring sunset beginning to arrange itself to the west, she heard the cars slow down out front and turn into the driveway. She called to Ross, who had retired to his room to read the latest Captain Marvel comic. A trifle recalcitrant about being sent on a errand just as his father came home, he reluctantly agreed to make the trip, the carrot of a dime to spend at Pop's removing the steam from any argument he might have had. He slipped into his light spring jacket and was out the door in no time, taking the stairs two at a time, as usual. Fay estimated that he would be gone for at least forty-five minutes, depending on how philosophical Pop felt on this particular Sunday afternoon. As the door closed behind Ross, she had an insane thought to run after him, and for the two of them to keep right on going, to where she had no idea. The thought, one of those random, ridiculous musings everyone gets now and then, vanished as quickly as it came. With her stomach threatening to turn itself inside out, she moved her favorite chair slightly toward the front window, settled back, and watched as the clouds lined up for their chance to glow in the sinking sun.

Ethan Becker, perhaps sensing that something waited for him inside the house, brushed aside his normal fanaticism for detail and put off unloading the race car until after supper. He assured his friends that he could handle it himself and sent them home to their wives and girlfriends to try once again to explain the attraction of becoming encased in a combination of dirt, grime, oil, and dust while watching a car go in circles for hours on end.

He watched as the cars left the driveway then he proceeded toward the back fire escape entrance to his apartment, wondering why Ross hadn't performed his usual clambering down to greet the returning race warrior, as he liked to think of himself.

No sooner had he opened the door than he heard Fay call out. Something in her voice carried a cold draft with it as it drifted down the hall toward the kitchen.

"Would you come into the living room, please?" A simple enough question—so why did he have a sense of impending disaster?

The same day that Fay Becker was living in a state of gut-wrenching mental anguish, several miles to the south, in Lyndeboro, Jennie Proctor and her father spent the beautiful spring Sunday beginning to work on the flower beds around the house. Jennie, although only eight years old, worked like a trouper alongside Bob and loved the results of their labors. To her father, she was a wonder, but to Jennie the world was a wonder. She thrived on examining every little insect and worm, picking them up and gently holding them in her small hand. Bob would glance over at her and be amazed at the rapt expression on her face as she seemed to communicate with the tiniest of creatures, setting them back down in the dirt with a startlingly delicate softness. Late in the afternoon, as the brilliant sun and the fluffy spring clouds began to put on a spectacular show, Bob and Jennie gathered their gardening tools and returned them in the garage. Bob loved the weekends for the purely selfish reason of spending uninterrupted time with his precious daughter.

Over the last eight years, especially the past three after their move to Lyndeboro, he realized that not all fathers cherished the time with their children as he did. Jennie had to be his first priority without any question and he became distressed when some of the men at his plant wanted to work overtime at the expense of spending time with their families, compounding this offense with the daily tavern stops after work. He remained mystified why people would not want to be with those they loved. Long ago, he reached the conclusion that Jennie possessed unique qualities deserving of his complete attention and used the conclusion to explain why he was different from the other fathers of his acquaintance. In his heart he knew that he could not claim credit for being a good father; Jennie's matchless singularity, even peculiarity, gave him no choice but to be an attentive, flirting with obsessive, father.

Jennie and Bob closed the garage door and, hand in hand, began to walk around the house. With a regular ferocity, at times like this, memories of Jeanne aggressively pushed their way through Bob's subconscious. The well-manicured house, now with most of the gardens ready for planting, served as a constant reminder of their first house, all primed for their first child to come. To keep from weeping, Bob had simply to look over at Jennie and the despair would vanish as quickly as it came, like a puff of steam dissipating in the air above a boiling tea kettle.

"Daddy, may we watch the sun set from the swing, please, before we get supper?" Bob just smiled, as if he had any choice. "How many eight-year-olds want to watch a sunset with their fathers?" he wondered, once again realizing why he loved to spend time with his daughter.

After the two of them made a complete circle of the house, admiring their afternoon's work, they climbed the front steps and sat on the swinging divan, facing the west and the rapidly changing, color-laden sky. They sat in an awed silence at the display before them for a few minutes before Jennie broke the quiet.

"Do I frighten you, Daddy?" The simplicity and innocence with which Jennie phrased the question caused Bob to turn toward her. He placed the index finger of his right hand under her chin and pushed her face upward. Looking directly into Jennie's eyes was always a disquieting experience, ever since she was a baby. Her deep-set sparkly eyes could take on a troubling, brooding grayness that her father knew showed a wisdom far beyond her years. There was a direct correlation between the profundity of her question she asked and the degree of darkness in her eyes.

"What a silly question, Jen!" He always called her Jen when their conversations turned serious, and he knew that she did not ask silly questions. "Why would you think something like that?"

Her answer startled him into silence as he frantically searched his mind for a good, fatherly kind of gentle, soothing advice but he could find none.

"Because I frighten myself, Daddy. I don't like knowing so

much and I don't know if I always do the right thing." Bob cuddled her up against him and her tears dampened the shoulder of his light spring jacket.

Just as Jennifer Proctor leaned against her father for strength and support, Ethan Becker was reaching into the icebox for a cold beer to arm himself against whatever might happen when he went came face to face with Fay.

"What in the hell could be going on," he thought as he reached around the gradually melting block of ice to grab the last bottle of Schlitz from the top section of the icebox. He opened the drawer filled with miscellaneous kitchen utensils and rooted around until he found the bottle opener. After flipping off the cap, he chugged several hard swallows, then proceeded slowly to the living room. Trying to be casual, he leaned against the doorjamb with his right shoulder, holding the beer in his left hand. Fay looked across the room, infuriated by his cavalier, mocking attitude. The way his left arm extended toward her, with the foaming bottle of beer ever so slightly overflowing, she could only think of the paradoxical toast "Here's mud in your eye," whatever that meant.

"So, what's up, Doc!" Ethan began, trying desperately to disarm the apparent gravity of the situation with his poor imitation of Bugs Bunny, hoping Fay might smile. He received no reaction in return, other than what could be interpreted as utter disdain. The sunset had exploded into its full glory behind Fay, filling the living room with light and color. As she rose to face Ethan, she blocked the sun, creating a halo effect around her entire body. With the sun at her back, the brightness highlighted her hair but had the effect of blinding Ethan to the expression on her face. In a monotone, Fay began her well-rehearsed speech. Ethan never moved from the position he had assumed upon entering the room, still leaning and still holding his beer. Once Fay started to speak, he might as well have been cast in stone, the beer never coming to his lips and his shoulder seeming to be attached to the doorjamb.

"I had a phone call this morning, Ethan," Fay said, in such a calm voice that she surprised herself. The practice had helped. She spoke so quickly that the sentences seemed to Ethan to run together. He could not have interrupted, even had he wanted to.

The phone call had lasted only twenty seconds but Fay's version occupied the better part of five minutes. She was absolutely focused on having all actions and reactions to this conversation well over with before Ross arrived home, bringing his innocence with him.

Since the terrible phone call that morning, Fay had arranged a chronology of events and, in her mind, enough indisputable evidence to prove the call was not a prank. In her determination to have the upper hand in this dispute, Fay had not truly faced her desperate hope that Ethan had a plausible, logical, and truthful explanation for the phone call.

To her husband, Fay appeared to be a disembodied spirit and the words tumbling out could as easily have been coming from the radio in the corner. The same sunlight that kept Ethan from fully seeing Fay's face illuminated his. As her story continued, only his eyes changed at all. When she mentioned a phone call, they showed a degree of curiosity. When she mentioned Rose McGowen, they showed a degree of panic. When she mentioned the day of the Manley strike and his late arrival at the office, they shifted quickly from panic to acceptance at being caught. When she brought up the regular visitations during John McGowen's absences, she recognized immediately his glaring and frightening defiance.

"So what!" might as well have been written across his forehead. When she finished, the crushing awareness that all she said was true washed over her like a vicious, blindsiding wave at the shore.

"What happens now?" Ethan asked, finally pushing off of the doorframe and actually entering the room.

"I think we need to go and talk to Father Gallagher at St. Luke's. I've heard that he is good at helping people in trouble." Fay said this with hopefulness in her voice that belied the hopelessness in her heart.

"We are not people in trouble, Fay. We are person in trouble. You go to church regularly. You know that if you divorce, you're supposed to be on an express train to hell. Things are really starting to go well for us now. Manley is grooming me for a big job and with that Democrat Truman being voted out this November, the country is headed for good times. Rose and I are meaningless. It's just stuff that happens, that's all. I'd just like to get hold of the guy who made that call-it had to be someone wanting to get even. Anyway, you'll have it real good soon and Mr. Manley wants everything to look good, at least on the surface. If you want to talk to that priest, who can't know anything about marriage or sex for that matter, go right ahead. You can tell me all about it!" Ethan ended his mild tirade with one of his most obnoxious sneers and Fay knew that the discussion was over. Everything he said obviously made perfect sense to him. What he did not understand was that she won this argument. She knew she was right; he proved it by not threatening her with physical abuse of any sort. She saw their marriage quickly deteriorating to the live-and-let live category, as if it had not been for a long time.

The room grew darker, as if paralleling what had just happened between the two people standing in it. The sun finished providing its inspiration for the day and Fay's thoughts turned to greeting Ross when he returned home from the frivolous errand. She pulled the chain on the small hand-me-down table lamp by her chair and brushed by Ethan on her way to the kitchen to start dinner. The magnets were at work again, this time repelling her well beyond the three-foot circle surrounding Ethan Becker more powerfully than she had drawn Al into hers.

As June approached, Ethan Becker's regret at allowing Fay's family to move into the downstairs apartment increased in geometric proportions by the hour. Moving day, June 1, 1948, was greeted with what could only be called thundering apathy by Ethan Becker. During the previous week, he had drawn up all the papers, including leases, insurance, and any other protection he could manage. Since the first happened to be a Saturday, he rearranged his schedule to make sure that he had to work that day. Fay had never seemed happier. After the Sunday in April when Ethan's affair with Rose McGowen was exposed, his relationship with Fay could best be described as icy. To her credit, although some would say stupidity, she remained true to her upbringing and regularly met the conjugal responsibilities of a good Catholic wife. She did not speak with any of the priests in the parish, deciding instead to satisfy her need to talk by connecting with Al Stuart any chance she had. Now, she would have her family close by once again, providing a covey of confidants if necessary.

Moving day proceeded quite smoothly and by the time Ethan arrived home from work, Johnsons seemed to be everywhere. Only five of the children remained at home but that created a severe imbalance of power in the apartment house, at least to Ethan's way of thinking. Fay and Ross could not have been happier. Susan Johnson had in the last few years developed a matronly physical appearance that matched her matriarchal stability and dependability. Her strength of character was sufficient for the entire family to lean on and Ross looked forward to spending more time downstairs with his aunts and uncles rather than upstairs in the tension-ridden household of the Beckers.

Fay had not seen nor heard from Rose McGowen since the infamous Sunday-morning phone call back in April. She attributed the absence of contact to one of two things: Either Ethan had filled her in on what had happened, thereby confirming her suspicions that he still was seeing her or Rose herself had also received a phone call of some sort.

Now that her family surrounded her, she found herself feeling safer than she had in years. As Fay felt more protected, Ethan experienced a strong sense of déjà vu that once again a family conspiracy was forming against him. Every time he had any contact with the Johnsons, he believed they acted as if they knew some terrible secret of his. His simple solution to the increasing bouts of paranoia was to stay away more than ever. Work and racing became his cover for rarely being home.

His being forced to keep up the appearance of a happy marriage for his employer compounded the resentment of being trapped into joining Fay's family because of her pregnancy years before. As the summer months went by, Ethan became increasingly morose, dreading the onset of the cold weather when racing was finished and refuge provided by the garage would be virtually gone. Of course, the only tangible aspects of his deep frustration, unfounded anger and stomach churning tension slept next to him every night.

With the successful racing season winding down, Fay started to worry about how Ethan would deal with his obviously bottled-up emotions. Having her family downstairs provided some measure of safety but she still lived in fear of Ethan's violent temper. On a chilly late-October night, the first night of the fall when it was too cold to work out in the garage, she understood just how tenuous and dangerous her existence was.

The rare occasion of a dinner at home with Fay and Ross turned into chaos, a scene that would be repeated with frightening regularity over the next two years. When Ethan called from work at around four o'clock to say that he would be home for dinner, Fay and Ross quickly walked to McGruder's Meat Market in the center of town and had Mr. McGruder cut a prime sirloin steak. Fay worried about the expense but hoped Ethan would be pleased with a special dinner. For months, Fay had fought with the ambivalence of trying to keep her husband happy and satisfied while ignoring the deep and abiding hatred for what he had done to her. She continually struggled with the accepted cultural concept that a straying husband must be the result of an inattentive wife. The steak could easily become the symbol for that ambivalence. While she tried desperately to please him, he could always find a way to be unhappy with her. Yet she continued to try simply because that was what women did.

Hurrying home with the prize cut of sirloin, both wife and son clung to a futile hope that perhaps this would be the night when everything would be made right. The human spirit does appear to be at times indomitable, continuing to hope even when by every rational measure all hope should be lost. Fay and Ross were pinning their hopes on a piece of meat and both knew, with unspoken sadness, that they were not sure what those hopes really were.

The veranda provided a perfect place for the Johnsons to gather after their own family dinner. This early-fall evening was alive with the crispness of the air seeming to turn the gently falling leaves brittle before they hit the ground. Fay and Ross walked the shortcut through the yard and came up the side steps on the porch. Ross settled right in with his aunts and uncles, surrogate brothers and sisters really, pushing himself up onto the rounded railing of the porch and leaning against one of the columns supporting the overhanging roof. His eyes asked if it would be all right to stay out on the porch until his father arrived home. His mother gave a hurried explanation of why she couldn't stay and visit but a simple nod indicated to Ross that he did not have to come up just yet.

Fay opened the door at the bottom of the stairs and slowly climbed toward her apartment. She was thankful for her family but also knew that they were probably discussing her marriage situation as soon as she closed the door behind her. Now that they lived in the same house, Fay's anxiety was impossible to hide. Even in the two minutes she just spent telling them how excited she was that Ethan would be home for dinner, not one of them would have taken a bet that she believed what she herself was saying.

In front of Ross, Susan Johnson and her children were careful not to let their feelings toward Ethan Becker enter into the discussion. However, even his youth could not ignore the tightness that would come into his grandmother's voice whenever his father's name was mentioned. Now, as he waited eagerly for his father to come home to the wonderful dinner, he looked around at the usually mischievous bunch sitting on the porch and disappointingly caught the not-too-subtle animosity toward his father. Had he been able to put the situation into words, it would have seemed as if they knew something about Ethan that he obviously did not.

"I guess I'll go help Mom get the dinner ready," Ross said as he slid off his perch on the railing. He loved the lighthearted joking that was usually an integral part of any Johnson family gathering. Now, more with each passing day, he realized that the Johnsons' collective sense of humor disappeared in the presence of his father or any discussion concerning his father. He had just crossed the porch to the door when Ethan's car slowed out front and made the turn into the driveway. Ross raced up the stairs to tell his mother to get ready.

"Daddy's home," he called twice before he reached the door off the second landing leading to the apartment.

When Fay heard the car turn into the drive, the sound turned her knees to water. The physical reaction told her, as if she did not already know, that she had been placing too much importance on this dinner. Ross opened the door, full of wonderful and boundless vitality. This evening, the vitality was intertwined with a devastating innocence, the constant innocence of youth that shouts that everything will be all right, that problems are either going to be solved or they are going to disappear.

"Is everything ready, Mom? This is going to be great!" Fay looked across the kitchen at Ross and tried desperately to absorb just a small portion of his optimism. The effort practically broke her heart.

"We'll let your father relax with the paper while I finish things up, OK, Ross?" A battle against an overwhelming temptation to hide the steak and just to heat up some canned Dinty Moore stew had to be fought and won. Fay's mind raced through a perfect catalog of incidents when she tried to win Ethan's approval over their years together. Not a single time did he react the way she thought he would. She went to the rear kitchen window and watched as he got out of his car, trying without success to read his mood from his body language as he strode toward the house.

Ross could hear her mumbling as he went past the kitchen door and into his room. He felt the familiar sense of dread rising through his stomach and stopping in his throat.

"He'll really like this dinner, I know it!" he said aloud, but not convincingly. He too had been present at many of the incidents parading through Fay's mind at practically the same time. Over the years, the old cliché about walking on eggshells had become a science in the Becker household. Ross knew that he and his mother were about to practice the delicate steps once again, at least until Ethan indicated his state of mind.

The plodding footfalls on the step finally reached the door and Fay approached her husband with a genuine enthusiasm, born primarily out of her need for Ross to have a decent family unit. She reached around Ethan and pulled him to her, a strong hug that included a slight but definite pelvic pressure against him. She backed slightly so she could search his eyes, perhaps to find some clues about what sort of night it might be. No clues were to be had. Ross came out of his room and stood somewhat tentatively in the background.

"Hi, Dad," he said in a soft voice. Sometime in his eighth year, he started to call Ethan "Dad," shortening the child's term of endearment from its original "Daddie." The subtle change had gone unnoticed to everyone except his mother. As he grew older,

Ross felt more respect and awe for his father, not realizing that the unconditional love of a child for a parent diminishes as a degree of fear creeps into the relationship. Without ever knowing it, the young boy's feelings for his father had evolved from absolute devotion to a mixture of fear, admiration, and veneration. His mother saw it happening and only she really knew why the delicate change from Daddy to Dad had occurred.

"Hey, boy, how're you doing?" Ethan asked the superfluous question as he gently but definitively nudged Fay away and started toward the living room.

"The paper in here?" he asked, calling back over his shoulder. Ethan continued without waiting for an answer and found his way to his favorite recliner in the corner of the room, picking the paper off the couch as he passed by.

Fay and Ross, left standing in the hallway, began their dance around the eggs once more. Ross ventured into the living room and took a seat diagonally across from his father, who had vanished behind the fully extended newspaper.

On the rare occasions when this type of scene played in the Becker house, Ross seemed content just to be in the same room with his father, even if no conversation took place. As he sat there, he could be assured that he would be privy to Ethan's running commentary on the news of the day, even though he did not understand most of it.

"Goddamn Truman!" Ethan muttered. "How in the name of living hell he thinks he has a chance is beyond me. Tom Dewey will get us back on track for sure."

Ross sat listening to the headless voice drifting over and around the edges of the newspaper. The traditional sounds of a wife at work clattered down the hall from the kitchen.Ross thought of interrupting his father's newspaper reading to tell him of the surprise they were to have for dinner that evening, but he thought better of it. He did not even dare to turn on the radio and so sat waiting for his mother to call them to dinner.

When the call finally came, Ross jumped off the couch and ran to the kitchen. After much rustling of paper in the living room, Ethan made his way to the kitchen.

Ross thought his mother never looked more beautiful. She

had changed out of her dull blue housedress and into an outfit she usually reserved for Parent-Teacher meetings. The pleated red skirt and bulky sweater accentuated her figure and the flesh-colored nylons displayed her shapely legs. He was happy that Fay had removed her apron to serve dinner and he could not help but notice his father staring at her as he pulled his chair out to sit down at the gracefully set table, a picture of charming simplicity.

Ross became more convinced than ever that this would be a good night. Like their parents, children expend much of their energy on trying to make the ebb and flow of life around them more comfortable, and Ross wanted very badly for this night to bring some stability to his home. He was certain that his father and mother loved each other and why they fought so often remained a mystifying enigma to him.

"So, what's the special occasion, Fay?" Ethan raised the question in a surprisingly gentle voice, a tone that both his son and wife were not used to hearing. Ross's frame of mind improved even further as he caught the positive inflection of the voice and the glimmer of a smile on his father's face. Now he knew that this indeed would be a good night.

Fay had her back turned to Ethan when she heard him ask the question and she spun around, making sure that it truly was her husband who sat at the table.

"It's always a special occasion when you get home for dinner, Ethan. I could ask you the same thing." Ross caught the barely perceptible edge to Fay's response and hoped that his father had missed it.

"Come on, Fay. You know how hard it is make a living. I'm just lucky to have a good job, one that's getting better by the day. I'd love to be able to be here every night for dinner with you and Ross but someone's got to be looking after our future."

Fay decided for Ross's sake to let this comment go. She knew Ethan could invent a profusion of reasons not to come home, some of them valid but most were just excuses. With deliberate effort, she kept the momentum of the conversation heading in what she thought would be a safe and wifely direction.

"How did work go today, Ethan? Anything new in the car business?" Safe but superficial-depth could come later, Fay thought.

"Biggest news is that Mr. Manley thinks we'll be able to keep our practice track for another couple of years anyway. The development plan for the property's going to be done in stages and the last phase won't be started for another four or five years. That's the section where the track is." The gleam in Ross's eyes became brighter, realizing that his father had just spoken more civil words to his mother than he had heard in a year. He watched as Fay began to dish the food onto the plates, her back to the table once again.

"What are you frying over there, Fay? Smells like an awful good grade of hamburger to me." Ethan directed his attention to Ross as the dinner preparations were completed. "You seem pretty happy today, boy. What is going on?" His father speaking directly to him invariably had the effect of making Ross become practically tongue-tied. He managed to gather his wits and respond with a slight stutter.

"Guess I-I'm just excited about the steak, Dad."

"Hey, Fay—what the hell's this about steak for dinner?" Suddenly the cheery atmosphere shifted into a darker place. Ross could almost see his mother begin to tread lightly around the eggshells on the floor between her and the table. She brought over two of the well-presented plates, the medium-rare steaks sizzling in the center surrounded by baked potato, freshly sliced tomato, and green beans. She smiled broadly, truly proud of her creation, and placed the full plates down in front of her men.

"Oh, Ethan! It is a special occasion. We have stew or soup or hash almost every night. It should be special when you're able to grace us with your presence!" Fay wanted to suck the last few words of the sentence back into her mouth before they escaped but both mother and son knew her regret came a second too late.

For some insane reason, the new escalators at Gimbel's Department Store in Philadelphia flashed into Fay's mind. She thought of her stern admonition to Ross that once he stood on the first moving stair, he had to keep going to the top. There could be no turning back. Now, she saw both of them on an escalator right here in their own kitchen, her smart "grace us" remark placing them on the first step. Escalation was unavoidable. She turned away from the table to get the other plate and heard the ominous deep voice behind her.

"Dammit, Fay. You don't need to make me feel guilty about this too. I do the best I can and I'll be damned if you don't go spending money we don't have." Ethan's descent into one of his irrational tirades happened in matter of seconds. He followed his cursing of Fay's extravagance with a leap-frog series of unrelated frustrations, from Harry Truman to unmotivated union workers to the ungrateful tenants downstairs. Ethan's mention of her family, as always in derogatory fashion, spun Fay around toward Ethan once again. Ross, not believing that all this could be happening again within such a short time, pushed his chair back and assumed his defensive posture, ready to flee at any moment. He recognized the signs of Ethan's rising temper clearly and hoped that his father would just leave relatively quietly.

"Please, Ethan. Don't ruin this. I don't care what you think of me, which obviously isn't much, but think of Ross for a change!" Fay's voice trailed off pitifully. "Why don't you go in your room for a minute, Ross? I'll keep your dinner warm." She looked at him, the hurt and sadness in her eyes bringing tears to his. He stood, politely muttered, "Excuse me," and disappeared around the corner and into his room, pushing the door closed behind him.

"This is why I don't come home, for God's sake, Fay. You're always after me for something." Ethan had risen from his chair and now leaned forward in a menacing attitude, his hands on the table in front of him.

"If things are so bad, Ethan, why don't you just give it up? You could go to your precious Rose or Dorothy or any one of your other women friends." Her voice came out in a low hiss.

"You're trapped because of your religion and my good financial support. I'm trapped because I just wanted to have some fun and you got pregnant. Now, Manley wants his managers to have a picture-perfect American family. That's all there is to that. We're both stuck so let's make it look good, as least." Ethan spoke in a controlled voice and Fay experienced a sense of relief that perhaps he would just leave this time and at least she and Ross could enjoy the special dinner.

Fay called to Ross to come back to the table. Her cheerful invitation ignited an illogical rage in Ethan.

"Calling him back to protect you, huh! Well, here's what you can do with your damned special-occasion dinner!" Ross came out of his room and into the doorway just in time to see the dinner, plate and all, hurtling toward his mother across the kitchen. By the time it struck the icebox behind her, the dinner was flying in all directions. The china plate shattered and before it hit the ground, Ethan disappeared down the hall and out the door, slamming it behind him. Ross could only stand by the kitchen entrance, helpless, as he watched his mother's body sag, as if under some invisible weight. Unaware of his presence, she bent over and began to pick up the pieces of the broken dish, feeling as though she was looking at her life scattered across the floor.

"I'm only twenty-four years old," she whispered, at the moment dreading the possibility that she would have many more years of this existence. She suddenly had an urgent need to see her mother, just to see her, with no intention of relating the ugly scene just played out. From her position on the floor among the splinters of china and the grease streak where the special-occasion steak had slid across the floor, she reached for an empty milk bottle under the sink. With one hand, she knocked the bottle firmly on the floor one time, hesitated for thirty seconds, then and knocked again.

The Beckers' kitchen was almost centered over the Johnsons' apartment and the milk-bottle code found its way clearly to the Johnsons' living room. Fay and Susan Johnson had established the code as a temporary solution to the one-telephone problem. Until the Johnsons could afford their own, Fay, with Ethan's grudging approval, had agreed that anyone living downstairs could use her phone number as a contact point. The milk-bottle signals ran in descending age order, with one knock indicating that Susan had a phone call. When Susan heard the knock over her head, with the pause and then another, she left her apartment, quickly climbing the stairs to answer what she thought was a telephone call. She knew Ethan had come home for dinner but had heard his heavy footsteps coming down the stairs after the door slammed and wondered where he had gone. Ross had described this special dinner to her and she surely did not want to intrude on the family, well aware of the glaring tension in her daughter's life. When she knocked lightly on the door, Fay greeted her and escorted her directly into the living room, explaining that Ethan had been called away to work for some emergency and she just felt like visiting. Susan caught a fleeting glimpse of Ross, sitting at the kitchen table by himself, eating his dinner. Her mother's intuition and her innate wisdom told her to not ask any questions but to follow Fay's direction. Even the most disinterested observer could pick up the clues that the special occasion had turned out to be anything but that. Susan felt her stomach churn once more, desperately wishing for her daughter's happiness but aware that her chance of finding it with Ethan were between slim and none.

The Magnets Collide

Fay found her anticipation of Friday nights disconcerting, annoying, and bothersome, yet brimming with excitement. Ethan always worked late, and she and Ross usually ate an early supper, Ross finishing quickly so he could join his aunts and uncles downstairs. He often remarked to Fay that they "always seem to be having fun down there!" She could not disagree and after doing the dishes and straightening up, more often than not she joined them for their card games or just ordinary conversation. Some Fridays, she would come down a little later, her tardiness caused by the reason that she now prepared for Fridays with considerable excitement. On many Friday evenings, Al Stuart dropped by, ostensibly to look in on his car, even though it remained in the same spot as he had left it in late October. After checking his car, he would climb the back fire escape and ask if Fay had any coffee. She always did, of course.

The Friday-night visits became a ritual for Al two weeks after the surprise presidential election of 1948. Up to that time, he had come by regularly but not every week. What Fay told him that Friday in mid-November made him determined that he would check in every week, perhaps even more often.

The Wednesday morning after Thomas Dewey's incredible defeat, Ethan Becker and John Manley had their early-morning coffee as usual in Manley's spacious office overlooking the sprawling dealership. The *Courier Gazette* sat on the owner's desk, front-page up and screaming.

"Truman Wins!" The headline seemed to take up the top half of the paper, right to its fold. Only slightly smaller, the sub headline reinforced the cloud of depression hanging over the two men. "Dewey Upset Stunning!"

"Can you fucking believe this, Ethan?" John Manley was convinced that the country as they knew it would vanish if the Democrats won the White House again. He loved talking politics with Ethan because they agreed on everything, commiserating with each other when things were not going their way and celebrating when they were.

For two hours, the men sat in Manley's version of the Oval Office, railing against a populace who could be hoodwinked by a man like Truman. They decided that the collective stupidity of the American people was at new level. They would never admit, even to each other in their inner sanctum, that had Dewey been triumphant, they would have been celebrating the incisive, perceptive intelligence of these same people.

Ethan's agitation continued to increase during the remainder of the workday as conversation throughout the company centered on what many pundits were calling the major political upset of the century. As the last of the employees required to punch the time clock inserted his card and heard the familiar stamp of the machine, Ethan needed desperately to separate from the environment of the blue-collar unionists. He watched the last of the day-shift workers drive away from the parking lot and walked over to John Manley's office. Seeing the heavy oak door ajar and no one with his boss, he knocked lightly, providing enough momentum so that the door swung open a few inches wider. Manley looked up from his enormous desk and motioned for Ethan to come in. Ethan just leaned in and called out.

"I need to get out of here for a while, Mr. Manley, if it's all right with you. If I hear one more word about the earthy, regular guy Mr. Truman, I'll probably lose my lunch!"

"Sure, Ethan, I completely understand. I've heard quite enough gloating to last me a long time. Damned idiots! I'll see you tomorrow but you take it easy." Manley gave a quick wave of dismissal and returned his attention to the papers on his desk.

Ethan conducted a marvelous debate inside his head as he left the dealership and started across the lot toward his car. He could go home, surprising Fay and dealing once more with her ridiculous, fawning apologies for not having a better dinner and not being ready for him, even though it was not her fault at all. He could stop by at Mel's for a quick beer with the after-work bunch, who were sure to be railing on and on about the election. At least at Mel's he would have some support. He knew that Fay and the Johnsons would continue to be unbearable, probably for the next four years. When his personal debate ended, no question remained. He would make a quick stop at Mel's and try to improve his mood before facing the uninviting home front.

Fay and Ross were in the plainly furnished living room of the Johnson's apartment. The topic of conversation all evening long was the election, ranging from the reminiscences of the day Truman assumed the presidency from Roosevelt to his courage in using the bomb to end the war with Japan. Fay sat on an old leather hassock in front of Susan Johnson's faded maroon chair, crocheted white doilies hiding the badly worn corners of the arms. Mention of Roosevelt transported Fay back to the park monument and the first time she shared her feelings with Al. Ross sat on the floor next to his grandmother, leaning sideways and absorbing the loving camaraderie of the five Johnson children. He could not have felt safer as Susan softly hung her arm over the chair and patted him lightly on the shoulder.

The familiar vibration of the slam of Ethan's car door brought Fay straight out of her chair. "Come on, Ross. Your father's home." Everyone caught the unmistakable edge of panic in her voice. Her reaction startled her family with its passion, as though she had been caught doing something as a child that would be putting her in deep trouble. She crossed the room and grabbed Ross firmly by the hand, pulling him to a standing position in one movement.

"We'll see you later," she called back over her shoulder as she drew the door closed, still pulling and pushing Ross out ahead of her. The Johnsons heard the two of them stumbling up the steps to their apartment. Fay's family could only look at each other and shake their heads sadly. Unspoken but in the hearts of her mother and siblings was an undeniable fact-Fay was terrified of Ethan Becker.

Within minutes of hearing Ethan climb the apartment steps, they cringed as they heard and felt the first, loud volleys of an escalating argument from the floor above. Susan Johnson remembered the very recent special occasion in the Becker family and wondered how much more her daughter could take. Harold and Greg Johnson had developed an effective defense mechanism when one of these unpleasant scenes played out above their heads. The apartment house had a cellar level, available for any of the tenants to use as storage. It housed the boilers for heat and hot water and an enormous coal bin in one corner, providing all manners of creative possibilities for playing or hiding. With Susan's permission, they retreated out of the apartment, jumping from the porch and making their way down through the heavy metal hatchway to the basement so they would not have to listen to whatever was going on upstairs. Once in the safety of the cellar, they wished that somehow Ross could be with them at times like these. Susan and the three girls attempted to fool each other by burying themselves in whatever reading material they had in front of them. None of them could have remembered a word of what they read as the battle raged upstairs. They wished, but despairingly, that somehow they could help Fay and Ross.

Unbelievably, the brief Becker quarrel began when Fay once again asked the innocent, innocuous, wifely sort of question.

"How did work go today, Ethan?" Ethan senselessly used the question as a vehicle to launch into a vicious tirade about how many stupid employees of Manley Motors had voted for Truman. When Fay had the temerity to suggest that perhaps they had good reasons for their choice, he turned his daylong frustrations toward her with a vengeance. Ross had already backtracked into his room, recognizing immediately the vibrations that always preceded a furious storm.

Fay felt Ethan's presence close behind her as she stood facing the sink. She wanted to see his face in order to judge his rationality at the moment and turned around.

"You *always* think you know what you're talking about, don't you? Well, you're wrong again, Fay. You and those other damn fools are going to get what you deserve. You ought to see who butters the bread around here, for God's sake!" Ethan's voice had risen in volume enough so that Susan and her girls downstairs looked up to the ceiling when he said "For God's sake!"

Her question about his rationality answered, Fay's conscience called on her one more time to speak out for what is right.

"Ethan, you aren't being fair. You're just such a poor loser. Why don't you grow up? And keep your voice down, you'll scare Ross." The verbal portion of the argument ended right there.

Susan Johnson, eyes riveted on her book but seeing nothing, relaxed as the sounds of spoken combat subsided quickly from upstairs. The floorboards between the two apartments prevented the softer sounds of the argument from permeating to the lower level.

Ethan had responded to Fay's final volley not with words but with actions. With the two beers he had downed at Mel's Tavern helping to remove his inhibitions even more than usual, his violent temper overtook him. As uncontrolled as he had been while attempting to run down a striker two years before, he lashed out at Fay, striking her hard with a balled fist, directly under her left eye. Fay did not recoil, standing her ground. She raised her left hand and covered her eye, trying to rub away the shooting stars streaking across her retina. She confronted Ethan with her right eye, wordlessly glaring at him with a malevolent stare. Ethan glared in return but finally had to turn away.

"Stupid bitch", he muttered as he turned and sauntered down the hallway to the living room. Fay followed him and, before she turned into her bedroom, called to him just as he sat down with the newspaper.

"I'll be in our room tonight. Please take care of Ross." Ethan grunted an affirmative response and Fay disappeared behind the bedroom door.

On the Friday night following the election, Al Stuart arrived at the rear door of the Beckers' apartment at his usual time. After knocking loudly four times, Ross finally heard him above the radio and came to the door. Excited as he was to see Al, his mother had told him that under no circumstances was he to allow Al into the house. She did not feel well and hoped that Al could return next week when she felt better. Ross did exactly as he had been told, even though he had not seen his mother in the two days since his parents' last argument. She had done all of her communicating through the closed bedroom door. Ross was puzzled and confused even more when she told him to tell the Johnsons that she had the grippe, didn't feel well but needed no help.

After Ross's unsatisfactory explanation, Al left. He knew something serious had happened but felt that he had no choice but to honor Fay's wishes. After an entire Friday night of worrying about Fay and Ross, he called Ethan early Saturday morning, waking him from a sound sleep. Hearing Ethan's flimsy reason for Fay's behavior, he felt even worse, sensing that Ethan was withholding something. Al spent the remainder of the week tormented by speculation about what happened to Fay. He could not wait until the next Friday to see her.

Nine days after Ethan struck her, Fay Becker spent the day preparing for her meeting with Al. She had not heard from him since Ross had given him the transparent excuse the previous week. Other than Ethan's caustic announcement that Al had asked about her health, she had no indication that he had the vaguest idea of her desperate need to talk to him. She only hoped that he was able to read between the lines of her refusal to see him and the insensitive manner in which Ethan dismissed her "illness" when Al had inquired about her in the Saturday-morning phone call.

The Johnsons had plans for an extended Friday-night Monopoly game and asked Fay and Ross to join them. The two loved to take part in these riotous family games, enjoying the lighthearted fun that seemed to enfold the whole family when they were together. For this particular Friday night, Fay asked if Ross could come down by himself, just on the chance that Al might stop by. Susan Johnson, the perceptive matriarch, who at times appeared to have a prescient gift, took Fay's excuse as just a chance to be by herself. Fay had done a masterful job of hiding the deep purple bruise on her upper cheek with powder and rouge, passing off the blackened eye as a "ran-into-a-door" accident. The family, sensitive to Fay's delicate balance in her marriage, accepted the evasion without question to her face, but filed away the injury as one more reason to distrust and even hate Ethan Becker.

Fay and Ross sat down to an early-Friday dinner, meatless in the Catholic tradition. Ross never understood the significance of this prohibition, despite his Catholic schooling. Any questions about it resulted in the usual non-answers from the nuns so he gave up and put in it on his list of things he did not need to confess. The dinner, tomato soup and a tuna fish sandwich, took only about ten minutes to eat and they were just beginning to clear the bowls and plates when Al Stuart drove into the backyard. Fay still tried to convince herself that her feelings toward Al could be managed in their "solid friendship" format. However, dismissing the shiver of excitement she felt when she knew he had arrived presented a very real problem. First of all, there was much more than a solid friendship sort of feeling, and second, and just maybe more important, she hung on his promise that things would be all right. If she handled the situation carefully, Al could be the personal knight, the kind that saves damsel in distress.

She heard his car door slam, the rattle from the loose window rising the two floors into the apartment. Expecting that he would go over to the garage to look at his race car, she set the dishes down on the drain by the sink and went to the window. He was coming across the yard toward the house, not stopping at the garage. She quickly suggested to Ross that he start downstairs to the Monopoly game, but Ross would not hear of it, not until he said hello to Al.

Al made the trip up the back stairs in record time and knocked at the door. Fay told Ross to let him in while she busied herself with the dishes at the sink. For no reason that she could think of, her hands shook with a sweaty nervousness and her knees actually wobbled.

Ross greeted Al in his usual way, a firm handshake and a childlike hug around his neck as Al bent to meet him halfway. Fay turned from the sink, her emotions in a state of disarray. She watched as Al and Ross connected on a level that she knew to be far beyond the physical and her eyes glistened. When Al stood up from the hug, he shot a penetrating look toward Fay.

"It's really good to see you, Al." Their eyes locked and neither of them could pull away.

"Same here, Fay. How are you doing? Do you have any coffee brewing?" Ross, standing between them, looked from one to the other but obviously was not being noticed. He finally spoke loudly to his mother.

"Al asked about coffee, Mom. You going to answer him?" His voice broke the silence, forcing Fay to respond. She was able to redirect her attention from Al to Ross only through a concentrated physical effort.

"Of course, dear. Now, why don't you go ahead down to your grandmother's for the game?" Her gentle tone asked the question but hid the underlying necessity. Ross understood that the question was not meant as a choice for him. It was time to go downstairs. "I'll try to come down later, OK?" Under other circumstances, Ross would have rather just sit close by Al during his visit, but the beckoning amusement of playing a long, bedtime-breaking game with his uncles and aunts provided enough enticement to propel Ross toward the door.

"See you later, Al!" Ross shouted as he turned the door knob. The door closed behind him. Fay and Al did not move from their original positions in the kitchen as they listened. His steps could be heard all the way down to the lower door, then out across the porch. When the Johnsons' closed, Fay broke the palpable silence and tension with an invitation to come sit in the living room while the coffee finished brewing. She led the way down the hall, sensing Al's presence as he followed behind her. She sat on the sofa and, as Al started across to a chair under the window, she patted the couch, indicating that he should sit next to her. Too late, she realized that he would be sitting on her left side, exposing the fading but still apparent bruise and discoloration above her eye.

Earlier in the day, as she prepared for what she hoped would be a visit from Al, Fay had wrestled with what to wear on this Friday evening. Looking through her somewhat limited wardrobe, she remembered how happy Ross was to see her in the outfit she had worn the night of the special-occasion steak fiasco. She admitted to herself that she enjoyed the effect that the tailored sweater and skirt seemed to have on men, even catching Father Gallagher casting a hesitant but admiring glance in her direction at the PTA meeting the previous month.

Now, as she motioned for Al to join her, she thought she sensed that the outfit affected him in much the same way. Crossing the room toward her, he was struck by how beautiful she was. The white, bulky-knit sweater served only to accentuate her figure as it settled on her full breasts, clinging to the contours of her body. As she patted the cushion once more, she slowly crossed her legs, the red pleated skirt rising briefly above her knees. Al thought once more of his childhood magnets, hopelessly at the mercy of their nature. Fay's dark eyes sparkled, somewhat too provocatively, Al thought, as he helplessly but willingly followed the beckoning invitation. The pit of his stomach felt just as it did before a race, a wonderful nervousness bubbling and spreading throughout his being. He sat down as far from Fay as the space on the sofa allowed.

He turned toward her and once again their eyes met. He absorbed her face in a single glance and knew that she was the most beautiful woman he had ever seen. The blemish on her left side could not be ignored and Al had to ask.

"Oh, Fay, what on earth happened last week?" He reached out and took both of her hands. Her deep-set eyes filled with tears and her face remained beautiful though it now assumed a frighteningly desperate expression. Al moved closer. He let her hands drop in her lap while he reached around and pulled her toward him. What he intended, truly intended, to be a reassuring and friendly hug suddenly ignited feelings deep within him, feelings he had successfully turned aside until this moment. A rising wave of passion, fueled by the years of self-denial, washed over both of them. Fay moved against him, her arms encircling him. She pulled back far enough to look briefly into his eyes, then moved her mouth to meet his. The kiss fired a long-denied frenzy, and the "solid" friendship disappeared into a furious yet subdued sensuality. Fay frantically pulled her sweater over her head. She had deliberately not worn a slip, enjoying the sensuality of the wool sweater. Al was kissing her exposed skin as he gently pushed her back onto the sofa. He reached behind her and unhooked the clasp of her bra. He slid the straps from her shoulders and, in a single movement, exposed her breasts as he dropped the garment to the floor. Their urgency carried them through the stages of lovemaking at an adolescence couple's pace. Feverishly, they helped each other remove any remaining remnants of clothing and finally lay languorously intertwined on the sofa. The gradual but inexorable process of falling deeply in love over the last four years provided all the foreplay and stimulus they needed to take the final steps to intimacy. Fay's long, sexual fantasies in the bathtub flitted deliciously through her head, heightening her anticipation as she moved under him.

Al felt as if he was being swept away in a surreal but wonderful reverie. He had truly lost control and knew nothing could come between them from this moment on. He was torn between his naturally gentle nature and urges that simply could not be denied. Fay positioned herself to receive him and raised her pelvis slightly. She stared up at him, her eyes glazed with desire. Al spread her legs apart, exposing her even further. He guided himself toward her and firmly pushed his way inside. Once again a sense of the deepest urgency created a rhythm and an increasing tempo, which they rode to an explosive mutual climax, a transcendent physical and spiritual bonding far beyond what either ever imagined.

Physically exhausted but emotionally charged, they lay in perfect stillness, wrapped in each other's arms, enfolded in what Fay would come to call her haven, her very safe haven. After what seemed an eternity but was but a few minutes of Al's gently stroking her cheek and dragging his fingertips down her neck and across her breasts, Fay opened her eyes and the reality of their environment crashed over her. It was almost physically painful to ask Al to stop caressing her and extricate himself from the delicious curves of her body. She became acutely aware of their situation, the emotional roller coaster having reached the pinnacle of the hill just moments before but now hurtling toward the station, ready for the brakes to be applied.

"Al, I'm really sorry but we've got to get up!" A bit of panic curled around the edges of Fay's voice.

Al, lost in his own private heaven, stopped his caress as it reached her breast and he leaned over and kissed her, thanking God for her presence in his life. His lovemaking had been superb, ravenous and needy but in a deliberate and gentle way, but now her panic spread quietly to him. He awkwardly pushed himself off the sofa, feeling somewhat embarrassed as he fumbled clumsily with his clothes, strewn all over the floor. With a slight smile, he looked down at Fay, still reclining in utter nakedness on the sofa.

"Now I know how Adam must have felt after eating the apple," he said lightly, gathering his clothes and covering himself as best he could with the rumpled ball of pants and shirt and underwear. He nodded toward her bedroom door with a questioning glance and she nodded back. He turned, the jumbled material covering his front side but leaving his rear completely exposed, and hurried into her bedroom to dress.

Fay, her panic now under control, sat up and reached down between the sofa cushions to where a small white patch of her silk panties showed itself against the dark green material. She was completely dressed by the time Al emerged from her bedroom, also fully dressed.

The electric gaze they exchanged told each other that they had stepped over a line, a line that might as well be a steep cliff. There would be no turning back, even though they both knew that the course they were taking would be dangerous. For Fay, as if she cared, her soul carried a continuing mortal sin in the eyes of her church.

The rest of this Friday evening would be spent with the flushed excitement of the new lovers tempered by Fay's revelations of the true character of her husband, revelations that Al had guessed about his best friend but could not bring himself to accept. Fay sat in her favorite chair next to the bay window and Al sat in Ethan's green recliner across the room, as if neither of them dared to be exposed again to the passion of earlier in the evening. When Al first came out of her bedroom, they had sat on the sofa again but Al explained that he had trouble concentrating on what she was saying when he moved within his three-foot circle, especially now. Fay had just smiled, finally relieved of the stress of the physical tension between them and able to love him simply for being who he was.

When Ross opened the door much later that evening, he did not expect Al to be there but was happy to see him and regaled him with the tales of the Monopoly board. Shortly afterward, Al stood up to leave and Ross walked him to the back door. Al reached for Ross's hand for the traditional handshake and looked back up the hall to the living room where Fay still sat in her chair. He waved to her with his left hand and held it out with fingers extended, as though he could still feel her warm, unbearably pleasurable skin beneath them. Finally lowering his wave, he gave Ross his usual good-natured squeeze. As he left, he called back to Fay: "Thanks for a wonderful evening. I'll see you next Friday!" The inflection he put on the words soared over Ross's head but directly to Fay's heart. She quickly began developing plans to ensure Ross's continued absence on Friday nights and prayed that Ethan would continue his Friday work schedule.

"See you later, Ross. You take care of your mom, hear?" Again, the depth of feeling hidden in those few innocuous words made Fay smile more broadly than she had in months.

Al's knees still wobbled as he descended the fire escape and jogged across the backyard to his car. He had never in his life experienced anything like the last few hours. The explosiveness of the attraction he felt for Fay had been building for so long that now, as he sat in his old rumble-seated 1937 Ford sedan, he could ecstatically declare to himself that at last he would not have to keep it inside anymore. He had known for years, actually ever since Fay confided to him during the Roosevelt walk, that she had special feelings for him also. Since that time and perhaps even before, they seemed to be participating in a primitive mating dance, darting in and out of the dangerous shadows around the fire, tentatively circling closer and closer but always receding into the darkness before the flames consumed them. Tonight, finally, they had allowed themselves to be deliciously devoured by the fire, and things would never be the same for either of them. The sexual interlude was so powerful and all encompassing that afterward Al easily absorbed Fay's extensive sharing of details of her life with Ethan for later examination. The switching on of the car's ignition corresponded to another kind of internal switching in Al's mind. The engine being brought to life by pressing the foot starter simultaneously with the accelerator forced him to exchange the still quivering sensual nerve endings demanding all of his attention, replacing them with his infinitely more normal and rational thinking mode. This clear-headedness, found with some effort on Al's part, allowed him to concentrate on Fay's story of married life with Ethan Becker. Some of the tale he knew but one aspect of her continuing story created a rising swell of anger in him, an anger more deeply felt now than ever.

"How could he be so abusive to such a wonderful woman?" he thought. A vision of Fay reclining on the sofa drifted through his mind and he forced it aside, wanting instead to concentrate of the whole of her story rather than descending into the marvelous fantasy-come-true just hours before.

Although Al knew about some of Ethan's violent incidents, he did not realize the frequency or the degree. He had no reason to doubt Fay's description; she had always been truthful with him. All the way home, each of the incidents Fay related to Al on this very special Friday night floated before his eyes in a dreamlike mist. She didn't deserve what she had been through in the nine years with Ethan Becker, that much he knew. By the time he arrived home on the watershed Friday, he had revisited through the mist of his mind all of Fay's humiliation, the physical and verbal abuse, the emotional mistreatment and the violation by a doctor she had trusted. An irrevocable change occurred. He decided emphatically and without question that he would be the one to implement a plan for Fay's freedom, even knowing in his heart that it may come at a very high price. The question now moved into the realm of the when and how. He completely set aside the "if" possibility. In the meantime, he would protect her and her son in every way.

The first dream image that night as Al finally fell into a troubled, shallow sleep that night was of Fay, sprawled naked across a bed. It was not a sexual image at all. A dark figure had removed something from her body and held it up to the light while she cowered, then turned and sobbed into her pillow. The vision brought Al to a sitting position in bed, the depth of the rage he felt toward Ethan Becker taking him by surprise.

The extraordinary haven that Al Stuart provided for Fay Becker kept her sanity in place for almost a year and a half. The Friday nights they spent together evolved into a successful pattern of finding at least two hours, sometimes more, to be alone in some safe location, usually the Beckers' apartment. On rare occasions, the lovers found some other time to see each other, but the Friday-night "visits" became the staple for their relationship. Unbelievably, Ethan continued his own Friday-night pattern, coming home on only one occasion when he didn't feel well. Al's anger toward Ethan increased in almost direct proportion to the expanding and increasingly powerful love he felt for Fay. Al, much to his own surprise, rose to levels of duplicity he never thought he was capable of. He managed to hide his feelings for Fay under a facade of friendship, a facade easily accepted by the other men in the racing crews, including Ethan. They obviously detected no no change in their relationship. Al continued to be the butt of the jokes about his lack of female companionship, dealing with the crude male barbs in his usually good-humored way.

"If you're ever in the shower with Al, boys, don't bend over if you drop the soap." Al would just smile, knowing that none of the boys gave even the most remote consideration of anything going on between him and Fay. As the friendship between Al and Ethan cooled, imperceptibly to everyone but Al, Charlie Beckholdt gradually filled Al's human need for a close confidant of the same gender. Charlie had worked with Al and his race car for several years and the two had moved beyond the casual acquaintance stage into a friendship. Charlie Beckholdt would never know the role he played in the murderous scheme borne out of Al's overpowering love for Fay combined, with his burgeoning hatred for Ethan Becker.

Monday, May 23, 1950

WORKING THINGS OUT

As the racing season approached, Al Stuart's pit crew, a formidable title his three buddies had bestowed upon themselves, gathered on Monday nights for a "war-story" session. These sessions generally lasted well into the night, becoming longer each season as the stories became more numerous and inevitably embellished almost beyond recognition. Just as an avid golfer may recall every single shot of a particularly memorable round, Al and his friends could amuse each other for hours with detailed stories of races past. Al could reenact the drama of careening around the track in a reckless disregard for life and limb with such specificity that anyone listening absorbed the vicarious experience with a suitable intensity.

This Monday night, they prepared for the first major race card of the season on the following Monday, Memorial Day, with the usual reminiscences of death-cheating accidents, crowd-pleasing finishes and the competition and camaraderie among the recreational weekend racers. Somewhere around the middle of the evening, quite inadvertently, Charlie Beckholdt planted a seed of an idea in Al Stuart's mind, a forbidden thought that Al could not dwell on until his friends had left for the night.

Charlie had a magnificent sense of humor and held everyone's attention whenever he had the floor. The story he told that triggered a silent and subtle response deep inside Al's subconscious was not a funny one, although Charlie had started out with everyone laughing at his description of the trip to the racetrack that day.

Two years before, in midsummer oppressive heat and breath-draining humidity, the two crews of Al Stuart and Ethan Becker had set out for a small track in Bethlehem, Pennsylvania. A comedy of errors began with a tire going flat on the trailer immediately after they loaded the car. When they backed the car off the trailer and removed the five-gallon cans of aviation fuel strapped to the side of the trailer, they fixed the flat. In an anxiety-driven rush to get going so as not to miss the time trials and the qualifying heats, they pushed the car back onto the trailer. All three then jumped in the truck, backed the trailer down the drive and realized forty miles later that the two gas cans were still sitting on the edge of the driveway. Charlie was one of the few storytellers who could make the scene a funny one, describing each man's reaction as he discovered what they had done. The misadventures of the day continued even after they arrived at the track: Engine problems developed because of the quality of the hastily borrowed gas, a humiliating embarrassment for all. Sunday Blue Laws in Pennsylvania allowed for no chance to purchase anything and the crucial timing of the engine suffered with the lower-grade fuel. Charlie had his little audience enjoying the revisit of the disastrous day and making it appear that they all had a wonderful time, although the car never raced in a single heat.

The second part of Charlie's story could not be told in any way that might show off his sense of humor. He remembered an accident that day, not a fatal one, but one that resulted in serious injuries to one of their comrades.

"A single loose bolt, remember that, guys? One silly little bolt, the size of my little finger could have killed old Jeff..."

Charlie added detail after detail but the detail that caught Al's attention was Charlie's off-handed and understated comment about the importance of tie rod ends in the steering system. The connecting tie rod bolt on the right side of the race car had worked its way loose during the six laps of the qualifying second heat and left Jeff Knowlton with no steering as he rumbled down the backstretch. He could do nothing as he approached the third turn, trying to brake without causing the cars behind to lose control as well.

"...hit that fence so damn hard his rear wheels went straight up in the air...pushed his head right into the concrete wall...thought we had lost him that day...."

Charlie's voice trailed off, out of respect for the fine young man whose story he had just told.

"...at this very minute probably sitting in his wheelchair, wondering why he ever took up racing in the first place...."

Somewhat subdued, Charlie mentioned that he had seen Jeff just last month, with the prognosis just as it was when the accident occurred. "Can't move anything but his mouth," Charlie said, his voice trembling.

After everyone left, Al went to bed and let his conscious mind listen to the whisper of the thought he had plunged into a black recess of a place he hated to admit even existed. He wondered aloud in the darkness of his bedroom if everyone had one of these places, a section of the mind cordoned off from any intruders, a storage area for thoughts that shock and terrify, creating doubts about one's sanity. Always in the dark, as he lay in bed these days, the synapses of his brain seemed to break open the physical senses and let the residual memories of Fay enter in. The power she held over him was so strong that it frightened him in a strange, delicious way. He could feel her smooth skin on his chest; he could taste her lightly glossed lips; he could see her eyes imploring him for help; his nostrils filled with her natural, fragrantly delicious scent; he could hear her soft voice professing her love. He experienced nothing but pleasure during these times, even surrendering on occasion to an adolescent sexual urge when her ethereal presence occupied his bed with him. Tonight, a strong and negative intrusiveness could not be turned away. He had admitted to himself that he had to do something, even long before his relationship with Fay attained such startling status. He decided to allow the forbidden whisper to come to the surface of his consciousness.

Although their friendship had grown slightly sour, Ethan trusted Al implicitly with testing his car on race day. The rituals of superstition must be followed. The volume of the forbidden whisper grew louder in his head.

"What if," it asked, "what if, after testing the car during the practice laps just before the qualifier, I crawled under the car to check something or other and ever so slightly loosened one of the bolts on the tie rod ends?" The volume stepped up another notch.

"The heats are eight laps in duration; surely the bolt might vibrate loose over that time?"

The whisper became so loud in his head that his mouth actually formed the words.

"Ethan Becker will fall, an unfortunate victim of the vagaries of destiny in the dangerous hobby of auto racing." Al sat straight up in disbelief at the words that came out of his mouth, but he knew in some strange way that they were true. In that moment, he realized he was capable of murder. From some other compartment, another thought found its way to the surface, a thought from some long-forgotten high school English class discussion on the philosophy of Karl Marx or Aristotle or somebody. Continuing his conversation with himself, he speculated that in this case, the end surely justified the means. He drifted into a sound sleep, knowing that at least something had been settled, and if all went well with the embryo plan taking shape in his mind, he perhaps could begin to anticipate a long and happy life with Fay and Ross.

Friday, May 28, 1950

WORKING THINGS OUT
PART TWO

Ross greeted Al Stuart with a wide smile. He now watched eagerly for Al's car to arrive on Friday nights. His relationship with Al the last year and a half had intensified from a big-brother type of give-and-take hero worship to a more sublime and meaningful one, almost father and son in nature. The change corresponded with a distinct transition in Ross's attitude toward his father, a transition not uncommon in father-son relationships.

Ethan Becker leapfrogged up the ladder of success at Manley Ford, vaulting over the other assistant managers and positioning himself for consideration as general manager when Manley decided it was time to distance himself from his involvement in the day-to-day operations of the dealership. Ethan's philosophy of work first and family second won the favor of John Manley, as long as the marriage to Fay gave the outward appearance of being a loving one.

The wifely support necessary for success in the business world provided an unexpected niche for Fay, one that allowed her to mingle with other managers' wives at social events. As she wondered whether anything would ever come of Al's promises, she decided it would not hurt to hedge her bets. There certainly could be no harm in playing the role of executive's wife while waiting for some other possibility to surface. Ethan's interest in having her be a part of what she referred to as the country club hopefuls did surprise her but she knew it was purely pretense. For Fay, mixing with the women provided an outlet she had not experienced before and she decided, at least for the present, it would be worth while to take advantage of it. Of course, her favorite activities with the "hopefuls" were the shopping trips to the city, excursions that required Ethan to provide her with the financial resources needed to blend in with the other women.

The appearance of the marriage, both Ethan and Fay knew, was a sham. The tension at home continued unabated, although Ethan noticed that Fay seemed more docile and actually happier than she had ever been. She still performed her marital duties with even more enthusiasm than ever, much to Ethan's delight. He would not have been nearly so delighted if he could penetrate the sullen eyes (he took them for lustful) to see what she was thinking during their most intimate moments. Ross's respect and admiration for his father's business abilities continued to grow, as did his fear. The eggshell dances that both he and his mother had mastered stood both of them in good stead most of the time. Fay knew that respect and admiration often could grow into love but the fear that Ethan instilled in his young son prevented that from happening. It was obvious to Fay that Ross looked toward Al more as a father figure than he did his own father and she did not worry about it one bit.

Fay became quite talented at faking a calm and reserved reaction when she saw Al, in contradiction to the spasms of excitement in her heart. As Al and Ross proceeded through their greeting rituals, she watched from a distance and waited for them to finish. This late-spring evening had turned out very warm and she knew that Ross would be walking down to Pop's to visit with him as he sat out in front of his shop, waiting for the local movie crowd to pour in for their post-movie sundae or shake. She appreciated Al more than ever on those rare Fridays that Ross stayed around the house instead of visiting with the Johnsons downstairs or playing with friends outside. As the three played Old Maid or some other children's game on those nights, the glances and smiles the lovers shared clearly indicated that their minds were not exactly on the game at hand. Al easily imagined what it might be like for the three of them to be a family unit and these times became as almost as precious as the cherished moments when he and Fay were alone together. When Al passed on his usual greeting to Fay, he thought of those special times and, with a twinge of nervousness in his stomach, decided that after the races on Memorial Day, perhaps the impediment to a permanent living arrangement would be removed.

True to her expectations, Ross soon said goodbye to his mother and Al, declaring that Pop would be lonely tonight and he should go visit him for a while but would be home before dark. The instant he closed the door behind him, Al reached for Fay's hand and led her to the living room. Still standing, they kissed passionately but then Al retreated slightly. The timing of his subtle withdrawal turned out to be fortunate, as Ross came running back up the stairs and charged through the door. The innocence of a young boy prevented Ross from noticing how close his mother stood to Al and he thought nothing of it.

"Hey, Al. I forgot to tell you. My dad says that I can be in the pits for the Memorial Day races. First time he's let me do that!" Fay smiled at the boy's exuberance but was puzzled by Al's strained, almost wooden reaction. Ross disappeared as quickly as he came, his promise to be home by dark floating back through the closed door.

"Are you all right, Al? Is something wrong with Ross being in the pits on Monday?" Fay asked the questions with no concern in her voice; she trusted Al's judgment completely.

Al's mind spun in turmoil as he thought about Ross being that close to the track. Then, in an exercise in strange, somewhat warped reasoning, he thought of the closure the day would provide to Ross if he was present and he let it go.

"No, no, everything's fine. The pits'll be a good place for Ross. I'll have my boys keep an eye on him. Fay, I promised you that things would work out. I have a plan and you're going have to trust me. I can't really explain it because you need to be honest if you get asked any questions. If everything goes according to my plan, we'll all be together after Monday's races." Fay's questioning glance turned to a troubled one.

"Al?" Before she could say anything else, he kissed her again, this time not pulling away but drawing her into the cauldron of passion that always seemed to bubbling between them. She sank under the spell of sensuality, leaving behind the compelling fear that Al's announcement had created. Fay quickly led Al into the bedroom, having managed to overcome the nagging guilt of making love to him in the bed she shared with Ethan. She no longer considered the sexual aspect of her relationship with her husband as making love; to use the word *love* in the context of what happened in their bedroom would have given it a meaning that no longer existed. Instead, Fay found that she could use her lively and creative imagination when Ethan insisted on initiating sex. She became very resourceful in fantasizing about Al even before they began their intimate relationship. Now, with the many experiences she could resurrect from memories of their lovemaking sessions, she found that she actually anticipated her encounters with Ethan, simply replacing him with Al in her imagination. This, Fay knew, constituted yet another of those sins in thought but she just added them to the list of other sins that someday she would confess; in the meantime, she allowed herself the luxury of enjoying her youthful sexuality, and sublimated any guilt associated with it.

The fearful hint that Al mentioned when he first arrived heightened Fay's level of excitement, more than the usual urgency enveloping them. Every touch carried a nuance not present before. In less than an hour, Fay and Al made love in several different ways, each one bringing Fay to increasingly intense orgasms as Al waited and watched, joining her at the final moment with his own, leaving them both gasping for breath.

Later that night, when Al had left and Ross had gone to bed, she sat at the front window, staring out at the reflection of the streetlights bouncing off the fully leafed trees of late spring. She thought about the conversation she and Al had shared after the exhilarating evening of physical closeness, certainly the most sublime since their affair began. How she hated the word affair! It did not begin to describe their relationship, casting a negative cloud over what had kept her rational and prudent over the years. She realized that she could not imagine her life without Al. During the last year and a half, the introduction of intimacy into the relationship only intensified her feelings for him. They talked about the future, with a careful avoidance of any mention of what Al had meant about his "plan." She found it amazing that she could remember conversations with Al practically verbatim, even as long ago as when they were good friends, not lovers. A gentle breeze rattled the trees outside as she thought about the underlying confidence that Al seemed to possess this particular night. In many ways, she found his certitude about their future together somewhat disconcerting. For whatever reason, she found herself thinking about Al when she first met him.

Fay had been a mother for two years, even though only seventeen. She remembered how she thought that he perfectly represented the definition of the phrase "painfully shy," with the emphasis on *painfully*. Ethan had described him as a grease monkey from a local filling station, interested only in cars and racing. She wasn't sure what she had expected but she had definitely not expected Al to be so easy to talk to. Although only eighteen himself, he possessed an air of worldly experience, an air she would discover later came from losing both his parents during his early teens and fending for himself ever since. His shyness she attributed to his inexperience with the opposite sex. When he appeared on the scene as Ethan's new friend, she pretended not to notice his lean but rugged good looks, punctuated by piercing brown eyes, eyes most often cast down when he was in her presence.

Her little reverie was interrupted by the headlights of a car approaching up Virginia Avenue. The car slowed and turned into the driveway and she knew it would be Ethan. Her last thought as she rose from the chair to prepare to greet her husband came as a revelation. The frightening but electrifying realization explained the fervor and the passion of the evening with Al. It made Fay gasp so loud that she worried that it may have awakened Ross in the next room. As clearly as if Al had explained his plan in detail, the comprehension of what he meant erupted in her mind. Al's apparent concern about Ross and his being permitted to be in the pits for the first time helped to crystallize her insight. The emotional floodtide crashing over her sent her scurrying to the kitchen to splash cold water on her flushing face. She had never been so excited or so terrified in her life.

Monday, May 30, 1950 (Memorial Day)

WORKING THINGS OUT
PART THREE

Bob and Jennie Proctor had just begun their trip to the racetrack when Jennie looked across the seat at her father. He could feel her eyes on him and knew she was about to say something that would launch a discussion lasting the entire drive. Bob often felt as if the two of them could sit in close proximity, completely wordless, and communicate more effectively than most parents did while engaged in active conversation with their children. He also knew that the single reason for this unique situation had nothing to do with him but everything to do with Jennie.

"Daddy, I know something is going to happen today. I don't want you to be afraid but I just know it!" Almost before she finished the sentence, Bob slowed the car and looked for a safe place to pull over. The tone of Jennie's voice whenever one of these predicaments presented itself left no room for interpretation. He loved his daughter more than she could possibly know but he knew that her strange ability upset her, and the unsettling effect on her had become stronger with age. With most children, the age of reason means moving from innocence to a knowledge of the difference between right and wrong. Jennie retained the innocence of her childhood, clearly knowing the difference between right and wrong, but wrong never appeared to be a choice for her. Only one aspect of her life seemed to be more bothersome and obviously became more deeply disturbing as she grew older. Her concern for her father and the knowledge that he might be afraid joined the two issues.

Jennie Proctor exemplified the traits that any parent might long for in his children. She had long demonstrated a matchless depth of compassion and a level of caring for everyone around her, far exceeding any degree of realistic expectations for someone her age. The teachers and children at her school loved her, although she often appeared to exist on a different plane, a trait some found fascinating yet frightening. She was the gentlest, kindest child in the Lyndeboro Elementary School, yet no children would take advantage of her. "Held in awe" was a frequent phrase her teachers used to describe her presence. Of course, none of this came as a surprise to her father. He had experienced firsthand the almost spiritual demeanor of his daughter. As disconcerting as all of this happened to be, he thanked God for Jennie every day of his life. He worried about her perceptive sensitivity, knowing that children may be hurt beyond measure by the unkind actions and words of others. Her wispy, almost fragile, appearance seemed to accentuate her vulnerability and Bob often just wanted to enfold her in his arms for protection. Usually, Jennie appeared to be more acutely aware of his concern at times like those and she would casually reassure her father that everything was fine and he needn't worry.

The eerie episodes when Jennie's unique gift became apparent caused both her father and Jennie the most difficulty. As she grew older, Jennie often told her father that she knew things that she did not want to know but she did not understand how she could avoid knowing them. She said that she always felt as if she had to do something about what she was being told.

Bob finally found a place to pull the car off the road. Bringing his black, wood-paneled Ford station wagon to a stop, he turned and looked at her. Her sparkling eyes met his and he recognized the look. She had "been told something." Other descriptions of being told something were always the same. She did not hear voices; she did not go into a trancelike state; she just *knew*! She *knew* the boy was caught on the train tracks. She *knew* the toaster was shorting out at the Baranellos'. She *knew* the squirrel was going to be hit by the car.

"What is it, Jennie? What should we do?" Bob always felt their roles reverse when Jennie "knew" something. He became the child, waiting to be told by his ten-year-old daughter what he should do. "Should we turn around, Jen, maybe head back home?" In his heart, he hoped that she would say yes. Home equaled a safe haven for both of them. The directness of Jennie's answer, unequivocal and indisputable, startled even her father.

"We have to go to the races." Bob had learned long ago that the obvious question "Why?" was superfluous. Jennie did not know why and only became more agitated because she didn't have an answer for her own father. He now knew enough not to ask. Without another word, he checked his rear-view mirror and pulled back onto the highway, heading for the races and wondering with fatherly concern what the day had waiting for Jennie.

Al and his pit crew without Charlie Bechholdt, who had not been feeling well since the middle of the week, drove up the Pike to Ethan Becker's early in the morning. Billie Jensen and Johnnie Crusoe wondered why Al had been so insistent that they get an early start. They had always traveled in tandem with Ethan Becker, and the Laurelwood track certainly posed no problem as to travel time. Like any good pit crew, their loyalty overcame any questions they might have. They were sure that the Indianapolis pit crews of drivers like Bill Vukovich and Tony Bettenhausen didn't question their jockeys on race day, so they went along with Al's request, positive he had good reasons for what he was doing.

After arriving at Ethan's garage so early that it looked as if no one in the apartment house was even awake, they loaded the race car on the trailer as quietly as possible and in record time. Al left a note on the door of the garage saying that he decided to get to the track early to check out some things on his car and did not want to bother Ethan and his family.

When they arrived at the track, the gates to the pits had just opened and, in the tradition of first come, first served, were given a good pit position, just a short way from the starting line. One of the crews that had come in earlier already had its car off the trailer. The four men were swarming over it in preparation for the practice runs before the time trials, so intent on their jobs that they didn't notice Al and his entourage slide by into the pit in front of them. Billie and Johnnie could not help but notice that Al, known as one of the calmest drivers on the loop, seemed to have his adrenaline flowing copiously, even this early in the day. They both wished that good old Charlie wasn't under the weather; perhaps he could have calmed Al down a bit.

About an hour later, his car prepared for the time trials, Al leaned against the vehicle and waved to Ethan, Ross and the rest of his crew as the passed by on the way to their position much farther down the line.

"What the hell-you're pretty anxious today." Ethan hollered from his truck window. Al glanced at him but found that he could not make eye contact; instead, he looked at the top of the truck. His adrenaline was indeed working overtime at the moment.

"Sorry, Ethan. We just decided to come a bit early and didn't want to bother you. Still the same deal, right? I'll test-run you and you'll do the same?"

Al had no idea what he'd if Ethan decided against their traditional arrangement but he wasn't really worried. He felt more than confident that everything would work out as planned. Ethan clutched superstitions as if they were the word of God handed down from Mount Sinai and he wouldn't change anything if he could help it.

"Of course, man! We don't change anything we don't have to. I'll catch up with you after the time trials." The surging relief that Al felt quickly became as emotional as it was physical. He had to get at Ethan's car just before the race started and now he saw that at least that part of his plan would work. Determined as he was to see the plan through, he wondered if either his increasing hatred for Ethan Becker and his fully ripened love for Ethan Becker's wife would be strong enough to force his final step.

The time trials continued all morning long. By noon, the roofed grandstand behind the starter had filled, the true race fans enjoying the qualifying efforts of the drivers even though they were not actually competing with each other. Today's racing card included six heats of eight laps with sixteen cars in each. The formation of each heat would be established strictly on the basis of the time trials. A rotation system determined which cars raced in which heat, the ultimate goal being to have the twenty-five-lap feature race at the end of the card composed of the fastest cars. The feature event comprised the top three cars in each of the heats, a total of eighteen cars. The owners of the track were always being petitioned by the drivers to allow fewer cars to race in each event, as the danger factor on the half-mile oval increased proportionally to the number of cars racing. The promoters, of course, were well aware that the danger factor filled the stands with paying customers and were reluctant to take away the excitement inherent in having sixteen to eighteen cars jockeying for position.

Al Stuart and Ethan Becker pushed their cars to the limit during the time trials. Al drove especially hard to win the pole position, given to the fastest car in each heat. He wanted to be in front when the race started and in front when it finished. Starting on the inside, in the first row, would make his race easier as long as his car held up.

At twelve-thirty, the announcer read off the names of the drivers, their car numbers, and their starting positions for each heat. Al and his crew cheered lustily when his position in the second heat was announced. He had won the pole position with an average lap speed of eighty-six miles per hour. Ethan Becker, whose car did not perform quite as well, would be racing in the same heat, but starting in the fifth row.

One more brick of the foundation of Al's plan had fallen into place. If they were both racing in the same heat, they would be testing each other's car at the same time, with little or no time for Ethan to discover anything amiss with his car until it would be too late.

Al began to feel as if fate or destiny or some other force had taken over, struggling to rationalize his murderous strategy as nothing more than justice being served; there would be no stopping the momentum now.

The first heat had just concluded, an exciting race for the true fans but not so exciting for the thrill seekers. All sixteen cars actually finished the heat, with the battle for third place and a spot in the feature race providing the most excitement. It was a dead heat, impossible to call, as the checkered flag waved and the cars crossed the finish line in a blur. The loudspeaker blared that an official decision would be announced momentarily. The competitors in the second heat were given permission to take to the track for practice and warm-ups. As was their tradition, Al's crew helped to start Ethan Becker's car. They pushed Al out onto the track in Ethan's number 21. Al drove slowly at first, letting the car warm to its peak efficiency. As he came past the pit area after his first test lap, he noticed his car, with Ethan driving, being pushed out onto the track.

Al, thinking more clearly and calmly than he could have imagined, estimated he would have less than two minutes alone with Ethan's car. He had chosen a place in the pits where he would stop, instead of driving to Ethan's assigned area. By the time Ethan's crew maneuvered through the pit area, crowded with vehicles of every description, he could have been under the car and "checked out" the problem. When Ethan arrived, the announcer would have already called the cars to the track for heat two, leaving no time for any last minute checking.

Al decided to take two additional laps, then pull into the pit area. He opened the throttle and wove in and out of the cars on the track in various stages of warm-up and preparation. As he passed Ethan on the outer lane of the track, he formed an O with his thumb and index finger, raised the other three fingers and flashed the OK sign. He continued speeding around the track and, according to plan, pulled in and stopped the car in his carefully selected place. He quickly pulled on the hand brake, unsnapped his seat belt and pushed himself up and out of the car. Across the infield, at the far end of the pit area, he saw Billie and Johnnie talking with Ethan's crew. They had just noticed that Al had stopped, giving him just the time he had calculated he would need. The crews and drivers surrounding him were so absorbed in their own cars and problems that he might as well have been alone. He knelt down by the right front wheel and looked over his shoulder. No one paid the slightest attention to him. Lying quickly on his back, he slid partially under the car and reached for the tie rod end, pulling his adjustable wrench out of his pocket. In fifteen seconds he had taken several turns on the bolt, making it loose enough to turn by hand. Satisfied, he wiggled across the ground and assumed a kneeling position by the front wheel once again. He looked back around and saw Ethan making his way through the maze of trucks and cars and people filling the pits. Ross and the two crews trailed close behind. He stood up and brushed off the knees and backside of his pants.

"What's up, Al?" Ethan called, still a distance away. Al gathered himself for the next step.

"Oh, it's OK, Ethan. Thought I felt a bubble on the tire and wanted to check it out without going too far. Must have been one of those washboard sections on the backstretch. The car's perking along. Sure wish I was in some other heat than yours." Al couldn't believe how calmly he was able to lie.

"You'd better get back to your car, Al. They've called us. Good luck and...hey, Al...thanks a lot for checking." In that instant, Al looked past Ethan and saw Ross standing behind him. A phantom freight train loaded with guilt practically knocked him from his feet. A tornado blew through his mind, picking up debris from his years of friendship with Ethan and his special relationship with Ross. He was reeling, but Ross's voice broke through the whirling sludge stirred from the bottom layers of his memory.

"COME ON, AL! The race is going to start without you!"

"Why don't you watch with Billie, Ross?" Al called back over his shoulder as he sprinted to his own car, wishing sadly that he had more time to arrange exactly where Ross would be seeing the race. To regain his composure, he allowed an image of a picnic with Ross and Fay to block out the young boy's excited face. The three of them lay spread out on a blanket, laughing. Then he was at his car, climbing in and snapping on his seat belt as the boys pushed him toward the track.

Fay had heard the call from the starter for the cars to get on the track for the second heat. She had been to enough races to know that it would be about ten minutes before the process of lining up the cars for the start would be completed. She had time to find her way out of the grandstand and out to the spectator parking lot behind. She slowly made her way out to Billie Jensen's car, twenty or so rows back in the lot. Loretta Jensen had been drawn into the race scene by her husband's interest, which she referred to as more of an obsession. She enjoyed watching the races with Fay Becker. She knew that when any race involved Fay's husband, Fay spent the entire time engaged in saying the rosary in someone's car. It really didn't matter whose as long as the car was far from the track and Loretta was happy to oblige her request. Today Loretta thought Fay seemed more anxious than usual, but attributed that to this being her son Ross's first time in the pit area with his father instead of sitting with her. Loretta turned and watched through the space between the long splintered boards that made up the grandstand seats to be sure that Fay found her car, then directed her attention to the dusty track as the drivers arranged their cars into the proper starting alignment. Al Stuart had his dark red number 8 out in front, already aligned in the pole position. Several rows back, still finding his place, Ethan Becker throttled down to let three or four cars pass and then settled back into the fifth row. From her seat near the top of the grandstand, she had an outstanding view of the track. She looked down to her right at the first turn and the ominous embankment beyond the fence. A newspaper or magazine photographer had set his camera there, apparently for an attempt to capture in a still picture the thrill of the start as all sixteen cars came thundering toward him. For the spectator, the running start of a sprint-car race could be one of the most exciting and most dangerous moments in any sport. The misjudgment of a fraction of a second or a fraction of an inch on the part of any driver could cause a devastating multicar collision. Loretta, typical of most of the fans, felt her heart pick up its pace in tandem with the drivers picking up the pace as they approached the starter's green flag.

In the Jensen's car, Fay began her ritual of the rosary. The difference today was that she felt such a profound crisis of guilt, religious doubt, and ambivalence that she was sure that even the most merciful God could never forgive her. She thought of the Christmas Eve services when Ethan would set foot in the church for his once-a-year visit and the jokes from her family about lightning striking or the roof caving in. Using the rosary to pray for the outcome of this race suddenly seemed to her to be the most sacrilegious act she had ever committed. She stopped in mid "Hail Mary" and rolled the length of the beads into a ball and clasped both hands around them. She closed her eyes and lowered her head, determined to stay that way until someone came to tell her the outcome. She fervently hoped that someone would be Al Stuart.

As the second heat careened to its climax, Jennie knew, she *knew*, she had to do something. She glanced over at her father, saw that he had been absorbed in the dramatic last lap of the race, and quietly slipped out of her seat. Not knowing why, she exited the grandstand by the rear stairs and started toward the first turn of the track. Behind her, she heard the crowd cheering and she walked faster.

"I'm supposed to be there to help." A burly man with a cheerful face was walking beside her. Jennie looked up at him and knew he was right. She found this aspect of her gift most disturbing; the older she became, the more disturbing the knowledge that she always knew what was supposed to happen. This man needed to be there to help also. She *knew* it!

"Thank you!" Jennie replied, as if whatever was happening occurred on a daily basis. Nothing else needed to be said.

At that moment, a loud crack, like a rifle shot, drew Jennie's attention back to the racetrack. The cheers of the crowd, exhorting on their favorite on, turned to a loud, collective gasp. Jennie saw the white pieces of the broken fence on the first turn settling back to earth and, within seconds, was caught up in the spectators' rush to the scene of the accident. The starter bypassed the yellow warning flag and frantically waved the red flag, telling the drivers to stop. Jennie, in front of the surging crowd, ducked under the outside fence, looked back toward the stands, saw the other cars slowing to a halt, and crossed the dirt track. She sprinted into the infield and noticed Ross among the gathering circle of pit crews and other drivers. She made her way to him, asked him the question, and delivered her message, all within seconds. His affirmative answer sent her scurrying across the track and partially down the embankment toward the overturned car. She felt almost invisible to the masses of people collecting on all sides of the accident. Gas fumes filtered up the hill and her nostrils filled with the toxic odor of aviation fuel. She felt a presence sidle up to her and knew now that her only responsibility was to nod to the muscular man standing beside her.

Ethan Becker, upside down and trapped by the white hot exhaust pipe laying across his only exit route, struggled to unsnap his seat belt. In the brief time required for the brawny, cheerful man to pull the exhaust pipe clear enough for Ethan to escape, Jennie had mingled with the crowd, gradually working her way back to her panicked father. Ethan had climbed the embankment, his "I'm OK" wave to the crowd becoming a shout to clear the area. The track fire equipment and crews arrived at the top of the first turn just in time to witness the explosion behind Ethan as the leaking fuel ignited after accumulating on the underside of the engine. The large trees surrounding the car absorbed the strongest part of the blast, providing a protective cushion for the crowds still straining to view the accident. Ethan Becker's number 21 racecar was now nothing but a smoldering, blackened skeleton of twisted metal.

Al Stuart had led the race from start to finish. From his position on the pole, he exploded out of the start in full throttle, ahead of the pack into the first turn and never looking back after that. He kept waiting, actually hoping, to see any of the warning flags waving from the starter's platform each time he came sliding out of the fourth turn. By the fifth lap, he began to worry that Ethan's car had not suffered any problems as a result of his tampering. Comfortably ahead, or so he thought, he throttled back his engine just a bit and became more aware of the total track environment. He thought of Fay and, knew exactly what she would be doing at this precise moment. He had no way of knowing that she had stopped saying the rosary. The intrusive and powerful thoughts of Fay preoccupied him so much that his racing concentration suffered. Midway through the sixth lap, as he cruised down the backstretch, he heard the rumbleof another car, the deep resonating sound echoing off the tall trees lining the far side of the track.

With just two and a half laps to go, he felt confident that he could respond to any challenge on the track, but the thought of facing Fay with the failure of his wonderful plan presented a different problem. He had no idea how he would handle that. Coming off the second turn and barreling down the backstretch, Al glanced over his right shoulder and saw the familiar 21 painted on the nose of the car now pushing him for the lead.

"Ethan!" he thought, the irony slapping him in the face. Not only was the plan a flop but now he could even lose the race to the man he had thought could be dead by now. The two cars leaned deeply into the third turn. Al kept his car low through the turn, forcing Ethan to stay high on the banked curve, unable to gain any ground. As they came off the fourth turn, Ethan closed the gap by pushing his car to its limit. The starter signaled one lap to go and they could both sense the tension in the crowd as they roared by. As the front of Ethan's car moved into Al's peripheral vision, he thought he noticed a slight wobble in the front end. He looked farther back and saw Ethan beginning to fight the steering wheel. Unconsciously, Al slowed his car and looked over again. The first turn loomed ahead, microseconds away, and he saw Ethan cover his face with his hands and give up. Al's shoulders sagged as he realized that Ethan was going through the fence. Concerned with maneuvering his own car through the turn, Al didn't see the car leave the track, but even the noise of his engine couldn't cover the collective sigh of the crowd that resounded across the track. Al began to construct the upcoming scenario with Fay and Ross, a scenario that once again was blocked out by the guilt-ladened, onrushing freight train. He crossed the finish line and pulled into the pits, his mind spinning in chaos.

Fay had sat in Loretta's car, head bowed for almost twenty-five minutes. She was not aware of the commotion at the first turn until the loud but muffled explosion slightly rocked the car. She looked toward the far end of the track, saw the rising plume of smoke, and thought of Ross with a suffocating mother's guilt. Her hands were wrapped around the ball of rosary beads for so long that the cross made a deep indentation in her palm. She opened her profusely sweating hands, shaking out the beads into their original shape. She had never been so afraid in her life. She sat, numb, shocked, yet tingling with excitement at what she had become a part of, waiting for the next chapter to begin. She closed her eyes once more, not at all sure that she would ever be able to pray again.

Loretta Jensen's hand reached through the car window and touched Fay gently on the shoulder, not wanting to frighten her. Fay opened her eyes, startled to see Loretta and not Al.

Loretta had obviously been crying but her eyes were clear now.

"He's OK! He's OK!" Fay's state of mind prevented her from immediately comprehending exactly what Loretta meant. Gradually, the crushing reality of what Loretta was telling her washed over her like a wind-driven high tide, leaving in its wake a return to the despair and hopelessness she knew before she and Al fell in love. Suddenly, she needed desperately to see Al, as if maybe the failure of his plan had changed his feelings toward her.

Loretta launched into a vivid account of the terrifying accident, throwing in the phrase "lucky to be alive" at regular intervals. Finally, Fay pushed open the car door and said she needed to find Ross. She set off across the parking lot, her legs made of rubber and her stomach in a nervous network of knots.

Within days of the accident and of the unfortunate Charlie Beckholdt's funeral, the lives of the Beckers and Al Stuart resumed their normal pattern. Ethan was quite worried about his sanity, as he was convinced that the large, muscular man who helped him escape before the explosion was the affable Charlie Beckholdt. The events of the day had proved that to be impossible. The timing of Charlie's death was duly recorded and had occurred at least a half hour before the accident at the track. The appearance of the little girl with Charlie, and Ross's contact with her, remained a puzzle but the trials of everyday life have a way of trampling on the mysteries, submerging them deep beneath the realities. It would be three years before the mystery again became a factor in the life of the Beckers.

Al Stuart and Fay Becker resumed their Friday-night escapes, discouraged by the result of the abortive attempt to change the direction of their lives. For the immediate future, they mutually agreed that neither of them could generate enough energy or courage for another try, perhaps waiting for a just destiny to intervene in some other way. They did not believe for an instant that divine or human intervention of any sort was on the horizon. No choice existed for them. Teetering on the edge of reality and illusion, they struggled to maintain their meager grip on prudence and good judgment.

Friday, April 4, 1951

WORKING THINGS OUT
ETHAN BECKER'S VERSION

Another racing season was on its way after a long and colder than usual winter. Fay Becker and Al Stuart decided to work at keeping Al's friendship with Ethan as a high priority. It provided Al with excuse after excuse to visit the Becker household and to continue to strengthen his relationship with Ross. Any suspicion that Ethan might entertain could be deflected under the guise of a mutual friendship. As distasteful as Al found the arrangement, he agreed with Fay that their relationship was so important that they needed to handle it this way, at least for the present.

The regular Friday-night pattern proceeded without interruption throughout the winter. Ross joined them on only one or two occasions; the attraction of the festive Johnson household provided much more to him than any games that Fay and Al could offer. The time Al spent with Fay only increased in importance and intensity since the debacle of what they now referred to as the Ethan's "mystery survival," an event they added to their list of euphemisms, in the same category of the "Roosevelt walk" and the "bathrobe incident." When either of them mentioned any of the special shared events, a perfect catalog of memories would be triggered, shared silently if others were present.

Fay planned to make this Friday a very special one. One of Ross's uncles had offered to take him to the theater for the new 3-D movie, "Fort Ti," replete with a cartoon and Three Stooges short subject, all in 3-D as well. Ethan said he was sure to be home late from work and Fay could not wait for Al to arrive.

Ross left for the movie before Al arrived. Fay went directly to her room, undressed and put her on freshly washed silken bathrobe. A few minutes later, she heard Al climbing the back stairs. She stood back in the hall away from any light as he knocked on the door.

From the darkness of the interior hall, she called softly, "It's open, come on in."

A little hesitantly, Al entered the kitchen. Expecting Fay to be in the living room, he started down the hall. Fay reached behind her and switched on the overhead light , at the same time untying the sash on her robe and letting it fall open.

"Care to have another bathrobe incident?" she asked provocatively. Al quickly slipped his arms around her back under her robe. His hands relished the feel of the smoothness of her skin on his palms and fingers on the front and the silk of her robe as he pulled her to him. After one long, passionate kiss, he led her into the bedroom. Fay glanced at the clock as she reclined on the bed, watching Al undress.

"Six-thirty," she thought. "We have at least two and a half hours." She found herself shivering in anticipation.

What had been scheduled as a three-hour dinner meeting with all of the department managers at Manley Ford came to an abrupt end after only an hour. After the meal, John Manley stood, called the meeting to order, and announced that all departments had met or surpassed the established quotas for the month of March. He was extremely pleased with everyone's performance and had just one other announcement before the meeting adjourned. He called Ethan Becker to the front of the room and, to the surprise of all present, including Ethan, read the announcement that would be posted throughout the dealership in the morning.

"Effective May 1, 1951, Ethan Becker will become general manager of Manley Ford. He will oversee the managers of all departments and should be considered as acting in my stead in the event that I am absent from the dealership. He will be second in command of the entire operation." Manley made the announcement in his usual booming and authoritarian voice, leaving no doubt what it meant.

"This meeting is adjourned." He reached over and shook Ethan's hand, whispering in his ear that of course a substantial raise would be forthcoming with the position.

Ethan could only stammer "Thank you" before John Manley disappeared. Ethan's managers, for they were indeed now "his" managers, instantly surrounded him, patting his back and shaking his hand. Trying to outperform one another, they began immediately to ingratiate themselves. In a short time, Ethan decided he had enough of them falling all over him and excused himself. He had no doubt that many, if not most, of the department managers had visualized Manley bestowing the same honor on them. For tonight, the professional but often petty jealousy could be put aside, but he realized that at some point in the future it would certainly show itself again. For now, at age thirty, he was sure he was the youngest dealership general manager in the entire Ford organization, perhaps even in the auto industry.

Ethan had told Fay about the late dinner meeting and thought he just might hit Mel's on the way home to celebrate a little. As he walked to his car, he decided instead to proceed right home. He loved every chance he could get to rub the noses of the Johnson family in his success, and for once, he looked forward to getting home. He thought Al might be working in the garage also, and he would be glad to share this news with anyone who would listen. He glanced at his watch; this would be the earliest he had come on a Friday for years.

Fay and Al, preoccupied, didn't hear Ethan's car crunch its way up the driveway. When he slammed the car door, they both sat straight up in bed.

"Oh God, it's Ethan! I know it is. What the hell?" Fay did not answer her own question, nor did Al. He grabbed his clothes, scattered over two chairs and the floor, and tried to put on everything at once. His predicament would have made a wonderful sight gag for Red Skelton but he knew this could be serious. Fay shouted for him to take everything into the bathroom and dress there. She, meanwhile, slipped into a pair of slacks hanging on the door and put on a work-around-the-house sweater, not taking the time for her panties or a bra. She smoothed the bedspread and looked at herself in the mirror. She thought she looked as if she should have a scarlet "A" stamped on her forehead.

Ethan had seen Al's car but no lights in the garage and figured he must be visiting Fay and Ross. He quickly crossed the yard and took the fire escape two steps at a time. From the bathroom just off the hall, Al heard the back door open. He didn't know what to expect when he came out, and wondered how Fay could possibly cover the situation. He took several deep breaths, almost hyperventilating, but finally brought his heart rate down to a rapid thud in his chest, an improvement from the chaotic fluttering of moments before. He glanced in the mirror and was relieved to see that his cheeks were drained of the bright red flush of sexual excitement and had returned to a relatively normal color. Through the hollow wooden door, he heard Ethan call out to Fay, who somehow was now sitting in her favorite living room chair.

"Surprised to see me, aren't you? Well, I've got some good news and I wanted to tell you about it." Entering the living room, Ethan quickly scanned the room. "I thought Al was here. His car's out back."

"He just went to the bathroom a minute ago. He'll be right out, I'm sure." Fay listened closely to her own voice, pleased that it sounded relatively normal.

"What about Ross; where is he?" Ethan listened as Fay explained that Ross had an invitation to go the movies, the 3-D movies, as if that made any difference to her husband. He thought she was speaking rather rapidly, more excited than the occasion warranted.

When the bathroom door opened, he turned to greet Al as he came into the room.

"Got some great news, Al! Mr. Manley is making me a general manager of the whole agency." Ethan enthusiastically embarked on a description of the dinner meeting, the wonderful way that Manley had made the announcement, and the jealousy of the other managers. He closed his story with the mention of the "substantial raise," a grin spreading across his face.

Al and Fay communicated by eye contact across the room, a bold relief shining in both their faces. Ethan, as usual, was so caught up in his own selfish world that he didn't suspect anything.

"We probably could've been sitting on the couch holding hands and he wouldn't have noticed," Fay thought to herself.

Al, remembering the old saying that discretion is often the better part of valor, congratulated Ethan and apologized for needing to be on his way. He said goodnight to Fay and quickly walked toward the back door.

"See you on Sunday, Ethan," he called back, remembering that this was the first spring day to run their race cars at the practice oval. "Supposed to be good weather, I think." Then he was out the door. Fay listened to his fading footsteps and, a minute later, heard his car start.

In that instant, as she looked over at Ethan, already sitting in his chair with the newspaper in front of him, she wished with all her heart that Al's plan of last Memorial Day had been successful. She stood, drawing Ethan's attention from his paper. "That's really great news, Ethan. When does it start again?"

"First of May. I'll ask for a few more details about the raise tomorrow." An even wider grin split Ethan's face, almost in half, it seemed. This smile, more of a smirk really, carried something else with it, something unsettling to Fay. His smile gradually turned into a familiar Ethan Becker leer.

"Come on over here, Fay. I think we should celebrate a little tonight." An icy shiver shot through Fay. She had hoped to beat an inconspicuous path to her bedroom and change into her nightgown.

Fay's mind whirled as she fought to remain calm. "Let me change into something a little more comfortable," she said, hoping to sound at least a trifle interested. The line came out sounding like something from a poorly written movie script. Ethan didn't fall for it. He motioned with an infuriating wave for Fay to join him over at his favorite recliner. She was paralyzed with fear, with loathing, with a catalog of negative emotions. She slowly crossed over to him, not knowing what would happen next, feeling that it would be a very interesting scene to watch but certainly not to be a participant in.

Predictably, as soon as she was within his grasp, he slid his hands under her old sweater. If finding her naked surprised him, he didn't show it. Instead, he methodically caressed her right breast, sliding his left hand down past the elastic waistband of her slacks. When his hand reached the smooth skin of her well-rounded derriere, he stopped moving altogether. He quickly withdrew both hands and folded them in his lap.

"Perhaps it would be better if you changed into something more comfortable, Fay." When Fay looked down at him, his expression had changed from one of lust to a blazing, unadulterated anger and she wondered why he seemed to be allowing her to escape.

"OK, Ethan. I'll see you in the bedroom." Fay tried, valiantly but probably unsuccessfully to keep up the facade of piqued desire. Knowing intuitively that Ethan had lost interest, she knew that was not a good sign. She turned away and practically ran to the bedroom, leaving Ethan sitting perfectly still, his hands still folded in his lap.

Ethan didn't move from his chair for a long time. He was remembering in detail a scene from a long time past. During a furious lovemaking session with Rose McGowen, a door-to-door salesman had rapped loudly on Rose's door, causing a panic in the two lovers, who were certain they had been caught. They had frantically gathered their clothes, Ethan heading for the bathroom and Rose slipping on anything she could find to cover herself. After she sent the salesman scurrying down her walk, muttering to himself about her unfriendly, even vicious reception, they had reconvened in her bedroom. Ethan had laughed about her ingenuity in getting dressed so quickly, whereupon Rose unzipped her slacks. As they slipped to the floor, she pulled her old sweater up over her head, smiling at Ethan as she stood there in radiant nakedness.

"That bastard, screwing my wife in my own house!" His next thought concerned vengeance and how best to extract it. Then he went to the bedroom, as if nothing had happened, and made angry, violent love to his adulterous wife.

The first Sunday of the new spring race season dawned clear but with a residual chill of winter still hanging in the morning air. It had taken all winter for Ethan to build his new car, working often in below-freezing temperatures in the garage and with abominable lighting conditions. Ethan had spent the entire season the year before looking for rides after his accident, usually able to find one each Sunday. His driving reputation was sound and there always seemed to be someone looking for a driver. This year he had his own car again and was desperately anxious to try it out on Sunday.

Al's crew were able to get his car ready for a few practice runs by working at Ethan's garage most of Saturday while Al had to work. Obsessed with what happened the night before, Ethan took Saturday off to prepare his car as well. He thoroughly enjoyed the company of Billie Jensen and Johnnie Crusoe as they rehashed race story after race story; there seemed no end to the possibilities. As they worked on preparing the cars for the first tests of the year, many of the reminiscences involved their old comrade Charlie Beckholdt. He had been an integral part of the group that gathered at Ethan's garage and everyone missed him dearly. In his muddled state, Ethan chose not to resurrect his belief that Charlie had saved his life, along with that little girl, whoever she might be. Instead, he quietly worked on his own car, the mechanical focus relieving some of the building need for suitable revenge against the duplicity and betrayal of his wife and best friend.

A short while after the lunch break, Billie Jensen lay on his back on the mechanic's dolly under Al's car, checking the dozens of bolts that needed close attention. From his awkward position looking up through the engine compartment, he had just directed his attention to the tie rod ends when he remembered one of Charlie's favorite stories.

"Hey, remember Charlie talking about Jeff Knowlton's horrible accident, all because of a tie rod bolt?" Billie called up to no one in particular. "Better check yours carefully, Ethan, especially in that new rig you'll be chauffeuring."

Ethan was practically upside down in his engine compartment, focusing intently on the bolts holding the heads and head gaskets in place. As Billie's suggestion drifted over to him, he filed it away in the "to-do" part of his brain. He had never been able to reconstruct what had caused his other car to crash, the explosion obliterating any evidence.

Suddenly, his focus shifted from the mechanical process in front of him to the day of the accident. Pieces of a frightening puzzle began to slide toward each other. Jeff Knowlton had lost his steering due to tie rod malfunction, a fact that Al Stuart would have been well aware of because of Charlie's memorable way of telling his stories. The day of the accident, Al tested his car right before the race, parking it in a place where it would be impossible to determine what he may have done to it. Finally, Ethan had noticed the handling of the car gradually becoming more difficult as the race proceeded, culminating in the tight race down the straightaway past the grandstand, when the steering finally gave out altogether. The interlocking pieces of the puzzle snapped into place.

"They tried to kill me and damn near succeeded." The realization that his friend and possibly even his wife were involved in a plot to take his life was numbing. Rationally, he knew that what happened last night made all the other pieces perfectly logical as well. He extracted his body from the engine, straightened up and stretched, trying to loosen the muscle kinks as he regained his composure. The cry for revenge, last night a whisper, now screamed inside his head. He looked around the garage at the two cars, the men working on them, the sun streaming through the window, the tools hanging neatly on the wall, and everything turned into surreal images, floating before his eyes. One of the very few biblical verses he knew echoed in his head.

"Vengeance is mine, saith the Lord!" Ethan Becker knew, right then and right there, that vengeance would be his, and soon.

The blank, cold look on Ethan's face should have attracted Al's attention that Sunday morning, particularly after the Friday-night adventure. Instead, he went directly to the task of preparing the cars for the trip to the gravel pit. Initial loading everything in the spring required considerably more time and almost two hours passed before the two were on the trailers and ready to go. Ross came home from Sunday Mass. Resuming the tradition, he changed and came down to the garage to announce that Fay had the coffee brewed. Al was the first to respond to the invitation, asking if anyone would like him to bring the coffee out to the garage. No one accepted his offer so he followed Ross to the house, thankful that the other boys were still engaged in the various details of preparation. Perhaps he could have a brief visit with Fay before they had to leave. By the time Al and Ross reached the top of the fire escape, Ethan was on his way across the yard to the apartment. Al pushed open the door and found Fay in the kitchen, seemingly calm but with small worry lines creasing her face. Her reserved greeting remained unchanged as she saw Ross immediately behind him. With barely enough time to say hello before Ethan came into the kitchen, Fay could not communicate her concern. Ethan had been acting strangely quiet and cold since he had come to their bed Friday night. She had never seen Ethan so aroused and she matched his passion with her own, thinking about Al the entire time. As Ethan neared his climax, he had grabbed her hands and pinned them over her head, forcing himself deeper and deeper inside. As he began to groan with pleasure, she had opened her eyes to find him looking down at her, his eyes filled with a strange mixture of ecstasy, anger, and hatred. The look had thoroughly frightened her, especially when he spoke not a single word afterward, just moving off her, turning his back, and falling asleep almost instantly. After the Saturday work session on the cars, his quiet attitude had assumed ever more frightening proportions. She fervently wished for just a moment alone with Al but Ethan's presence in the apartment made that impossible.

Ethan, who always asked Ross to bring his coffee out to the garage, surprised them by pouring his own cup and picking up a cream-filled pastry to take with him. He did not acknowledge either Fay or Al's presence, instead directing his attention to Ross.

"Hey, boy, how'd you like to come and watch the practices today?" Ross could not believe what he heard. "I think maybe today your Uncle Al and I will put on a show. What do you think, Al?"

Now it was Al's turn to be surprised. "Sure, Ethan, whatever you say." Fay, Al, and Ross exchanged glances, all for differing reasons, none of them knowing how to take the offer. The excited look in Ross's eyes offset the worried look in Fay's. Al still searched Fay's expression for some clue, but found nothing but anxiety and apprehension, a look that could easily have said, "Please be careful!"

"OK, then let's go get this over with", Ethan announced, with some degree of resignation. The subtlety with which Ethan expressed his "let's move it out" order was lost on his audience of three in the Becker's kitchen. The two men, followed by an increasingly vociferous and excited young boy, picked up their coffee and pastries and headed out to the waiting trailers. Fay moved to the window and saw Al look back up to her, his left hand extended almost in a salute. She suddenly experienced a sense of foreboding sharing the kitchen with her, so heavy that its tangible quality threatened to envelop her. She found herself swinging her arms back and forth, as if the breeze she created could make it disappear.

Since the first time Ethan Becker had brought his friends to the gravel pit oval, the development around it had begun in earnest. John Manley's fortune was a reality and several huge tracts of land now were home to housing developments. The homes for the most part were of the inexpensive variety, catering to the thriving and ever-expanding lower middle class. As promised by a succession of politicians, they searched for the classic American dream-their own home with a car in every garage and a chicken in every pot. The population density around the practice oval had thickened to the point that visionary commercial developers could foresee large profits on the horizon from shopping centers, supermarkets, and all sorts of other enterprises.

Ethan knew that in the near future, Manley would be selling the practice oval, even though it was located in the least desirable area of his enormous landholdings. He had even thought that this might be the last year for the oval to be available to the two crews, but he regularly expressed his appreciation to his boss for allowing them to use it for the time they had. As the trucks and race car trailers drove to the oval now, the boys had to pass through several town roads and saw houses in various stages of construction. By next year, people would be living in these houses and would certainly be more than a little averse to listening to the throbbing, unmuffled noise of sprint cars roaring around what, in reality, was their neighborhood.

This late Sunday morning, the prospect of development of his private practice area could not have been farther from Ethan Becker's mind. The weekend had been a blur of charged emotions, all of them negative. Since Friday night, when he realized that his faithless wife and his scheming, disloyal friend had hung the horns of the cuckold around his neck, he had thought of nothing but revenge. On Saturday, as the men worked on the cars and the pieces of that repulsive puzzle came together, he knew that exacting his retribution could not wait. Any evidence that Al had tampered with his car last Memorial Day had long since been eradicated and he knew that he would sound like a foolish paranoiac if he tried to explain to the police that his wife and friend tried to kill him. No, he had to do this on his own, with no one else allowed in on the scheme. He spent much of Saturday night lying next to his slut of a wife, staring at the ceiling above his head, replaying in his mind every twist and turn of the practice oval. Eventually, the ceiling took on the characteristics of a movie screen and he watched his plan come to fruition time after time.

Ethan was sure he could entice Al into a practice run where they would push the limits of safe speeds but could also practice driving the cars in extremely close proximity. Al had often mentioned that this was a weak point in his driving ability and he needed to eliminate the bad habit of backing his car off ever so slightly when he was challenged. Two race cars at full throttle down a straightaway fighting for the lead in the race often were within inches of each other. Ethan knew Al would accept his offer to practice the split-second maneuvering, even though the actual start of the race season was still weeks away. Ethan watched this practice session on the on the ceiling over and over, perfecting his technique during a night of restlessness and malevolent conspiring within himself. The brilliant idea to bring Ross along had come much later in the night. What better way to heap more suffering on Fay than to have her son witness her lover's death? Hadn't that bitch allowed Ross to be in the pits when she probably knew that his own father would be killed? Ethan thought of that day so long ago when he forced Ross to drown the kitten and relished the chance to build yet more character in his young son. He knew how Ross idolized Al Stuart.

The cars circled the track for a full fifteen minutes and were well warmed up. Ethan was more than satisfied with the performance of his new car. He and Al had kept the usual practice separation of five hundred feet, but now the time came for Ethan to transfer his plan from the bedroom ceiling to the track. As they passed a small group of curious onlookers, Ethan slowed his car, drifting toward the left side of the track, and motioned for Al to come up along side of him. The engine noise from the two cars obliterated any chance of conversation between the two drivers but they had worked out the logistics of practicing the close-proximity strategies ahead of time. If both cars were performing well after a lengthy warm-up, they would spend several laps practicing what Al had said he really needed to work on. Ethan made a circular motion with his right hand and held up three fingers, indicating that they would take three more laps around the track as they had planned. Al responded with a nod and moved into position on the outside of the track, his car just inches ahead of Ethan's. In tandem, they gained speed, keeping the two cars in their identical positions. They passed their crews, now watching with renewed interest as their drivers began to practice some of the finer points of racing. The sand-and-gravel track had not received the benefit of an exact land survey and the banking on the turns was somewhat uneven, forcing the drivers to slow so the cars did not slide off into the soft shoulders edging the packed surface. As they came off the second turn and entered the backstretch, both drivers accelerated, disappearing from the view of their crews as the land contours sloped away. Ross, never having been to the oval before, watched as the cars seemed to vanish into the clouds of dust hovering close to the ground. In just seconds, they rose out of the slope and roared into the third turn, so close that they appeared from the distance to be one car with eight wheels. Shifting down and braking for the turn, they stayed together and soon were speeding by the excited crews, then slowing for the first turn. They disappeared beyond the slope once again and Ross looked to the end of the backstretch for their appearance out of the dust and fumes. From just behind, Ross heard the voice of Billie Jensen exclaiming, "*Holy shit*!" Ross's head jerked back to look at Billie, his glance ricocheting from Billie's eyes across the track in the same motion. Ross could not comprehend what he was seeing. One of the cars was completing the third of a series of end-over-end flips, only coming into view above the slope when the car was up on end. The distance across the track absorbed most of the sound of the crash, creating a strange silent-film effect. Billie already was on the dead run toward his truck when the other race car emerged from the dust on the backstretch and made the turn, not braking at all this time. As the car came out of the final turn,

Ross watched intently and a deep sense of shame settled in the pit of his stomach. A disturbing comprehension spread over him. He guiltily understood that he was hoping to see Al's car come out of the clouds of exhaust and dust. Instead, the gleaming maroon paint of his father's new # 21 reflected the sun as it came hurtling down the straightaway. The car skidded to a long, slow stop on the sand and gravel, throwing dirt in every direction. Ethan had his seat belt unsnapped before the car stopped and started barking directions before he even got out of the car.

"Somebody find a phone and get an ambulance here quick", he shouted. "Al's crashed," Ross, on the verge of going into shock, thought irrationally of the second grade nun explaining with painful patience the difference between declaratory and exclamatory sentences. As he sprinted toward his father, he wondered how Ethan could be using simple declaratory sentences in a situation that cried out for exclamations.

As Ethan had spent most of Saturday and Saturday night tracing every nuance of the practice oval, he arrived at the logical conclusion that the Sunday practice presented a perfect opportunity to satisfy his obsessive need to get even. He knew it was highly unlikely that anyone suspected what he knew about Al and Fay but even the most remote possibility that someone could find out sent tremors of rage through him. He had to bring closure to the issue in an indisputable fashion and his practice track provided a fitting and just location for vengeance.

Over the years, the sand and gravel had become solidly packed in the two racing lanes, although the narrow shoulder was still soft. If a car drifted onto the shoulder at anything approaching a racing speed, the effect would be the same as being drawn into a deep, soft puddle of mud. Any effort to steer out of it would be like trying to steer out of a snowbank; the car would develop a tendency to slide even farther to the right. The backstretch was actually seven or eight feet lower than the beginning of the oval. The difference could not be detected by the naked eye; it was so subtle that it would have taken a survey crew to establish it. For a practice track, the slope was fine, although no actual racetrack would have been built without correcting such a flaw. As Ethan went over the track in his mind, the fact that the backstretch could not be seen from where the crews always set up to observe practice would work dramatically to his advantage. He thought again of the Lord exacting His revenge and decided it must be fate that the track happened to be arranged in this configuration.

Unlike the abortive attempt of Al Stuart to remove Ethan from the planet, Ethan's scheme worked to perfection. As the cars were taken from their trailers, Ethan issued a casual invitation to Al to practice a few racing techniques, an invitation eagerly accepted. When Ethan motioned to Al to pull up alongside, both cars were running well and there appeared to be no reason not to proceed with the practice. The two cars passed the watching crews the second time and rounded the second turn, sliding into the backstretch and disappearing from sight. Ethan had edged quickly ahead by half a car length and looked to his left, seeming to be distracted. The distraction had been carefully incorporated into his plan. He wanted an alibi should Al survive the crash. The cars had reached peak straightaway speed when Ethan's car suddenly lurched to the right. Al reacted instinctively to avoid a collision, pulling the car sharply to the right as well. The right front wheel dug into the sandy shoulder, softer than usual from the spring rains. Ethan glanced quickly over his right shoulder and saw the right side of Al's car dip sharply, the tail end beginning to rise from the ground. Ethan moved out farther to his left and slowed slightly, enough so he could again glance backward. Al's car had begun its end-for-end flip, hopelessly beyond control. Ethan sped off into the third turn, preparing to play out his next part as panicked comrade and he hoped, grief-stricken friend.

"Vengeance is mine, saith the Lord," he thought.

In the flash of the instant Al knew he was about to die, his adrenaline rush slowing everything to a crawl, he knew everything, struck with a sadness he had no time to savor. He watched an instantaneous flashback, a picnic with Fay and Ross sprawled out on a blanket, beckoning him to join them. Then, everything went black.

The ambulance arrived, sirens wailing and lights flashing, but everyone surrounding the crushed skeleton of the car knew they might as well have called the hearse. Ross watched from behind the inner ring of people surrounding the car, experiencing for the second time in less than a year the terrifying feeling that he had lost someone very important to him. For some reason he did not cry, even as the rescue workers pulled Al from the wreckage and placed him on the stretcher. They proceeded through the motions of helping him hold on to life, trying valiantly to save him the indignity of dying in front of this small crowd.

As soon as Al had been placed in the ambulance, Ethan took Ross by the hand. They went to the truck and followed the ambulance to the hospital. Even at age eleven, Ross understood why the ambulance did not run any red lights or speed past other cars. Billie and Johnnie followed in their truck as well, leaving Ethan's crew to pick up what they could, knowing that they would be coming back for what remained of Al's racing gear and car.

Even without speeding, the flashing lights got the ambulance to the hospital first. After Ethan and Ross parked the car following a silent trip, they found their way to the emergency room and were directed to take a seat in a small, windowless office just off the hallway leading to the ER. They were joined there moments later by Billie and Johnnie, their eyes glazed over with shock, looking as if their world had just ended. They were not yet seated when the door to Room 3 opened and Dr. DeGregorio walked straight toward them. The young doctor looked like an adolescent, a smattering of acne just fading from his face. His lean build seemed unable to bear the invisible burden he carried on his shoulders, and his entrance was somewhat hesitant, as though he would have done anything to be somewhere else at the moment.

Ethan stood as the doctor clumsily introduced himself to all four of them. All but Ross shook his hand. He came directly to the point, speaking in staccato phrases.

"Truly sorry...nothing we could do...severe head trauma...dead at the scene...."

Ethan took charge, telling the doctor that he would be back to him with arrangements and thanked him for his efforts.

"Sweet Jesus, I can't believe it," Billie whispered. "First Charlie, now this. Damn!"

Ross remained seated, staring straight ahead but hearing the conversation. He muttered a hollow goodbye to Billie and Johnnie as they left. Both men asked Ethan to call them as soon as he knew anything. The young doctor, his unpleasant task completed, left the waiting room, almost seeming to bow as he left. Alone now with his father, Ross dissolved as all his efforts to be grown up disappeared and any semblance of composure left him. His chin dropped to his chest and he sobbed uncontrollably.

"I really loved Al, Daddy," he managed to whimper, the first time he had called Ethan Daddy instead of Dad in years. The vulnerability of his son caught Ethan off guard momentarily, until he remembered why Al was under the sheet in the other room. With an insipid harshness, Ethan instructed his son to pull himself together.

"Let's go tell your mother," Ethan said, and Ross once again wondered about the use of a simple declarative sentence. The boy didn't notice the hint of gleeful anticipation lurking beneath the surface.

Memorial Day, May 30, 1951

BEGINNING THE DESCENT

> "And then, down we came with a sweep, a slide and a plunge that made me feel sick and dizzy, as if I was falling from some lofty mountaintop in a dream."
>
> —Edgar Allan Poe, *A Descent into the Maelstrom*

Fay knelt on the lightly padded but still uncomfortable bench in the last pew of St. Luke's Catholic Church. Ruefully, she thought back to the day exactly one year before when she became convinced she would never again be able to pray. Life is full of "if onlys," and Al's unsuccessful plan certainly fit into that category. If only Ethan Becker had died a dramatic racing death that day, this might have been the day she discarded her widow's weeds and started to prepare for a wonderful new life with Al Stuart.

"If only...." she said in a quiet and bitter whisper.

In the nearly two months since Al died, she came to the church in desperation, looking for answers. The despair and hopelessness she had thought would dissipate instead grew more overwhelming by the minute, or so it seemed. Her half-hearted prayer sessions had not made any difference other than to provide a physical haven for her while she sat in church. As soon as she walked into the bright, late spring sunshine, she was reminded of the hope Al had given her, the only real hope she had felt since her father died. She thought of Sandy Johnson often these days, remembering how certain she had been that some day he would return home, not just with trinkets from some merchant marine junket but with resources that could have pulled the family out of the life cycle of the poor. Then, he had been taken away from the family, and now she had lost Al, her salvation from the tyranny of Ethan Becker.

There was no doubt in her mind that Ethan had something to do with Al's death. When he came home that day with the news, he first sent a sobbing and disconsolate Ross to his room. Then he took her hand, not very gently, led her into the living room and made her sit on the sofa instead of in her favorite chair by the window. The apprehension she had felt that Sunday morning had led to premonitions all day long and she knew not only that Ethan had awful news, but also that it concerned Al.

"Al's dead-killed in an accident at the track today," he said. He followed this spirit-crushing news with another pronouncement, one spoken with an infuriating smugness.

"But you know all about unfortunate accidents, don't you? I'm sure you have many fond memories of Al that will keep you going." Without another word, he left the room. Fay sat there, stunned at first but strangely not surprised. She slowly stood up and went to Ross's room. He lay face down on the bed, his head buried in his pillow. She walked lightly over to him and shook his shoulder gently. He looked up and her heart broke. She held out her hand, pulled him up, and together they went downstairs to the Johnsons'.

Fay had always felt that Al's protective shell kept her sane. At times, playing the proverbial games of both ends against the middle, she had been ready to jump to whichever side held out the most hope. Now, there was only one end, and less than two months after Al had been killed, she believed she would go insane. She had stopped using the phrase "when Al died," substituting instead "when he was killed." In racing, if a driver had the misfortune to die in a crash at a track, the "he was killed" phrase was accepted as appropriate. For Fay, the simple but harsh phrase carried a far more sinister significance. Everyone at the site the day of Al's death agreed that what happened at the practice oval was an accident. Al had made a judgmental error, a microsecond in time, causing him to catch his right wheel in the soft shoulder. For her part, Fay would continue to use the phrase "he was killed' as an accurate description of what must have happened.

Ethan's apparent lack of grief for his friend, a disassociation from Al shown only in her presence, provided enough reason for her to think the worst. His callousness and aloofness toward both

Ross and her practically shouted that he attained some level of satisfaction in Al's death. When finally she came to accept without question that Ethan had somehow known about the affair and, most probably, about the Memorial Day accident plan, Fay's tenuous hold on her mental balance loosened. She had no idea how far the deterioration would go and was paralyzed with fear.

September 1954

THE ASCENT FROM THE MAELSTROM

For Ross, the three years following Al Stuart's death were a blur of bleak desolation, melancholy, and misery. He approached the new school year with a faint hope that attending Collins Heights High would broaden his scope of friends. His eight years in St. Luke's left him with a sound education and, at least the nuns hoped, a firm foundation in the faith that would survive the iniquities of the public school system. The anticipation of the first day of school filled Ross with the expected fear and trepidation of any freshman in a new school, although he did count among his friends a number of non-Catholics who would be joining him in the ninth grade. Many were the same friends who, the Dominican nuns had assured him, were already well on their way to hell, a constant puzzlement to Ross, who thought they were as good or better morally than he was.

Fay Becker had decided long before that eight years of Catholic school was sufficient to set Ross on the correct course. When Ross made the request to attend Collins Heights, her thinking was so muddled that she seemed hardly to understand what he was talking about. Witnessing his mother's gradual but inexorable withdrawal from active participation in his life had increased his dependency on the Johnsons, especially his grandmother. The public high school had certainly been good enough for her children. When her mother told Fay that she thought Ross would do just fine there, Fay numbly agreed to it.

The first day of high school was over, it seemed to Ross, before it began. The change in routine contained many dramatic differences from the one-nun classrooms of St.Luke's. His initial contact with the frenetic schedule of changing classes included a cleverly designed, motivational math game and an interesting lecture from Mrs. Ambruster on the wonders of Edgar Allan Poe. He met only half of his teachers on his first day, as each class time was doubled for orientation purposes. After an interminable homeroom period spent filling out forms, only enough time remained for double sessions of English and Introductory Algebra, with a double dose of physical education after lunch.

Ross received no math homework for the night but Mrs. Ambruster, determined to retain her status as the "toughest teacher in the department," assigned Poe's short story, "The Descent into the Maelstrom." She admonished the wide-eyed freshmen to look deep into the story, beyond the surface, and they sat and wondered what on earth she meant. Although her orientation speech convinced most of the students that they would never pass her class, she then had her freshmen hanging on every word as she ingeniously guided them toward truly wanting to read Poe's story. Whetting their appetites with tales of his personal life, Mrs. Ambruster had her students peeking at the story in their anthology even as she spoke. Ross actually looked forward to this reading assignment that night.

When the bell rang at the end of the day, Ross followed his ritual of the last several years, even though his route was slightly longer than it had been from St. Luke's. After a ten-minute walk to the downtown shopping area, during which the crowds of students heading home gradually thinned, he arrived at Pop's.

His brief visits with Pop had become a daily occurrence. His mother was not interested in anything he did these days and Pop would listen to him endlessly, or so it seemed to Ross. As he sat at the counter sipping his specially made chocolate milk shake, he filled Pop in on his first day at Collins Heights High School. Pop busily filled ice cream and frappe and shake orders for the noisy crowd of exuberant students filling his shop and Ross continued to talk to him, knowing he was listening from the occasional wink cast in his direction. Ross knew that if he returned later, when no one was in the shop, Pop would be able to question him about his day at school, remembering every detail of what Ross had told him. When he finished his shake, Ross slid off the stool, caught Pop's eye, and just nodded. The two exchanged glances and silently agreed that they would see each other the next day. As he walked the last three blocks home, he thought about how fortunate he was to know someone like Pop Hiller, and about why Pop had dropped into his life when he most needed him.

No one would be home yet at the Johnsons'. Ross reluctantly climbed the stairs to his apartment. He dreaded opening the door; he was never sure what state of mind his mother might be in. He hoped, somewhat guiltily, that she would be in her room. He slowly opened the apartment door, relieved that he could not hear the television in the living room. He closed the door quietly behind him and walked down the hall into his room, and softly shut the bedroom door. He threw his book bag on the bed and thought of how Fay greeted him when he came home from St. Luke's after the first day of a new school year. The crushing waves of sadness since Al's accident were less frequent, but thinking about his mother's old enthusiasm and interest generated a wave of misery. He sat down on the bed and stared out the window, embarrassing adolescent tears welling up in his eyes. He sorely missed the reassuring presence of Al Stuart, and now, sitting alone in his room, he realized that he missed his mother even more, and a pervading sense of hopelessness washed over him.

Ross reached into the book bag, and pulled out a new spiral notebook and his English anthology. He opened the almost virgin notebook to the inside front cover, glancing at the class schedule he had taped there. The classes for the second day also were doubled and he wondered if the Social Studies and the General Science teachers could match the good impressions made by the two academic teachers he had seen today. The family grapevine provided the information on Mr. Hancock. His science classes were lively, hands-on laboratories and Ross thought that could be interesting. Having just meager experience with science at St. Luke's, Ross already looked forward to General Science class the next day. He opened the notebook to the section he had set aside for English and looked at the first page, just Mrs. Ambruster's name and the reading assignment adorning it. Leaving the notebook open, he flipped through the anthology to the small piece of paper marking the assigned Poe story. With a picture of Mrs. Ambruster firmly in his mind, he decided that hc wanted desperately to be off to a good start in his new school and especially with his "tough" English teacher. Marking the page of his textbook with this finger, he rose from the bed, and crossed to the small desk in the corner. He set his book face down on the desk and reached over his head to the single shelf holding the few old St. Luke's books that he had not pitched onto the railroad tracks from the overpass that last day of school in June. Finding the thick hardbound copy of *Webster's World Dictionary,* Ross quickly searched for the word, *maelstrom.* Mrs. Ambruster had only hinted at its definition and he wanted to impress her if he had the chance in the next class. He noticed that the word was primarily defined as a large and dangerous whirlpool but it was the second definition that caught his attention. Perhaps this was what she had meant with her admonition to look beneath the surface. The maelstrom could also be applied to a mental condition, a dangerously agitated or violently confused state of mind. Ross picked up his notebook and scribbled both definitions under the assignment. "My first high school notes," he thought to himself. Then he filed the definitions away in his mind and began to read the story.

An excited and enthusiastic Jennie Proctor greeted her father with her usual rambunctious hug and began immediately to tell him every detail of her first day at Collins Heights High School. The transition from the small Lyndeboro Elementary School, with one self-contained classroom for each of the eight grades, to the large high school had been a great concern for Bob Proctor. Jennie had flourished in the small school and her classmates accepted her as she was, a sensitive young girl with an unusual inner glow. Many of them found her unique personality somewhat discomfiting but not at all unpleasant. With high school looming on the horizon, Bob had thought about sending her to the more protective environment of a private boarding school. Jennie categorically dismissed that idea, allaying Bob's fears with her customary self-confidence that she would be just fine. After all, her entire eighth-grade class was moving on to Collins Heights; it wasn't as it she would be alone. Besides, the practical matter of the expense of a private school should be considered as well. Bob knew Jennie was right. He had to face the difficult fact that she was indeed growing into a beautiful young woman, which again cast a pall of sadness over him. Jeanne would have loved this stage of Jennie's life; for a single father, it was a stage charged with potential danger and anxiety.

Jennie spent the better part of an hour re-creating her day at school for Bob. The teachers were wonderful, the new people she met were wonderful; in short and not unexpectedly, Jennie found everything at Collins Heights as positive and exhilarating as she found everything else about life. Jennie finished her exhaustive narration and was off to start her homework, calling back to Bob as she left the room, "Tomorrow, I'll get to meet my General Science teacher, Daddy. Everyone says he's really good!"

Bob Proctor just shook his head and wondered how any human being could have so much positive energy, and tried hard to absorb some of it for himself.

When he finished reading about the descent of a small boat into the unforgiving whirlpool, Ross sat numbly at his desk. In a subconscious act, he had superimposed the second definition of *maelstrom* over the entire story. Never in his life had he been so affected by reading. Before he entered Mrs. Ambruster's classroom, he knew exactly what a whirlpool was but had never heard of a maelstrom. As he read the story, he visualized his family being dragged deeper and deeper into an ever-descending watery pit, the steep sides allowing no chance of escape. The descent had begun with Al Stuart's tragic accident. After that, nothing was the same.

The tension in his home reached an unbearable level soon after Al's funeral. He began to live in the downstairs apartment during waking hours, gaining a small measure of stability from the Johnsons. A final, pivotal argument, almost one year to the day after Ethan's accident, reached vicious and frightening proportions, sending Ross to the kitchen in terror. He slammed the milk bottle on the floor over and over, a desperate call for help from downstairs. When none was forthcoming, he ran into the living room and stood between his parents, begging between fearful sobs for them to stop fighting. His presence only provoked his father. Ethan pushed him out of the way; he lost his balance and fell against the recliner. From this prone position, Ross looked up to see his mother, an ferocious expression on her face, close on

Ethan and begin to pummel him with her fists. He watched as Fay's attack continued unabated for a full minute, then her highly agitated anger seemed to drain from her, almost as air flows out of a balloon with a pin hole in it. Her words came out in a deflated but still seething whisper.

"You killed him...you killed him...you..." She seemed to lose strength and then sagged to the floor, thoroughly beaten. At first, Ross had no concept of what she could possibly mean. Then, a hideous thought struck him as savagely as a hard punch to the stomach. He watched as his father looked down at the two of them for a silent minute, then turned and left the room. Reeling from the idea that somehow his father had been involved in Al Stuart's death, Ross managed to crawl over to Fay, who now made no sound whatsoever, and asked quietly if she was all right. Fay looked back at him, a blank, absurd pout on her face. Ross felt as though she were staring straight through him and wondered if she was aware of who he was at that moment. As he slowly picked himself up, a darkening cloud of sadness mixed with youthful fear enveloped him. He simply did not know what to do. Leaving Fay sitting silently on the floor, he quietly went down the hall, slipped out and down the steps to see his grandmother. The blinding tears made him think of the many times he had found his way to Susan Johnson's comforting presence in the dark at the old farmhouse. When he pushed open the door to the Johnsons, as if by divine intervention, none of his aunts and uncles was in the living room. His grandmother, sitting in her usual place, motioned to him. As he moved closer, he could see that she too had been crying. She reached out for him.

"I'm sorry, Ross. We just can't interfere; you know that, don't you?" He knew they had heard his frantic pounding, and without any doubt or hesitation, accepted her brief explanation as truth. Much as he had done as a small child, he leaned against her, absorbing a measure of the strength emanating from her and he felt safe.

Ethan Becker suggested that it was time for Fay to "get some help," as he delicately phrased it. He had achieved an affluence far beyond what Fay or her family had imagined but Fay was dazedly walking through the motions. The vibrant spirit and the zest for living she exhibited while waiting for Al Stuart's promises to be fulfilled had vanished, replaced by a resignation and dullness that permeated her heart and soul. Amazing herself but mostly for Ross's sake, she developed an ability to show one personality to the world outside of her immediate family. Still a realist, she worked hard at fulfilling her social responsibilities as an increasingly important businessman's wife. Her true personality, the self that frightened her, became more subdued by the day, functioning but at times barely aware of the world around her. Whenever possible, she avoided social interaction, preferring instead to spend her time alone. At home there were times when her depression threatened to overwhelm her. Her rare smiles usually came when she was by herself on the sofa where she and Al had first made love. She found that she could re-create the sensations of his presence in vivid detail, reveling in them until reality slapped her face; then, the depression galloped back, more confounding and upsetting than ever. When it was necessary to satisfy others, she could exemplify the ideal housewife and mother and could even fool her perceptive mother most of the time. Her relationship with Ethan had deteriorated into nonexistence. Trapped into pretense by the cultural and social pressures of her church and her community, she became a magnificent actress when the need arose. Alone with Ethan, she had no need to act. If Ross were present with both of them, she could manage, just barely, to be civil.

The desperate irony of their situation was obvious to both of them. Ethan knew that he almost became a murder victim of his wife and best friend, yet could do nothing about it. Fay knew her husband was responsible for the death of her lover and potential savior yet would be viewed as a raving lunatic should she to try to expose him. As they settled into their tense routine of numbing acceptance, Fay felt herself drawn ever closer to a looming precipice, somewhere in the distance. She knew that when she reached the edge, nothing would be able to stop her from leaping from it. In her darker moments, alone with memories of Al, she thought seriously of how wonderful it might be to join him.

Periodically, Ethan and Fay Becker engaged in what Ethan termed a "logistics session," a business meeting of sorts, to work out financial details of their relationship. During one of these talks, Ethan tentatively suggested that Fay see a psychiatrist. She flatly refused. Ethan's immediate withdrawal of the suggestion prompted the contrary side of Fay to consider it more seriously. Her secret thoughts were becoming more frightening and perhaps just talking about them might help. Fay greeted Ethan's suggestion that she speak first with Dr. Judson with utter disbelief. In the years since her first meeting with the infamous doctor, he had been indicted but not tried on illegal abortion charges and was the subject of all sorts of rumors about other nefarious activities. She remembered well the physical and emotional pain he had inflicted, at Ethan's insistence. If she were to visit a psychiatrist, she could very well do it without a referral from their old family doctor.

With no indication to anyone that she had decided to "get some help," Fay contacted a psychiatrist she had overheard some of the PTO ladies speaking about. After just three sessions, Fay admitted to herself that the plan was not a good one. He was a competent interviewer, drawing from Fay in their second meeting some of her deepest and most well-guarded secrets. By the end of the third session, she felt as though she had been sliced open and the pieces of her life spread out before her in a series of broken, unsolvable dilemmas. After profusely thanking the good doctor for his help, she said she needed to think a little more and would get back to him about her next appointment. The close examination of her life sent her spiraling toward an even deeper depression. She never returned.

Fay offered no explanation for her behavior to her family or to Ross. Since the vicious argument with Ethan, when he virtually admitted that he was responsible for Al's death, she withdrew further.The Johnsons, despite the bitterness and hostility of Ethan Becker, provided a sanctuary for Ross. Susan Johnson often attended the activities that Fay used to go to at school, and acted as surrogate mother for Ross. Only on special occasions, such as Ross's birthday, did Fay manage to be anything like the Fay Becker they all knew before Al's death. Even those happy occasions frequently ended with Fay's descent into deeper valleys of melancholy despondency. She wondered if a time would come when she would not be able to climb back up the slippery slope to reality.

As Ross sat on the edge of his bed, thinking about the Becker family's descent into its own private maelstrom, an image of Pop Hiller came to mind. Pop was someone who would understand if Ross told him about the disturbing tailspin of the Beckers. Pop usually just listened, rarely offering anything but a kind smile and a safe cliché. For the last three years, Ross had been dropping by to visit almost every day and Pop never seemed too busy for him. He decided to try out this idea of the whirlpool and see if Pop might had a suggestion for how to throw a life raft to his mother. Fay Becker certainly existed in an obviously disturbed and dangerous state of mind as she followed a path into the vortex toward oblivion.

The story gave Ross a rather graphic image of the apparent hopelessness of his family situation. In a strange way, the image helped him realize that despair may have become his mother's prevalent state of mind but that it was not his. An ominous feeling swept over him. He suddenly understood that he needed to be involved in finding a way out of this torrent of problems that threatened to sweep his mother and him into the black nothingness at the bottom of the maelstrom.

Mr. Hancock's first *Introduction to General Science* class exceeded all of Ross's expectations. The teacher's dynamic presentations involved every student, setting a relaxed but businesslike tone in the classroom, an environment that would last throughout the year. In just his second day at Collins Heights, Ross knew the decision to come to the public school had been a good one and Mr. Hancock's class confirmed that belief.

Before the gifted instructor began to work his magic on his students, he delivered a brief but inspirational lecture on the importance of the entire class acting as a team.

"You will learn as much from each other as you do from me," he said, and no one doubted his sincerity, although the students were dubious about the content of his remark. He followed his speech with the timeworn activity that every freshman who had ever taken his class dreaded. He asked his students to stand and introduce themselves, giving only their names and their hometown.

"If we are going to be a good team, we need to know who we are", he said with obvious logic. The class was a mixture of students from several towns, and, on this, the second day of school, most of them had been happy to find their way to the classroom. There was no time to make new friends or try to socialize with perfect strangers. Mr. Hancock, of course, was well aware of this. The exercise enabled each student to attach a name to himself and required the others to turn in their seats and look directly at their classmates as they recited names and towns. Ross was seated in the first row, first seat as there were no students whose names began with an A. Mr. Hancock glanced up from his class roster. His kind, gentle expression drew Ross out of his seat. He turned toward the rest of the class and spoke in a firm but quiet voice, "Ross Becker, Collins Heights." His eyes skimmed over the heads of his attentive audience. After he sat down, a residual vision of a girl in the third or fourth row, toward the rear of the classroom, floated before his eyes. The introductions continued as he tried to refocus on the image but he needed to swivel in his seat to be sure that he did as his already favorite teacher requested. He couldn't wait to see the girl whose face was the only one he noticed during his introduction.

One by one, up and down the aisles, the students did exactly as Mr. Hancock requested, their collective comfort level rising with each self-introduction. Finally, the girl in the fourth row, fifth seat rose. In a wispy but clearly articulated voice, she pronounced her name. The three words she uttered became the first notes in the science section of his spiral notebook.

"Jennifer Proctor, Lyndeboro," she said and he knew he had heard that voice before. She quickly sat down, disappearing from Ross's view behind the sea of heads between them. In another minute, the introductions were completed. They accomplished exactly what Mr. Hancock intended and he now called the class back to business. Ross was reminded of the new television show "Mr. Wizard" as the remainder of his class featured a series of expertly performed science demonstrations that captured his attention and inspired his imagination. As fascinating as the class was, Ross could not help casting backward glances toward the fourth row, fifth seat, always thwarted from catching a glimpse of Jennifer Proctor by the bobbing and nodding heads of his classmates. As the harsh buzzer sounded, indicating the end of the class, Mr. Hancock had just finished his hilarious demonstration of what helium does to a person's vocal cords when inhaled. In a high, squeaky voice, he managed to dismiss the class, reminding them that the next day regular schedules would begin. With the final syllable of "Class dismissed," Ross stood and quickly turned toward the back of the room. The science rooms exited from the rear for safety reasons, although Ross could not imagine Mr. Hancock having any problems with his experiments in front of the class. Ross looked directly at where Jennifer had been sitting as he blindly reached for his books scattered across the top of the lab table. Clumsily, he knocked his notebook to the floor. A bit frantic and embarrassed, he bent to retrieve it, standing up again as quickly as he could. He started to the door but the aisles were clogged with students gathering their materials and beginning to flex their social muscles with the new names of those around them. Ross, giving in to the frustration, stopped trying to get anywhere. Instead, standing on his toes, he tried in vain to see Jennie. For a brief instant, he caught sight of her mingling with the other students pressing to move through the door, then she seemed to vanish into the crowd. As she disappeared into the energized crowd of students in the hall, a lightning flash of comprehension, so powerful that he felt his knees buckle, consumed him. He propped himself against the table for support, his mind reeling.

"Jennifer Proctor, Lyndeboro," he thought as he scanned his notebook. He had finally found the girl who had saved his father's life.

Ross already was eagerly anticipating Mr. Hancock's class the next day, for a whole variety of reasons, not the least of which was Jennifer Proctor, Lyndeboro.

The second day of high school was of momentous importance to Ross. After his initial contact with Jennie Proctor, he spent the remainder of the school day searching in vain for her in other classes, in the cafeteria, and in the hallways. He was carried back to the Memorial Day holiday of four years earlier when he had spent an afternoon searching for the ethereal young girl who had appeared and disappeared as easily as a puddle mirage on a hot highway. Now, when the dismissal bell rang, Ross knew he just had to wait for the next school day, and he would see her again in the wizard's science class. As he left school for his daily visit with Pop, he circled the block before taking his usual route home. He had no idea which of the long line of school buses was heading for Lyndeboro, but made a silent and firm resolution to discover that information the next day.

By taking his long detour around the block surrounding the high school, Ross let the usual crowd of students who stopped at Pop's get a head start. When he finally arrived, Pop, inundated with requests for every kind of sweet dairy product imaginable, still found time to glance up at Ross standing behind the row of red, leather-covered stools. Every stool and booth in the shop was filled, and the noise seemed to coalesce into a single loud but pleasant hum. The students on the stools watched as Pop alternately buried his head in the various containers of homemade ice cream, amazed as he always came up with a perfect scoop and a smile. As he had on several other busy occasions, Pop nodded his head to Ross, a signal to come behind the counter and act as his assistant.

The crowd dispersed after an hour or so, and Ross moved around the counter to take his place on his favorite stool. Pop offered him his usual, mentioning that it was getting close to dinnertime and perhaps his mom might not want him to have such a sinfully and deliciously filling shake. Ross just shrugged.

"It really doesn't matter, Pop. I'll just heat up the canned stew when I get hungry. Mom doesn't eat with me too often anymore. She's kind of tired a lot of the time." The pathetic resignation Pop heard from across the counter caused him to look up from the pile of dirty dishes in the sink. His heart skipped sadly as he caught the tail end of a dark, gloomy expression just leaving Ross's face.

"But wait till you hear this, Pop!" Some enthusiasm returned in an instant. Ross initiated a long monologue starting with his first reading assignment for Mrs. Ambruster.

"Old arm buster!" Pop interjected, his vast experience in hearing student counter conversations showing. They were the only words he managed to squeeze in as Ross interpreted Poe's story and the maelstrom that he thought described so well the collapse of his own family. With a growing excitement, Ross moved onto a topic that Pop had not heard about for some time. The dirty dishes now washed and draining, he came around to sit on the stool next to Ross. The maelstrom analogy concerned Pop Hiller. He had learned most of what he knew about the Beckers' problems, particularly Fay's withdrawal, directly from Ross's innocent confusion about what had happened to his mother over the last three years. Again, his heart ached for Ross. He had always admired Fay Becker; she made such an effort to appear as a wonderful, attentive mother and he wondered what could possibly have brought about such a dramatic change. He pushed the family concerns out of his mind as Ross, somewhat breathlessly, transitioned abruptly from the whirlpool of the Beckers to what had happened at school that day.

"I've finally found her, Pop. She's in my science class. I know she's the one who was at the track that day. I just know it from her voice." Pop listened intently as Ross provided detail after detail of his adventures in Mr. Hancock's class that morning. Pop calculated that it had been over a year since Ross had mentioned the events of that Memorial Day race, and Pop had hoped the illusion that a little girl had fatefully intervened somehow was a fading glimmer in his memory. Pop would be the first to admit the story had an intriguing side, but his innate realism would not let him entertain the possibility with too much seriousness.

Ross finished his vivid descriptions, both of the whirlpool story and the Jennifer Proctor story.

"I want you to meet her, Pop. I'm going to get her here to meet you, really!" He breathed deeply and looked at Pop, whom he had come to regard as a very special person in his life. To Ross, Pop Hiller was one of those "drop-in" people, people who slip into one's life, usually subtly, but exert a profoundly positive influence. Ross often wondered how he could get along without Pop, a universal characteristic of "drop-ins"; they occupy an indispensable place for varying amounts of time before fading away as subtly as they came. Al Stuart had certainly qualified as a drop-in for Ross, and Fay had not been the same person since he died. As he waited for a response from Pop Hiller, Ross thought of Jennie, who assuredly had no idea of the effect her drop-in had on that fateful Memorial Day. Now he was sure she was about to drop in again.

Pop draped his right arm around Ross's shoulders and looked straight into his eyes.

"You've become like a son to me, Ross. I have no idea why we have made this connection but it's there, no denying it. I wish I had answers for you, but I don't. You just have to know I'm here to help you, in any way I can. Now, about that young lady. I'd love to meet her, but I think probably you'd better meet her first!" Pop finished with a twinkle in his eyes, a wide smile crinkling his jovial face.

"Now why don't you go on home and invite your mom to share some of that stew with you? Tell her I said she should!"

Ross could only smile himself, looking at Pop with a combination of love, admiration, and respect that embarrassed the older man into glancing at his shoe tops.

"Thanks a lot, Pop! I'm going to bring her here, you just wait!" With that, Ross got off the stool and walked toward the door. He looked back as he opened the heavy door. Pop remained on the stool, gazing after him. Ross waved and was off down the street, the same bounce in his step that he always had after a nice chat with Pop Hiller.

The lively bounce lasted only until he knocked gently on his mother's bedroom door, inviting her out to eat stew with him. He felt the maelstrom begin to swirl once again when she called faintly through the door.

"I'm really tired, Ross. You go ahead and I'll join you some other time."

Dejected but not discouraged, Ross made his way to the kitchen and once again opened a can of Dinty Moore, poured it into a saucepan and turned on the gas burner. He sat at the kitchen table and reached into his book bag, his fingers finding the metal spirals on his notebook. He took it out and opened to the science section, read "Jennifer Proctor, Lyndeboro," and imagined that perhaps she might join him for some stew some day.

Christmas Eve 1954

THE ASCENT CONTINUES

Ross lounged on his bed, waiting to go to Christmas Eve Mass. He thought of attending Mass on Christmas Day to fulfill the Holy Day obligation, but Jennie had invited him over for Christmas dinner. He would gladly sit through an hour and a half of a High Liturgical Mass in the middle of the night if meant being able to spend time with her. His mother had even agreed to come to Mass with him, and with adolescent optimism, he thought this special time of the year might bring about some change in her.

As he put his head back on the pillow and closed his eyes, he engaged the movie camera of his mind and began reliving some of the scenes of last four months.

Ross thought Jennie Proctor was the most beautiful girl he had ever known. After a brief period of shy and awkward adolescent jousting, he and Jennie had become the best of friends. He felt he should send a thank-you card to Mr. Hancock for his determination in making sure that his class embraced the team concept. Every day he divided the class into different groups, providing a different personality and chemical mix. On the day after he assured Pop that he would meet Jennie, Ross rushed from his English class, charging through the crowded hallways with the agility of a deer navigating the thick woods. He had just finished impressing Mrs. Ambruster (whom he now had to consciously avoid calling Mrs. arm buster) with his preparation of the reading assignment on "The Descent into the Maelstrom." That success had already been pushed to the back of his mind, as he wanted desperately to be at the science class door before Miss Jennifer Proctor arrived. His heart, racing from his flight through the hallowed halls of old CHHS, practically doubled its rate when he saw her approach from the far end of the hall. He tried to be casual as she neared, and stood examining the natural wood doorjamb as if it were a wood shop assignment. When she was closer, Ross's intense image of her girlish face four years ago superimposed itself over her maturing, womanly countenance and the two blended into one. The effect of the combination of the two images stunned him into an inability to say or do anything. He nodded to her as she passed, a puzzled expression crossing her face when their eyes connected briefly.

Now, four months later, lying on his bed on this magical night, Ross smiled at his utter foolishness as his vivid imagination brought the scene back to life. He had wondered if there was a possibility that she'd recognize him, but dismissed that as a romantic fantasy. He attributed her puzzled look as part of his appearing so stupid, standing in the doorway for no apparent reason. As he found out later, the look did indicate a degree of awareness, but he certainly never thought so at the time. As Mr. Hancock continued his wizardry in class that day, Ross could not believe his good fortune as the final fifteen minutes of class were devoted to group work.

"Teach each other!" the Wizard announced as he called off the names of the students for each group. "Becker, Jennings, MacDonald, Proctor, and Seward, group one" Mr. Hancock called and Ross had stiffened in shy anticipation.

"How could I have been so lucky?" Ross thought as the movie continued to play in his mind.

The first group learning session in Mr. Hancock's class soared far beyond even the Wizard's most outrageous expectations for Ross and Jennie. Each of the lab tables accommodated six students and when Ross made his way across the room to group one, everyone was already seated. The two empty chairs at the table presented Ross with a difficult adolescent dilemma. One vacant seat was across from Jennie Proctor, the other next to her. As the last to arrive at the table, Ross found the others looking up at him, creating yet another degree of nervousness. He looked anxiously around the table, and saw Jennie's eyes raised to meet his. She lowered her eyes to the seat opposite her, and Ross took the subtle cue, if that indeed was what it was. For the next fifteen minutes, while the other four students diligently pursued the learning outcomes established for the group lessons, Ross could concentrate on nothing but Jennifer Proctor. He felt as if he could happily stay in this group for the next twenty years, if Jen stayed opposite him. When the session ended, Ross quickly asked Jennie if he could sit with her in the cafeteria for lunch. She readily agreed. His memory of the remainder of that morning was a blur, as he had never anticipated lunch so much in his life.

Ross checked the Big Ben alarm clock ticking away on his bureau, saw that he had another ten minutes before leaving for Midnight Mass, and had more than enough time to revisit his first lunch with Jennie. It had been a typically hurried high school lunch, but as he remembered it, he believed the fifteen minutes spent with Jennie represented the beginning of his clawing his way up the side of the swirling maelstrom of his life.

He waited just a few minutes before asking the question. She seemed to know it was coming and had her answer prepared.

"I am the girl you saw at the races that day, Ross. Perhaps as we get to know each other better, I'll be able to explain things a little more completely, but not now. I hope things have been good for you." Her answer was so straightforward and simple that Ross had been taken aback. Responding to Jen's reticence, he switched the conversation into safer areas, asking about her other classes, her teachers, and where she lived.

It was not until a warm fall day late in October, when they had arranged to ride their bikes to school, that Ross summoned enough courage to ask the second big question. Over her father's protective objections, Jennie rode her bike to school alone, explaining that she would have company all the way home so he needn't worry. She would take smaller back roads and be careful at the major intersections, saying all the right things to make a father feel better about allowing a daughter to ride a bike three miles to school. Ross planned on riding home with her, then continuing on to his house, a six-mile round trip, but well worth it for the extra time he could spend with Jen.

The ride home through the small streets of Collins Heights and Lyndeboro was mostly a silent but pleasant one. Many of the residents had raked their leaves into the curbside and now, as late afternoon approached, were burning them, sending the unique pungency of leaf smoke drifting through the air. After they arrived at Jennie's house and she and her father had given each other their usual warm, loving greeting, Ross met Bob Proctor for the first time. It was a stilted social occasion for Ross but Bob made him feel comfortable, joking about Jen's first boyfriend, the teenagers blushing crimson. Bob left them sitting on the porch and went inside to prepare dinner.

When a slight pause occurred in the conversation, Ross cleared his throat, straightened his back against the wooden porch column, and asked the second question he needed answered about the Memorial Day race.

"Jen, do you remember what you said to me that day, about the favor?" He watched closely for her reaction and knew that he did not have to say any more. Her eyes radiated such a fusion of innocence, intelligence, honesty, and purity that goose bumps rose on Ross's arms.

"Of course, I do, Ross. I told you that the favor would have to be returned sometime later." Jen said this in the same matter-of-fact tone she had used when she admitted being the girl at the races.

"What does that mean, Jen?" Ross began to stutter. "I mean, how…when…?"

Jen responded by leaning back against the matching column on her side of the porch and sighing heavily. "I don't know, Ross. I wish I did but I don't. I have no idea why I said that, other than it seemed the right thing to say. I just don't know…"

From across the porch, Ross could see Jennie's eyes watering. He stood quickly and crossed over to her. "Jen, I'm so sorry; I didn't mean to upset you." Ross never felt more awkward or more unhappy with himself.

"It's not you, Ross. It's me. I know things I don't want to know and I feel that I need to do things I don't want to do. And I don't even know why!" Jennie voice rose to a heartbreakingly frail pitch. Ross heard the front door open. Bob Proctor came out onto the porch and went immediately to Jennie, brushing Ross aside.

"Oh, Daddy, why do I have to have this?" the tears now flowing freely.

To Ross, she could have been speaking about some dreaded disease but her father seemed well aware of what was happening.

"I think you'd better go on home, now, Ross. Ride carefully, it's getting on toward dusk."

Bob Proctor did not seem at all angry with Ross, who by now was feeling that he had caused some major problem. Bob actually gave his direction to go home with a gentleness and kindness in his voice that Ross found surprising.

"I'll see you tomorrow, Jen. Thanks for letting me ride home with you." Ross jumped down the steps from the porch. He rolled up his right pant leg to keep it from getting caught in the bicycle chain, waved to Jen, now looking at him from the porch, and was relieved to see her return his wave, a small smile compensating for her tear-stained face.

As Ross watched the scene played again with the wonderful gift of hindsight, he wished the following day at school had not turned out the way that it did for Jennie, even as he realized their young relationship was taking on a depth he had never imagined.

He thought of Jen's profuse apology when she saw him in science class the next day. When they met later in the cafeteria for lunch, Jennie accepted his invitation to meet his father and mother. In retrospect, it was a foolish decision but Ross told his parents that he had met the girl who saved his father's life. The state of his parents' relationship negated any possibility of telling them together and certainly made it impossible for Jennie to meet both at the same time. He could not imagine the two of them in the same room with Jennie; she surely would see through the tension of the relationship. After observing the loving and warm father-daughter relationship of the Proctors, Ross had developed a fear that Jennie would not be able to understand the icy connection between his mother and father. He told himself that he could explain it to her sometime later, but he didn't really believe it.

Fay expressed a lukewarm interest in meeting Jennie, at first a very puzzling reaction in Ross's mind. Ethan had a different reaction and wanted to meet her immediately. He could still reconstruct, even after over four years, the sight of the young girl and Charlie Beckholdt, or "whoever the hell it was," standing by the accident as he hung upside down.

He knew he would remember her, if indeed this was the same girl.

The two occasions when Jennie walked home with Ross would be forever etched into his memory. The maelstrom that he had hoped to escape when he met Jennie only increased in intensity with each meeting.

On a chilly, gray afternoon early in November, Jennie walked home from school with Ross. Her father planned to pick her up at the Beckers' around four o'clock. Ross expected, or at least hoped, that his mother could rise to the occasion and visit with Jennie for a few minutes at least. He had prepared Pop as well that he would be stopping by with Jennie and he happily introduced her to him as they entered the shop. Pop had saved a booth for them, turning away several groups who arrived before them. After they were settled in the booth, Pop signaled for Ross to go behind the counter and make whatever he would like for the young lady. Ross beamed, proud to show his expertise as well as Pop's trust in him. He whipped up two double chocolate shakes and served them with as elegant a flair as he could muster. Jennie smiled broadly, seeing through the attempt to impress her but enjoying it immensely. Ross felt that he had just moved another step or two toward the top of the whirlpool. They had no time for much of a discussion with Pop but he made Jennie promise that she would return in a quieter time so they could talk. They devoured their shakes in record time and were about to leave when Pop called them back.

"You got a real special young man there, Jennie. Don't you forget it!" For the second time since they met, Jennie and Ross blushed in matching scarlet.

When they reached the apartment house, Ross decided against introducing Jennie to his grandmother and aunts and uncles. He wanted to spare both of them the potential of blushing in unison once again, as he knew that the Johnsons would be merciless in their good-natured kidding of the young couple. Instead, he opened the door for Jennie and they went upstairs to the Beckers' apartment. Opening the door hesitantly, he felt a rush of nervousness wash over him. After a quick silent prayer that his mother would be in one of her lucid states, he escorted Jennie into the hallway and took her coat to the closet. As he turned from the closet, he was startled to see Fay standing in the living room doorway. He had been sure that he would have to call her out from her bedroom.

"Come on in", Fay said, in a voice more cheerful than Ross had heard in months. The relief buoyed him and he moved quickly down the hall to hug Fay, who responded as she might have years before. Jennie stood by, smiling at what appeared to be a warm relationship.

"This is Jennie, Mom, the girl I've told you about." Ross's enthusiasm radiated through the room as the three sat down. His mother's first question to Jennie, harmless enough, made Ross nervous and a little wary of where this meeting might head.

"So, you're the little girl who saved my husband's life?"

Jennie seemed unsure of how to respond and just nodded tentatively.

"I just knew something was going to happen, Mrs. Becker. Someone else really did it." Her answer was so simple and so direct that Ross wondered how Fay would proceed. A change in Fay's expression and body language sounded an alarm but Ross, hampered by youth and inexperience, did not know what to do.

"My next question, young lady, is what gave you the right to intervene? Everything would be fine now if you had stayed out of it." A flush appeared on Fay's cheeks and Ross could see an irrational anger toward Jennie bubbling up from some deep crevice of her mind. Then he realized why his mother had that puzzling reaction when he had first told her about Jennie. Absurdly, Fay Becker somehow placed the ultimate blame for her descent on Jennie!

"The maelstrom," he thought and he knew he had to get Jennie out of there.

"Come on Jennie, we'll go downtown and wait for your father." A full-fledged panic was settling over Ross. He crossed the room and took Jennie's hand.

"Come on," he said, now with deeper urgency. He didn't understand why Jennie had no reaction. She remained seated even as he tugged at her arm.

In an environment that seemed teetering on chaos, Jennie responded with a deliberate calmness that in itself Ross found unsettling. She replied in the same placid tone she had used in answering his questions.

"I'm sorry, Mrs. Becker. I didn't realize the situation. Please forgive me." Jennie's demeanor managed in the space of just a few words to convert Fay's illogical anger into a despairing acceptance.

Fay sank back in her chair. She looked like a rag doll that had just been shaken by a puppy, and quietly began to cry. Again, Ross felt his grip on the sidewall of the maelstrom slipping as his mother's words began a sinister infiltration of his consciousness.

"Come on, Jennie, we'll wait for your father on the front porch." He had not released his hold on her arm and now, with a more insistent tug, he lifted her from the chair. Fay Becker did not look up as they left the room. They got their coats and quietly left the apartment.

Neither of them heard Fay whisper to herself, "Please come back and visit again, Jennie."

The reminiscences playing out in Ross's head faded as he heard his mother call from the hall.

"Mass starts in just twenty minutes, Ross. We'll need to get going soon." Whatever happened to Fay Becker in the two months since Jennie's visit mystified him but made Ross happy at the same time. Her voice took on a strong hint of the intensity she used to have and she seemed to be reacting to the world around her more positively. He clicked his personal memory bank into a faster speed and brought back the rest of Jennie's visit that day.

They had left the apartment and Fay behind. A stunning numbness crept over Ross as they descended the stairs. When they reached the veranda, they found their way to the two large white wicker chairs that had not yet been put away for the winter. Neither had spoken a word after the apartment door closed behind them. Jennie's father would not be along for at least another fifteen minutes and Ross slumped into one of the chairs, staring out toward the railroad tracks across the street. The brief exchange between Fay Becker and Jennie revealed so much that he felt his emotional stability beginning to unravel. Jennie moved the second chair close to his and sat beside him. He looked over at her, an unbelieving and frightening expression locked in place. His body tensed. Jennie Proctor, in that single, significant moment released a tangible mist of tranquillity toward Ross. When he finally directed his wild, emotion-laden attention to her, she reflected back a serenity that Ross found momentarily maddening, until the pleasant mist enveloped him.

"What's happening, Jennie?" Ross asked, grimly trying to recover from the revelation of just moments ago. His mother's vehement reaction to Jennie's interference on the day of the accident had clearly indicated that she wished Ethan Becker died. At the same time, he had remembered his intuition that he had a choice in his answer to Jennie's question that day. Suppose he had answered no, that he did not want his father to be all right?

"I'm truly sorry but you needed to know this, Ross." When her father finally pulled up to the curb at the front of the house, Ross resisted the urge to ask her to stay just a little longer. In that fifteen minutes, she had helped him slow his whirling descent into the deep despair that encased his mother, explaining in precise terms why he needed to talk to Fay about what had happened.

Less than a week later, Jennie was back at the Becker household, this time on a Sunday morning while Fay was at Mass. Ross had awakened early, knowing that Jennie would be coming that morning to meet his father. He bolted down a bowl of Wheaties, bade a hurried goodbye to his mother and made the required trip to St. Luke's for what everyone called the "quickie Mass." He loved meeting his Sunday obligation with a half hour Mass, with no sermon and sparse attendance. Often tempted to spend the time hiding at the elementary school playground, Ross could not ignore the mortal sin of missing Sunday mass. "Die with an unconfessed mortal sin on your soul and you'll go straight to hell!" That constant admonition from the nuns and priests for eight years echoed in his head as he walked briskly to church, passing the playground and not yielding to temptation. He anticipated this morning's meeting with Jennie and his father with a mixture of dread and positive energy. It was something that had to be done and Jennie Proctor seemed able to lift people's spirits just by being the same room with them.

Ross and his mother actually had several meaningful conversations since Jennie's visit and the change in Fay's emotional state bordered on the miraculous. Ross, at Jennie's suggestion, had decided to wait to ask his mother what she meant by saying that "everything would be fine now" without Jennie's intervention. His determination to postpone the nagging question left him during one of the long dinnertime conversations he and his mother shared. Fay had started speaking about Al Stuart and was unable to control her emotions. She started to cry and Ross came around behind her. He gently placed his hands on her shoulders, trying to console her, but he didn't know what to say. He couldn't see the expression on his mother's face but her distress was obvious.

"I really loved Al, you know, Ross?" Fay said quietly. Ross had no realization of what she really meant, interpreting her declaration as that of love for a dear friend.

"I loved him too, Mom", Ross said, with a small loss of composure. To Ross, the timing seemed appropriate to ask how things could possibly have been fine now if only Jennie hadn't gone to the races that fateful Memorial Day.

Fay had reached up and taken his hands in hers. She asked him to sit down and looked directly into his eyes.

"Al had a plan," she began. By the time she finished, the maelstrom whirled out of control and Ross was desperately grasping at the sides to keep from drowning.

During the brief Mass, Ross thought of nothing else. He believed Jennie had indeed provided some momentum for the family to begin its ascent out of the vicious whirlpool of their lives. He was sure the meeting between Jennie and his father would produce only positive results.

Shortly after Fay left for the ten o'clock Mass, Bob Proctor and Jennie pulled up to the front of the house. Ross was waiting on the front porch and ran down the walk to greet her.

"Hi, Mr. Proctor. Thanks for bringing Jennie over. Would you like to come in for a minute?" Ross extended the offer, knowing that Jennie probably had already told her father that he should just drop her off this time.

"Maybe another time, Ross. I've got some things to do; I'll be back in about an hour, if that's all right." Ross had already developed a fondness for Bob Proctor. He recognized the profound love he had for his daughter and appreciated that he allowed Jennie her freedom to make whatever choices she felt were right.

"Sure, we'll see you later, and thanks again!" They waited until Bob drove away and then turned toward the house. Ross began to feel a dull, ill-defined nervousness in the pit of his stomach. He had no doubt that Jennie would handle the meeting with his father with her usual good nature and clarity of purpose. He attributed the sudden, bewildering nervousness to a flashback he had had the night. He was lying in bed, thinking about his father finally getting to meet Jennie. Just as he drifted into the nebulous space between wakefulness and sleep, a sharp image of his mother appeared, her fists flailing at Ethan. She kept repeating: "You killed him, you killed him." He had sat up in bed, thinking, but also saying to himself in a croaking whisper, "My God, I'm living in a house with a murderer!" And now they were climbing the stairs, and Jennie was about to meet him.

Ethan was waiting in the living room, seated in his favorite chair. When Jennie and Ross entered the room, he motioned for them to sit down on the sofa, perfunctorily acknowledging Jennie without any formal introduction. He came directly to the point, knowing immediately that this was most certainly the girl he had seen from his upside-down vantage point that Memorial Day.

"So, Jennie, how did you do it?" Jennie appeared to be expecting the straightforward question, and she disarmed the hostile tone Ethan had used in phrasing it.

"First of all, it's nice to meet you, Mr. Becker" Jennie said, her sincerity and sweetness taking Ethan Becker back. He felt a bit guilty for his social rudeness and the edgy tone of his voice.

"As I told Mrs. Becker, I didn't do it. I had help. All I did that day was to come to the races as I had been told." Ross sat next to her and once again marveled at her poise and dignity. "Could she really be fourteen years old?" he thought.

"OK, Jennie. How did you get Charlie Beckholdt to help you? According to his wife, at the time the accident occurred, he had suffered a massive heart attack and most likely was dead. Explain that to me, if you can." Ethan's tone had resumed its antagonistic flavor.

Jennie, at her most fascinating and innocent, related the facts of the Memorial Day experience, fearless in the face of Ethan's obvious skepticism. She mentioned that her father almost turned back but she knew, she just *knew,* that they were supposed to be at the races that day. She didn't know why. Something had drawn her out of the grandstand, she didn't know what. She had met a burly, muscular man who said he would help. She didn't ask who he was or where he came from. She had watched as he moved the hot exhaust pipe so that Ethan could crawl out, then returned to her waiting and worried father. She didn't know where the brawny man went but he had disappeared before she could thank him for his help. When she finished her story, Ethan rose from his chair and paced around the room. His skepticism and incredulity became more obvious and his tone assumed a condescension that Ross resented, but Jennie didn't seem to notice.

"You're telling me that you knew I was going to crash and need help. You're telling me that it's possible that a guy who had died helped me get out of the car before it exploded. I was there and I know I saw you and someone who looked like old Charlie, but what I'm hearing is just too farfetched for words. It's been nice to meet you, Jennie, and you are a sweet girl. But your story is just a bunch of superstitious hogwash. Thanks for stopping by." Ethan quickly left the room and disappeared into the kitchen.

Ross couldn't believe what he had heard. He knew his father had no explanation for what happened that day. Ross had believed that Ethan would accept Jennie's account as credible, if hard to believe. As his resentment at his father's treatment of Jennie grew, his initial nervousness at the start of the meeting was replaced by a burgeoning anger.

Jennie, sitting quite close to him on the sofa, could feel the tenseness as it overcame him. She reached over and placed her right hand gently on his cheek, turning his face toward her.

"It's all right, Ross. Really! He has every right to doubt a story like that. I'm just sorry that I can't explain things more clearly, but I don't understand them either. Sometimes I have this strange feeling that I'm in the world but not really part of it, like I'm a connection between two worlds. It's just impossible to explain but sometimes I don't feel like I belong here."

Ross gazed into Jennie's eyes. She did not look away, even as her eyes began to water. His throat constricted as he was swept into her sad but wonderful world. At fourteen years of age, he now knew what it meant to be in love. In a humbling but vitalizing way, he knew he was in the presence of a remarkable human being. He also knew that his suspicions were correct; for the second time Jennie Proctor had "dropped in" to his life. He accepted without hesitation, unequivocally, that she had kept him from his ultimate dissolution at the bottom of the maelstrom. The realization of what his parents had done surely would have sent him twisting and turning, sinking without hope and without faith. With her and because of her, Ross Becker began an ascension toward the widening light at the top of the whirlpool, and he hoped he was dragging his mother behind him.

Fay's insistent calling rousted Ross from his intense recollections. "We've got to leave now if we're going make the midnight Mass, Ross!" He closed down the theater of his mind, reveling in the sweet memories of Jennie and eagerly anticipating a future in which she would play a major part.

June 1956

THE HILLERS DROP IN

Mary and Warren Hiller, better know as Mom and Pop, were ready to admit that they needed someone to help around the shop. "Not as young as we used to be, Mary," Pop would say, with a devilish twinkle in his eye. "Still can chase you around till you catch me, though!" Mary would giggle like a schoolgirl, the bonds of forty-five years of marriage tying them happily together.

As transportation into Philadelphia improved, the outlying towns on the Jersey side of the river blossomed. Collins Heights had expanded and was considered one of the most desirable places to settle in. Virtually every lot in town had been sold and most had houses already built or soon to be built on them. With the additional population, the confectionery portion of their shop had grown, requiring more of Pop's time in the back to assist Mary with the homemade candy.

One evening, just after school had closed down for the summer, Jennie and Ross paid one of their regular visits. They waited until a little after eight, when business had slowed enough to allow a leisurely conversation with Pop. Pop loved to see the two youngsters. They always added a vivaciousness and it was such a pleasure to watch the two of them interact with each other. Pop had grown very fond of Jennie; she certainly was the most sensitive and perceptive teenager he had ever known. The great change in Ross since he started seeing Jennie was not lost on Pop. He knew Ross had entered a difficult time at home just before meeting Jennie and he had been quite worried about him. In the first few months of his freshman year, coinciding with Jennie's entrance into the life of the Beckers, even Fay had undergone a noticeable change for the better. As he watched Ross and Jennie devouring their huge ice-cream sundaes, he didn't think he had ever seen two sixteen-year-olds more obviously in love. Their delight in being with each other made Pop smile. He waited until the sundaes had reached a manageable level in the bowl then called Mary out from the back room. The two of them approached the booth, and asked Ross and Jennie if they could join them. The only part of the request that seemed out of the ordinary was that Mom had come to the booth as well. The last remaining customers had made their way to the door and called a hearty goodbye to the high-backed booth, unable to see the occupants but aware that Pop and Mom were there.

Pop opened the conversation with a salesman's line, a line he had used before in joking with Ross. "Boy, have we got a deal for you!" He used the same exaggerated inflection that the local used car huckster might use.

"What are you talking about, Pop?" Ross responded, curious but still thinking there was a joke of some sort coming.

Pop had rehearsed his speech carefully, even practicing it in front of Mary. There was a part for her to play as well, but that would come later.

"How come you're having sundaes tonight? You always have shakes!" Pop asked the question as a transition; he didn't anticipate any special answer.

"We're kind of just celebrating," Jennie and Ross responded, in unison. "Two full years of high school down the drain," Ross continued. The meaning of their two years together remained unspoken but Pop knew how important they had been.

"Well, you probably haven't noticed, but Mom and I are getting a little older!" Now Ross really thought a joke was in the offing, but he said nothing. Pop continued as Jennie and Ross finished their sundaes, tipping the bowls up on their sides to scrape out every drop of ice cream and chocolate sauce that remained.

"We need some help here, some dependable help, and we thought you two might be interested." Pop's assessment proved correct. Jennie and Ross ceased their scraping, and turned their full attention to Mary and Warren Hiller, now suddenly cast in the role of potential employers.

"You're both so wrapped up in the academics at school that you don't take part in sports or anything and we thought you might like some extra money while you helped us out at the same time. We could work out a flexible schedule. We just can't keep up with our candy orders and it surely would help if you folks could cover the front every once in a while."

Then it was Mary's turn. "We can arrange it so it doesn't interfere with your schoolwork at all and, best of all, you could work together."

Pop watched the two for some sort of reaction and saw them glance at each other and smile, a sign he took to be positive. Jennie replied first. "I'll need to talk with my dad before I say yes, but I'm sure it will be all right, as long as I want to do it. And I do, Pop."

Ross echoed Jennie and everyone agreed to meet at the same booth the next night with decisions. Pop believed he would soon have two new employees and some of the stress of running his shop might be relieved, especially with two fine young people like Jennie Proctor and Ross Becker.

After bidding Mom and Pop goodbye, Jennie and Ross walked leisurely toward the Beckers' house on Virginia Avenue. They had become inseparable over the last two years. They shared experiences and found they could talk to each other comfortably about anything. Jennie often visited the Becker household, timing the visits for when only Fay was home. In her own mind, Fay drew rather close parallels between the anticipation she used to feel when Al Stuart would be coming and the expectancy she felt when Jennie was dropping in for a visit. Much as Al had been her haven of sanity, Jennie now had assumed a similar role.

His mother had emerged from her dangerous state of mind of two years before, and Ross gave full credit for the transformation to Jennie Proctor. Fay had even started to call Jennie her "little light," as if Jennie's presence acted as a beacon of safety across a rocky ocean inlet. With the estrangement of Ethan gradually moving into a chasm of separation, Fay drew much of her strength from Ross's young friend. When Jennie came to visit, they often had far-reaching philosophical discussions and Fay was constantly amazed at Jennie's perceptiveness and intelligence. On numerous occasions, she had even told Ross that it appeared as if Jennie had lived a full life already at the age of sixteen, her insightful observations on human nature bordering on the wonderfully frightening.

The last day of school, just before summer vacation began, had been designated a half-day session and Ross agreed to help the librarian pack up boxes of books for a sale later in the summer. Jennie had arranged to spend the afternoon with Fay Becker. They planned to share a picnic lunch at a small lake in an adjoining town while they waited for Ross to come home. Later, Fay would call this event her change-of-life lunch. She had come to know that her life was a spiritual and moral sham, badly in need of change. The discussion she had with Jennie Proctor that day sent her in new and wonderful directions.

That afternoon, Fay had asked Jennie about other events that might have been similar to the Memorial Day race, something they had not mentioned again since her first meeting with Fay almost two years before. Jennie shared many of the unusual events, and remarked that many of them had been unwelcome intrusions. The wide-ranging discussion eventually found its way around to how unhappy her gift made her on occasion. She hadn't asked for it and the older she became, the more she tried to sublimate it, even ignore it, but her attempts were always unsuccessful. When someone needed help and she knew about it, whatever the process, she had to respond. What disappointed her many times was how easily a good intention led to injurious results. Saving Ethan Becker's life had led only to a whole series of events that made many people suffer, including Fay and Ross Becker, and cost a fine man his life.

The life-changing discussion for Fay followed quickly after Jennie expressed her contention that she saw no purpose for her gift. The young boy she had helped escape from the railroad track had developed polio, most likely picked up at the municipal swimming pool, and was now confined to an iron lung. Jennie's agitation increased as she thought of other times she had used her gift. Fay stepped in, and steered the conversation toward what she thought was safer ground.

"Last year, I signed up for a class in religious theology for laymen at St. Luke's, Jennie. It was offered to anyone and at the time I was trying hard to find some tangible reason for my existence, so I decided to try it. Anyway, here's a question they posed for us. Do you think we are spiritual beings on a human journey or are we human beings on a spiritual quest? Would you like some time to think about that?" Fay asked lightly, intending to relieve some of the tension from the talk about Jennie's gift. The answer Jennie gave, without the slightest hesitation, supplied Fay with the courage to pursue a course of action to extricate herself from the destructive and unhealthy relationship she now shared with Ethan.

"We are all spiritual beings in human form. We are just passing through this planet. We came from somewhere and are going somewhere. There are times when I feel as if my feet are hardly touching the ground, Mrs. Becker." The answer was so simple, so direct, and so definitive that Fay could not find an adequate response. She looked at Jennie, whose attention seemed to be riveted on some point high above the lake, her eyes almost filmy.

"Thank you, Jennie," she said simply.

During the wonderful walk home through the warm summer evening, Jennie had shared with Ross most of the conversation she had had with his mother during their picnic. Ross once again expressed how much he appreciated what Jennie had done to preserve his mother's sanity. He was eager to hear his mother's version of the profound discussion they had.

Jennie and Ross had decided to accept Pop's offer, unless Bob Proctor or Fay had an objection. Following her usual selfless pattern, Jennie thought Pop appeared tired and that maybe this would help him out. When they climbed the steps to the apartment, Fay, who had heard the door open at the bottom of the stairs, greeted them as they came in.

"Hey, Mom. Wait till you hear the deal that Pop offered us!" They moved into the living room and Jennie and Ross, with barely controlled youthful enthusiasm, described the Hillers' employment offer. Fay responded much as they had guessed, offering support and encouragement tempered with a small amount of parental reservation.

"Before I drive Jennie home, there is something else I want to tell you." Ross thought his mother's voice had never sounded so strong and confident.

"I've told your father that I am leaving him. I cannot accept the life I am leading and need to change it. We have to take control of our own destiny while we are on this human journey, don't you agree, Jennie?"

Jennie looked over at Ross for some sign, some reaction, but could not see any.

"Yes, Mrs. Becker, I do agree." Ross glanced from one woman to the other. In his mind's eye, far in the distance, he saw the maelstrom drying up to nothing. He walked over to his mother, pulled her up from her chair, and hugged her tightly. Unashamedly, the three people in the room stood together, sharing cascading tears, but without a trace of sadness on their faces.

June 1958

THE ASCENT COMPLETED

Ross wondered aloud to Jennie if she thought his father would come to their graduation. He had sent the invitation early to the latest address he had for Ethan Becker and it had not come back, so he made the assumption that he had received it. He had not seen his father for a year and a half and he worried a bit about the scenario that might play out at the school when Fay and Ethan met but quickly dismissed it as not worth worrying about. His mother had, as she had vowed, taken control of her life and had no qualms about seeing Ethan again, although she doubted he would make an appearance at the graduation.

When John Manley had summarily fired Ethan Becker from his position as general manager of Manley Motors, Ross had actually felt sorry for his father. Manley had made good on his promise that anyone who brought negative publicity to his dealership would not be working for him very long. The day immediately following Ethan's feeble attempt to explain to him why Fay had filed for divorce, beginning the proceedings within the shortest time allowable by state law, John Manley had called Ethan to his office over the dealership intercom. As Ethan heard the call and began to walk through the showroom, the whispers of the other employees may as well have been shouts in his ears. The meeting lasted all of two minutes. Within an hour, Ethan Becker found himself leaving the executive parking lot for the last time.

St. Luke's entire parish reverberated with the scandal but no one could have been truly surprised. The rocky relationship between Ethan and Fay Becker had been gossip fodder for years and now it appeared that Fay was finally asserting herself.

If Ethan put in an appearance at his son's graduation, that would be fine. If he didn't, that would be fine too. His family, the family that had been his support and the family that mattered, would surround Ross. With Jennie Proctor at his side, he felt he could take on the world.

Ethan

"I don't need these ungrateful bastards," Ethan thought. His mind was racing, keeping pace with his brisk strides to the car after his final meeting with John Manley.

"For more years than I can remember, no one in that family, not even my own son, gave me credit for anything I did for them. I'm sick to death of their whole attitude and if John Manley couldn't see my value to this company then he's as stupid as the rest of them." Ethan shook with anger by the time he reached his car. He climbed in and put the key in the ignition then sat and looked back at the dealership.

"I have more friends and contacts than anybody else in this whole business. I'm the one who should be worn out from trying to keep everything going. Let Fay find someone else who can keep her as well as I did." He felt himself regaining some control of his incensed state of mind. "After that embarrassing scene in the showroom, all those people laughing behind my back, I've got half a mind to drive right over to the house and teach her a real good lesson," he thought.

As Ethan's anger continued to subside, an insight into what he should do came to him as clearly as if some had spoken to him. "That's probably just what they'd like but I'm smarter than that. They're not worth my trouble."

He began already to relish his freedom as he turned the key, and brought his car to life. He knew about so many good opportunities in the South and could almost hear Daytona Beach calling. Like a weight lifted off his back, he could say good riddance to the Johnsons and the narrow-mindedness of people like John Manley. He knew how they wanted him to react.

"I'm not going to fall into one of their traps again. I could care less if I ever see any of them again, including Ross and his psychotic girlfriend," he thought.

The Ascent Completed
(Continued)

Jennie and Ross intended to commute to the local branch of Rutgers, the State University, continuing to help the Hillers' with their ever-expanding business. Pop and Mom, now virtual adopted grandparents of both Jennie and Ross, planned on closing the shop during graduation ceremonies so they could both attend.

Jennie' gift, much to her relief, had apparently gone into a hibernation stage. She had not had any episodes, as she now called them, for over a year, the last being a warning to a bus student to step back, just before a novice driver accidentally rode up over the curb. Her warning had been heeded; otherwise the student would have been severely injured. Jennie credited the short supply of "episodes" as the result of her involvement with every good cause she could manage. She spent equal amounts of time as a student volunteer and an employee of Pop's. Ross's good-natured joking about her Florence Nightingale image at school was taken in the spirit in which was given. Already announced and publicized, the award for outstanding service to the school and the community would be hers at the graduation ceremony. Ross would have been proud to be counted just among her friends but their classmates and everyone else knew their relationship had gone far beyond the friendship stage.

The early summer morning of the Collins Heights High school graduation dripped humidity. The temperature had climbed into the low eighties before ten o'clock, threatening to break 100 before the evening ceremony. Ross asked his mother if he could borrow the car to run over to see Jennie for a few minutes. The drive took just a few minutes and Ross could barely contain his youthful joy at being alive. To be eighteen, in love with a wonderful girl like Jennie, have a stable life. Could it be any better?

As he pulled up to the curb, he saw Jennie come running through the door and down the sidewalk. The look on her face made his heart skip a beat and his stomach flip. Over her shoulder, he saw Bob Proctor hurrying down the walk toward the car. Ross got out and stood leaning against the car, an ominous dread dropping over him like a heavy blanket.

"Ross, we've got to get over to Pop's *now*!" Bob Proctor stood behind Jennie, nodding his head. She ran around to the passenger side, shouting "Hurry!" three times in quick succession. Ross slid back into the driver's seat. The engine was still running; he dropped the shift lever into drive position. As he made a sharp U-turn, the tires gave off a squeal. As they sped back toward Collins Heights, Ross felt the whole bench seat shake in unison with Jennie's shivering in the eighty degree heat.

Ross covered the three miles to the downtown Heights in five minutes, backing quickly into one of the few remaining parking spaces along the street. Jennie had said very little during the brief trip, mentioning only that she had been eating breakfast with her father when the episode began. She had called Ross at home but he had already started out for the Proctors' and she had no choice but to wait for him to arrive.

The hurried parking job left the car two feet from the curb, the chrome curb feelers not even close to touching the concrete edge of the sidewalk. Jennie was out of the car first and two steps ahead of Ross when they came to the door of Pop's shop. She pushed against the door and found it still locked. The huge four-sided clock in front of the Federal Savings Bank showed 8:50. Pop did not open until 9:00. They both leaned against the window in the center of the door, cupping their hands around their eyes to fend off the glare from the sun splashing across the storefront. There was no sign of activity inside the store. They backed away and looked at each other for direction. Ross moved close and knocked loudly on the metal push plate at eye level on the door. After what seemed like minutes but really was a few seconds, Pop opened the door. The relief on the young couple's face must have been painfully obvious.

"Are you OK, Pop?" Ross asked, with a small stammer. Pop clearly did not know what they were doing there.

"Of course I am! What are you two doing here at this hour, starting to celebrate graduation a little early?" he asked, his trademark crinkle forming around his smiling eyes. Jennie, wanting desperately to believe that everything was fine but knowing it probably was not, laughed lightly. She started to say they just wanted to drop by to say hello but did not get past the first word when Warren Hiller, their beloved Pop, put his right hand to his chest, muttered, "Oh shoot, not now," and collapsed in the doorway.

Ross couldn't believe that the ambulance wouldn't go faster. He and Jennie followed close behind, flashing the headlights of Fay's car with a wild desperation; neither of them wanted to verbalize what they were thinking. There just did not seem to be any urgency on the part of the ambulance driver.

Through the rear window of the emergency vehicle, they could see the two medics apparently working on him. Mrs. Hiller sat motionless in the jump seat just in front of the gurney. Ross irrationally thought of taking the lead and forcing the driver to try to get to the hospital faster. Jennie's hand lightly resting on his shoulder exerted a powerful calming influence, pushing the jumble of thoughts and emotions into a neat, controllable pile in a corner of his mind.

After what had seemed an interminable trip, the ambulance finally turned into the emergency entrance and Ross steered the car to the nearest parking lot.

More than seven years before, Ross had been with his father as they drove into this same parking lot, and now the fading memories of Al Stuart suddenly became vivid once more. Al might as well have been sitting on his shoulder; he could hear his voice; he could feel his firm handshake; he could feel his calming presence.

The memories became so real and intense that Ross felt as if a huge, powerful wave was crashing over him. He squeezed the car into a space bordering a no-parking zone and stopped. He reached for Jennie's hand, still resting on his shoulder. He pulled it to his cheek and pushed it hard into his face, as if she could stem the tide of tears the towering wave had started. Jennie leaned across the seat and hugged him, saying in her thin, gentle voice, "We need to go in; Mrs. Hiller might need us." The significance of Jennie's use of Mrs. Hiller, not Pop, did not occur to Ross until they sat in the waiting room opposite ER 3. The large wooden door was slightly ajar, just enough for Ross to see the medical staff moving around the room, not in any particular hurry, it seemed to him. If anything, the patient on the table appeared to be ignored as they went about their business. Then he knew; he despairingly knew why the ambulance did not speed; he knew why the staff in ER 3 did not hover over Pop; he knew what he had refused to admit when Jennie told him that they had to go to Pop's. Another of his "drop-ins" was gone and he wondered how he could cope with the loss of his wonderful friend. He looked over at Jennie, thought of graduation that afternoon, and wished with his whole being that Pop Hiller and Al Stuart could be there.

Then, as if some conspicuous duty had overtaken him, he stood up, walked over to Mary Hiller, and gripped her shoulders as the doctor approached them from ER 3. The man's hesitant step and hunched shoulders told them everything before he said a single word.

The afternoon after Pop's funeral, Ross and Jennie had walked directly from the Avalon Hills Cemetery to her house, just over three miles away. The walk was therapeutic and cathartic. In her inimitable fashion, Jennie used her uncanny ability to rise above her sensitive, deeply emotional state and examine the mysterious workings of the world in a concise, matter-of-fact way.

"Do you believe in God, Ross?" she asked.

"What a question, Jennie. You know I do. Why would you ask that now?" Ross had some doubts about his mental stability after the draining experience of Pop's funeral and burial and wondered where Jennie was going with the question.

"It all seems quite easy to me really, then. If we believe in God and what he promises, then we'll just be missing Pop for the short time we are here on earth. That's not really all that long, you know? The real test of faith comes in whether we truly think that people like Pop are indeed in a better place now then they were here. Do you believe that, Ross?" Ross had grown accustomed to deep discussions with Jennie and this one promised to last for their long walk home.

"I guess I do, Jennie. It's just hard to think about when it's so close to losing him. No, wait, you can scratch out the guess part of that. I do believe that there is a better place after this one." Ross caught the glimmer of a smile beginning to appear on Jennie's face.

"Well, then, we can be sad and miss him but be happy at the same time, right?"

All Ross could do was stop walking, turn to her and take both of her hands in his. Gazing into her mesmerizing eyes, those eyes that long ago had peered into Bob Proctor's very soul, he said softly, "I love you, Jennie Proctor. Don't you ever think of going to that better place without me, understand?"

That exchange ended the philosophical part of their discussion, and the remainder of the walk passed by quickly in relative silence, both thinking about Pop Hiller and wondering what Mary would do without him.

Two weeks after the Collins Heights High School graduation ceremony, Ross received a call from Mary Hiller asking him to come to work an hour early the next day. Ross's workday started at nine o'clock when the shop opened and he was more than slightly puzzled over Mrs. Hiller's request. He readily agreed and actually arrived at the shop before eight the next morning. Ross had wondered if he would be able to function in the shop with every movement he made weighted heavily by Pop's invisible but palpable presence, as though he was looking over Ross's shoulder at every sundae or shake that was served. Much to his relief, Ross found that having Pop lurking over every scoop of ice cream he funneled into a sundae and hovering over the sink as he washed the dishes actually felt just fine. As Jennie had said, Pop surely was in a happier place.

The front door was unlocked when he arrived and he went straight to the closet to put on his starched and bleached white coat, marred only by a few stubborn drips of various ice-cream flavors down the front. Mrs. Hiller had heard the gentle ting-a-ling of the bells triggered by the front door and came out of the back room.

"Good morning, Ross. I'd like you to come back here for a few minutes before we start work." Mrs. Hiller, always a behind–the-scenes person when Pop was out front, actually possessed an outgoing personality and her cheerful disposition effectively covered the undercurrent of sadness at losing her cherished husband of forty-five years.

She led Ross through the back of the shop and into the Hillers' living quarters, an apartment no larger than the one he shared with his mother. A tall man in a dark blue suit sat at the kitchen table as they came through the door. He stood and greeted Ross warmly, extended his hand and returned Ross's firm handshake. He spoke his name but Ross missed it as he looked around the kitchen. Standing in the middle of the room, he felt transported to the kitchen of the old farmhouse where he had spent so much of his childhood. Mary obviously had been up early that morning and the sweet aroma of freshly baked bread filled the air, mixing with the tantalizing aroma of homemade chocolates. Mary Hiller asked Ross to have a seat at the table and bustled into the corner to prepare a plate of warm, freshly sliced bread.

"I'm sorry, sir, I missed your name...daydreaming, I guess," Ross said.

"Quite all right, my boy. I'm Richard Lundquist, the Hillers' attorney." He sat in the chair opposite Ross and shuffled a raft of papers spread out in front of him.

"Would you like me to tell him, Mary, or do you want to?" Lundquist asked in a way that said that he preferred to tell him whatever it was. Ross began to squirm ever so slightly, a bit of nervousness settling in, despite the homey, relaxed setting.

"Pop Hiller must have thought a lot of you, Ross. With Mary's blessing, I'll explain the situation the way I see it and try to answer any questions you might have afterward.

Richard Lundquist picked up an important-looking document. "I won't bore you with the legal terminology, Ross, but this is Warren Hiller's will."

With that brief introduction, Lundquist explained in the easiest terms possible the provisions of Pop's will. If Ross Becker and Jennie Proctor agreed to allow Mary Hiller to live in the apartment behind the shop as long as she could care for herself and to share the profits of the shop on a fifty-fifty basis, the Hillers would deed the property, including all of the business rights, to the two parties heretofore named.

Ross glanced to the corner of the kitchen where Mary Hiller stood; it appeared that her hands were folded together as if in prayer. He was unable to speak, still digesting what he had just heard.

"In a nutshell, if I may use the vernacular, Ross," continued Lundquist, "this means that you and Miss Proctor have been deeded a successful business but only if you agree to see that Mrs. Hiller is taken care of for the rest of her life." Lundquist intoned this in as deep and theatrical voice. The lawyer truly seemed to be enjoying himself.

Mary Hiller spoke as she approached the table, the platter of sliced bread she held in her hands attracting Mr. Lundquist's undivided attention.

"Ross, Pop and I had talked about this; we just did not expect it to be happening so soon. I can't operate this shop by myself, and if I sold it I'd have to move to who knows where. You and Jennie were special to Pop and you are to me too. I'd love to hear you say that you would consider it." She offered the platter and Lundquist scooped two slices of the bread onto his napkin. Ross absent-mindedly reached for a slice as well.

"I'm really a bit dazed here, Mrs. Hiller. I guess I just need to ask for a little time to talk to Jennie, maybe her father and my mother also. Would that be all right?"

Richard Lundquist assumed his lawyer role: "We'll just need to know before probate, probably in the next week. Would that be an acceptable time frame?

Ross looked at Mrs. Hiller again. "Sure, yes, thank you!" He tried but failed to imagine Jennie's reaction.

Saturday, July 10, 1960

Bob Proctor had to keep telling himself that he would not be losing Jennie. His friends repeatedly threw at him: "You're not losing a daughter; you're gaining a son." How he had come to hate that cliché! He knew Ross Becker was a special young man and he should be thankful that Jennie would be marrying such a hard worker. Ross obviously adored Jennie, and Bob had no trouble with that part of it. Jennie had probably analyzed his feeling quite correctly several nights before.

"My mother will be at my wedding," she had assured him. He wondered again how Jennie could make a statement most people would consider as having come from a spiritual fanatic yet somehow, when she said it, it became utterly plausible. She said she *knew* her mother, dead for more than twenty years, would be at her wedding. Jennie knowing something carried an infinitely different meaning from other people knowing something. Living with her for twenty years had demonstrated that fact time and again.

He really didn't have any cause for concern. Ross and Jennie would be living close to him and their financial status had been secured by the wonderful arrangement the Hillers had provided. Business at Pop's Confectionery was never better and the youthful energy applied to the shop by Jennie and Ross continued the tradition Pop had developed. Bob regretted the necessary postponement of the young folks' college plans but Jennie had been able to fill her spare time with more volunteer and charitable causes than he knew existed. Her warm and caring spirit permeated everything she did, whether it was serving a customer an ice cream or sitting with an elderly patient at the County Home for the Aged. Anyone who knew Jennie spoke of her as though she occupied a position of uncanonized saint on earth.

In spite of every reassurance, on this, her wedding day, he worried about how he would deal with going home to the empty house this evening. He thought of Jeanne, sadly having to struggle to bring her face to mind. After twenty years, Jeanne's final words appeared truer than ever.

"You were right, my dearest Jeanne, she has been worth the sacrifice," he thought to himself, and he felt in his heart that Jennie had been right also. Jeanne would be at her daughter's wedding. As he thought of parents and weddings, a sense of unrelenting resentment suddenly came over him. His abiding fondness for Ross Becker corresponded to an intense dislike bordering on hatred for Ethan Becker, a man he had met just once, and then only briefly. How could a parent miss his own son's graduation from high school, and now, his wedding? It went beyond what a man of Bob Proctor's caliber could understand.

The Becker wedding, held at St. Luke's rectory as Jennie had not converted to Catholicism, had one memorable moment, not scripted by the rituals of the marriage ceremony. The small group of guests, the Johnson family tilting the balance far to the Becker side of the aisle, barely noticed the hitch and passed it off as a private joke between bride and groom.

In a brief lull between the vows, as Father Samuels temporarily lost his place in the missal, Ross leaned close to Jennie's ear. She felt him lean and moved closer. He whispered into her ear and she turned what could have been a loud guffaw into a muffled chuckle.

"At last", he said, "I've returned the favor. I'm letting you marry me!"

January 24, 1961

PRESIDENTIAL INAUGURATION DAY

The residents of Collins Heights as well as the entire eastern seaboard shivered through a bitter cold wave that had almost forced cancellation of the inauguration ceremonies for newly elected President John Fitzgerald Kennedy. A fierce storm had struck Washington overnight, dumping more than ten inches of snow and wreaking havoc with the plans to introduce the youthful president to the city. Jennie tried to hide her disappointment but was unsuccessful. Everyone knew that Jennie had worked tirelessly to see that Kennedy was elected and she anticipated staying tuned to the festivities all day on the small black-and-white television they had brought to Pop's Confectionery from home.

Winter, even in the moderate climate of New Jersey, did not lend itself to selling very much ice cream. After the Christmas candy rush, the three proprietors of Pop's Confectionery were able to relax a bit before the Valentine's Day crush for heart-shaped boxes full of Mom Hiller's chocolates. As they watched Dave Garroway in the morning, the snow had subsided in Washington and it appeared the inauguration might be held after all. Under duress, Ross carted the small but weighty television with its twelve-inch screen to the shop so Jennie could watch the man who had convinced her that he could be the Sir Galahad the American people were waiting for. While Ross supported the convincing campaign Kennedy had launched and even attached two Kennedy-Johnson bumper stickers on the front and back of his car, he let Jennie immerse herself in the local political scene.

Fay Becker and Bob Proctor had a wonderful time teasing their children about their political involvement, since neither one had yet attained voting age. Jennie accepted her father's happy-go-lucky banter, devoting herself to the cause and rejoicing when the noble JFK reached the electorate's equivalent of the Holy Grail-the Oval Office on Pennsylvania Avenue.

Ross set the television on the table in one of the booths where it could be seen from the counter. Jennie, having postponed her weekly trip to the children's wing of St. Mary's Hospital, watched every minute of the telecast, applauding with those attending the ceremonies when Kennedy issued the call for a new direction for the nation, led by people born in the twentieth century. Even Ross, straining to see the fuzzy screen from across the room, was moved by the dramatic and memorable phrases of the inaugural speech. When the new president finished with the rousing "Ask not what your country can do for you" portion of his speech, Jennie turned to Ross and Mary Hiller. They both had moved closer to the television, attracted by Kennedy's vivaciousness as well as his message.

"He will make a difference, I know he will. You can see it in his eyes!" Jennie's excitement spread to them and they both agreed; Mary Hiller added that she had never heard a president speak so forcefully or effectively. "And I'm pretty old," she added with a pleasant smile.

July 9, 1963

The Beckers had invited Fay and Mary Hiller to their tiny new home in Lyndeboro for a barbecue to help celebrate their third anniversary. Ross had checked with the hospital late Sunday afternoon and received a tentative clearance to pick up Jennie's father to come home for the festivities but that could change. Since Monday was the only day the shop was closed in the summer, they had decided to have the dinner on the day before their actual anniversary so that Mary could attend as well. She had become as one of the family and they wanted her there for the special occasion. As they began the preparations that Monday morning, Ross asked Jennie to sit with him for a few minutes on the old porch swing they had moved from the Virginia Avenue apartment house. At first, she objected, pointing out to Ross how much had to be done before the guests arrived. She reconsidered after just one look into his eyes at her rejection.

"OK, Ross, but just for minute!" He took her hand and led her out the rear door of the small bungalow. He deliberately walked her on a detour around the edge of the tiny fenced backyard. The enormous variety of flowers and shrubs she had planted were in full bloom, casting color and aromas in every direction. Walking slowly, they inhaled the garden environment she had created, even in the minuscule plot of ground. To Jennie, the garden represented a special place, a place where the handiwork of God and the hardy work of man blended with spectacular results. It was a silent walk, a squeeze of each other's hand the only communication. When they finally arrived at the large concrete front step, out of proportion to the rest of the house, Ross stepped ahead and, in an elegantly exaggerated motion, bowed before Jennie. He then ushered her to the waiting antique swing. She sat and waited for him to join her.

"Remember, Ross, one minute." He interrupted her directions by delicately placing his hands on her cheeks and, bending over, kissed her lightly on her forehead.

He gently sat down beside her, careful to keep the rickety old swing still, and reached for her hands. As he held them, he gazed into her eyes, damply sparkling in the sun. "I brought you here to tell you three things," he said, "and they will not take more than my allotted minute. So pay attention!" Ross spoke with a mock seriousness that made Jennie smile.

"First, I still owe you a favor. Second, I never dreamed I could have be as happy as you have made these past three years. Third, I love you more than even you could ever know, Jennie Becker. Now, that's all I have to say and it took less that forty-five seconds. I've left you fifteen to say whatever you want; that is, if you have anything you'd like to say."

Ross smiled as he saw the tears well up in Jennie's eyes.

"Darn you, Ross. You wanted to make me cry, didn't you!" They both stood at the same time, leaving the swing swaying behind them. Jennie grabbed Ross's hand and they followed the same tour back to the rear of the house, again in silence but with much more hand squeezing.

The anniversary cookout succeeded beyond expectations. Jennie's concern about bringing Bob Proctor home from the hospital for a day turned out to be unnecessary. Bob had been in a fairly stable and lucid period the week before and the day ended without incident. Ross agreed to drive Bob back to the hospital while Jennie had a chance to visit with Fay and Mary over the dishes.

The Favor Returned

Jen knew from previous visits that her father's condition was deteriorating. The hospital had agreed only under pressure to allow Robert Proctor to remain on the long-term-care wing, despite a policy that dementia patients would have a limited stay before being transferred to a mental health facility. Jennie had begged to keep her father where she knew he would receive the best treatment. Bob Proctor existed in a limbo of medical care, presenting a dilemma for the supervisors. Most of those associated with his case knew intellectually that it would be just a short time before it became necessary for his transfer, but emotionally would have kept him forever for Jennie's sake. She also knew that what had happened that day in the wing of the small Catholic hospital had been inevitable.

Jennie had perfected a personal preparation ritual that she practiced in the car on the fifteen-minute drive to the hospital. The visits usually ended with Bob Proctor sobbing and begging her to take him home, but she knew that soon after she left, he promptly forgot she had even been there. Her well-rehearsed ritual was designed to keep her on a sound emotional footing while projecting confidence and strength to her father. Jennie would spend the ride drawing vivid mental pictures of four of the happiest times of her life with her father. When she arrived at the hospital, the resurrected memories provided the armor that protected her from the breathtaking truth she faced when she saw him.

This day had been different. With her emotions firmly in check and the power of the positive memories giving her courage to see her father as he was now, she climbed the long, concrete steps and entered the hospital. Everything about these visits had become so familiar that she felt she easily could have closed her eyes and navigated through the maze of hallways to his room, greeting each of the nurses by name at each station without even seeing them. Almost without realizing it, she had come to Room 345, a corner room with two windows looking out over what was a colorful garden in the summer but now had the depressing deadness of late November. She pushed open the heavy door and saw her father sitting in the chair facing the dull flower garden with its withered plants, seemingly hoping for an early snow to cover their bleakness. Bob had turned in response to the sound of the door opening and instantly made eye contact with Jennie. Her cheerful smile, well practiced and delivered in spite of the circumstances, faded as quickly as it had come when Bob said, "Hello. Who are you?"

When Bob Proctor was first diagnosed with the early onset of dementia, Jennie had handled the news easily. He had none of the recognition problems when she was around and she could find dozens of reasons for his confusion when in the presence of others. When he went to the wrong bank and tried to withdraw money from his savings account, he made jokes about the attention he received. Her rational mind constantly told her she was in denial when she rejected what others saw happening to her father. Eventually, even she had to admit that Bob was becoming a danger to himself and others. Ross, who knew very well the importance of Jennie's father in her life, had stayed out of the situation entirely until it was obvious that something had to be done. He was pleasantly surprised at how effortlessly Jennie helped her father realize that he needed to be where he could be watched and cared for.

Ross had come to hate the euphemistic phrasing of "something needs to be done" or "he needs to be put someplace." He was very fond of Bob Proctor and appreciated his generous moral support several years before when he and Jennie decided to marry. It had been Ross whom the worried bank employee had called when Bob was insisting that he had money in their bank. By the time Ross arrived, Bob was apologizing profusely to anyone who would listen and the incident had been completely defused. Had that event been isolated, it could have been ignored, but the increasingly regular bizarre behaviors had forced the issue. Finally, under doctor's orders, Bob had been placed in the extended-care wing of the hospital, supposedly on a short-term basis, although Jennie had managed to extend his stay indefinitely.

Jennie's last visit to her father was devastating. After Bob's lack of recognition, Jennie tried with her usual patience to explain to him who she was and where he was and the entire situation. At one point, she even left the room and pleaded with the nurses to check him for a stroke, convinced that some catastrophic event had occurred overnight. They assured her everything was the same and that her father's symptoms were classic. They explained that sometimes it is almost as if the memory of someone in Bob's state is composed of doors that open and shut in random fashion. This morning, the door to the room that stored all recollections of Jennie had closed tightly and she, despite valiant and continued efforts, could not open it. When the futility of the visit became obvious after more than an hour of meaningless conversation between what might as well have been two strangers, Jennie politely excused herself.

Just before leaving, she had quickly crossed the room and kissed her father lightly on the forehead. A strange mixture of ambivalent feelings nearly overpowered her. The relief that she would not need to deal with the usual emotional weeping scene was overshadowed by the possibility that her father might never recognize her again. An even more powerful and unsettling sensation swept through her when Bob Proctor looked up at her after she had kissed him. His dark eyes still had the glassed-over look of confusion and the complete absence of recognition. In that brief moment of eye contact, a single tear formed in the corner of each eye. Before Jennie could retreat, he had reached out, squeezed her hand, and said quietly, "Thank you for coming." The phrase was uttered in the same tone so often heard by hospital visitors who have come in the role of good Samaritans, trying to improve the spirits of barely known acquaintances. In her fear and confusion, Jennie ran from the room, attracting the attention of all of the nurses as she set her rapid pace through the halls and past the hospital reception desk. As strong and as rational as she always had been, she could not shake the feeling that she was experiencing an anxiety attack. When she reached the car and pulled open the door, she tumbled into the seat and frantically searched her pocketbook to come up with the keys. She had to be moving, doing something, going somewhere. Finally the keys found their way into her hand. She forced herself to stop shaking long enough to shove the key into the ignition and start the car. She sped through the familiar twists and turns of the parking lot. She directed all of her energies to seeing that the car kept moving, pulling into traffic with hardly a glance. She had the sense that if she stopped, she would fall apart. Her mind raced over the last hour again and again. How could her father deteriorate so far in the space of a single day? She found that she could remember the entire conversation verbatim as the environment surrounding the car assumed a surreal appearance, passing by in nothing but a blur. The stable and calm person she had been on the trip to the hospital had disappeared, replaced by a person she didn't know even existed.

In just over ten minutes, she traveled the four miles to where the road widened into four lanes. The state had recently completed a long stretch of paved shoulder better to accommodate the rush-hour traffic. Jennie gathered herself enough to know that she had better pull over for a minute. The car had no sooner come to a full stop, squeezed against the small grassy mound on the right edge of the shoulder, than she shivered, put her head against the steering wheel and began to cry. The tears created a full-blown release for her and she felt the panic of the last twelve minutes or so drain ever so slowly to a point where she actually was able to think clearly again.

In her entire life, she had never felt so foolish or so useless. With her reasoning power once again in control, she knew she had to return to the hospital, apologize to the nurses for upsetting them, and sit with her father once again, whether or not he knew her. The catharsis that the tears brought about settled in and she resolutely sat up straighter in the car, determined to face and conquer this crisis as she had many others. She found her attention directed at the puzzlement over what her final minute with her father meant. Even in his delusionary state of mind, she was sure that the tears and the gentle squeeze of her hand were no accident. As she remembered these two gestures, she felt her usual optimism return. In the brief space of two minutes, she had moved from an angry despair to a cautious but deepening hope. Suddenly, she wanted desperately to be sitting at her father's bedside again. With her eyes once again filling s she remembered the touching squeeze of her hand, she put the small Ford Falcon into drive. A quick U-turn would start her on her way back to see the father who was the source of so many of her happy memories.

"I know that he is going to know me this time," she thought. After a cursory glance across the road at the northbound lanes, she wiped her eyes and started the sweeping turn.

The sparkling new Public Service Transit Authority building had been open for just over a week. It housed several of the newest buses in the entire commuter fleet and today Paul Devork had the unique honor to take the brand-new addition for its maiden voyage. The PSTA drivers always were involved in a friendly competition to see who would get to pilot a new bus on its first trip. Tradition held that the bus would be driven at exactly the correct and appropriate speed heading southbound on the Tilton Pike between Collins Heights and Laurelwood. Paul was feeling especially lucky to be driving the empty bus. The speed limit had just been raised to fifty-five along the five-mile stretch where the new paved shoulder had been added. After the first several miles, he would be able to put the high-powered diesel through its paces for a while. As the other drivers, preparing for their respective runs, waved jealously, Paul pulled the sleek, streamlined coach out onto the highway and headed south toward Laurelwood.

Becoming anxious to move through the more congested area of the beginning of the trip, he pulled away from the last stoplight before the newly paved section of road. As he looked ahead, he could see the road widen. He gradually increased pressure on the accelerator. As expected, the bus responded beautifully and smoothly moved in to the fifty-mile-per-hour range. About a half-mile ahead, he noticed a bright red Falcon parked far to the right on the shoulder and decided that it must be someone looking at a map or simply resting. Paul's driving record was a sterling one, admired by all of his colleagues, and he reacted to the parked car with his customary caution. As he closed in on the car, he became more convinced that the driver had chosen this new shoulder to rest for a moment. The speedometer in his temporarily personal limousine had quietly crept up to just over fifty-five. His eyes, which were focused on the road straight ahead, caught unexpected movement in his peripheral vision on the right. By the time he had time to react, Jennie's little Falcon had pulled out from the newly paved shoulder and crossed directly into his path. The bus, with its new and improved large windshield design, gave Paul a panoramic view of the road but he did not have time to slow the multi-ton vehicle before it struck Jennie's car broadside, directly at the driver's door. The adrenaline rush that the bus driver experienced just before impact etched the image of the scene forever on his mind. Later, as he stood by what was nothing but a pile of twisted metal ground into the front of the bus, the devastated bus driver would describe Jennie's face just before the crash as beatific, smiling, and completely distracted.

Two hours later, after the rescue crew had taken apart the Falcon piece by piece to extract Jennie from the wreckage, the ambulance finally arrived at the hospital. The nurses in the extended-care wing three floors above the emergency room heard the siren's wail as it approached but paid little attention. They were engaged in an animated discussion about the remarkable change in Bob Proctor since his daughter had fled past their station in such a highly charged emotional state. After Jennie had disappeared, one of them went directly into Bob's room to check on him and found him sitting on the edge of his bed, smiling and happy. He had looked up, seen her puzzled look, and said, "She really has been worth the sacrifice, you know." In the ensuing two hours, each of the nurses on the floor made it a point to drop by his room, for no reason other than to observe a patient whose spirit had undergone such a dramatic change.

The local police, as soon as they identified the owner of the car, sent a police car to the rectory of St. Luke's Church to escort a priest to Pop's Confectionery Shop downtown. Ross, his hands immersed in the same sink where he had watched Pop wash thousands of dishes, saw the car come to a stop in the No Parking zone in front of the busy store. He saw Danny Fischer, an old high school acquaintance new to the police force, and Father Samuels exit the car and walk toward the shop entrance.

The butterflies in his stomach were accompanied by a vivid mental flashback to the day the family found out about his grandfather's death in the war. In the years since, Ross had become quite aware that a priest coming to visit usually meant some sort of bad news. Even before the pair entered the shop, Ross had washed his hands and was drying them as Danny and Father Samuels came in. Even the most casual patron in the shop could sense that something was terribly wrong. Ross motioned his now unwelcome visitors toward the rear of the store and ushered them into his tiny office. The three men barely fit into the space. Ross closed the door.

"What's happened?" Ross asked without really wanting to know. He already was picturing how he was going to tell Jennie whatever this bad news was about her father. Danny and Father Sam, as he was affectionately called by his parishioners, had discussed who was going to say what. Now they looked at each other, searching for the right words, knowing that there are never the right words in this situation.

As Danny cleared his throat and began to speak, Ross thought, somewhat irrationally, how old he looked for a twenty-three-year-old.

"Jennie has been in an accident, Ross." Danny fairly blurted this out, the words running together and the sentence became more like a single word.

The presence of the priest made this announcement take on an ominous life of its own. Ross could not speak and numbly waited for the officer to continue. "Jennie" and "accident", the first and last words of the officer's garbled opening sentence, were echoing in Ross's mind as the initial nervous flutters in his stomach turned to a cold, shiver-producing fear. He felt as if he needed to grab Danny by the throat and force him to speak faster. Danny, for his part, could not even meet Ross's eyes.

Instead, it was Father Samuels who told Ross that he had better come with them in the police car to the hospital. Ross immediately knew the unspoken reason; it will be faster. Completing the logical progression of this thought, Ross realized that it probably meant that they did not have much time, if any.

He grabbed his coat off its hook with such force that it ripped the collar.

"Jennie can fix that," a thought immediately replaced by, "Oh my God, NO!"

The whole picture became unreal, and Ross, fighting back panic that was quickly taking over, called back to his patrons.

"I've got to leave. Please understand!" With the priest and the policeman close behind, Ross charged out into the cold November afternoon.

As Ross hunched over in the back seat, his head buried in his hands, Danny flipped a switch and the flashing blue lights mounted on the top of the cruiser came to life. Father Sam glanced over his shoulder from the passenger seat and could sense the fear emanating from Ross in the rear. He knew that any words of comfort would be futile. The mind of the priest, always inclined to the spiritual, could only manage the usual meaningless cliches, and he saw no reason to say anything. He had enough experience in this kind of situation to know that even the most faithful are not at all receptive to deep discussions of the spiritual big picture when they are feeling as if God is in the process of destroying their lives. The ride to the hospital, endless to the pathetic figure in the back, took barely twelve minutes. Danny expertly maneuvered the police cruiser through the noontime shopper traffic and drove directly to the emergency room entrance.

When the car stopped, Father Samuels scrambled out first and opened the rear door for Ross. During the brief ride to the hospital, Ross had recovered his composure somewhat and a bit of his youthful vigor had returned. His mind had clicked back into the optimistic mode that Jennie always insisted on. He climbed out of the car and walked briskly with Father Sam through the door, directly to the nurses station straight ahead. The priest stayed several steps behind, unintentionally, but subconsciously dreading the next few minutes. When Ross announced his name and inquired where he could find Jennie, the pleasant, smiling nurse behind the desk quickly looked down at something invisible on the counter in front of her. Averting any eye contact with either Ross or Father Sam, she came around the counter through a swinging gate and motioned for them to follow. Her reaction to his name was not lost on Ross and he felt his legs wobble a bit as they proceeded down the hall to ER #3.

The door was partially ajar and the frenetic but controlled activity taking place in the room made Ross feel even weaker. The optimism of just minutes ago was again replaced by a feeling of dread. In spite of his experience in this very emergency room on two other occasions, he was not prepared for what he saw as he tentatively pushed open the door. The nurse who had greeted him so cheerfully kept her eyes riveted on the floor as she escorted the two men into the room. One of the doctors, who seemed to be just an observer to what was happening, looked over. The nurse finally raised her eyes and made what must be a universal "this is family" emergency-room signal that brought the doctor quickly to their side. The large, well-equipped treatment room had a small waiting room attached and the doctor actually took Ross's arm and guided him toward the door, deftly keeping himself between the activity surrounding the patient on the table and the two visitors. As the door closed behind them, Ross realized that it could have been anyone on that table. All he had seen was a series of machines with what seemed to be at least two white-coated technicians for each one. Something about seeing all the attention she was getting once again raised his level of optimism. The doctor indicated the two chairs in the corners of the tiny room and he and Father Sam slowly sat down.

"She must be all right," he said to himself, but in a voice loud enough to be heard by the others. The group in the small waiting room now consisted of the well-trained emergency-room doctor along with the priest and Danny, who had come quietly into the room and stood along the back wall. The priest and the doctor were, of course, veteran witnesses to this kind of human drama and had seen Ross's initial denial coming. His conviction that Jennie had to be safe because she was in the best medical hands and receiving the best treatment was commonplace. After all, with all of the expert professional help surrounding her, surely she would be safe.

Dr. John Baring, of all of the doctors at the hospital, had the deepest degree of compassion for those whose lives were forever changed by what happened in the three emergency rooms. He was the star of many of the myriad stories of black humor that the staff often engaged in to keep their sanity around such human devastation. His reputation for sensitivity and understanding while handling the stricken families of emergency-room patients was almost legendary. When others on the staff realized they were scheduled to work with the affectionately dubbed Jolly Jack, they would begin to make what he called their sick jokes. These so-called jokes generally took the form of complaining that theirs would be a difficult shift because Jack always seemed to be on duty when the worst cases came in, just so he could the one to break the news to the unfortunate families.

Now, John Baring looked across the tiny room at the young man trying desperately to remain calm, even as he was grasping for plausible explanations why it was necessary for a police cruiser and a priest to bring him here. Dr. Baring knew that the blurted and almost plaintive cry of "She must be all right" had been uttered for Ross's benefit as much as for anyone else in the room.

It had been fifteen minutes since the sirens signaled the arrival of yet another emergency downstairs. The unofficial inter-hospital communication system, also known as the gossip brigade, had managed to spread the word to the third-floor extended care wing that a beautiful young woman had been involved in a horrible crash and the situation appeared rather grim. The medical staff, from doctors to nurses to candy stripers, took news of this sort with a sadness more profound than most outsiders would expect. For the most part, their decisions to enter the medical profession were based on a desire to help people and any senseless tragedy affected them at an almost personal level. Dealing with life and death every day did not diminish the personal involvement each of them felt.

No assignment in the hospital required more patience and understanding than the responsibility of dealing with dementia patients. Most of the patients would never go home; rather, they usually were transferred to hopeless mental asylums directly from the hospital. Many of them were not even sure exactly where they were at any given moment. Even as the nurses heard about the tragic accident victim being treated downstairs, Bob Proctor's behavior of the last two and a half hours or so had buoyed their spirits. As a group, they had been hoping that Jennie Becker would return to see him, even though she did not usually come back on the same day. During one of the rare times when four of the five nurses in the wing were gathered around the counter at the central station, the phone rang. Nancy, the youngest and least experienced of the group, was on watch at the desk, responsible for answering calls. The others quieted their ongoing discussion of the fate of the poor girl downstairs. Nancy's gasp caught their attention. All three looked at her at the same time and all saw her face go slack and lose all expression. Marybeth quickly moved behind the chair, ready to catch her as it appeared she was going to faint. Nancy slowly placed the phone back in the cradle. As her eyes filled, she could barely speak. "It's Jennie Becker." She managed to add "in the accident" before sobbing drained her of the strength to say any more.

From his position in the chair on the wall opposite the door to the waiting room, Ross had a skewed view of the hectic efforts taking place in ER #3. Even through the slightly opened door, he could sense the urgency in the room. His overloaded mind was able to form an incredible appreciation of the efficiency with which the ER team moved.

As he stared at the still-standing Dr. Baring, Ross managed to summon some strength from the reserve of optimism that his beloved Jennie had always supplied in abundance. He knew Dr. Baring would be truthful with him, but he could tell that the good doctor was experiencing some difficulty finding exactly the right words and the right opening to tell Ross what he was waiting to hear. In the exasperating few minutes, seconds really, that it took for the doctor to begin to speak, Ross's confidence that the news would be good had inexplicably risen to new heights. It was becoming one of those times when people simply go through the motions of life while waiting for real life to begin again. Several of Ross's human senses were operating at their highest level in what was a surreal setting. The mixtures of antiseptic, medicinal hospital smells were suffocating him. The constant, barely intelligible garble of the hospital address system paging an endless list of doctors with an endless variety of extension numbers echoed in his ears. The soft leather of the institutional chair combined with the usual unbearably warm hospital temperature made nervous sweat stick his shirt to his back. His eyes shifted between two focal points, quickly glancing back and forth between the barely opened door to the emergency room and the doctor, who finally seemed ready to say something. Everything else in the room blurred as he waited for the doctor to make his assurances that Jennie would have a difficult but rapid and complete recovery.

Dr. Baring, with his extensive experience, knew exactly what Ross was thinking. His hesitancy in starting to explain the nature of Jennie's injuries came from knowing that young people have a wonderful feeling of immortality and invincibility. Had this been a fifty-year-old man sitting opposite him, he would have taken a caring but much more direct approach. In his gentle, soft-spoken manner, Dr. Baring started to explain to Ross precisely what Jennie's injuries were.

"Ross," he said, making sure eye contact was made and that Ross was listening. "She is not conscious. We're doing everything we can but I'm afraid the outlook is not good." Dr. Baring sighed inaudibly and struggled to follow this terrible blow with something for Ross to cling to.

"She has youth, strength, and a strong will to live. I wish I could be convinced that could be enough. You know how wrong it would be to give you false hope, but the situation is not completely hopeless. I am truly sorry...." His voice trailed off to another sigh, this one heavy enough for everyone in the room to hear.

Dr. Baring watched carefully for the change he knew would come in Ross's eyes as his words slowly penetrated the wall of optimism Ross had carefully constructed over the last few minutes. He had deliberately paused, allowing the first impression to settle. The doctor continued only after he saw the confidence of youth fading into a more realistic look of concern. He knew Ross now had to know the seriousness, even desperation, of the measures being taken in the next room. Dr. Baring left his standing post near the door, walked over to Ross and took a seat next to him. He was starting to feel that he had made the necessary beginnings for Ross to accept the bleak prospects. He decided to attempt to keep this momentum going and continue, even before Ross raised any questions of his own.

"Jennie's injuries are severe. It's hard to imagine how she even survived the crash but somehow she did. As soon as we feel that she's stable enough, we'll be taking her up to the operating room and try to stop the internal bleeding."

Ross seized on every positive word the doctor had uttered and ignored the rest.

"Not completely hopeless", the doctor had said. The fact that they were taking her to an operating room where, in his mind, miracles could be performed was a good sign.

Dr. Baring, with his physician's intuition, immediately was aware that Ross was venturing to a place that he had not intended, a place in his mind where Jennie made a full recovery. In the next instant, he knew his intuition had not failed him.

"Can I see her before the operation"? Ross asked, with an innocence and optimism Dr. Baring found disheartening.

"Ross," he answered as calmly as he could, covering his agitation with himself for not clearly indicating Jennie's condition. "She's unconscious; we're using every bit of new technology we've got just to keep her alive. I don't think it would serve any purpose for you to see her now. Wait until we have a chance to stabilize her and get her out of danger."

"She's in danger?" Ross posed this question in such as way that Dr. Baring wondered what he possibly could have said just moments before to raise this young man's hopes so much.

"Ross," he said in his sternest voice, "she wouldn't be alive at all if we had not put her on to the new life-support systems we've just installed. She is comatose, Ross. She can't even breathe on her own."

Over the next several days, the hospital's mailroom staff had all it could handle to keep up with the cards and notes arriving for the beautiful young lady in Room 225. They marveled that a girl of just twenty-three could have had such an impact on so many people. The colorful receptionist at the front desk, having served the hospital in that capacity for more than twenty-five years, had never seen so many flowers delivered to one person. As reporters began to investigate what this young girl's life had been like before the accident, a clear picture emerged. Jennie Proctor Becker had been practically an angel to all who knew her. The interviews with friends and family revealed a thoughtful and caring person who exhibited a maturity well beyond her years.

Jennie's days on the life-saving machines stretched into a week and the stories of her struggle continued to fill the human-interest columns of the local papers. The soothing, calming effect this young woman had on the lives of those around her became more and more evident. A reporter had finally cornered Fay Becker and written a brilliant story about the inspirational and uplifting effect Jennie Becker had on the life of her mother-in-law. When Fay Becker read it, she fell apart as she recalled how much the human-interest stories in the paper had meant to her in the past. The notable difference with this one obviously was that the end had yet to be written. The universal question of why such tragedies happen to the good people of the world was constantly being raised, even in groups that would consider themselves without faith or religion.

Jennie lay now in a state of suspended animation, kept alive by a roomful of machines that performed every vital bodily function for her. The doctors, while encouraged by the success of the new technology, were in general agreement that she had little chance of recovering. They knew that sometime, in the near future, decisions would have to be made.

Ross had been shocked back to reality by Dr. Baring's commanding presence when he announced that Jennie could not breathe without the machines, and had gradually crumbled once again. The discussion with the doctor became more of a litany of the critical nature of Jen's injuries. Instead of subconsciously blocking out the negative, Ross now dwelled on it. Before the ten minutes of Dr. Baring's elaborate explanations were concluded, phrases like "irreversible coma," "severe internal injuries," and "lucky to be alive" were whirling through his mind. What he had seen as unreal before took on nightmarish qualities and he was unable to put together intelligent questions. Everything was blurring. For whatever reason, a conversation he had with his father-in-law just months before forced an intrusive reality on his rapidly deteriorating stability.

The conversation occurred following one of Bob's increasingly frequent bouts with dementia, one from which Ross had rescued him. Ross received the phone call from the local barber, Sam Durocher, at around eleven o'clock in the morning. Both Ross and his father-in-law were regular patrons of the popular Sam, a rather typical small-town barber with a sharp wit and a ready arsenal of philosophical wisdom. The shop was only two blocks from Pop's Confectionery and Sam did not indicate an emergency existed, so Ross finished serving the last customer and walked briskly down to Sam's. Bob had met him at the door but Sam was right behind, motioning to Ross to come in. Bob Proctor obviously wanted to leave with Ross right away and Ross practically had to push him out of the way to enter the shop. Bob followed him in but, surprisingly, walked to the rear of the shop, mumbling something about how embarrassed he was. He sat in a chair as far from Sam and Ross as possible and tried to be casual as he picked up a magazine. After the usual apologies for interrupting Ross at work, Sam explained that Bob had arrived a few minutes ago and asked if Sam could fit him in for a haircut. Perplexed, Ross could only ask, "So?"

Ross's heart sank as Sam told him that Bob had been in just two days before for a cut, shave, and trim, the "works," as it was called on the price schedule.

"He had no recollection of being here, even after I told him." Sam clearly was genuinely concerned and troubled.

Ross could only reply, "Thanks for the call, Sam. I'll take it from here." He walked back to Bob, who tried to appear absorbed in the magazine, but Ross had caught the quick, sidelong glance from his father-in-law as he had finished his conversation with Sam. Before Ross reached him, Bob had gotten up and was headed for the door. Ross turned to follow him.

Bob Proctor stopped in mid-step at the door, turned, and said, "I'm sorry for the trouble, Sam." Ross noticed that his eyes were moist.

Once the barbershop door closed behind them, Bob tentatively and almost in a whisper asked, "What's happening to me, Ross?" Ross didn't know how to answer and tried to direct the conversation into safer territory. He suggested that they walk the two blocks back to Pop's and Bob could return for his car later. Bob agreed and seemed to Ross to be completely himself, in full control of his mental faculties.

After a minute or two of silence, Bob slowed his step just a bit and said to Ross, "I'd like to tell you about Jeanne." The short, simple statement instantly brought Ross to a stop and he turned to stare at Bob. Any knowledge that Ross had of Jennie's long dead mother had come from Jennie, and that was sketchy at best. Jeanne Proctor had died shortly after giving birth to Jennie and Bob loved to tell Jennie in Ross's presence that she possessed all of the wonderful attributes of her mother. It was always clear that Jeanne had been enshrined in Bob's memory, and he seemed reluctant to share much of who she was to anyone, even her own daughter. Now, in this unlikely environment, in the center of the business district of the small town, Bob Proctor wanted to share something very special with his son-in-law.

Ross suggested they return to the store and talk in the privacy of his office. Bob agreed and the two of them began to walk again at a quickened pace. Ross thought all the way back that surely Bob would change his mind and instead of talking about Jeanne would opt to return to his car and drive home.

When they arrived at the shop, it was almost lunchtime and his part-time helper, a student involved in the high school business courses and serving an internship with Ross, was anxious to return to school. Ross sensed this but knew that he and Bob could never carry on any sort of conversation if he had to cover the shop at mealtime.

The brief walk back had convinced him that Bob Proctor wanted to talk, and he was afraid that this rare opportunity would be missed if it had to be postponed. In a sincere and contrite way, he approached the young girl and asked if she could possibly delay her return to school for about a half hour. He would be happy to supply her supervisor with a note, explaining the extenuating circumstances. She started to balk but something about the way Ross asked stopped her. With Jennie's father standing behind Ross and obviously troubled, she agreed to wait.

"Thanks, Celeste. I knew I could count on you." As he was saying the words, he and Bob started down the aisle toward the rear of the store and what Jennie referred to as his "so-called office." He realized that he was inexplicably very nervous, as if some dramatic revelation was coming.

They entered the office and Ross quietly shut the door. He noticed that Bob Proctor was fighting a severe case of the fidgets, as Susan Johnson used to call them. As Ross moved his chair closer and faced him, Jen's father got a look wild-eyed look on his face. Ross tried to initiate the conversation. If the attempt fell flat, he would not be surprised.

The topic of Jeanne Proctor had never come up in the course of even the most profound conversations he had had with his father-in-law, and Ross was prepared to let the matter drop if it seemed to be in Bob's best interest.

"So, um...you mentioned something about Jeanne back there." Ross practically squirmed in his chair; this was as awkward a position as he had ever been in with his father-in-law. He had no idea where the conversation would head and began to wish he had encouraged Bob to return home from the barbershop.

At the mention of Jeanne's name, the wild and frazzled look faded from Bob's face. Later, when he related the incident to Jennie, Ross described her father's look as becoming placid and serene. This moment, before Bob Proctor launched into his compulsive retelling of Jeanne's last few minutes on earth, truly touched Ross. The calming influence of a twenty-three-year-old memory clearly demonstrated a special, abiding love. Ross felt that by looking into Bob's eyes, he could almost see the vivid living image of Jeanne cast across the years. At the time, he shoved aside the creeping feeling of envy by substituting an image of his own, his beloved Jennie. He knew that they also had something special and could look forward to what he was sure would be a bright future. Just for an instant, the unnerving reality of the Proctors' tragedy intruded, but Bob's first words caught Ross's attention once again.

"She was beautiful, you know." Ross had no doubt that right then, Jeanne was as alive in Bob's mind as she had ever been. He pushed himself up straighter in his chair as Bob Proctor spoke, seemingly lost in a distant reverie.

For fifteen minutes, Ross found himself drawn into the world of two people passionately in love. Bob described the unbounded optimism of their youth as they prepared for the baby they were sure would be coming soon after their marriage. Jennie had already described the whole story to Ross but an entirely different prospective emerged as Bob recounted the years up to Jennie's birth.

As Bob continued his narrative, Ross began to dread the end of the story. He felt as if he were watching a sad movie for the second or third time, knowing the ending but somehow wishing it would turn out differently this time. Bob supplied some small details of the story that Ross had not known before but no startling revelations. He continued to wonder why Bob had been so insistent about talking with him. Perhaps he should just dismiss the whole request as part of the pattern of creeping senility that his father-in-law was sadly sinking into.

Bob Proctor had covered the twelve years of his marriage to Jeanne in less that fifteen minutes but the warmth and detail of the description had held Ross's keen interest.

"How utterly sad," Ross thought. "practically one minute for each year...." For whatever reason, Ross sensed that this conversation, a monologue really, was just about over.

Bob Proctor, his eyes glistening, had reached the trip to the hospital for the unbearably eager, soon-to-be parents. Ross, while extremely interested in the story, found himself trying to guess if indeed anything new would be forthcoming from Bob. Finally, as the twelve year story was reaching its conclusion, Bob pulled his chair the few steps across the office. Never missing a word, he sat down again, leaned forward and, with his face inches from Ross, made almost confrontational eye contact.

"I have never told a single soul the last words Jeanne spoke on this planet, Ross, not even Jennie." Ross had involuntarily recoiled because of Bob's proximity but now he subconsciously leaned forward himself. He knew all about the waiting room scene and often had thought that he would never be able to handle anything like it-an expectant father, excited beyond words, leaping across the room at the doctor's entrance, only to be taken into the hallway and given such devastating news. He had never heard anything about Jeanne Proctor's last words, other than he knew that Bob had not heard them. Jeanne was dead before he even had a chance to say goodbye.

During the fifteen minutes of Bob Proctor's monologue, Ross had given no verbal responses, only nodding now and then. Now his interest reached a new level and he could not contain himself. During Bob's deep breath following his intention to share this intimate information, Ross blurted out the question that had instantly come to mind.

"Dad, how in the world did you find out what your wife said at the end?" He immediately regretted the interruption of the story. His voice seemed to take Bob Proctor out of his reverie into a much less pleasant place, a place inhabited by far too much reality.

Bob stumbled over the words but they tumbled out as though they had a mission of their own. Ross now had the definite feeling that he was playing the role of intruder. Perhaps this was the reason for Bob's desire to tell Ross about Jeanne but the wild look in Bob's eyes told Ross that the territory they were traveling in now was not at all safe. This might be the time to change the direction of this scene, Ross thought, but when he tried to interrupt again, his father-in-law quieted him with a simple but forceful glare.

"The doctor, that absolute jerk, Judson..." Proctor seemed to Ross to be teetering on the edge of a breakdown and what was happening was suddenly very frightening.

Ross stood and took a half step toward Bob, who stared down at his feet but continued to speak.

"He could have been gentler, Ross." The composure Bob had displayed minutes earlier was rapidly disappearing. At twenty-three, Ross had been exposed to more tragedy than most people his age, but the appealing innocence everyone admired in him was making it impossible for him to handle this situation. In an effort to comfort the shaken man, he reached out to touch Bob's shoulder. In an attempt to finish what he had come for, Bob stood up, turned his back to Ross and started toward the door.

"She said that she loved me and that Jennie would be worth

the sacrifice." Barely audible, the words drifted back to Ross as he followed Bob from the office.

"That is all that has kept me together, Ross. I'm fine. Please don't come after me; I can get home all right." With that, he opened the door and walked quickly through the shop and out into the street.

Jennie's survival of the crash had been miraculous. The question of why she survived to live in her current state was a topic of hot debate among both religious and atheistic types. With her life dependent on the new technology and machinery, the argument centered on whether she really was alive or was merely a tool of a cruel and experimental process.

Ross naturally spent hours sitting next to her bed, holding her hand and watching for some small sign that she knew he was there. With nothing to do but think, Ross bordered on being driven crazy by two phrases that whirled through his mind and became interchangeable and irrational at the same time.

"This favor will have to be returned sometime later." Jennie and Ross had thrown that around for years, but it had been their secret. Jennie claimed she had no idea why she had said it at the racetrack other than it simply had to be said. At first, Ross was convinced that she knew something that she was not sharing. As he came to know her better, he knew that she could never lie to him and eventually the teasing about the promise made under the threat of losing his father faded.

With Jennie now in what certainly was a life-threatening situation, Ross began to imagine a whole variety of scenarios in which he could save her by repaying the favor. In the rare moments when he faced the stark and crushing reality of her condition, he despairingly would decide that perhaps her favor would never be repaid. He could not yet bring himself to face the possibility, actually more of a certainty, that she would die. Talks with the doctors always left him with the uneasy impression that they were just waiting for the right time to involve him in a decision that he had no intention of facing, not for a long time.

Mingling with the unending hope that a miracle would occur was the phrase that Jeanne Proctor had apparently spoken when she knew that her life on earth was finished. Granted it had been given to Bob in a harsh, second-hand fashion from a doctor who seemed determined to make sure that no fault for her death was aimed in his direction, but Ross had no reason to doubt its accuracy. He had first met Jennie at the racetrack more than thirteen years earlier and had come to know that she truly was a uniquely special individual. So many times, as he gazed at the beautiful young woman, connected to a myriad of tubes, cables, wires, and instruments, he wondered how this vital, compassionate person with so much to offer the world could be wasted by a crazy quirk of fate. He would run through the string of "what ifs" and always come to the same conclusion: Nothing really mattered.

He now knew the details of Jennie's last visit to her father and found nothing but yet another whole series of "what ifs." What if her father had recognized her that morning? She wouldn't have left his side. Why had she decided to turn back instead of just coming home that day? When the nurses told him that Bob Proctor had used the phrase, "She'll be worth the sacrifice," that morning after she had left and seemed to undergo a transformation, he wondered if Jennie had somehow known to come back. When all of this threatened to force him to the edge of rationality, his only savior became the promise extracted by Jen when he was ten years old.

"I still have a favor to return," he would say to himself. "She can't leave me yet."

He had shared this with friends and family and the sympathy they were feeling for him only deepened. The long, lonely vigils by her bedside were manageable only because he held out this hope, and they certainly were not going to take it from him.

Early on the morning of the eighth day after the accident, Ross received a call from Dr. Baring requesting a meeting with him and the team of doctors who had responsibility for the life-support technology that furnished Jennie's room in wall-to-wall fashion.

"We'll gather everyone at eleven this morning, Ross," said the doctor. "There are some things we need to talk about."

As he placed the receiver back into the cradle, Ross smiled somewhat ruefully, knowing that Dr. Baring was having difficulty living up to his Jolly Jack image, not sounding very jolly at all during that phone call. Ross knew in his heart that this meeting was not an "if" event but rather a "when" event. The huge expenditure of money coupled with an equally large investment of time and effort had to stop somewhere, even if the medical specialists were gaining valuable information during what Ross now knew for sure was simply an experiment-a caring and compassionate one, but undeniably still an experiment. He decided that he would need some additional support during this meeting and thought first of Father Samuels. That would be best, even though Ross would have loved to have his mother and grandmother sitting next to him. Jennie had regularly pointed to Fay Becker as one of the few examples of any good coming from her gift, although even that had happened in a convoluted way. He was sure that they would be willing but was not able to convince himself that they deserved the traumatic stress which he was sure would come out of this meeting. He decided it would be best to spare them at least this bit of heartache.

Ross spent the time during the short drive to the rectory steeling himself for the string of profound but still meaningless cliches that Father Samuels was sure to utter in a vain attempt to ease the tension. His expectations could not have been more correct. The entire ride to the hospital saw the good-hearted priest trying desperately to come up with just the right combination of words to dispel some of the dread from the upcoming meeting. To the hapless husband on his way to discuss life-or-death decisions regarding his young wife, any words would have been empty.

"It's all in God's strong hands."

"What's meant to be will be."

"God's plan is difficult to understand."

"Let the Lord's will be done."

"Whatever happens always happens for the best."

"Whatever happens will be a blessing."

Ross couldn't believe either the depth of faith or the total foolishness of this man of God. For eight days, he had been existing on an unshakable belief that somehow Jennie would make it. The blur of words emanating from Father Samuel's mouth were doing more to destroy that confidence than the priest could have imagined. During a brief pause in the apparently endless list of trite expressions the priest had at his disposal, Ross interjected a bit of philosophy of his own.

"Father, don't you ever wonder why all these things about the Lord's will and God's plan all point to human disappointment and even devastation?"

He followed this question, delivered in a soft, calm voice, with a much more heated declaration.

"If something happens to Jennie, it will *not* be a blessing; it will *not* be for the best. How anyone could say something so stupid is beyond me. What's for the best is for Jennie to recover and come home, to be able to keep being a human being who actually is able to give some hope to people she comes in contact with. Period and end of story!" Ross glanced sideways at the priest and saw that he was nodding. The nodding did not present any problem for Ross, but he was infuriated by the condescending smile that he had seen so many times on supposed holy men in the service of God. It was the kind of expression that said to the observer that they were seeing through the glass clearly. Ross would certainly admit that he was seeing through the glass darkly and had been for eight days. He did not need nor appreciate being reminded of it by his passenger. Ross was silent for the rest of the trip and wondered if he had made a mistake in choosing Father Samuels as his companion for this next assault on his sanity.

One floor above and several corridors away from where Jennie lay entangled in life-giving tubes, Bob Proctor was in a lucid period and wondering once again why it seemed so long since his daughter had come for a visit. He was not aware that directly beneath him, in a hospital conference room, decisions were about to be made that might finally put to rest the trauma so many people had suffered over the last eight days. He, of course, had no idea that his daughter had been the focus of so many directed prayers since she had fled his room just over one week earlier. He had not understood why the nurses kept referring to him as blessed. Only they knew that, for once, his state of mind was an advantage. As the poet said, it's always better to be an idiot than a wise man-that way, you can't be hurt so much. Bob Proctor had no concept that his state of blissful ignorance served as an emotionally protective shield. Everyone who knew him felt certain that had he known what had happened to Jennie, he would have lost his mind completely.

Ross had anticipated being intimidated by the gathering. He had spoken to no more than two of the doctors tending to Jennie at any one time. Yet here he was, facing all seven of the technical wizards who had managed to keep his life intact by somehow, miraculously, circulating Jennie's blood through her organs to keep her alive. Dr. Baring sat at the head of the table and motioned to Ross and Father Samuels to sit down. Ross fought the flight or fight instinct that had recently become the study fad in college psychology classes. He did not want to be here and physically forced himself to take the seat that was indicated, coincidentally directly to the right of the obvious moderator of the group, the famous Dr. Baring.

Dr. Baring cordially thanked Ross for coming and Ross simply stared at the kind doctor. John Baring knew that this was going to be a most difficult challenge for his reputation. He looked over at Father Samuels, who had taken the only other empty chair halfway down the table, and knew as well that it would be challenge for the priest but in an entirely different way. Faith proved to be an easy commodity to have when one was not faced with a meeting of this importance. The good Father Samuels, so faithfully confident in the car just a few minutes ago, felt a twinge of doubt about his ability to keep Ross together. The priest's eyes never rested, nervously darting from one doctor to another as though searching for something that was not going to be found. Anyone looking closely at the priest's face would have known immediately he was wishing that Ross had chosen someone else to be by his side during what was sure to be the most trying moments of his young life.

"Ross, we know this last week or so has been very difficult," John Baring began, infinitely understating the obvious. The doctor followed this with a long, detailed explanation of how well the new equipment had performed in keeping Jennie in a stable but vegetative state. Ross had to force himself to be an impassive observer so that he could absorb all that was being said. At times he felt like only Dr. Baring was aware of his presence. The other doctors would break into Baring's description occasionally with excited additions to the wonders of the technology without, it seemed to Ross, any regard for the human being who lay on the table beneath it all.

He was reminded of his Uncle Joe's visit to Jennie two days ago. Joe brought his daughter along, thinking that somehow Jennie would recognize the lovely young girl she had baby-sat for so often. When his youngest cousin ventured close to Jennie's bed, she had looked long and hard at her before turning to Ross and asking the question that once again broke his heart.

"Is there a person in there?" she had asked in complete innocence.

Ross's attention snapped back. He listened to what had turned into a discussion of the virtues of modern medicine and resisted the urge to scream. Dr. Baring, sensing the palpable tension coming from his right, quickly brought the animated group of doctors back to the purpose of the meeting. He turned to Ross and saw a look on his face similar to that of a poorly educated parent facing a battery of his child's teachers at a parent-teacher conference. Ross was intimidated, not really knowing what they were talking about but trying desperately to understand what it had to do with him and, more important, what it had to with his beloved Jennie. Dr. Baring knew that it was time to get to the point or the permission they needed from Ross might be lost and the experiment would come to an end.

"Ross, we can keep Jennie alive indefinitely. We would like to continue this treatment with the hope that someday she'll come out of the coma. If we take her off the machines, she will not survive. What we need is your permission to continue." Dr. Baring never looked away from Ross's eyes.

"You have my permission to treat her, Doctor. What's changed?" As he finished the question, the obvious answer came to him simultaneously. "The cost!" he thought.

Jolly John Baring used his special perceptive ability to read what Ross was thinking. "The hospital will cover the entire cost of the treatment, Ross," he said. It's the least we can do under the circumstances."

Ross became very confused. First of all, the treatment, as they kept calling it, was not really treatment at all. Treatment of a disease or injury held out some hope of improvement; from what Ross had been able to see, Jennie had not shown any improvement. In reality, she seemed more frail than ever. Second, what were the circumstances under which the hospital would assume the exorbitant costs of the new technology? The inexpensive Blue Cross/Blue Shield health insurance plan Ross had purchased had no provision for the type of treatment Jennie required, but as long as the carrot of hope dangled, no thought of taking Jennie off the machines had surfaced. No price could be placed on Jennie's life and Ross had dismissed any discussion of alternatives. The hospital's offer to cover the expense had the effect of raising Ross's optimism once more. The question of why went unanswered; no one, including Ross and his priest companion, really wanted to ask it.

The high-powered team of experts sitting around the table began to shift in their seats as Dr. Baring repeated his request for permission to keep Jennie on life support for what could be an indefinite amount of time. Ross looked over at Father Samuels, who managed to turn a shrug into a positive gesture. No logical reason existed for Ross to hesitate in accepting the offer.

"Of course, I'll give you the permission, Doctor." As the words left his mouth, he suddenly had an unbearable, desperate urge to spend a few minutes with Jennie. "Would you mind if I saw Jennie for a while?" The question was posed in such a quiet, touching way that the seven doctors nodded almost in unison and began to get up from the table.

"Stop by my office when you're ready, Ross. I'll have the paperwork all set for you to sign. It'll take just a minute of two. And, Ross, it's the right thing to do. Trust me, Jennie is very important to us here." With that, John Baring escorted Ross and Father Samuels to the door.

Once in the hall, Ross asked Father Samuels if he would mind waiting for another few minutes before returning home. The priest agreed, reminding Ross that he had many parishioners he could visit here while he was waiting. He actually loved visiting people in the hospital; they were always so receptive to seeing their parish priest. Father Sam had decided that they must be reassured by his presence, as if nothing bad could happen to them if he was there.

In the conference room, the team of doctors quietly congratulated John Baring on his handling of the meeting. He had done it with his usual compassion and never had to force the issue of obtaining permission from Ross to continue the treatment. It had been as easy convincing him as it had been convincing the hospital administrators to allow him to make the financial offer to Ross. After all, everyone could see that for the last eight days, as the struggle to keep Jennie alive received more and more publicity, the hospital was the beneficiary of volumes of positive public reaction. Anyone associated with the funding of hospitals, administrators and doctors alike, knew the power of positive imagery when the time came for grant writing and fund-raising. None of the doctors, Baring included, would have any difficulty rationalizing the use of poor Jennie Becker as a catalyst for bringing the hospital to the attention of possible donors, especially rich ones. The longer Jennie is kept on this earth, the better the chance of fulfilling the long-range plan and vision they had for the hospital. What could possibly be wrong with that?

As Ross walked toward Jennie's room, he wondered about Dr. Baring's offer, but his emotional state would not permit him to dwell on it. There was absolutely no reason to refuse it. He would accept it gratefully and, as Dr. Baring said, put his trust in those who know what they are doing. He would just check in on Jennie quickly, then go to the doctor's office and sign whatever he wanted signed. As he arrived at Jennie's room, he had no idea that everything would change in little more than five minutes.

Every time Ross entered Jennie's room, a thick layer of sadness would settle over him. Until the moment he sat down next to her and took her hand, she lived vividly and vibrantly in his mind. He would raise her cool hand to his lips and kiss the back of it, slowly look up toward her face, and be jolted back to the grim reality that she did not even know he was there. The crush of the machines around her and the tubes and the whirring noises and the beeping sounds were an integral part of her environment and Ross had come to accept them. He could concentrate on her face; for most of his visits, he would just sit quietly, holding and stroking her hand and looking at her. For the last eight days, during countless hours of bedside vigils, there had been no response, no indication that she was alive other than the mechanically induced measured breathing. For Ross, these times were precious, despite the despair always lurking in his mind.

Today, Ross went through his rituals as usual, pulling the chair up close to the bed, searching for Jennie's hand under the blanket, drawing it close to his face, and finally kissing it lightly. He kept her hand entwined with his and gently placed it back on the bed. As he followed the lines of tubing up toward her angelic face, he felt an unmistakable squeeze of his hand. The hair on his neck prickled as the sensation traveled through the synapses of his brain. In that instant, the feathery squeeze was gone. He desperately tried to recapture the feeling but it had disappeared in all but his imagination. Jennie's head rested on two pillows, slightly raised and turned toward Ross. He had learned to ignore the intrusive modern medical marvels of tubes running in and out of her nose and concentrated instead on her pale cheeks and closed eyes.

"Please, Jennie, squeeze again", he begged, in a voice loud enough to startle the nurse assigned to the desk by the door. She looked over briefly but just as quickly went back to her paper work.

Ross realized that he was trembling, excitement mixing with a fear that he had imagined the phantomlike squeeze. Just as he had decided to call the nurse over, Jen's eyes blinked open and locked onto his. Something in her eyes stopped him from screaming for the nurse.

"The eyes are the window of the soul" the old cliché went. At that moment, Ross would have sworn to God himself that this was absolutely true.

At exactly the moment Ross was one floor below staring into the depths of Jennie's soul, Bob Proctor was calling frantically for help. Marybeth and Nancy reacted in a second. The two highly skilled and profession nurses knew only too well the precarious mental state of their patient. The inflection in his voice demanded an immediate response. They found Jennie's father scrambling around his room, picking up any loose clothing and generally behaving as though he was about to have a very special visitor.

"She's coming; please help me get fixed up here," he said. Nancy was first to react to Bob's exclamation.

"Who, Mr Proctor? What do you mean?" Her well-trained mind echoed with the credo she learned early on when she decided to specialize in care of the elderly: "Don't confront. Be patient and let them tell you what they want to tell you when they want to tell you." Her favorite professor's voice came up from her subconscious but he might just as well have been standing behind her.

"My daughter, Nancy. My daughter will be here any minute for a visit and I want everything to be perfect." Bob Proctor said this in such a plain, matter-of-fact way that both Nancy and Marybeth knew that the only role they should play in this scenario was the one Mr. Proctor wanted them to.

"Well, that is exciting, Mr. Proctor. We'll be glad to help." They had to stifle a chuckle as they realized that they had responded virtually in unison.

"I just want it right, that's all," Bob said calmly.

Ross felt another light squeeze of his hand as he sat mesmerized by what he saw in Jennie's eyes. In that instant, it was recognition of him, of the world around her, and of her situation. Later, Ross would thank God for the two-hour midday period when the breathing tubes ran only through her nose, the tube for her mouth and throat temporarily removed to provide a chance for the throat irritation to subside.

Jennie seemed to struggle at first but finally spoke, softly as always. The sound of her voice made Ross's eyes blur with tears.

"Tell them to let me go, Ross. I need to be let go. It's time for the favor to be returned. I'm sorry but you must do this. I love you." As she said the last word, her eyes closed slowly once again. Ross felt one more gentle squeeze but this one was different, as different as the emotional greeting hug of two long-separated lovers is from the fatalistic farewell hug. In an instant, the squeeze was gone, leaving Ross dazed, his stomach churning and his mind reeling.

He continued to hold Jennie's quiet hand as he waited for the nurse behind him to say something about what had just happened. He slowly turned, fully expecting to see her standing behind, matching his psychological state. He was shocked to see her sitting at the desk, head down, absorbed in shuffling through the pile of papers in front of her.

"Did you hear her?" For the second time, the nurse jumped, startled at the sharpness and the volume of his voice.

A bit afraid and with a great deal of hesitancy, she almost whispered, "No, Mr. Becker, I'm sorry. What exactly did you hear?"

Ross smiled slightly even in the frustration of the moment. Being the husband of such a tragic celebrity appeared to bring an automatic respect. It was the first time he had been called Mr. Becker by anyone other than those who worked for him. He could only stammer in answer to her question. He could not believe that no one else had heard Jennie speak. Turning his attention back to Jennie with the fading hope that he would see her awake, he grasped her right hand and sandwiched it between both of his, as if to warm it. It seemed more lifeless than ever.

"No, Jennie, please." Ross could not form the words with this mouth but thought them loud enough so that they reverberated in his head.

He felt an immediate need to escape from Jennie's presence and just think. Prodding doubts that she had indeed spoken to him were rapidly galloping across his memory banks and he needed desperately to sort them out in a different environment. As long as he stayed here, he would wait for her to awake again. He had to get to a place where he could fight the intruding reality that Jennie probably would never wake again, at least not on this earth.

Ross mumbled a pathetic apology to the concerned nurse and walked quickly to the flight of stairs leading to the lobby, keeping his head down and avoiding eye contact with anyone. He did not want to see people now, nor need to explain anything, especially things that he could not understand himself. He waited for the newly installed automatic door opener to function.

"Another stupid technological improvement," he muttered as he exited. He found a vacant wooden bench in one of the patient exercise parks and sat facing the sun. He felt the unusually warm mid-November air on his skin. Ross had always been proud of his ability to think logically and clearly. He thought of himself as an excellent problem solver and now he tried valiantly to approach his present situation analytically. After a few minutes of contemplation, he came to two conclusions: first, no amount of reason or logic could explain what had happened just minutes before; second, he had to tell Dr. Baring that he could not give permission to keep Jennie on the respirator any longer. He based his first conclusion on the fact that he had been able to put emotion aside during his visits to Jennie after just the first few days. Had she spoken to him during the early days, he surely would have thought he had imagined it, his muddled mental state clouding his judgment. Now, he approached each visit with no expectations, and when he first felt the hand squeeze, he had managed to remain relatively calm. He knew he was not in a vulnerable frame of mind when Jennie opened her eyes and spoke. Actually, he remembered feeling almost like a detached observer, perhaps not a scientific one but accurate, at least. The conclusion now seemed irrefutable. She had spoken to him and had given specific instructions. With surprisingly little difficulty, the decision was made to move forward with what had to be done.

"Why am I so calm about all of this?" Ross kept asking himself. He knew the answer, but only because he had come to know Jennie so well. The phrase she used so often took form as clearly as if he were reading it from a billboard; "I feel like I'm in this world but not of it." Jennie seemed perplexed over her gifts, gifts she had tried to explain to Ross, usually with a distinct lack of success. She never complained about anything but could not understand why God let her know things which others did not.

"It's as if He is letting me on secrets, some that I would rather not know," she had once said after using her knowledge of a "secret" to make a high school classmate step back from a curb to avoid a carelessly driven school bus.

Ross, about to lose the most precious part of his life, became increasingly convinced by the minute that he had heard Jennie speak to him and that he had no choice but to follow her instructions. He left the bench and headed for Dr. Baring's office.

* * *

"Shocking," the doctor was exclaiming, his Jolly Jack exterior fading in Ross's presence for the first time. He had anticipated something of a problem after Jennie's nurse had reported the incident involving Ross. His fear then was that Ross might be experiencing the trendy new phenomenon the psychiatrists were labeling post-traumatic stress syndrome, the only truly new aspect of it being the name. Dr. Baring knew of many cases in which the surviving spouse became delusional, his senses fooled by the power of the mind. The doctor had been prepared to handle that but the nurse did not know exactly what Jennie supposedly had told Ross. He was utterly unprepared to respond coherently to the preposterous request that Ross Becker was making.

"I simply can't do that, Ross," he said. "It flies in the face of everything I believe in. We have to work to keep Jennie alive as long as possible in the hope that she'll come out of her coma."

When Ross was escorted into Dr. Baring's office by his nurse, the doctor had been somewhat relieved by his appearance. He was expecting the worst after Jennie's shaken nurse had relayed the message that Ross claimed that Jennie had spoken to him. The nurse, whom Dr. Baring knew to be capable and highly skilled, was not one to lose her composure. In her brief intercom report, she repeated twice her belief that Ross did not seem unsettled and actually had been rather collected, even resigned, during the entire incident. Dr. Baring was well aware of the power of the mind and expected that Ross would need some gentle, therapeutic calming when he came in to sign the permission forms. He was sure in his own mind that if Ross thought Jennie had indeed awakened, however briefly, it would make the signing a formality. Ross would have some hope, even though the doctor would not let the generally held professional opinion slip into the conversation. There was no hope and there was not a doctor on the staff who believed that Jennie would ever be anything but what she was now-an experiment. The medical staff easily rationalized why this opinion should not play a role in Ross's decision. They all knew by now that Jennie Becker might as well have been a saint on earth during her brief life. Were she the one making the decision, she would certainly choose to continue the treatment out of compassion for those who might benefit in the future.

Dr. Baring signaled for Ross to take a seat in the overstuffed chair across from his and peered through the family pictures in frames scattered over his desk. Being sure to make eye contact, his round face filling with the most sincere, caring look he could construct, he had asked, quite easily, "How're you doing, Ross?" Even as he asked the question, his hand found the forms and began to slide them through the maze of pictures toward the serious young man facing him. The first words from Ross brought Dr. Baring straight up from his chair.

"I can't give you permission to continue, Dr. Baring. You must suspend the treatment as soon as possible." Ross amazed himself at how easily the words came out. Across the desk, Dr. Baring stopped moving the papers and sat stunned.

"Shocking!" he exclaimed. "What in the name of God are you thinking of?"

"It's really very simple, Doctor. Jennie woke up and told me what I had to do." The doctor, rarely at a loss to find the correct words to defuse any situation, struggled to regain the upper hand. Trying to determine the best approach to bring the young husband's thinking back to a rational level, Dr. Baring just stared at Ross. Where he hoped to find some evidence of confusion, some weakness in Ross's psychological armor, all he could see was an almost preternatural strength of conviction. He found Ross's demeanor under the circumstances rather unnerving. The meeting had lasted less than two minutes and already Dr. Baring began to map his strategy for informing his colleagues that their experiment was soon to be over.

Without agonizing any further, Dr. John Baring realized that something very special was going on. Much of his vast medical experience had come in the ER, where the terrible thin line between life and death was so often drawn. He learned long before that some things simply couldn't be explained in a logical way.

He knew it would be best for all concerned if the dreams for the future of the hospital, conjured up by the unfortunate and tragic accident that placed Jennie Becker in their care, were put aside for the moment. Dr. Baring, shocked first by Ross's pronouncement, now found himself shocked even more by his own thoughts. Ross was correct. His intuition told him that, by what means he had no idea. He knew also that he needed to put forth a token argument so that he could honestly inform his colleagues of his effort to convince Ross of the mistake he was making.

"Ross, are you sure you know what you're doing?" The doctor's question simply hung in the air, a rhetorical question if ever there was one. John Baring knew it; and Ross knew it but Ross understood that he must follow the rituals of the game.

"Yes, Dr. Baring, I know what I'm doing. Please let everyone know how much the loving care for Jennie has meant to me." Ross felt as if he was sixty-three years old instead of twenty-three. In this short conversation with the doctor, he had ensured the imminent death of his young wife. In a bizarre way, though, he felt a sense of relief. He remembered having similar feelings twice before in this very hospital.

After Al Stuart and Pop Hiller died, he had experienced the overwhelming grief, but strangely mixed with a weird sensation that at some point in his life he would have lost these special people anyway. It could have been years or it may have been days; one never knew. "Why not get the grief over with sooner rather than ," he had thought, somewhat irrationally.

"Will you do me a favor, Dr. Baring?" he asked, knowing that the answer would be yes. "Please let me know the details of what I can expect at the time, when the respirator is disconnected; I'll need to be prepared."

"I'll handle things from here and will be back in touch later today," Baring said. "I must warn you that you'll probably have to explain your decision to the press. There has been a lot of public interest out there for Jennie and I wish you luck with that." The doctor, much to his own surprise, had resumed his role of compassionate and caring physician, and Ross was grateful for his effort to help.

"I'll expect to hear from you later today, then." Ross stood and extended his hand. "Thank you, Doctor. Thanks for avoiding the speech I was sure I'd be getting." The two men looked at each other with the shared loss apparent in their eyes. A husband losing a wife and a doctor losing a patient are not all that dissimilar, Ross decided.

As Ross was leaving, Dr. Baring called after him. "There have been miracles before, Ross. It's not hopeless."

"I'm afraid it is, Doctor. Jennie told me so herself." For the first time since their meeting began, Ross felt the insidious doubt infiltrating his heart once again.

"Did she really tell me that?" he wondered as the door closed behind him.

The lecture that Ross expected from Dr. Baring came instead from Father Samuels as they drove home from the hospital. As was the case on the trip in, Ross was able to let the thoughts of what he had just done cover the priest's diatribe on modern medicine's effects on the ethics of life and death. He thanked Father Samuels profusely for coming with him, sparing the priest his true feelings.

"I'll let you know the arrangements as soon as I know anything, Father", Ross said as the car door slammed. He quickly realized the irony of his use of the word *arrangements,* as though he were already arranging for Jennie's funeral. The disturbing insight led to a profound sadness, softened only by the knowledge that Jennie had indeed spoken with him. The arrangements were not his but hers. He knew that if he was going to be able to maintain his sanity, he had to believe that she had told him what to do. It would be impossible if he assumed even a small part of the responsibility for letting Jennie go.

By the time Ross arrived at his house, he had decided to spend the afternoon at home instead of returning to the shop. His high school assistants and other part-time employees had understood and been helpful to the point that Ross felt guilty placing any additional burden on them, but today he just could not face any more people.

He placed the perfunctory phone call as soon as he came through the door. Celeste answered and she knew immediately why he was calling. She told Ross she understood before he had finished his sentence.

"We can handle everything, Mr. Becker," she said, with an air of confidence that made Ross believe her.

"They've really come through for me", he thought, as he

replaced the receiver.

He went into the kitchen, grabbed a cold beer and a bag of potato chips. He hadn't felt like eating since Jennie's accident and knew she never would have approved of his diet of the last eight days.

"Not that it really matters, now, I guess." Ross found that he was speaking out loud and was amused, embarrassed, and devastated all at the same time.

"This will be the pattern for the future. I'll just walk around eating chips and talking to myself." In spite of himself, he laughed lightly, knowing that Jennie would have laughed right along with him. He found himself becoming agitated over his referral to her in the past tense, something he had not done until she gave him his directions that morning. Taking his so-called lunch into the living room, he flicked on the television and plunked down in his favorite recliner. He glanced over at the twenty-one-inch RCA console, the first new television he and Jen ever had. It was to be their combination birthday and Christmas presents. "For the next ten years," she mildly scolded him. They had even wrapped a bow around one leg of it and agreed that the bow would stay on until Christmas so everyone would know that it was a gift. Here it was, November 21, and it was only the second time in the two weeks since they had purchased the set that he actually sat down to watch it.

The local station, WCAU-TV, Channel 10, was closing its midday half-hour news program. When the file picture of Jennie came on the screen, Ross jumped from the recliner without even lowering the footrest. The anchorman, speaking in a deep resonant tone reflective of his radio background, gave the kicker that indicated that an update on the condition of Jennie Becker would be announced at the hospital at four o'clock that afternoon. The doctors who were treating Jennie would hold a press conference at that time, he said, and Channel 10, knowing how interested in this story its audience was, would carry it live.

In a matter of seconds, Ross had Dr. Baring on the phone.

"It's really just a formality, Ross. The press has asked for updates on her condition on a regular basis and now we felt we should let them know the next step. It's not a big deal. I was going to call you later to tell you about it. There's no need for you to be there or anything." It was John Baring at his best, setting Ross at ease and managing to put everything into perspective.

"Of course," Ross said apologetically. "I'm sorry to have bothered you. You're still going to get back to me with details about what happens next, right?"

Dr. Baring supplied the necessary assurances and Ross, temporarily feeling slightly better, cradled the phone once more.

Dr. John Baring and his six colleagues spent more than two hours in a meeting that went nowhere. The only conclusion everyone could agree on was the importance of changing Ross's mind and subtly forcing him into signing the permission. Dr. Baring, while agreeing that it would be helpful if they could show Ross that he was making a huge mistake, did not believe for an instant that they would be successful. He alone of the professionals in the room knew that there was much more to this than they could imagine, and even he could not come close to understanding his own behavior earlier in the day. As he reenacted his meeting with Ross, he could not discover what intuitive force made him give in so easily. He certainly was not going to expose himself to this group, none of whom would believe for a second that Jennie had communicated any sort of message to Ross. Instead, he simply agreed to the plan of holding a news conference, at which the doctors would explain that a family decision to remove Jennie Becker from all life-support systems had been made. Then they would let Ross explain why he would not follow the advice and counsel of this group of medical experts, all of them convinced that taking away her machines would mean her death.

At three-thirty that afternoon, Ross received the call he had been waiting for. Dr. Baring, in his most professional and forthright manner, explained that tomorrow morning at ten, all of Jennie's connections with the life-supporting machinery would be severed. The use of the word *severed* unnerved Ross, but he continued undaunted in his push to carry out the wishes of his beloved wife. Dr. Baring suggested that he arrive at the hospital no later than nine o'clock. He would be permitted to stay with Jennie as long as he wished after the initial preparations for disconnection were completed. Ross wanted to be at the hospital earlier but was advised that it would be better to come at nine. Some of the procedures would be upsetting to anyone, let alone a loved one, and there was no point in putting yourself through that, Dr. Baring had explained. Ross had reluctantly agreed.

Dr. Baring hesitated on the other end of the line. "One other bit of advice, Ross; you'd better have a story ready for the reporters. You're going to have to answer for this decision. Jennie is a very popular figure. Everyone is rooting for her. I suggest that you watch the press conference."

Ross closed the conversation, shaken but unbowed. "Thanks, Doctor. I'll be in tonight for the usual vigil, then I'll see you tomorrow before nine. What I'm doing is right. She would not have asked me otherwise."

He disconnected the call and dialed Fay Becker to make his request for privacy and to explain what he was doing. Not surprisingly, she seemed to understand; she had come to know Jennie like few others did. She agreed to spread the news to the family before the press conference that afternoon. The end of the conversation once again bought tears to Ross's eyes and he hung up abruptly with a hurried "Love you too, Mom."

Fay had said simply, "We both know she'll be going to a better place, Ross. I love you."

For the next half hour, as he waited for the news conference to be televised, he reclined in the chair and stared at the ceiling. A mindless soap opera provided background noise for him to shut out the world. As he had done as an adolescent in the bloom of first love, he used the blank white ceiling as a screen and projected his scene with Jennie across it. To Ross, the image was so vivid that it could have been in Cinerama. The scene played in a continuous loop, from the first squeeze of his hand to her request, from the final squeeze to his leaving the room. By the time the announcer's voice broke through his reverie, Ross was more convinced than ever that Jennie had told him exactly what to do. He turned his attention to the television as the special report began.

Incredibly, all seven of the doctors involved were standing behind a single podium, looking rather silly, Ross thought. The imposing John Baring stood in the forefront and had control of the microphone. After thanking the reporters in the crowded hospital lecture hall for coming, he said he would read a statement, after which they could ask questions for up to fifteen minutes. He prefaced his statement with the warning that this was an extremely difficult time for all concerned and pleaded with the news people to have some understanding of the depth of the tragedy for the family and friends of Jennie Becker. Ross thought Dr. Baring deserved his reputation as the "Dr. Kildare" of the staff. His aura of competence and professionalism combined with his compassionate bedside manner came across, even through the television screen. Ross knew that there would be no difficult questions for the good doctor. Dr. Baring reached into his inside pocket and pulled out half a sheet of paper. He placed it on the podium, smoothed the wrinkles and read the statement in a firm, steady voice:

"At a meeting with Ross Becker, Jennie's husband, and his priest this morning, an offer was made by the hospital to continue the life-support systems for Jennifer Becker indefinitely, with the cost of the treatment being borne by the hospital. The offer was the result of professional consultations that concluded that was a viable and legitimate treatment, and we held out some optimism for Mrs. Becker's ultimate recovery. Mr. Becker asked for time to consider this. Within a half hour, he returned to my office and rejected the offer. As you know, we have no jurisdiction or authority to continue this course of action without permission; therefore, tomorrow morning at ten o'clock, all artificial life-support systems will be disconnected from Mrs. Becker. Of course, we will be by her side to see that she is comfortable."

Ross slowly walked across the room to turn off the television. He did not need to hear the questions. He had just been made the villain in the piece and knew his phone would be ringing within seconds. There was one phrase in Dr. Baring's terse statement that bothered but did not really surprise him, considering the forum in which it was made. No medical professional, including Dr. Baring and his six partners, had ever indicated that they "held out some optimism for Mrs. Becker's ultimate recovery." He wondered if the transparency of the effort to let public reaction force him to let Jennie exist for a while longer was as obvious to anyone else as it was to him. Ross was astonished at the calm manner in which he was handling this. He did not even become angry with the doctors, who so clearly had hidden agendas beside Jennie's well-being. As he thought about it, he had been calm since Jennie had awakened. The course had been set and there was no turning back. Ross knew it had to be right. He picked up the phone, dialed his grandmother's number, and told her he would be unreachable for the rest of the day and night. When she protested that everyone would be looking for him after the news conference, he told her that the questioning could wait until after ten o'clock tomorrow. Just in case anything happened that needed his presence or attention, he explained where he would be. He trusted her to honor his request. Thankfully, she assured him that she believed in his decision, even though the doctors presented a strong case. The fragility of his mental state could handle only one conversation with his family for now, so he asked her to call his mother to check on her.

After putting down the phone, Ross hurriedly threw some clothes into a gym bag, wondering the whole time where he would be if not for Susan Johnson. In five minutes, as he was closing the front door behind him, he heard the phone ring for the first time of many, he was sure. The impossible decision was based on the strength of his convictions but he didn't know how he would be able to face the inevitable questions. He could not chance the return of the doubts about what he was doing. In his heart, Ross knew that Jennie needed to move beyond this world, and he was the only one who could help her. He had to return the favor; he had promised.

Ross was out of the cheap motel by eight o'clock on the morning of Thursday, November 22. After a quick stop at home to shower and dress for the hospital, he drove a circuitous route so that he could stop in and see his mother in person, wanting to see in her eyes that she truly believed in his decision. The visit was brief but long enough to fortify him with additional strength to face this day. She told him of the reporters' phone calls and visits, some of them rather harsh, but said she had handled them calmly, keeping her emotions in check. Fay loved Jennie as if she were her own daughter, but for Ross's sake summoned the courage to be strong as she sent him off to the hospital, alone as he had asked.

It was 8:45 when Ross walked through the automatic door, which finally operated smoothly for the first time since he started coming there. The hospital lobby was quiet; visiting privileges would not start for another four hours. Avoiding all eye contact, much as he done the day before, he proceeded quickly to Dr. Baring's office on the second floor.

The receptionist saw him coming, and stood before he had closed the door. A pleasant woman in her late forties, she had always been the epitome of what a receptionist should be-smiling, cordial and helpful, almost to a fault. To Ross, it seemed now that she glared at him just before she turned to knock on the doctor's door. He heard Doctor Baring give her permission to enter. She opened the door and said simply, "He's here." He could not see John Baring's expression but the receptionist nodded and turned to Ross.

"He's ready for you. You may go in," she announced in a cold, methodical voice.

"Good morning, Ross. Close the door, will you please?" John Baring motioned for him to take a seat.

"Did you have a good night? I know some people would have liked to have chance to talk with you but you were nowhere to be found." The edge in the doctor's voice was unmistakable. "We were hoping you might have had a change of heart overnight. Have you seen the morning papers yet?" Ross's blank look indicated that he had not but Dr. Baring could have had no idea that he had deliberately avoided the paper lying on the front step at home.

John Baring picked up the folded newspaper sitting on the corner of his desk and opened it to the front page. He turned it around so Ross could read the headline.

"JENNIE TO DIE TODAY" slapped Ross in the face. In smaller print below it read, "HUSBAND DECIDES."

"I have not changed my mind, Dr. Baring." Ross made the statement with an apologetic yet defiant tone to his voice.

"I'm not surprised, Ross, not at all. I really don't understand what's happening here but your behavior is not anything like most people would expect. I took the liberty of misleading the press about your time of arrival; that's why no one was waiting for you in the lobby. By the time that crowd is gathering to pounce on you, we'll be in the room with Jennie. I can't really protect you afterward but I'll do my best." After hesitating for an instant, he said in a low voice, as though he could not believe what he was saying. "I'd deny ever saying this to anyone, Ross, but I think that what you're doing is right and I admire your courage for going through with it. Now, let me explain what we'll be doing up there."

Ross, overwhelmed by the doctor's admission, now sat up and listened intently to the description of the heart wrenching medical process that would send Jennie to the world where she had always thought she belonged.

The two nurses in Jennie's room greeted Dr. Baring with a respect bordering on awe. Their reaction to Ross was similar to what he received from Dr. Baring's receptionist but they had come to know Ross and his dedication to Jennie. They contained some of the personal animosity they were feeling and reached for a degree of medical professionalism. For all of them, this situation was uncharted territory and even Dr. Baring was not sure how the next hour would unfold.

Jennie, looking more vulnerable and helpless than ever, was in her usual position on the bed. Ross felt his knees buckle when he saw her. He wished that he had come back last night as promised and spent his usual two-hour vigil by her bed. After watching the news conference, returning to the hospital did not seem like a smart idea. Actively resenting the intrusion of outsiders in this very private experience, he likened them to the once-a-year fans at the races, the "occasionals," who came hoping to see a spectacular crash, thriving on the misfortune of others. Had he come to see Jennie last night, there would have been some reporters waiting, hoping to get that elusive personal touch for their story. As he looked at her now, he tried, with a touch of desperation, to imagine her opening her eyes and speaking to him. If he was making a mistake, she needed to communicate again to him.

"Jen, you're going to have to help me here," he thought, and the thought became a prayer in his mind. The nurses, waiting for Dr. Baring's instructions, stood at the foot of the slightly raised hospital bed. Ross brought over a chair to the side of the bed that had no machinery, no tubes, and no hovering medical personnel. Dr. Baring had warned him about the "death rattle," the final sound many human beings make as they transition to what all hope will be a better place. Earlier that morning, a tracheotomy had been performed so that Jennie's breathing, if there was to be any, would be easier after the machine was turned off. Ross reached across and took Jen's left hand, gently caressing it with both of his. Dr. Baring said he would proceed as soon as Dr. Leonetti arrived, Leonetti being the only doctor beside Baring who agreed to be present when life support was suspended.

Ross found himself closing his eyes. He held Jen's hand and prayed that Dr. Leonetti would never arrive. At exactly five minutes to ten, the young doctor came through the door. After mumbled greetings to everyone in the room, he told John Baring that he was ready.

As complicated as the breathing apparatus seemed, the act of shutting it down was quite simple. Dr. Baring glanced over at Ross and asked, for one last time, if he was sure that he wanted to do this. Never looking up or opening his eyes, Ross replied in a firm voice, "Yes." Dr. Leonetti stood by the respirator and, at Dr. Baring's signal, flipped the two switches that silenced the machine. The silence in the room was deafening as Dr. Baring carefully removed the tube from Jennie's throat. All five people in the room tried in vain to breathe for the poor young woman in the bed. After what seemed an eternity, the covers on Jennie's chest move upward ever so slightly as she valiantly tried to pull in air. Without a sound, the movement stopped. Ross felt a strong squeeze of his hands and Jennie's eyes opened wide.

She looked straight at Ross and whispered "Thank you. I love you." The exclamation point for the final words Jennifer Proctor Becker spoke on this earth was a loud alarm signaling cardiac arrest. Dr. Baring motioned to the nurse standing by to turn off that machine as well.

Epilogue

Assisted by several of the nurses I had come to know over the last nine days, I made my way through the labyrinth of corridors under the hospital. Finally emerging on the side of the building exactly opposite the entrance, I hugged the brick walls and slipped around to the front parking area. I scanned the lot for my car, barely remembering parking it. I expected to see a horde of reporters but there were none. I crossed the lot quickly, crouching as I twisted through the other cars, hoping desperately to avoid detection.

Placing the key in the ignition, I slowly turned it until the engine came to life. There was no vehicle parked in front of mine and I was able to ease the Ford Fairlane out of the lot, moving very deliberately. Once on the highway, I put the car through its paces and sped toward home.

My churning stomach repeatedly forced a sour bile up into my throat. When I finally turned into the driveway, I noticed the porch swing rocking gently in the breeze. The crushing reality that never again would Jennie and I sit on that swing caused a vicious trembling that began in my hands and spread throughout my body.

Suddenly and fervently, I hoped that my mother and grandmother would not honor my request to be left alone. For no apparent reason, I stopped the car midway up the driveway and shakily turned the key. The engine died with a shudder. Any decision-making capabilities had been drained from me, ironically after making the most important one of my life. I couldn't even decide whether to go into the house or just keep walking around the yard.

I walked through the small gate into the back yard. Wandering among beds of dead flowers along the fence, I thought about what a fitting season it was. The desolation of the fast-approaching winter somehow connected to my personal devastation and made the walk around the yard a bit easier.

As I came closer to the large rhododendron that had been the pride of Jennie's flowering shrubs, the late November sun glinted off what looked to be a bright red piece of wrapping paper. I continued on, absentmindedly reaching for the paper while dazedly seeing nothing but hazy blurs around me. As soon as I grasped the colorful paper, I discovered it was not at all what I thought.

Sinking to my knees, I began to sob, unable any longer to hold my composure. With both hands, I reached toward the brilliant red flower, as beautiful a rhododendron blossom as I had ever seen. I thought of the day months ago when Jennie and I had sat on the swing. I gently cradled the flower between my hands and bent over and kissed it.

"Thank you, Jennie," I whispered. As I knelt by the bush for several minutes, my mind performed quantum leaps from past to present and back again, reliving the thirteen years since Jennifer Proctor Becker had dropped into my life. Finally I stood and entered the house, leaving the bloom to its rest.

I aimlessly found my way to the living room and flipped the switch on the new television, still sporting the red ribbon around the leg. I plopped myself down into the recliner, my mind rapidly fading into an idle blank from the feverish activity of moments before.

Walter Cronkite, his trained newscaster's voice quivering, drew my attention to the television. He seemed to be forcing out the words; "It has been confirmed that President John Fitzgerald Kennedy has been shot by a sniper in Dallas, Texas, just minutes ago. His condition is unknown at present. Please stay tuned for further details."

I rose from the chair, flicked off the television, and watched as the picture disappeared into an ever-decreasing circle until it was just a pinpoint of light. I thought crazily of how much the effect looked like a whirlpool, a maelstrom perhaps. I walked over to the picture window facing the street and drew the heavy, lined drapes across it, shutting the light from the room. When the drapes finally met in the center, all light had receded into the corners, the television still casting an eerie glow as the picture tube cooled down.

I sat back down in the darkened room and said aloud, with a touch of despair creeping into my voice, "There must be a better place!" Finally, I had returned the favor. I felt Jennie's presence in the room, gently chiding me. Maybe we are all in the world but not of it, and we just don't know it. My gloom began to lift as I remembered her irrefutable logic when we lost Pop: "...we'll just be missing Pop for the short time we are here on earth.... Well, then, we can be sad and miss him but be happy at the same time, right?"

I got up, opened the drapes, turned on the television and went to the kitchen for a beer and some chips.

About the Author

Duke Southard is a retired educator. He has published professional articles in *Media and Methods* and served as president of the New Hampshire Educational Media Association. In 1997, he was presented an "EDie," the New Hampshire Excellence in Education Award, for his contribution to the school library/media profession in the state. His educational credentials include a BS from Villanova University, a MA in English Education from Glassboro State University and a CAGS in Library/Media Technology from Boston University. He is married, the father of three children and lives in Tuftonboro, New Hampshire.

A Favor Returned is his first novel.